The Daughter of River Valley

Victoria Cornwall

Cornish Tales

Where heroes are like chocolate – irresistible!

Published 2019 by Choc Lit Limited
Penrose House, Crawley Drive, Camberley, Surrey GU15 2AB, UK
www.choc-lit.com

A CIP catalogue record for this book is available
from the British Library

ISBN: 978-1-78189-380-7

Printed and bound in Great Britain by Clays Ltd, Elcograf S.p.A.

When an ordinary person offers help and support to another, they become extraordinary. I would like to dedicate this novel to my family, who have each been extraordinary in their own unique way.

Acknowledgements

I wrote *The Daughter of River Valley* several years ago. Although it was shortlisted for the New Talent Award at the Festival of Romantic Fiction, I lacked the confidence to submit it to agents and publishers. Instead I self-published it under the title *The Gossamer Trail* and hoped readers would discover it.

There it would have continued to languish in the sea of books available online, if it had not been for my publisher, Choc Lit, who had more confidence in my writing than I did at the time and asked to see it. The Choc Lit Tasting Panel assessed it and subsequently recommended it for traditional publication and I am truly grateful for this. A special thank you to the readers involved, namely Dimi E, Rosie F, Alma H, Debbie S, Jenny K, Peggy H, Hilary B, Elisabeth H and Elaine R. I would also like to acknowledge my editor, who helped me breathe new life into Beth Jago's story.

I would also like to thank my husband, Ross, and my son, Sean, for their interest and support over the years, however a special thank you and acknowledgement must go to my daughter, Jade, who has been my greatest support and whose feedback is always appreciated.

Lastly, but by no means least, I would like to thank Hugo White, author of *One and All, A History of the Duke of Cornwall's Light Infantry 1702–1959* and Cornwall's Regimental Museum, Bodmin, Cornwall for their advice and help.

Memories

Remember me and you will smile,
Like echoes in the mind.
Tender, happy, loving moments,
Of another place in time.
Yet I can torment you, make you shake,
I'm your demons in a cage.
Vivid spectres of your past,
Crying out in rage.
Treat me kindly, or I will leave,
On the breeze, I will float away.
Delicate, evasive, like gossamer,
Leaving you in disarray ...

Victoria Cornwall

Chapter One

A muscle moved in the man's jaw. He had been watching the cottage for some time. Despite its isolation and ramshackle appearance, laundry on a washing line and wood stacked by the door were clear signs it was inhabited. Yet he had seen no one. His eyes narrowed in the fading light, as gulls screeched in the distance and the cool Atlantic breeze chilled his skin. Finally, a young woman emerged from the cottage to peg a garment on the washing line. Her long black hair and skirts lifted and tossed in the breeze as she did so, before she disappeared again behind the old cottage door. The man's jaw tightened at the sight of her. He had seen enough.

Without taking his eyes off the cottage, he gradually made his way down to the wooded embankment. The earthy track he followed, although narrow and ancient, held firm beneath him and he did not fear falling. The cottage was nestled amongst the trees of the beautiful River Valley, which had been carved by the Trevillet River. The river entered it by way of a waterfall, before making its way towards the jagged coastline, made of slate, and the deep blue sea beyond. As he neared his destination the joyful gurgling of the river welcomed his arrival but he found no pleasure in it or the beauty of his surroundings. It was the lone woman he wanted to see. She would not put up too much of a fight. The door of the cottage was closed, but he did not care. It gave way easily to his pressure and he entered with no announcement or cursory greeting. Within seconds a cloak of painful blackness engulfed him and the ground he stood upon came up to meet his face. As he fell unconscious to the floor, the reason for his

1

arrival, his plans, his past, indeed even his own name, was wiped from his memory.

Beth Jago's body shook as a mixture of fear and exhilaration coursed through her veins. She had experienced the intangible feeling of being watched for several days, and her sixth sense had now been proved right. The man lying on her slate floor was all the proof she needed. Unfortunately, his still body suggested she had injured him badly. Even so, her grip remained tight on the frying pan in her hand, ready to use it as a weapon again should she need to.

Fearing the unconscious stranger would suddenly reach for her, she took a step backwards on stiff, jerky legs. Her hands began to tremble violently and she found she could bear the weight of the heavy pan no longer. She slowly lowered it and made a concerted effort to calm her rapid breathing. She had sensed the man's arrival before she had seen him open her door. Acting on impulse she had reached for a weapon and swung it at the intruder. She had done such a good job defending her home that the man now appeared dead at her feet.

With some relief she saw his chest rise and fall. She relaxed a little and allowed herself the luxury of looking at him more closely. He was probably about thirty years of age, with the darkest brown hair, verging on black, cut short, neat and slightly longer on top, causing it to fall slightly tousled to one side as if he had not long run his hand through it. He was clean-shaven, with neat, well-shaped sideburns that did not distract from his handsome features. He was healthy looking, with broad shoulders and muscular thighs. However, his face carried the signs of solemnity in the form of two deep furrows between his brows and faint shadows below his eyes. His clothes, though hardy and splattered with mud, were well made and did not hint at his profession. His boots were made of expensive leather and, thought Beth, probably stolen. Who was this man and what did he want from her?

2

Lost in thought, she did not notice the slight flicker in his eyes. When she finally retraced his body and looked upon his face she realised, with a start, that a pair of hazel eyes were looking at her. She lifted the pan in readiness but his expression did not change. He continued to stare, his eyes narrowing as if he struggled to focus upon her. He attempted to lift his head, but the effort was too much. He groaned and his head fell back. Slowly he lifted his gaze to look at her again but, as if he could not bear the sight of her, he slowly closed his eyes and turned his head away to shut her out.

Beth let out the breath she had been holding and lowered the pan once more. The intruder was too ill to be a threat at the moment, she realised, but at some point he would recover and then what was he capable of doing? Beth gnawed at her bottom lip as she considered her next move. She wanted him out of her home and the only way to do that was to remove him before he regained full consciousness. From the length of him he looked to be six feet tall when standing, but he was not overweight. She mentally measured the distance to the door. If she managed to drag him to the other side of the threshold she could lock him outside before he recovered. He was a man, so hunger and a need for a drink would soon send him on his way – at least she hoped they would.

She placed her pan on the table and walked around his inert body, careful not to disturb him. He was all muscle and sinew, but each limb was well shaped and strong, perfect for dragging him across the room with. Beth decided to grab hold of one of his legs as it was booted and clothed and she would not have to touch the man himself.

Beth watched his face for signs of waking as she crouched down and carefully lifted his right foot. The polished leather was soft and smooth to the touch, but the leg felt far heavier than she had expected. Fearing the boot would come off in her hands when she pulled, Beth cradled it under her arm and held on to his knee. She paused for a moment, reflecting on the ridiculousness of the situation. This morning, when she woke to birdsong and the sun streaming through her bedroom window, she had not expected that only a few hours later she would be holding the leg of a man in her arms. Beth braced herself and gradually pulled. The task was more cumbersome than she had anticipated and despite using all her strength, the intruder moved very little. She attempted to pick up both his legs with the vain hope it would make the task easier, but holding two at the same time was unwieldy and it was difficult to obtain a secure grip. She lowered each leg in turn and decided to try his arms instead.

Beth briskly circled the man again, crouched on her haunches and selected a wrist. It was warm and well-shaped, with a fine scattering of dark hairs disappearing under the sleeve of his jacket and white cotton shirt. This intimate discovery caught her off guard and set off a train of thought as to whether his arms and chest were similarly covered. Beth gave herself a mental shake and forced herself to concentrate on obtaining a secure grip. She turned his hand over to reveal the smooth, fragile underside of his wrist. Protected from the sun, his skin was paler here and threaded with blue-corded veins. Mesmerised by the delicate pattern they made, she stroked a finger across them. She felt his heart pulsate beneath her touch and realised it matched the wild throbbing of her own.

His soft moan startled her and she immediately dropped his hand. She glanced at his face and was relieved to find that he remained unconscious and unaware of her. Beth stood up and placed her hands on her hips as she wondered what to do. Her plan to move him was proving more difficult than she had anticipated and to make matters worse he was oblivious to the trouble he was causing. Frustrated, and more than a little resentful, she realised she would have to wait until he woke and was able to stand. Only then could she force him to leave on his own two feet. She looked around for an appropriate weapon and selected a broom. The length of it would enable her to beat him from a distance if he gave her cause. She had done it before when a drunk from the village had wandered into the valley, so she felt confident that she could do it again if needed. Next time the intruder stirred he wouldn't find her feeling his heartbeat as it throbbed through his body. Next time, Beth Jago would be waiting for him with the sharp edge of her broom.

The blackness was thick and heavy, weighing him down so he could not move. His limbs felt numb and useless, yet his head throbbed with pulsating fire. Was this what it was like to be dead? Alone, helpless and in pain for all eternity? Without warning, the pain intensified to one small area, as if a rat had found a favourite spot and was gnawing at his brain. He wanted to brush it away, but the task seemed too complicated and insurmountable for his muddled thoughts. A rhythmic prodding of his body, from a world beyond the darkness, offered him a lifeline and something to focus on. With all his concentration, he slowly opened his eyes. A woman, with long raven hair, stood above him, prodding the side of his body with the head of a broom in an attempt to brush him up as if he was a pile of rubbish. He frowned. Her behaviour made no sense. The woman stopped, but continued to glare at him.

With difficulty, he eased himself to a sitting position against the stony wall of what appeared to be someone's home. He searched with shaking hands for the source of the pain and winced when he found a large bump on his head. If he was hoping the woman would offer him sympathy, he was wrong.

'It's time for you to leave,' she said calmly as she raised her broom. He looked about him and realised he did not recognise the granite walls and inglenook fireplace; furthermore, they began to sway alarmingly before his eyes. His confusion must have been clearly etched on his face, but the woman chose to ignore it. She prodded him with the broom again. 'Stand up. I want you gone.'

He returned his foggy mind to the woman. She was a little blurred, but he could tell she was angry with him, which confused him too, as he was the one lying hurt on the floor, not her. However, he would curb his tongue and remain civil as he had the uncomfortable feeling he was at her mercy. He searched for the bump on his head again. He winced. It still hurt.

He shook his head slowly and the pain intensified, whilst his stomach churned at the thought of standing up.

'My head hurts. I don't think I can stand up.'

The broom withdrew a little. 'You have not tried. This is my home and I don't want you in it.'

He tried to gather his thoughts, retracing his steps on how he came to be here. He frowned as he realised nothing came to mind. Another irritating prod of her broom jolted him back to the present. This time he attempted to swipe it away. It was a feeble challenge, no stronger than a babe in arms, and it embarrassed him. He dared to look up to see if the woman had noticed. She had finally stopped brandishing her broom, which told him that she probably had.

'I feel too sick to stand. I think I need to rest awhile.'

The woman arched an eyebrow, clearly unimpressed by his excuse. 'You must think me a fool.'

Concern for his own health finally caused him to snap. 'I have no opinion of you, madam, to think you a fool or otherwise!' His rebuke startled her and he immediately felt guilty for frightening her. 'I am sorry. I did not mean to shout. Please ... just tell me what has happened?' The woman tilted her head to look at him, but did not answer. 'Did I fall?'

The woman frowned. 'You don't remember?'

He shook his head slowly. The movement hurt forcing him to shut his eyes briefly until the pain eased. When he opened them again the woman was still looking at him.

'You broke into my home so I hit you on the head with a pan to defend myself.' The woman picked up a frying pan and held it aloft. 'And I will use it again if you do not get up and leave.'

Her explanation both horrified and confused him, but he could not help feeling there must be a grain of truth in it. After all, he did not recognise his surroundings so it could not be his house and therefore she had every right to ask him to leave. He slowly made an effort to stand. As he did so the room began to spin and the headache of pulsating fire returned with a vengeance. He reached for the wall and used it to slowly ease himself down on the floor again. The woman watched him struggle but remained where she was. Did she fear him that much that she felt a need to keep her distance?

'I can't leave ... not yet. The room is spinning and my head hurts like the devil has it in its grip.'

The woman took a step forward. She was a little clearer now, with a curious look upon her face as if he was a freak in a sideshow for her to view. He grew wary.

'Who are you?' she asked.

It was a simple question and one, he realised with horror, he could not answer. 'I don't know.'

'You don't remember who you are?' She took another step closer. 'Why did you break into my house?'

'I only have your word that I did.' He glanced at the open door. 'The door is open. It hardly presents as a break in.' The effort to come to that conclusion drained him of any strength he had. His head began to throb again and he could only cradle it in his hands hoping the pain would pass. The woman waited silently for him to recover. As suddenly as the pain arrived, it began to ease away. In its place was the realisation of the difficulty he was in. Dear Lord, he really didn't know his own name! He lifted his gaze to the woman standing no more than an arm's reach away.

'You did this to me. If I should die you will be culpable.'

The woman set her broom aside. 'You are not going to die.'

He rubbed the back of his neck to check for further injuries. 'I might.'

The woman placed her hands on her hips. 'I will not be made to feel it was wrong to have defended myself in my own home. Get up.'

'By your own words you attacked me,' he said as he attempted to stand again. His legs felt weak and trembled beneath him, but at least he was up. 'What if my reason for being here was an innocent one?' She refused to look at him. 'I should report you to the constable.'

His last remark goaded her into action, but it was not what he was hoping for. Unsympathetically, she opened the door wider, marched over to him and grabbed his arm. With an almighty pull she succeeded in dragging him to the door and, following a giant push, out of the house. The woman was stronger than she looked.

'I don't care if you do die. You are a crook and a thug and I want you gone. Stay away, do you hear?' she shouted before unceremoniously slamming the door in his face.

He stared at the wood panelled door as he listened to her drawing several bolts across to lock him out. He took a moment to steady himself before he turned around. He found himself in a deep recessed valley that stretched out towards a blue sea in the distance. Trees, of various shades of green, lined the slate scarred banks and waved their leaves at him, whilst down below was a silver tipped river gurgling in the sunshine. He recognised none of it and realised he should have considered the consequences of goading the only person who could help him.

Chapter Two

Beth stood at her window and watched the man. He sat on one of the boulders of slate scattered on the valley bank, his figure clearly silhouetted against the red sky as the sun prepared to set on the horizon of the sea. She glanced at the bolts on her door. She had felt for some time that she was being watched and had had them fitted only the week before, but despite her need for them, it was impossible to have her door bolted every minute of the day.

She returned her attention to the man outside. Despite her limited view of him, she could see that he remained unwell. He sat with his head cradled in his hands and his elbows balanced on his knees. He had attempted to stand twice but had become unsteady and was forced to sit down again. She bit her lip, his words echoing in her mind that should he die she would be culpable. She did not want a man's death on her conscience and although an hour had passed since she had evicted him from her home, he was no nearer to leaving the valley than when he had arrived. Suddenly she saw him retch. The stark contrast between the beautiful tranquil sunset and the ugliness and noise of retching finally forced her to act. She could no longer stand by and do nothing. Besides, it was difficult to enjoy the beauty of nature with his body blotting the view.

The man did not hear her approach and only realised she was there when she calmly offered him the tankard of water she had brought him. He lifted his head, nodded his thanks and silently took it. His trembling fingers grazed hers as he did so. Unknown to him, thought Beth, it was the second time their hands had touched that day, but a fragile truce had been formed – at least for now. The tankard shook in his grasp and Beth fought the urge to help guide it to his lips. He arched his neck and drank deeply, but his coordination remained poor and water trickled down his chin. He glanced up at her, embarrassed, and hastily wiped it away. Despite his strength and earlier dubious intentions, Beth was sure that this man was no threat to her now.

'It will be dark soon,' she said reluctantly to his bowed head as she took the tankard from him. 'You had better come back inside.'

The man did not reply. Beth braced herself. She would not beg to treat him, although she did not want his death on her hands.

'I know someone who could give you something for your retching. It might make you feel better. But you will have to behave – I want no funny business.'

The man gave a wry smile but finally nodded in agreement, then he slowly stood and promptly vomited on the ground at her feet. For the first time, Beth wondered if he would survive until morning. The enormity of what she had done, and the implications of his possible death, loomed in front of her and made her feel sick too.

Carefully they retraced the short walk back to her home. He stumbled several times and she had to resort to supporting his body and guiding him along the path down the steep valley bank. As luck would have it Beth noticed her neighbour's son, Tom Kitto, amongst the trees behind her house. Tall, clumsy and on the verge of manhood, he carried a bundle of wooden sticks he had gathered for kindling, but it was not his frame or his passion for collecting wood that Beth recognised. It was his unruly red hair blowing in the breeze that confirmed his identity, as no one but Tom had hair so bright. She called out to him.

'Tom, run home and fetch your mother for me. A man has fallen on the path and banged his head.' The boy clutched his sticks tighter to him and frowned at them. 'Do you understand, Tom? I need your help. Please get Martha for me.'

The boy, always eager to please Beth, suddenly smiled. Holding his sticks tightly, he ran off on his errand with the speed and agility of a pixie. Beth watched his pale, skinny frame disappear amongst the trees whilst offering an apology to the Lord for her little lie. Tom would only be upset if he had known the truth. The man she held appeared not to hear her explanation or even that she had asked someone for help. Instead he left her side and, with great effort and concentration, stumbled towards the door of her cottage. Beth followed close behind. Upon entering her home he grabbed a chair with a trembling hand, collapsed into it and closed his eyes to rest. Beth looked down on him and wondered, not for the first time that evening, what on earth she had done.

Beth was unsure how long it would take for Martha to arrive. She was an old woman and it would take time for her to walk to the valley from the village where she lived – too much time to be alone with the stranger. Beth envisaged stilted conversations and tension-filled silences stretching out before her as she watched the bowed head of the man in question from a safe distance on the other side of the room. What an odd situation to find herself in. Alone with a man she did not trust, yet did not now feel threatened by. A man she wanted gone, but who needed to stay so he could recover and not die. He was strong, yet, at the moment, so weak, and, the most odd thing of all, he was a stranger, not only to her, but to himself too. Beth looked at the chair he was sitting in. He also looked very uncomfortable. He needed to relax and rest while they waited for Martha to heal him. She caught herself imagining nursing him back to health by soothing his pain away with a wet, cool compress and feeding him broth, and was angry with herself for thinking such thoughts.

'I am going to find you some blankets so you can lie by the fire,' she muttered more sharply than she intended, before hastily leaving the room.

The dramatic sunset had faded by the time Tom's mother arrived. Martha was a portly woman, with untidy grey hair, a rugged complexion and an audible wheeze when she overexerted herself. Her arthritic hips gave her a rocking gait and her breathlessness gave the impression she had hurried, but despite these afflictions she was a robust, reliable and kindly woman who many of the villagers depended upon for her home-made remedies. The ingredients she used were a closely guarded secret and she would often be seen gathering the plants and seeds by the roadside as the sun rose and set. She was called upon to treat everyone from young babes to those in their twilight years and when death was imminent and the pain too much to bear, her face was the one they wanted to see to end their anguish. The villagers trusted Martha's wisdom more than any physician, as she had learnt her unique knowledge as a direct result of her own despair – for she had given birth to Tom and that was a heavy burden to carry. Beth welcomed her inside.

'Tom said a man 'ad fallen and 'urt 'is 'ead. I don't need to know all the ins and outs, just let me see 'im and I will make up my own mind.'

She handed Beth a basket of bottles and waddled over to the man lying on a makeshift bed by the fire. Since lying down he had not moved at all. Beth chewed her bottom lip and hoped he hadn't died while her back was turned. Martha knelt beside him to start her examination. The man's arm moved and Beth breathed a sigh of relief. He was still alive after all.

Beth strained to listen, but they spoke in hushed tones and she could only make out the odd word. After some minutes, Martha straightened her creaking joints and stood up.

'You 'ave 'ad a bad bang on the 'ead, lad. You must rest for a few days. The sickness, dizzy spells, and problems with your eyes are common symptoms in cases such as this. The loss of your memory is a rare thing, but is caused by the same injury.'

The man slowly propped himself up on his elbow. 'Will it come back?'

'Maybe.'

'Maybe? But I can't remember anything: my name, my age. It is like I am suspended with no reference to connect my life to.'

Beth dropped her gaze and fiddled with the bottles in the basket. Despite feeling he had brought it upon himself, she still couldn't help feeling a twinge of guilt.

Martha gave an empathetic nod. 'Can't be nice for you. 'Tis fortunate Beth found you. There is none kinder to provide the rest that you need. With God's 'elp, your memory will return. It may return like a dripping well pump, bit by bit, or it may come all at once. I've known a few people in my time who 'ave 'ad the same trouble. These things 'appen. 'T ain't nice.'

'So you think it will return?' said the man.

'In some rare cases the memory does not. In others it becomes like a sieve, unable to 'old on to new memories. I'm sorry to bear such bad news, but we must be 'opeful. I will leave you something to ease the pain and sickness. It will 'elp you rest.' Martha handed two bottles to Beth. 'But it is time, good food and gentle nursing you need, not my remedies. You must not move. Remain in bed until the sickness passes. God willing, I see no reason why 'e should not recover.'

'Gentle nursing? By the woman who almost k—' The man lay back down and rested a forearm across his brow. 'I'm doomed,' he muttered under his breath.

Beth opened her mouth to retaliate, but Martha stopped her with a pat on her arm.

''E's not right in the 'ead at the moment, maid. 'E will be feeling irritable and unsettled, like a pig on a beach. Don't take 'is mutterings to 'eart.'

Beth relented and followed Martha to the door. 'I had hoped you would make him better so he could leave tonight.'

''E needs time and rest, Beth.'

'I suppose I could put him in the shed to sleep.'

Martha shook her head. ''E needs warmth and someone to watch 'im. 'E could get worse.'

Beth reached for her arm. 'Are you saying he could still die?'

The two women glanced at the man by the fire. He had turned his back to them and did not appear to be listening.

''E might, but then 'e may not. Would you like me to stay?'

Beth shook her head. 'No. You have Tom to look after. He will be upset if you stay overnight here. He won't understand.'

'No, 'e won't.' Martha jerked her head towards her new patient. ''E will be too sick to give you much trouble over the next few days.' She turned to leave and noticed the bolts on the door. Everyone knew everyone in Port Carrek. The villagers' loyalties were strong and their family ties even stronger. It was a community where no one felt the need to lock their doors, yet Beth now did and Martha wanted to know why.

'You 'aving trouble, maid? Perhaps I should stay after all.'

Beth made light of her new bolts. 'I am fine. Since grandfather's death, I thought I would feel less vulnerable if I could lock my door. A woman living on her own can never be too careful.' She heard the sound of soft snoring coming from the figure lying next to the fire. Unfortunately, she wasn't alone any more.

Martha gave her arm a squeeze. 'Very wise. 'Ow long is it since he passed on? Must be almost three months now.'

Beth dragged her attention back to Martha. 'Yes.' She smiled reassuringly at her. 'There is no need to worry about me, Martha. My rounds taking in mending from the villagers who can no longer do close needlework keeps me busy and I have started to take orders too. I have already made two dresses this month. I get by and at least I have my own home, which is more than most.'

Martha took her basket from Beth and prepared to leave.

'What are you going to do with 'im when 'e is feeling better? 'E can't stay 'ere alone with you.' They heard him reach for a bucket and begin to retch. 'There is your reputation to think of. You know 'ow people will gossip. You taking care of an injured man they might understand, but if they knew you 'ad a young, 'ealthy one under your roof ... and an 'andsome one at that.'

'Handsome?' Beth glanced over at the broad shouldered figure by the fire. The man's head turned slightly in her direction. 'I hadn't noticed,' Beth lied.

Martha paused on the threshold to speak a few last words before opening the door and disappearing into the darkness. Beth bolted the door behind her and turned back to the stranger. He lay on his back on the temporary bed and stared at the ceiling, his hands cradled behind his head in a makeshift cushion.

'Do you really not remember anything?' asked Beth.

'No. I have lost my memory, remember?' came his curt reply. Beth turned away, but his next words halted her. 'I'm sorry for my rudeness. I had hoped your friend would cure me.' His sad confessional pulled at her heart as he continued to stare stoically at the ceiling above. His tightly interlaced fingers, bleached of blood from tension, showed his frustration and anger with the situation. A situation she had helped place him in.

Beth forced a brittle smile. 'Well, let's hope, for all our sakes, that your memory returns soon so you can leave.'

He did not reply. The firelight danced on his features as it warmed the room but the atmosphere had changed. It felt out of sorts, like an ill-fitting boot.

'It seems,' Beth added, 'that you may not be as doomed as you think.'

He turned to look at her. Beth lifted her basket, piled high with mending, and dropped it heavily onto the table. The man winced at the noise it made.

'Martha has discovered something about you that may encourage your memory to return.' He eased himself onto his elbow again to look at her. She had caught his attention. 'You did not walk here,' she said. 'Tied to a tree at the back of the cottage is a horse, and as I don't own one, it must be yours.'

She left him with two thick slices of buttered, homemade bread and two boiled eggs and went outside to see to his horse. She had expected a fine-boned creature, to match the man's fine leather boots, but instead his horse was a large, thickset cob, with a muddy coat and well-worn saddle. Would a thief arrive on such a big beast? Wouldn't it be more likely that he would creep up on the house unseen? Perhaps she had acted too hastily after all.

After a nervous start and a lot of fumbling, she managed to unsaddle the horse and lead it up the track, through the wood, to the road above her cottage. She was glad to be rid of the unpredictable beast as she waved her arms and shooed it into a neighbouring field. She watched it gallop a full circle before settling to graze and promised herself that she would explain how it came to be there to the farmer in the morning.

By the time she returned to her cottage it was fully dark but for the glow from the fire. Martha's remedy had taken effect and the man was asleep. He had not touched his food and Beth wondered how long it had been since he had eaten. She looked down at his still, peaceful figure. Martha was right, he was handsome and was a man she might have found attractive if the circumstances had been different. However, the reality was that he had barged into her home without knocking, and therefore his purpose and intent must be called into question. She fed the fire with another log so it would continue to burn well into the night and then replaced one of his blankets that had fallen from his body. She would sleep downstairs tonight, she decided, so she could be on hand should he need her. She would also ensure her broom was nearby – just in case.

He opened his eyes to see an unfamiliar room cast in the flickering warm glow of an oil lamp and the dying flames of a fire. The unfamiliar morphed into the familiar and he turned his head to see a woman asleep in a chair beside him, a basket of clothing at her feet and a shirt with a needle and thread hanging from her lap. Beth. At least that was what the old lady had called her. He knew the woman's name, if not his own, and she was the reason he was here. However, he admitted to himself, she had arranged for someone to treat him and offered him a bed for the night so her character was not so very flawed. The injury had disturbed his vision at first, spinning the world and turning her into nothing more than a shadowy figure, but over the hours she had become clearer, and at this moment her image was the clearest yet – almost perfect.

He eased himself onto his side to have a better look at her. He believed she was no lady, for she sat with one leg hitched over the arm of the chair and her hair loose about her shoulders. Yet he could not help thinking that he was rushing his assessment of her.

Time was on his side so he made himself more comfortable and restarted his study, starting with her feet. She had discarded her boots, which were practical and worn, and now lay haphazardly by her chair. A small foot, in a well-darned stocking, hung limply off the chair. Her skirt was made from an assortment of fabrics, which gave it a vibrant mixture of colour, yet it was clean and fitted her well. She wore no corset underneath, he decided, as there was no stiffness in her posture. Her waist was small, with a man's leather belt about it, and he noticed that its holes had been altered to fit her. The masculinity of the belt and labourer's shirt accentuated her femininity, which could easily entice a man if he allowed it. She had no use of a parasol, as her skin was tanned with a healthy glow and a hint of colour on her cheeks. Her hair was as black as coal, with gentle waves like an autumn sea, and it shone like black diamonds in the soft light. Her lips, slightly parted, were full and pale pink and he could not help his eyes lingering on her mouth a while before he continued his appraisal of her. Finally he noted her long black lashes, which lay fanned on her cheeks. Beneath those closed lids he knew there were the darkest, sapphire-blue eyes he had ever seen. If the circumstances had been different, he mused, if he had met her at another time and place, he would have thought her beautiful, unconventional and mysterious. Unfortunately, she had acted without restraint or caution, and her actions had almost killed him. She had robbed him of his memory and with it his past life and his present. How was he to return home, when he did not even know where his home was? Right now, despite her beauty and vulnerability as she slept before him, he had to acknowledge that he should hate her for what she had done as he was not a bad person and did not deserve such an attack. Yet strangely he did not hate her. Did this mean that on some subconscious level he knew he deserved her assault or was he simply letting her pretty features affect him so? He should at least resent her. He certainly felt capable of such a feeling. The more he thought about his circumstances the darker the emotion it conjured up within became. Such darkness, he realised, was not unknown to him and, more worryingly, felt like an old friend.

The hand on his shoulder woke him instantly. His eyes flew open, every nerve in his body alert and pulsating. It was Beth and she had just placed a dish of broth beside him.

'It's only me,' she reassured him. 'It's midday. You have slept non-stop since Martha's visit yesterday. I thought I should wake you. You should eat something, even if it's only a spoonful or two.'

He sank back on the bed, relieved that he had recognised her. It seemed he could retain fresh memories if not recall old ones, although, he had to admit, Beth was not a woman a man could easily forget.

'Not all night. I woke once.'

Her eyes widened and he realised he had unnerved her.

'Rest assured, I did not have the urge to attack you while you were sleeping.' He eased himself into a sitting position and took the bowl she offered him. She remained wary and he realised he had made light of a situation where she had felt frightened. He stared at the meal, frowning, unable to shake her worried expression from his mind. 'I have to ask ... did I hurt you?'

'When?'

'When I first arrived here. I hope I am not the sort of man who would lay a hand on a woman.' He glanced up at her. 'I want the truth.'

Beth fidgeted. 'I had a right to defend myself ...'

His stomach lurched at the thought that he may have harmed her.

'... but no, you did not harm me.'

He began to stir the broth with his spoon. An uneasy silence descended. Despite her reply, he could not help wondering if the only reason he had not harmed her was because she had stopped him in time.

'As you cannot recall your own name, what shall I call you?'

Beth's question caught him off guard. He did not want to pick a name at random and claim it as his own. His appetite left him as suddenly as it had appeared.

He rested the spoon in the bowl. 'I want my own name.'

'I have to call you something.'

'Call me what you like. I won't promise to answer to it.' He returned the bowl to her, lay down again and covered his eyes with the crook of his arm. To accept another name meant he was accepting his present state and he was not ready to do that yet.

'You have not eaten your broth.'

'I have no appetite. I am afraid that your time has been wasted, but I thank you for the sentiment behind it. Water will suffice for now.'

Beth stood up with the bowl in her hands. He thought she would leave, but instead she hesitated as if she was unsure whether to insist or let him dictate what his body needed. To his surprise, she decided on the former.

She sat down beside him again. 'Eat half of it and I will leave you in peace.' She held out a spoon filled with the broth she had made. He looked at it as it hovered above his chest.

'I am not a baby to be fed.'

'Then stop behaving like one,' retorted Beth.

He kept his lips firmly closed, but Beth would not be put off and the spoon remained. The aroma of the meaty broth wafted up his nostrils to tempt his appetite.

'If you don't eat it, it will spill and burn you. Let us stop playing games. You know, and I know, that to recover a body must sleep, eat and drink. So far you have done only two of those things since Martha's visit.'

He shot her a glance. Being ordered to do something felt both familiar yet unusual, which was unsettling, but he also saw the wisdom in her words. He wanted to discover his identity and to do that he needed to be well. He sat up again and took the spoon and bowl from her. Their fingers grazed and jogged a more recent memory. They had touched before, when she had handed him the tankard of water, only he was too unwell for the sensation to affect him. This time it affected him very much. He glanced up at her, interested to see if she had felt it too. If she did, she hid it well.

He decided to concentrate on eating and soon settled into the rhythm of a hungry man.

'I shall call you Luke until you remember your name. The Good Samaritan story is told in the Book Of Luke.' He continued to eat as if she had not spoken as he had no intention of accepting the name. 'I am talking about the Bible. Do you remember the story? It tells of a man who was attacked and badly injured, but who is later cared for by his enemy.'

He paused to look at her. 'And you are the enemy?'

Beth almost laughed, until she realised he was serious. 'Well, no.'

'I have only your word for that.'

'Which is more reliable than yours at the moment.'

He grudgingly accepted her retort. She had a quick wit, which was to be admired. He finished the soup and returned the empty bowl to her. When he was better he would be able to spar with her on more equal terms.

'I will call you Luke. It is up to you if you answer,' said Beth, getting up. She was leaving and he realised he had not thanked her. He tried, but the words did not come easy to him.

'The soup ... it was good.' His voice, barely above a whisper, stopped her in mid step. She hesitated, probably doubting she had heard the paltry compliment. She turned to look at him. Under her gaze he felt strangely exposed and vulnerable. He lay down again and stared at the ceiling as if he had not spoken and was just waiting for sleep. She turned away and he felt he had failed in some way. He forced himself to say the words he really wanted to say and this time he spoke more clearly so there was no denying his meaning.

'I am glad I did not hurt you when I entered your home.' Beth turned and as she was leaving, he lifted on his elbow to watch. She was smiling. Hopefully she would now believe her intruder was not so very dangerous after all.

Chapter Three

The mud sucked at his boots, hampering his progress and balance, causing him to lose his footing like a drunkard. With each step the mud became deeper, as pools of dirty water filled the voids left by other men's footfalls. Sharp white stones, hidden in the stinking mess, cut at his hands and knees with each fall and soon his blood flowed into the brown puddles around him. He stopped, exhausted and unable to go further, and looked about him.

With growing horror, he realised the white stones were in fact human bones. Some protruded out of the mud at odd angles, whilst others lay flat and slowly sank in the quagmire. He struggled to his feet as skeletal limbs rose from the depths to reach for him. They clawed at his body, pulling him downwards into the darkness and away from the light. He could smell and taste the stench of gangrene as it infiltrated his nostrils and clawed at his throat. He found himself drowning in the decomposed tissue. He battled to reach the surface and cry for help but no matter how hard he fought for survival, the dead were claiming him as one of their own.

He woke suddenly, sweating, breathless and alert. He sat up and ran a trembling hand through his hair, relieved he was no longer in the hell he had dreamt about. Having refused further doses of Martha's medicine, he had been tortured by nightmares ever since. He had not confided in Beth about his dreams during the three days he had stayed with her. How do you explain to a woman that you dream of death when she still remains wary of your presence? He did not want to frighten her. He was scared enough for the both of them.

He glanced at the stairs and hoped he had not woken her. The stairs were cast in shadow, but the cottage remained silent so he felt increasingly confident that Beth remained asleep in her bed. He lay down, cradled the back of his head in his arms and stared at the beams above him. He was no nearer to remembering who he was. A search of his clothing gave no clue to his identity as his pockets were empty but for a few coins. However, despite his nightmares, he had made some progress. Yesterday he had started to feel better. His appetite was back to normal, whatever normal was, and he was able to walk around the room without feeling dizzy. Physically he was well, although he had to admit that inside he still felt vulnerable and weak. Call it masculine pride, but he did not want Beth to know and was glad she had not heard him cry out in his sleep.

Beth Jago. What a strange creature she was. Independent, feisty, and with a tongue as sharp as flint. Her energy was hard to tolerate when he felt so ill as was the name she had insisted on giving him. Luke. He had refused to answer to it. He was an impatient invalid and a frustrated man. The combination made him sullen company and, to his shame, he had snapped at her several times. Yet she had continued to let him stay despite the risk he might pose to her. He knew she did not trust him completely and wanted him gone, whilst he could not help but still blame her for the situation he now found himself in. It was not a good mixture to build a friendship on.

Tomorrow might see an end to both their problems as he planned to visit his horse. The beast might just evoke a memory and provide a key to who he was. He could be leaving tomorrow and they would never have to see one another again. The thought both pleased and unsettled him. He closed his eyes and waited for a more peaceful sleep to claim him and take him away from his troubles.

Beth sat in the shadows at the top of the stairs. Luke's cries had pulled at her heart, but her instinct made her keep her distance so she had remained hidden. She waited until she could hear his breathing settle into the slow rhythm of deep sleep before she silently retraced her steps to her bedroom. She slipped beneath the covers in her box bed and snuggled deeper under them. It was the third nightmare he had had in as many days. It took some time before she finally fell into a fitful sleep.

Beth's grandfather's shed appeared on the verge of falling down. Its door hung precariously from the hinges, and the rotten wood, with its telltale pinprick holes of woodworm infestation, provided poor security for the shed. The peeling paint and boarded up window emphasised its longstanding neglect, but once inside it was apparent that it was far sturdier than it looked. Luke entered and looked around with disgust at the scattered tools and dust. Beth followed him in. Feeling a little embarrassed by the state of the shed, she stood quietly beside him and waited. Laid out on the bench were the saddle and bridle, and although well used, it was also well made. The neglected shed had disgusted Luke, but the tack appeared to give the man hope.

Beth sat patiently on her grandfather's workbench while he ran his hand along the saddle's worn brown leather. Next, he tested the metal stirrup's weight in his hand, before examining the horse's bit, taking note of its shape and type. Finally, he lifted the saddle flaps in turn for signs of ownership and even smelt the leather in the hope it would evoke a memory inside his blank mind. She waited quietly, but after five long minutes she could wait no longer.

'Does it bring back any memories?'

Luke shook his head. In a fit of anger that startled her, he threw the reins across the shed. They hit the wall and crumpled to the floor in a tangled heap.

'Martha said it may take a while. You must be patient.'

'I don't want to be patient!' shouted Luke. 'I have a life out there that might need me. What if I have a business, a family ... people who rely on me?' He shot her a scowling glance. There was no mistaking who he blamed for his predicament.

Beth jumped down from the bench, picked up the reins and set about untangling them until they hung neatly from her hand. She would not be made to feel guilty for protecting her home. Martha had warned her Luke would feel out-of-sorts, 'like a pig on a beach', so she would remain patient with him.

'Come and see your horse. Perhaps he will stir a memory. I put him in a field on the other side of the trees. A walk through the wood will do you the world of good.'

Luke did not look convinced but Beth ignored him. Once he saw the beauty of the branches and leaves against the blue sky, spotted the entrances to burrows in the embankment and heard the birds in the trees, his mood was bound to lighten.

She was wrong. Luke took no pleasure in his surroundings and his scowl remained firmly on his face as he followed her through the woods. So when he finally saw his big boned horse, his shocked expression gave her a perverse sense of pleasure and she allowed herself a smile. It seemed that he too had expected a thoroughbred rather than the muddy, muscular cob that grazed in the field beyond the gate.

'Perhaps the high and mighty life you think you lead is not so high and mighty,' she said, sounding as smug as she felt. 'Perhaps you are a farmer or a rag and bone man?' The worried glance he threw her made her laugh. 'I'm sure I can find a sack for you to start your rag and bone *business* again,' she teased.

The warm summer breeze gently lifted her hair as she began to laugh. Luke's eyes dropped to her exposed neck and for a moment it was unclear what he was thinking. Did he want to touch her there to caress or throttle her? Her heart skipped a beat. He turned briskly away and stared at the animal. The horse disappointed him.

Beth stopped laughing. 'I'm sorry. I shouldn't be making fun of you.' She came to stand beside him and leant against the fence too. They stood in silence and watched the horse eat in the sunshine, his grazing continuous despite the occasional flick of his tail to ward away the flies. A rabbit popped its head above the tall meadow grass. It furtively looked about and quickly disappeared from view, only to re-emerge nearer the hedge. Beth glanced at Luke to see if he had seen it too, but he showed no interest. He had other things on his mind.

'I don't remember the horse. It feels like I'm seeing it for the first time.'

'Something will jog your memory, Luke.'

He braced his shoulders. 'Don't call me that. I want my own name.' The horse briefly lifted its head to look at them, but soon returned to its grazing. Luke made a decision. 'I will go and speak with a constable.'

Beth was horrified. 'And say what?'

'I will tell him the truth.'

'That I hit you?'

'Everything.'

'But I may not be believed. *You* don't believe me.' Beth's heart began to race as she tried her best to remain calm. 'You are trying too hard, Luke.'

'Don't call me Luke.'

'I'm sure that memories are best coaxed to return, rather than forced. Come stroke the horse to see if that helps.'

'Someone will have reported me missing.'

Beth tried to open the gate – the sooner he met the horse the better – but the gate was old, hung badly from its hinges and would not budge. The constable would never believe her. She had no injuries to warrant almost killing a man. 'The horse will recognise you. Come meet him first.' Beth took to shaking the gate with frustration, as it would still not open. Luke ignored her.

'I will tell the constable that you fetched help, but what has been done cannot be undone. Let this be a lesson to you.'

Beth's frustration turned to anger. She had had enough. Hitching her skirts, she climbed the gate and straddled it, pausing momentarily to look down on Luke's surprised face. It seems that he had never seen a woman climb before.

'You are the most rude and ungrateful man I have ever met,' Beth seethed. 'I have given you a roof, nursed you and fed you for four days and all the thanks I get is to be arrested for violence. I wish I hadn't hit you on the head with a pan,' she said as she prepared to climb down the other side. 'I wish I had used a brick!'

With a vice-like grip Luke grabbed her, his fingers easily circling her small wrist. Beth was too angry to be scared.

'You are not the victim, Mr Luke Whoever-you-are. You forced open my door. There was no knock, no greeting. Tell me, what good reason would you have to enter a woman's home without announcing yourself? At best you have no manners, at worst you are a thief, so don't preach to me about what is right or wrong.'

Luke's grip remained tight but she had seen a flicker of surprise and concern in his eyes. It was fleeting but it was there all the same, passing across his face like a dark cloud on a sunny day. Yet even when it had gone she remained transfixed by those expressive hazel eyes as they held hers as effectively as his hold on her wrist.

She attempted to pull away. 'And you are the most unlikeable man I have ever met,' she added for good measure.

The concern in his eyes had gone, but it was too late – she had seen it and it had told her what he had not. He was finally beginning to question his reason for visiting her. Beth relented, for anger would get them nowhere. 'Come, meet your horse,' she coaxed.

Luke's fingers loosened, allowing her to peel her arm away and climb down on the other side of the gate.

'I'm sorry,' she said. 'I should not have lost my temper.'

'No, you shouldn't have.'

They stared at each other, both a little breathless and shaken by their argument.

Desperate to put some distance between them, Beth turned on her heels.

'But you are right, I have not been easy to live with these past few days.'

Beth inhaled deeply. It was not an apology, but it would have to do. Without replying she left him at the gate and made her way quickly across the meadow. Her body trembled with rage, or perhaps it was exhilaration; she did not know for sure which. She glanced over her shoulder. Luke was swinging his body over the gate with ease, as if he had done it a hundred times before. She marched on, annoyed that he had made it look so easy. A man's voice called out to them and stopped her in her tracks.

An old man, with a dog bounding at his heels, came towards them, cutting a trail through the colourful flowers that peppered the tall grass. His walk, although slow, had an air of proprietary confidence. Beth instantly recognised him. It was Bill, the farmer who owned the field.

'Hello, Bill,' called Beth. 'This is the man who owns the horse.'

The farmer's watery blue eyes narrowed as he scrutinised the younger man as he approached. With the benefit of some distance between them, Beth found herself appreciating Luke's healthy physique as he strode through the long grass towards them. The last shadows of her anger faded away with each step he took. Bill turned his head and spat on the ground, the fluid dart streaking a straight trail through the air.

'No, he's not the owner of the horse,' he replied.

Luke arrived. 'You know me?'

The farmer removed his cap to only replace it again immediately with great care and precision, as if giving himself extra time to think.

'Nope, don't reckon I do. But I know the owner, and it's not you.'

Beth grew apprehensive. 'Do you think this man *stole* the horse?'

'Now, Beth, I didn't say that. Look here.' The farmer led them to the horse and ran his hand over its belly and a branded mark, partially hidden by mud. 'This is a loan horse owned by Treligga over at Killygrew.' He straightened. 'I suggest you take him back soon as the bugger will charge you for each day he's gone.'

Beth and Luke exchanged glances. This was the lead they had been waiting for.

'Where is Killygrew? I must speak with Mr Treligga. He will know who hired his horse. He will know me.'

Bill rubbed the back of his neck with a weathered hand. 'Now that's not easy to explain. 'Tis a complicated route.'

'I will take you,' interrupted Beth. Both men looked at her. Her offer surprised both of them, but no one more than her. She shrugged, a little embarrassed. 'I want to make sure you don't get lost.'

Luke's hazel eyes narrowed. 'There is no need. I can make my own way.'

Bill was not convinced he could. 'Beth knows the way. She wants to help.'

'She wants to be rid of me.'

Beth placed her hands on her hips. 'I am offering to help. Take it or leave it.'

Luke remained sceptical. 'And how do you intend getting home again?'

'Like everyone around here who does not own a horse … by walking or accepting a lift. You need not concern yourself.'

A muscle in Luke's jaw moved. 'Then I will not concern myself and your offer is accepted.'

The farmer began to chuckle at their sparring.

'Loss of memory is no laughing matter, Bill. You have a name, I do not.'

'Then let me give you one, boy,' said the farmer, hitting away a swarm of midges that came to settle near the horse.

'Thank you, but no.' He looked pointedly at Beth. 'Despite Beth christening me with another man's name, I want my own name. And I have a feeling I will find it at Killygrew.' He undid his belt and secured it around the horse's neck.

'What are you doing?' Beth asked.

'I see no reason to wait. I will saddle the horse and meet you at the shed.' He turned to Bill and shook his hand. 'Thank you for your help, sir. I am grateful and hope I will not have to trouble you again.'

Beth watched him lead the horse carefully from the field. He had been living with her for several days now, but she still knew so little about him. They had been forced together for the briefest of time by circumstance and mishap. His lack of identity, a basic human quality, formed an invisible barrier and kept him a stranger to her. Their time together was drawing to a close and soon he would be gone. She should be glad it was almost over.

'Thank you, Bill, for allowing the horse to graze in your field.'

She watched Luke open the gate with ease and she couldn't help but feel annoyed that he managed it while also leading a horse. Why were her feelings towards him so confused? They seemed to swing precariously from concern to frustration. She felt unable to drag her eyes from him until he was out of sight, a fact that was not lost on Bill.

'When you told me about the horse, you said you found him lying on the ground outside.'

'Yes. He fell.'

Bill raised an eyebrow at her. Beth felt her cheeks burn with shame for lying. She had known Bill since she was a child and trusted him, yet for some strange reason she did not want him to know the truth. He would wonder why she had taken it upon herself to care for a man who had broken into her home. It was something she wondered about herself.

'Well, maid, you are in a pickle. If you want me to help, just let me know. We have a barn he can sleep in. I don't like to think of you alone in a house with a strange man.'

'Luke will probably be gone by tonight so there is no need to worry.' Remembering his disturbing dreams, Beth added, 'I should be scared of him, but I'm not. At this moment, he is in more distress than I am. He reminds me of a dog that has been badly treated, snarling and snapping at everyone who tries to help. You won't tell anyone that I have a man living with me, will you, Bill? Martha and Tom know, but Martha won't tell and Tom ... well, you know what Tom's like.'

The farmer shook his head. 'No, I won't, maid. Hopefully you won't see him again after today. Good luck in Killygrew.'

'Thank you.' She kissed his whiskery cheek, which made him blush, before hurriedly following the trail of crushed grass Luke and his horse had made as they left the field.

Bill remained in the meadow, smiling to himself. It had been a long time since a pretty girl had kissed his cheek. The man was too wrapped up with his own problems to notice just how pretty Beth was, but Bill had no doubt that he would if he stayed around any longer. *If* he stayed around. He felt a sense of unease, as if he had forgotten something but did not know what it was. The troubled feeling remained with him for some time and it was only when he sat down to eat his wife's meat and potato pie later in the day that the uneasy feeling finally faded away.

Beth stroked the horse's nose as Luke put the saddle on. He found that he was efficient and competent in the task, which was a relief as Beth was watching his every move. He mounted with ease and offered her his hand to help her up. To his surprise, she declined it.

'No, thank you. I will walk.'

He frowned. Only a woman could deflate a man's ego so fast. 'You told me it is three miles to Killygrew. If you don't find a lift home it will be six for you.'

Beth shielded her eyes from the sun as she looked up at him. 'I have walked six miles before.' She looked nervously at the horse as it shook its head.

'But not in my company. What sort of man would I be if I let you walk?'

'That is why we are going to Killygrew, to find out what sort of man you are.'

'I did not have you down as a prude,' goaded Luke.

Beth ignored him and began to follow the track out of the valley. Frustrated, he followed her.

'You straddled a gate. I am sure you can straddle a horse too.' He caught up with her. 'Is it because you don't want to sit close to me? I can assure you that the only thing I am interested in is finding out who I am.'

Beth marched on. She really was a stubborn woman. He eased his horse into her path, forcing her to stop. The horse stamped impatiently and she hastily retreated a few steps.

'We will get there quicker if you ride behind me. Don't be so stubborn and accept my offer of a ride, as I accepted your offer to be my guide.'

Luke leaned down and offered his hand again. It was fascinating to watch her thoughts play out in her eyes as she stared at it and seriously considered his offer. He saw a mixture of fear and longing. She gave the horse a furtive, nervous glance, before reaching for his hand. He lifted her onto the saddle behind him and quickly eased the horse into a brisk walk before she could change her mind.

The first part of the journey took them along the coastal bridleway. After a mile, they turned east and followed a track through a sparse, quiet wood, which later joined a track through the open countryside. Luke kept the horse at a brisk walk, eager to reach Killygrew. He felt comfortable in the saddle and discovered his horsemanship felt natural to him. This discovery was comforting and he was keen to learn more about himself. Beth sat behind him, but if it hadn't been for her grip on his jacket to maintain her balance, and the occasional offer of directions, he would have thought he rode alone. He had seen the flash of fear in her eyes as she realised she would have to ride behind him. It seemed she had not ridden before, but he was beginning to realise she was a woman of substance and that she would not let her fear of a big horse prevent her from getting rid of him. Bravely, she had grabbed his hand and heaved herself up behind him, being careful not to lean to heavily against his body once she was seated. Unlike some women she did not partake in idle chatter, allowing them both free to retreat into their own thoughts. It suited him well to ride in silence, with her comforting light grip on his coat to aid her balance.

His lack of memory irritated him as it made him question the source of every thought and every word he uttered. Had he known women who would chatter and annoy him or was he just making a sweeping generalisation with this thought? Was he an intolerant man in general? If so, why? There were so many questions that spun around in his head, twisting his thoughts and taunting him. Beth's voice broke into them, giving him a new direction to take. He followed her instructions and turned the horse to follow the new track. Her voice was gentle with a soft accent that was comforting and warm. Instinctively he felt the desire to be comforted but he did not know what comfort he wanted. Did he just want a soft woman in his arms or somewhere to rest from his troubles?

He was tired, he knew that, but was he tired of life or just suffering from fatigue? He had not slept well for a long time and last night two nightmares, in quick succession, had fractured his sleep. He clenched his jaw, as if to brace himself for the memory of the second. His other dreams had been surreal, a parody of his demons, yet last night the dream that bothered him most had been realistic and all the more terrifying for it. He had dreamt he had killed a man, knifed him beneath the ribs in an upward thrust to pierce his heart.

In his dream he had felt the knife in his grip as surely as if he held it now. He had felt the slice of the metal through the flesh and the grate of the man's rib on the edge of the blade as it buried deeper inside him. Even now he smelt the sickly sweet smell and felt the warmth of his blood as it flowed over his knuckles. The victim had looked into his eyes with disbelief, but as the knife became embedded to the hilt and the whole blade lay within his body, his eyes had become glazed as his spirit left him. He had watched the man's life fall away, as did the wrinkles in his face as he relaxed into death before him. He could still remember the dead man's weight slumping onto the blade as his legs ceased to support him. Finally he had allowed the man to crumple to the ground at his feet.

What sickened him the most was not the death – although he could see the man's face as clearly now as he had in his dreams – but that he had felt no remorse or guilt in taking his life. Shamefully, he had felt exhilarated, and this glimpse of the man he might be worried him. Had Beth seen it when he entered her home? Was he a deranged killer planning to murder her? Beth was speaking and he answered her more sharply than he would have wished if he had not been dwelling on such thoughts. Hurt by his rebuke, she loosened her grip on his jacket as she withdrew from him, and this only added to the ugly feeling of self-loathing he felt for the man he might be.

Beth had remained quiet for some time. Luke could bear her withdrawal no longer, if only because he needed a diversion from his own sombre thoughts. Glancing behind him he saw her face in profile and realised that while he festered and mulled over each word and each thought, she had moved on and was enjoying the views all around her. The higher position allowed her to see more of the countryside than she could on foot. The green and brown hedges no longer obscured her view, and she was delighted to see the patchwork of fields stretched out on either side. She turned her head and smiled up at him and he had a sudden stab of jealousy that she appeared to enjoy the simple pleasures in life so fully, with no worries to trouble her mind. He wished he could experience her joy and his envy of her turned to resentment. His scowl saw her smile fade and he turned away from her.

The remainder of the journey was in silence; no more directions were needed and neither had anything they wished to share. He had destroyed her happiness, yet perversely he yearned to turn around again to check if this was true. Did he want to see the sadness in her eyes or did he want to see her pretty face? I'm doing it again, he thought, over-analysing each thought, each deed. Irritated, he squeezed his heels into the horse and it obediently broke into a trot on his command. He felt Beth's grip tighten on his coat. The sooner the journey was over and they parted, the better for the both of them, he decided.

The road grew wider and busier with carts and carriages heading to Killygrew. They joined them and together they approached the southern side of the busy market town. Soon they were able to hear the growing noise of the market traders, animals and the gathering crowds as it carried towards them on the wind.

'It's Market Day,' said Beth from behind him. 'I've just seen a neighbour from Port Carrek.'

He could hear the excitement in her voice and it told him she rarely had the opportunity to see a market like this one. Suddenly he wanted to make amends for his earlier rudeness to her, yet the feeling of wanting to be nice felt alien to him. Nevertheless, he decided to follow the urge to put the smile back on her face.

'We can look at some stalls on the way to Treligga's stables if it is what you would like.' He sensed her surprise and delight, though she hid it well in her reply.

'Yes, I would like that,' she said flatly, but he had noticed her grip on his jacket tighten in her excitement. He felt a warmth flow inside him for making her happy and for once he forgot his nightmares. He urged the horse on and realised he now looked forward to the rest of the day as they entered the bustling town of Killygrew.

They dismounted and entered the market area. Luke remained on the road, which cut through the centre of the busy trading area. It allowed him to be able to watch from a distance as Beth meandered through the colourful noisy traders and hawkers. They walked in parallel. Whilst he led the horse, quiet and observant, Beth took delight in looking at the different stalls, exchanging a few words with each stallholder and tasting samples of treats that were offered to her. Sometimes she would briefly disappear from view, obscured by passing crowds or animals for sale and he would find himself searching for her, only for her to reappear and give him a reassuring smile. It was as if they were in two different worlds, he thought, hers vibrant and colourful, his lonely and barren.

The market stretched for some distance. As they neared its end, the quality of the stalls increased and their customers reflected this. Pens full of livestock were replaced by richly decorated carriages for sale. Traders selling cheap trinkets were replaced by merchants selling rolls of silk. The customers now held parasols rather than the hands of raggedy children. Their only hangers-on were servants carrying their purchases.

Luke saw Beth's smile leave her face as she self-consciously ran a hand through her loose hair. She no longer blended in with the people about her as she looked poor, yet exotic, with a mixture of gypsy and Spanish blood in her veins. He noticed two women turn to look at her then exchange a few words before laughing and continuing on their way. Beth tilted her chin in defiance but he had already seen how she had placed her hand over a patch on her sleeve. She no longer stopped to look at the stalls but walked bravely on through the well-dressed throng, refusing to be intimidated by their presence.

A crowd of dandies came towards her and spoke to her. Their exchange of words was no more than youthful banter and Beth replied in kind, but he had seen the lust in their gazes even if Beth had not. Luke held his tongue. He had no right to interfere, he told himself. Soon she would be out of his life and he would be returning home. Yet when a man on his own approached her, similar in age as himself, with a top hat and over-shiny shoes, he had had enough and called her name more irritably than he intended.

'Beth, it's getting late. We must be about our business.'

Moments later she was by his side and they were on their way to the horse loaner, leaving the bustle of the market traders behind them.

Treligga was the only *jobmaster* in Killygrew, supplying horses, drivers and carriages for hire to those who had the money to pay. His stables were conveniently sited in a purpose-built courtyard behind the Killy Coaching Inn, and it had a constant stream of horse-drawn carriages and riders entering and leaving the yard through its ornate, gothic, red-brick archway. Yet despite the chaos and noise, Treligga spied the newcomers immediately.

'Ben! Where have you been?' John Treligga walked briskly towards them, with his arms outstretched. He was a portly man, with a shaggy grey beard and a bulbous red nose that betrayed his fondness for ale. He appeared pleased to see them and as he approached his pungent smell confirmed his trade with horses.

Luke and Beth halted, momentarily stunned that they had finally met someone who knew him. The hope quickly died as the man greeted the horse. He stroked the horse's nose and buried his own face into his neck.

'I thought you were *a goner*, Ben,' Treligga whispered softly into the gelding's coat. 'You should never have been loaned out like you were.' He turned on Luke. 'I should have you arrested. You were meant to return him the same day.'

Luke apologised and explained the reason for his delay. He extracted the only coins he had in his pockets and offered them in way of payment for the extra days the horse was in his care. After checking his horse thoroughly for injuries, Treligga accepted them and placed them in his own pocket. Money proved to be a good tonic for his anger.

'No memory, you say? That's unusual. And you think I can help?'

'I had hoped you would hold some details, my name and address for example.'

Treligga snorted. 'Normally I would, but the day you hired Ben I was seeing to someone else and my nephew served you. I now know that the stupid boy can't be trusted. He has loaned horses that were not for loaning ... as with Ben who is my favourite horse ... and not taken the details of the men who he gave them to. Right mess he has made of things. I had no details of you and if it wasn't for you offering something in way of a payment I would have not only lost Ben but the fee as well.'

'What did he give you?' asked Beth hopefully.

'Wait here, I'll fetch it.' Treligga disappeared into his stables, leading his favourite horse behind him.

They waited in silence as people walked past them on either side. To casual observers, they might have appeared to be a couple who had been together so long that no displays of intimacy or affection were needed. If only they knew, thought Beth, of the unusual circumstances that brought them to Killygrew. It had been strange having Luke in her house. She did not have much contact with young men in general, as her customers were mainly women or the elderly. In the past there had been no time for courting, as all her spare time had been spent caring for her grandfather. Young men were like a rare species she had not encountered before, and Luke's presence had ignited a curiosity within her that she did not know she had. Since his arrival, this curiosity had insidiously removed the fear she had of him, and despite his occasional bitter retorts, there was no air of impending threat from him. She could not pinpoint when this had started to change, but it was hard to continue to feel threatened by someone who had been so unwell and vulnerable. It would be strange to be alone again and she could not help but feel uneasy at the idea of it.

'Luke?'

'Yes?' He had answered without thinking. The irony that he had accepted her name for him at a time when they were a little closer to finding out his identity was not lost on them.

Beth tried to smile, but found she couldn't. 'I hope that whatever he has gone to fetch helps you to find your way home.'

Luke nodded stoically, but did not reply.

As they waited, a man's voice called out to Beth offering her a lift home. It was the man from Port Carrek she'd seen earlier. He was standing by his cart filled with hay in the process of hiring a horse to replace his own that had gone lame. It would be a comfortable ride home and Beth would be a fool not to accept it. She thanked him, but remained where she was until he was ready to leave.

'I'm glad you do not have to walk home alone. You have looked after me well and I thank you for it.'

Luke was preparing to say goodbye and they both knew it.

'What will you do?' Beth asked as she watched the new horse being secured to the cart.

'Make some enquiries; perhaps someone in Killygrew will remember my arrival.'

'If anyone did it does not mean they learnt anything about you. You do not strike me as the type of person to share details of his life with a passing acquaintance. Will you enlist a constable's help?'

'Perhaps,' he answered noncommittally. 'If I do I will not implicate you.'

Beth thanked him.

'I don't deserve your thanks. The truth of it is I may run the risk of being arrested myself. What if I am a wanted criminal? According to you, I did enter your home uninvited.'

'You are welcome to stay with me until your memory returns. I could make up a bed in the shed for you.' Beth kept her gaze fixed on the horse and cart. 'My roof leaks in the rain and there are fallen trees to chop for winter logs. My grandfather would do these chores if he was still alive. I am no good at such jobs. My grandfather used to say I am a menace when I have an axe in my hand.'

A slight smile curved Luke's lips. 'I can well believe it.'

Beth looked at him and found herself smiling too. Perhaps under different circumstances, they could have become friends.

Before they could speak again Treligga returned. In his grimy hand he held a gold fob watch. He gave it to Luke.

'I think you have more need of this than me. Keep it. I am just thankful that Ben has returned and is unharmed.' He left them alone to stare at the watch in Luke's hand.

It was made of gold and lay heavy in his palm. Its face was engraved with a swirl of leaves and flowers at its centre and Roman numerals around the edge. Luke flicked open the cover which revealed an 18K stamp alongside a serial number. It was an item of value and the patches of worn gold were evidence that it had once been well loved. Luke snapped the cover shut and turned the watch over with a flick of his fingers. The movement came easily to him as if he had done it many times in the past. The rear was also heavily engraved with the same decorative floral pattern but for the centre, which displayed a heartfelt inscription, thoughtfully and lovingly commissioned.

To Joss, my darling husband,
from your loving and devoted wife, Charlotte.

'My name is Joss.' Joss swallowed down the emotion rising up in his throat. He repeated the unfamiliar name several times, softly at first then more clearly as he tested it on his tongue.

'You are married.' Beth's voice was barely a whisper at his shoulder.

'Joss is a good name, but I don't remember it.'

'You have a wife.'

Joss ran a thumb over the engraving. 'So it seems,' he muttered. Charlotte. The name seemed more familiar to him, although the woman behind the name did not. The man who had offered Beth a lift called out to her. He was getting ready to leave and Beth appeared torn about what to do.

'Go,' said Joss. 'You will miss your ride.' He slipped the watch into his pocket. He felt he had learnt nothing yet everything all at the same time. And stranger still, he mourned the single man known as Luke. It made no sense.

'Did the watch help?' she asked urgently. 'Have you remembered anything else? I don't like to leave you like this.'

Joss shook his head. 'No. Nothing.' The cart driver called to Beth again. 'You should go,' he said thickly. 'Don't worry about me.'

He watched her run to the cart, climb on board and sit on the pile of fresh hay. He focused hard on the wheels. He had troubled her enough. It was time to part. Beth sat looking at him but he did not meet her gaze. He watched the cart pull away and take Beth out of his life. She had injured him, shouted at him, nursed him and fed him. She had helped him and supported him yet he would probably never see her again. He tried hard, but he could not avert his gaze from her for long.

The sun shone on her black hair as she sat cross-legged in the hay like an ethereal woodland fairy hitching a ride.

He had a wife waiting for him yet he did not know who or where. He had a life waiting for him, yet it concerned him what sort of life it was. Beth was his only reality. His only friend. She offered him a roof and somewhere to rest while his memory returned. She offered him peace and work to occupy him. The alternative was the parish constable who might just arrest him, at best for vagrancy, at worst for murder if his dreams were based on fact.

Suddenly Joss was running, the soles of his leather boots hitting the rough ground in a rhythmical beat that grew faster and faster as he raced after the cart. Beth leaned forward and reached out her hand, spurring Joss on to run faster. His lungs hurt with the exertion yet his speed increased. Their fingers touched briefly in the air and the warmth of her skin spurred him on for one final effort. He grabbed her hand, and with a foot on the tailgate climbed aboard. He fell forward, twisting his body in mid-air so he did not land on her. Joss heard Beth laughing beside him at his sudden change of mind. He turned to look at her face full of joy and he couldn't help smiling too. As her laughter died they realised they were still holding hands. Embarrassed, Beth withdrew hers, an endearing blush brightening her cheeks.

Joss turned his head and looked up at the blue sky above him. He felt he had never taken the time to do this before. He relaxed into the sweet smelling hay to watch the occasional white cloud pass by above them as they travelled back to River Valley. As he lay in the hay next to Beth, he realised his broad smile, although short lived, had felt alien to him. It had worked muscles in his face that he had not used for a very long time. Although this new knowledge was worrying, the movement of the cart calmed his thoughts and eventually his tiredness overwhelmed him and he fell asleep. For once the nightmares did not haunt him and he slept deeply, while the watch lay in his pocket, forgotten by everyone but the woman at his side.

Chapter Four

Beth and Joss watched the cart leave. They stood alone on the road at the start of the dirt track that led to her cottage in the valley. An awkwardness had descended between them. The first time Joss had entered her home he was an intruder. The second time he had been unwell and needed her care. Beth felt she had little choice in either situation. But this time she had *invited* him to stay. A single woman had invited a man she did not know to share her home. He may still have no memory, but physically he was well and he was a married man. Beth felt she had dug herself a big hole and wondered how she was going to get out of it. However, she had her reasons for offering him somewhere to stay. Had he gone to the constable he may have changed his mind and told them how he had been injured. She had enough troubles without worrying about getting a knock on her door and her imminent arrest. Beth gave Joss what she hoped was a charming smile.

'If anyone asks, you are doing some odd jobs for me,' she said, turning and making her way down the track through the trees. She could hear him following, their footsteps muffled on the carpet of wild strawberries that grew in abundance beneath the leafy canopy above. The trees grew sparser as they neared the valley edge, and for the first time they could hear the sound of the waterfall that brought the river to its namesake. Beth glanced across to see if Joss could hear it, but he was frowning and looking up at the valley banks made of rock and slate. She realised that it was not the blue mesmeric sea in the distance that captured his attention, but how he may have gained access to the valley.

'I must have ridden the horse through the trees when I arrived here,' he said quietly to himself. 'The only tracks I can see are too narrow.'

'There is another route. It's a short cut.' Beth pointed to the other side of the valley. 'See the track that winds up the valley bank? It is wide enough for two horses to pass. At the bottom there is a bridge to cross the river. A confident rider may choose that route. From the cliff edge at the top you can see the full length of the valley.'

They looked at each other and Beth wondered if he had come in that way, observing the house and waiting for his chance to enter her home. They had come to a stop, the calming sound of the running river beneath them at odds with the uneasy thoughts in her mind.

'I won't harm you,' Joss said gently, as if reading her thoughts. 'If it was originally my intention to do you harm, it is not now.'

Beth nodded. 'You need a change of clothing,' she said briskly, wanting to change the subject. 'I have some clothes that belonged to my grandfather. You can wear them.' She picked a flower and twirled it in her fingers as she walked. 'We can move your makeshift bed into the shed. You can sleep in there from now on.' She glanced at him. 'People will talk otherwise.'

Beth turned and followed the remainder of the track. It zigzagged haphazardly until it arrived at the granite stone cottage with its white peeling windows. 'Welcome to Kynance Cottage,' she said formally, opening its battered door. 'Kynance means ravine in Cornish,' she added as an afterthought.

'I know,' replied Joss as he followed her inside.

Beth suddenly felt self-conscious about having him in her home again. Her mind raced with what she should do next. She did not think to question how he knew the meaning of the name of her little home in a Celtic language that was fast disappearing from usage. Instead she rolled up his makeshift bed by the fire so it was ready to take out to the shed later. 'My grandfather's clothes are in his room. It's this way.' She led him upstairs. 'While you are staying here I want no funny business,' she told him, trying her best to sound authoritative. 'I won't stand for it. I might be offering you a place to stay, but it doesn't mean you can take liberties.'

'I wouldn't dare,' Joss replied as he followed her up the narrow stairs, bending his head to avoid the low beam.

Beth suspected he was making fun of her, but chose to ignore him.

'This is grandfather's room. He was very dear to me so treat his clothes and tools with respect.' She stood aside to allow Joss to enter a tiny room with one small window, a bed, a chest of drawers and little else. As if by way of explanation, she added, 'He was a simple man and took pleasure in the outside world rather than material things.'

Joss stood in the centre, looking around him as he nodded slowly. 'Simple is good,' he said quietly. 'Life can be too complicated sometimes.'

He looked at her, his hazel eyes meeting her blue ones for the first time since he jumped into the cart. Beth felt herself begin to blush. She quickly turned to the chest of drawers and pulled one out. She riffled through the clothing hoping to look busy.

'These are some of his clothes,' she said, pulling out a checked shirt made of heavy cotton and throwing it behind her. 'A shirt,' she rummaged for more. 'Socks, waist jacket and trousers.' The clothes, a mixture of fustian, cotton and corduroy, lay at his feet in an untidy pile. 'Your boots are made of good leather, but your clothes are hardy and dirty. I cannot provide you with fine clothes to match your boots ...' Beth added a cloth cap and kerchief to the pile. '... but I can replace your clothes with a cleaner set.'

Joss slowly crouched, picked up the shirt and felt the texture in his hands. Beth winced as she realised she had been insensitive. She watched him gently stroke the material, deep in thought, and wished she had not made the sarcastic remark about not matching his fine leather boots. What did he care about fashion when he did not know who he was?

'It will feel strange to wear another man's clothing,' he eventually said.

'My grandfather was a practical man. He would not want them to go to waste.'

'Yes, I can believe that.' Joss picked up the cloth cap and felt the worn lining inside where once another man's head had fitted snugly.

'Anyway, it's wash day soon, and if you wear his clothes I will be able to wash yours in the river.'

'What happened to him?' It was a simple question but one Beth hated answering. It often conjured up the overwhelming grief she kept so well hidden. However, Joss had a right to know, if he was to wear his clothes.

'He was a miner and from the age of twelve worked below ground. He worked in the mines until he was almost forty. Not many last that long,' she added proudly. 'The dust and fumes from ten-hour shifts, six days a week, finally started to rot his lungs. He gave up mining and started general labouring but miners' lung had already taken hold. It is a wasting disease and it took its time, but it finally got him in the end.'

Beth took a deep breath; it was the first time she had managed to speak about it without tears choking her throat. The last few years of his life had been torture for him as he struggled to breathe, and it had been torture for her to see him suffer.

'My grandfather continued to take on odd jobs right up to the end, despite his ill health. He had a strong will and always ensured we had food on the table.'

Joss remained silent until she had finished. His frown and words showed his concern for her, but there was no emotion in his tone.

'Death is never a welcome visitor, however it announces its arrival.' He looked at her and added, 'I'm sorry for your loss.'

Beth was about to thank him for his words of condolence when, to her surprise, Joss suddenly stood up again. 'It will be good to have a change of clothes,' he said quietly, taking off his shirt. 'Thank you for lending them to me.'

While Beth remembered her loving grandfather's awful death, Joss had no such memories of him. He had died as many miners had died before him – of the acceptable occupational hazard of lung disease. Beth did not have time to look away and she stared, open-mouthed, at the man half-naked in front of her. Joss did not seem to care and reached for the clean shirt, but as he stretched to put it on Beth cried out his name. He turned to look at her as it was the first time she had used it. All thoughts of her grandfather were gone.

'Look at your back!' Beth cried. Joss frowned. 'You have a scar that stretches right across your back. Lord knows how you survived it.' She moved around him. 'And here's another.' Without thinking she placed her hand on his chest, touching the smaller jagged scar, no more than an inch long. 'You have been in a fight.' She looked up at him, intrigued. 'Who *are* you?' she asked. 'What has happened to you?'

Joss remained silent as he looked down on her. His hazel eyes darkened as his chest rose and fell beneath her fingers. He smelt of leather, horse and fragrant memories of Killygrew Market, whilst his warm skin invited her to explore further. Beth felt the drum of his heartbeat quicken, or was it her own? Skin inviting skin to explore it. Breath to match breath. Heart to race heart. Some type of magic was at play here, for it moved from Joss and entered her fingertips, before diving into her very soul. For the briefest of moments, she forgot how to breathe.

'Don't.' Joss stepped away from her touch, leaving her hand open in mid-air. Beth quickly withdrew her hand and hid it behind her back. She had over-stepped the boundaries of decency that she herself had lain down. 'You'd better leave,' he said gruffly, quickly covering the scars with the clean shirt.

'Are you remembering something?' she asked him as she watched the scars disappear under the cloth of his shirt.

'I will tell you when I remember something. Don't keep asking me,' he snapped. 'Now leave me to change.' Beth did not move. 'I am going to change the rest of my clothes, whether you stay or not, Beth. What is it to be?' His hand held the top button at his waist as he waited for her answer. Beth's gaze lowered briefly to his waist, before she turned and fled down the stairs.

Beth was running out of money. Feeding two mouths instead of one had taken all of the savings she had under her mattress. Joss had offered to help out, but Beth knew he would not find work in the area. People were suspicious of strangers with no references knocking on their door looking for employment. She had told him there was no need, yet Beth's unwillingness to leave Joss alone in the house while she went about her usual rounds meant she had not earned any money since his unexpected arrival. She could not afford to let his presence interfere with her work any longer. She had made the decision to allow him to stay, so now she must trust him not to steal from her while she was away. Not that she had much to steal now as all of her money was gone.

She wheeled her wooden wheelbarrow quietly from the side of the shed, being careful not to disturb Joss, who she could hear gently snoring in his makeshift bed. Despite not being impressed by the dilapidated building, Joss had settled into his new bedroom without complaint. He had even tidied it to a small degree, so it appeared much larger inside. She steered the wheelbarrow to the cottage door and started to load it with the clothes she had mended, all neatly packaged, labelled and ready for delivery. Movement caught her eye and she looked up to see the letter carrier from the village making his way through the trees towards her. Her stomach churned with anxiety.

He had visited her a month ago for the first time. Despite her grief for the loss of her grandfather, Beth couldn't help feeling excited when he had placed that first letter in her hand. She had never had a letter posted to her before. It was thrilling to hold an envelope made of good quality paper, with her address written neatly upon it. In fact it had been the first time she had ever seen a penny black stamp up close. It did not matter that the letter had not actually been addressed to her by name, just the words *The Occupier, Kynance Cottage, River Valley*. What did matter was that first letter was intended for *her* as she was the sole occupier. Confirmation of her belief that it was not intended for her late grandfather became abundantly clear as soon as she had begun to read it. There had been no heartfelt words of condolence at his death; in fact the words acknowledging his death were businesslike, almost brutal in their subsequent demand. To make matters worse, the letter, which had only minutes before felt precious, had become threatening and ominous in her hands when she saw the letterhead and signature. In good quality ink, and with the flourish born of absolute confidence in his power and standing in the community, was the signature of Mr Tremayne, of Tremayne and Goldsmith Solicitors, Truro.

The memory of that moment now churned Beth's stomach as she watched the letter carrier tentatively make his way down the path strewn with protruding tree roots. Her hand shook as she received the second letter and quickly hid it deep into her pocket so no one else would see.

When the letter carrier was gone and was no longer in sight, Beth turned and made her way down the gently sloping bank to the river. Her wheelbarrow, with its carefully packed and precious load, was now forgotten. Her best boots became slightly muddied from the descent, and within minutes she was standing at the river's edge, staring into the gurgling fast moving water below. She took out the unopened envelope and slowly and deliberately tore the thick paper into strips and dropped them one by one into the river. Her blank expression did not change. Any anxiety she had felt had been numbed when her decision was made. The current took the white fragments and toyed with them, spinning them around and around in a frantic whirlpool. Beth watched as the dark blue ink bled into the fibres and spread out like butterfly wings of the brightest blue. Suddenly they were off, like scurrying children running away, erratic in their journey down the river and out to the North Atlantic. Beth stayed until she could no longer see them, as she wanted to be sure they were gone. Satisfied the letter had been destroyed, and with it the demands it had made upon her, she turned and made her way back to her wheelbarrow. Taking in a deep breath in order to start her day afresh, she lifted the handles and began to walk the mile-long trek to the neighbouring village and start her rounds.

Port Carrek was a pretty village. Its steep, narrow main street was like a grey trail left by a bouncing ball as it rolled down the hill, passing small, whitewashed cottages as if by accident, to the bustling harbour below. It was said that the village was built on pilchards' bones, which was partly true, as the wealth that had come from fishing pilchards had helped make the village what it was today. Although it was still called a village by those who lived there, it was growing in size and had begun to resemble a small town. However, its quaintness still remained and the little fish could be seen everywhere by the discerning traveller, from the engravings above the fishermen's cottage doors, to the boats in the harbour. Even the main ale house of the village was called The Hevva Hevva, taking its name from the cry that the look-outs shouted to alert the fishermen that a gigantic shoal was in sight. On hearing the alarm, the fishermen would drop what they were doing and run to their boats. Working together, they would cast their large nets to catch the shoal as it swam near to the coast to feed in late summer. As the hardened fishermen worked, their lives dictated by the changing rhythm of the wind and waves, their women waited on the quayside. They sat with their baskets, ready to salt and press the fish with heavy weights and catch the oil that seeped from them which would be used for lighting lamps at a later date. It was heavy work, hard work, smelly work, but the women waited and prayed for it all the same.

If Beth ever had to leave River Valley, Port Carrek would be the place she would choose to live, not that she had much knowledge of the other villages and towns in the county. Her world was small and that was the way she liked it. She had started her round at the top of the village, which gave her a wide view of the beautiful harbour below. All the boats were in and the fishermen were busy preparing them and mending their nets so they would be ready for August when the pilchard season began in earnest.

Beth took a moment to look at the picturesque scene, but she knew all was not as idyllic as it seemed. There were two boats missing, along with their crews, the result of a ferocious and unexpected storm that had blown in from the North the month before. It left two women mourning the loss of their sons, and two widowed. The close-knit community still felt the loss, preferring to postpone Golowan Feast Day on St Peter's Eve in June for a later date. After all, no one felt like celebrating the patron saint of fishermen on the very day that the Lord had taken their own.

Beth had already visited four customers and been referred to two more villagers who wanted some mending done. Over the past four years her round had grown. It had provided her with a little money to help supplement what her grandfather was able to earn from general labouring, despite his poor health. She could not help but admire how he continued to bring money home. Without it, her earnings would not have been enough to support them both. Her regular visits and good standard of sewing had helped build her clientele, but there was a limit to how much she could take on. To fulfil an order Beth often stayed up late and sewed into the night, but good quality candles were costly and the flickering poor light strained her eyes. This meant that she had to do most of her sewing during daylight hours. Days shortened in the winter and she could only sew so fast, so she had resigned to the fact that she would not earn her fortune from her trade.

She arrived at her next customer's house and she could hear Jacca's children before he opened his door. The volume of shouting and crying doubled as the widower, tired and frustrated, leant against the open door. To Beth's eyes he looked as if he was contemplating escaping.

'Hello, Beth. Want a child?' he said, with a lopsided smile. Beth smiled back.

'Not today, Jacca.' Beth lifted out her parcel and held it out to him. 'Four knees mended and two trousers lengthened,' she announced proudly.

Jacca grabbed the parcel. 'Beth, you are a saint! I'd do it myself if I had the patience. Sarah used to do all the mending, God bless her soul.'

'How are you bearing up? Ten children to look after can't be easy for you.'

Jacca turned his head and shouted to the children in the house to be quiet.

'It's not been good, maid. People have helped out and been so kind, but I can't keep putting on people. They have their own lives to lead and I need to work. It's been six months and I have children that need a mother. Do you know anyone?'

Beth had known Jacca for many years and he was a good man. To some it may sound harsh that after seeing his wife die in childbirth a mere six months ago he was already looking to replace her, but the people of Port Carrek were practical folk and he had the interest of his children at heart.

'There is Amy on Hogshead Road. She was caring for her invalid mother, but she died in January of dropsy.'

Jacca thought for a moment. 'Widow or spinster?'

'Spinster,' Beth replied. 'You know her, Jacca, she lives in the house with the blue gate.'

'Ah, the run-down one,' Jacca said as he considered the woman. 'She's plain, but that doesn't matter. I'm no oil painting and she might like to live in a house that isn't about to fall down. I hear that row of houses might have their rent put up next year. Could be to my advantage.'

'She may be a spinster, but it does not mean she is desperate, Jacca.'

Jacca smiled. 'Don't worry, maid. A marriage may suit us both well. I will court her proper. I won't rush her but I will make my intention clear. No point wasting anyone's time and if it's the woman I think it is she will be past her childbearing years very soon and that is a good thing. I've got enough children without having any more.' He shouted again at the noisy children inside to be quiet before turning to Beth again. 'It will be your turn next, and you will be having a family of your own.'

Beth laughed. She thought of Joss and her laughter faded. 'I don't think so, Jacca. I have too much on my plate at the moment.'

Jacca paid her, retreated back inside his house with his parcel and closed the door. Beth shouted through it before she left. 'Put on a clean shirt before you go calling on Amy!'

His reply could be heard in the depths of the house. 'I will, if I can find one under all this mess.'

Beth's next stop was Mrs Tilly's fabric shop, and her entrance was marked by the ringing of a bell on the door, alerting not only Mrs Tilly, but also the only other customer she had, Gladys Pratt. The shop was small, dark and cluttered inside, resulting in Beth being temporarily blinded until her eyes adjusted to the change in light. Large shelves behind the main counter displayed bolts of fabric in every colour, whilst an array of jars, filled with buttons and ribbons, were displayed on every available counter space, but it wasn't any of these items that Mrs Tilly and Gladys Pratt were looking at. Placed proudly on the counter was a highly polished sewing machine, gleaming black and decorated in swirls of gold paint. Beth was immediately drawn to it too and watched in awe at the beauty of its movement and sound as Mrs Tilly proudly demonstrated how it worked. She also noticed the price tag. It was a purchase she would never be able to afford. Eventually Mrs Tilly looked up.

'Hello, Beth. Do you want another yard of the blue material?' Beth's cheeks reddened with embarrassment, particularly as Gladys Pratt had overheard. Now it would be all over the village that Beth could only afford to make a dress as long as she bought the material a yard at a time.

'Yes please, Mrs Tilly,' she answered, avoiding Gladys's gaze. The shopkeeper took out a roll from under the counter.

'I hid the last amount as I wasn't sure if I would be able to get any more. You have spent so long making your dress that I was afraid I would run out before you had time to finish it.' It was a very thoughtful thing for the shopkeeper to do, but her explanation increased Beth's embarrassment. Beth handed over the money.

'This is the last yard. It will be finished once I sew in this panel. Thank you for keeping the material back for me.'

Mrs Tilly puffed her chest out. She liked her customers to feel they were well looked after. She carefully wrapped the material for Beth.

'Mrs Tabb's eyes are playing up again and she wants you to drop by. She will think I have not passed on the message, but you didn't come to the village on Friday.' Mrs Tilly handed her the parcel. 'Martha wants you to drop in on her too.'

Beth took it and held it carefully in her arms. 'I have been a little busy these last few days,' she replied, hoping the two women would not press her. 'I must be on my way. Goodbye,

Mrs Tilly.' She nodded to Gladys Pratt. 'Goodbye, Mrs Pratt.' Beth hurried out of the shop before any questions were asked.

Mrs Tilly and Gladys Pratt watched Beth hurry past the window.

'Beth is a sweet girl. Which reminds me, did I see your son in the village the other day?' asked Mrs Tilly.

Gladys made a show of looking at some ribbons, the new sewing machine now forgotten. 'Yes. He has grown into a fine looking young man, if I say so myself.'

Mrs Tilly released the material she had used for the demonstration from the sewing machine. 'Will he be looking for a pretty local maid to take as a wife?'

Gladys shook her head with conviction. 'No, Mrs Tilly. I think we both know that Sam has outgrown Port Carrek's girls. He is educated now and destined for better things.' She gave her a smug smile.

Mrs Tilly accepted the rebuttal with a lift of her chin. She carried the sewing machine across the shop and placed it in the window. She turned it slightly, this way and that, until the sun caught it just right, but the temptation to goad the pompous woman was too much to resist.

'Beth would make a good match for Sam. He liked her a lot when they were children.'

'Oh, I don't think Beth is suitable at all.' Gladys discarded the ribbon she had been inspecting. 'She's very friendly with Martha and that son of hers. I don't know what she sees in them. Martha is rough as old boots and that son of hers is very strange.'

Mrs Tilly had to agree. 'Tom does have odd ways. Martha thinks it's because she ate a handful of unripe blackberries when she was carrying him.'

'Is that so? I had a friend who had a child who was simple in the head and it was because she fell over when she was four months gone. She thinks the fall damaged his head. Of course Tom may have got it from his father. He was odd.'

'No, Tom's father was all right. He just didn't like you.'

Gladys was about to deny it but then decided she had to agree. Neither of them had liked one another when he was alive.

'Beth could do with a man to look after her now that her grandfather is dead.'

'Sam must aim higher than a miner's granddaughter, Mrs Tilly. Besides ...' Gladys looked at the door to ensure no one was about to come in. '... it can't be denied that children do take after their parents.' She leant over the counter and lowered her voice. 'I think Beth is more like her mother than we realised.'

Mrs Tilly was all ears. 'What do you mean?' she asked.

Gladys looked about her. 'I mean a bad apple doesn't fall far from the tree.'

'It wasn't her mother's fault she fell in love with a man and he left her.'

'It was her fault she fell in love with a married man, ran off with him and got herself into trouble. If you do something silly like that you have no one but yourself to blame when the man tires of his fun and games and heads home to his wife.'

'Well, she paid for it in more ways than one. Beth won't do that, she's more sensible.'

Gladys raised her eyebrows, hinting at the secret knowledge she had.

Mrs Tilly, hating herself for indulging in gossip, could not resist asking. 'What do you know that I don't?' She took the jar of buttons that Gladys was pretending to examine away from her.

Gladys smiled. 'My son-in-law works for a farmer who lives near Beth. It seems he gave her a lift home from Killygrew and she was not alone.'

Mrs Tilly was disappointed. 'What is wrong with that? It is a long walk from Killygrew to River Valley.'

'Did you not hear me? I said she was not *alone*. A man was

with her and they were both dropped off at her track ... the track that leads to *her* house.'

'Did she know him? Was he local?' asked the shopkeeper. Gladys now had her full attention.

'No, he was not a local man and Beth had only just met him as she had only just found out his name. What respectable girl, living alone, would invite a strange man to her house?' Gladys's voice became a whisper. 'A girl that takes after her mother, that's who!'

'She will get a reputation for herself. Young men will be buzzing around her hoping for her favours.'

'Which is why I am keeping it to myself for now. Sam is doing well for himself at the moment and I don't want him to be tempted by a loose woman. The less Beth's name is mentioned in his presence, the better, I say.'

Beth had almost finished her round, as there was only Martha left to see. She always left her until last so they could have a chat and share in a dish of tea. Beth pushed her barrow, now laden with clothes that required mending, up the steep hill and paused to let an open carriage pass by. The carriage, however, came to a halt in front of her and the affluent occupants, three well-dressed ladies, stepped down onto the pavement one by one.

Beth pursed her lips. She had noticed a trend amongst affluent society to visit the countryside, particularly the seaside, in order to improve their health and partake of leisure activities by the sea. She couldn't help but feel resentment when she saw the different world of the rich, a world to which she would never belong. She watched the ladies pausing by the road, straightening their bell-shaped dresses by shaking their crinoline cages beneath in a well-practised movement. Despite her sullen expression, Beth could not help but admire the soft, beautifully braided fabric of their dresses. Their matching fitted jackets, again expertly made, showed off their small waists. Their hems fell elegantly over their skirts, matching their colour, shape and fullness as a result of perfect tailoring. Beth would never be able to afford dresses like that; the dress she was making for herself now seemed plain and cheap in comparison. Even their crinolines and straw hats – trimmed with velvet bows and extravagant plumage from birds the names of which Beth did not even know – were too expensive for Beth.

Beth hated the rich. She hated how they treated the countryside as a form of entertainment and were blind to the needs of the hard-working people who relied on it for their survival. She hated how they enjoyed all that life had to offer without having to do a day of work, but most of all she hated them for how they made her feel – ignorant, poor and rejected.

Her father had been rich, but he had also been a liar. He was already married. By abandoning her mother when she fell pregnant with Beth and returning to his wife, he left them destitute and bitter. Her grandfather had been furious when he had learnt of this and wanted to confront him, but by then her father was already cold in his grave, struck down by a sudden bout of pneumonia. At least that was what her mother had told her. As to his name? Beth's mother had kept his identity a secret to spare his family the shock and embarrassment of what he had done. Beth felt her father did not deserve such protection. His behaviour had been reckless and cowardly and his wife deserved to know. She never would now. Beth had been excised from his life as if she was a festering boil. It was only natural that her hatred and mistrust of those who had money to squander would continue to this day.

As the ladies began to walk towards the coast, the younger one noticed Beth standing by the barrow. The woman, who was similar in age to Beth, gave her a modest smile in acknowledgement. It was not unkindly meant. It was a simple greeting from one woman to another on a beautiful day and with the prospect of an exciting afternoon ahead, but Beth did not care. It was easy to smile when you have a day of leisure to waste. Beth ignored her. Lifting her chin in the air and her barrow by the handles, she turned abruptly and walked in the opposite direction. She had work to do, even if they did not.

Beth sat cross-legged on Martha Kitto's rug as the old woman sat in her favourite wooden chair. Tom's chair remained vacant behind her but she knew better than to sit in it and risk upsetting him when he came home. Tom was Martha's only child. His arrival into the world had been both a surprise and a blessing to Martha, as she had believed that her thickening waist was due to age and her childbearing years were well and truly over. Her early memories of her new-born son, enhanced by her joy of finally becoming a mother, were of a contented baby. Although his passive temperament did not last, her love and devotion to him continued to grow with each passing day and Beth admired her for it.

The two women supped from a dish of tea made from the leaves of the mugwort plant. Neither woman knew anyone who could afford real tea, but the bitter drink served as a cheaper substitute and was readily drunk by the working classes in Cornwall. Beth had been brought up on mugwort tea, and she smiled as she watched Martha over the rim of her dish.

''Ow is your patient?' asked Martha.

Beth thought of Joss looking down at her as her hand rested on his scar. A wild flutter rose up in her chest and caught at her breath. She swallowed it away.

'Much better. He has not regained his memory, but we now know his name is Joss. It was engraved on his watch. He's doing some odd jobs for me at the moment.'

Martha supped noisily from her dish as she watched Beth through the rising steam. 'Is 'e behaving?'

Beth smiled. 'Yes, Martha. He is behaving.'

Beth changed the subject and told her about the ladies from the carriage. Despite Martha having a face like a man, with hands to match, she broke into an infectious giggle like a young girl at Beth's description. Martha did not care about fancy clothes or heavily decorated hats. Her clothes were rough, simple and hardwearing, like the woman who wore them. Beth smiled as she took another sip, the taste of the dark liquid seeming less bitter with each mouthful. It was part of the joy she felt when visiting Martha, however an unlikely match they were. Neither judged one another in deed, looks or word and that suited them both just fine.

The small room, and Martha's company, gave Beth a feeling of protection and safety. Despite her busy day, the letter she had received remained on her mind and still troubled her. The letter may be destroyed, just as the first had been, but the threat it held remained. She looked at Martha, her face lined from a hard life and a difficult son. She did not want to worry her, but perhaps Martha could help by sharing her knowledge.

'Martha,' Beth said in a voice she hoped sounded conversational and light. 'When someone dies without leaving a will, their property goes to their next of kin, doesn't it?'

Martha's eyes darted up from her tea. She was not an educated woman, but she was sharp as any knife. 'What's up, maid? What's 'appened?'

'Nothing, I just wondered. Grandfather left no will and I was just making sure I had a right to stay in our house.' Beth took another sip of her tea, hiding behind her dish and trying to not look too concerned. Her acting seemed to work and Martha relaxed.

'Yea, it does, not that I 'ave owned anything. 'T ain't right that some work so 'ard but end up with nothing they can call their own.'

'Grandfather *did* own Kynance Cottage, didn't he? I never saw him pay rent and I never saw a landlord. When he was dying he said I need not worry ... that the house was mine to live in for the rest of my life.'

'I know of no landlord that will let a tenant stay if the rent is not paid. The 'ouse must 'ave been 'is then. If Will Jago said the 'ouse will be yours when 'e died then the 'ouse is yours, maid.' Martha dabbed her mouth with her apron, her thick, gnarled fingers at odds with the dainty movement. Even Martha had a feminine side to her, thought Beth smiling. Martha carefully laid her apron out straight on her lap. 'I did 'ear a tale about your grandfather once, and 'ow 'e came to live in River Valley.'

Beth nodded, she had heard it too. 'He saved the life of the mine owner's child. When his lungs went bad, he was given the house by the sea as a reward. My mother told me when I was little.'

''E was a lucky beggar. Saved the right life there, didn't 'e?' Martha started chuckling until her chest made her cough. 'The mine is closed now and the owner dead. Turns out your grandfather outlasted 'im and got a 'ouse for 'is troubles. Only your grandfather could fall in dung and come up smelling of roses!'

They sat in contented silence, Beth feeling reassured that the letter had no substance and Martha enjoying her memories of her younger days. Eventually the old woman moved her creaking knees and sat back in her chair.

'Tom came 'ome beaming from ear to ear the other night. 'Ee was so 'appy that you sent 'im to fetch me. Folk say 'e's simple, but 'e is not as simple as they think.'

'He did a good job, Martha. He fetched you straight away.'

Martha smiled a toothy smile and chuckled. ''E came 'ome and wouldn't sit still. Took a minute or two to understand what 'ad 'appened. The man fell, 'e said.'

Beth stared into her tea. She did not want to lie to Martha and was relieved when Martha did not pursue it.

'Tom is cleverer than they think. I know 'e 'as 'is funny

ways and fixations on things but there is no 'arm in 'im. 'E can name every type of tree. 'E knows their leaves, their seeds and where they like to grow. Not many folk 'as that knowledge.' She put her dish down and sat back again, contented with a warm belly and good company.

'Does he still collect their leaves?' asked Beth, remembering how Tom would entertain himself for hours looking through his collection and obsessively laying the pressed leaves out in straight lines. Neither had questioned this behaviour; it kept him happy and contented, which made Martha's day easier.

'No, not for a long time. 'E likes sticks now. 'E likes carrying a bundle in 'is bag, but they must be straight and the same length.'

Beth already knew this and took one that she had tucked in her belt. She handed it to Martha. 'I found this one on the way here. I thought he might like it.'

Martha heard the door open. 'You can give it to 'im yourself. Tom's come 'ome for his lunch.'

Tom Kitto stood in the doorway, rocking side to side in excitable agitation. He was beaming from ear to ear as he had just recognised the woman sitting on his mother's rug. His pale face was a stark contrast to his red unruly hair and crimson cheeks, yet despite his immediate recognition of Beth, his pale blue eyes darted everywhere except directly at the visitor who affected him so.

'Hello, Tom,' greeted Beth softly. Tom Kitto always brought the maternal instinct out in her, a fact that pleased Martha to see. He sat down next to Beth, encroaching on her personal space like no other man of his age would do. Beth discreetly moved away just a little to feel more comfortable. Tom did not notice. He was just happy that Beth was in his house. She showed him the stick and his eyes widened with innocent joy as he took the precious object in both his hands. He clasped it tightly to his chest and his smile broadened on his fragile, yet handsome features. Like a child, he showed his mother.

'Beth brought me a stick!'

'Say *thank you*, Tom,' said Martha.

Tom obediently did as he was asked.

Pleased that her gift had been accepted, Beth stood. 'I have to go now, I have mending to do.'

Martha saw her to the door.

Taking a quick look at Tom to see if he was settled, Martha whispered. 'If you are still unsure about your grandfather's promise you could always send 'im a message.'

Beth was not surprised by her suggestion. Martha often told her that flowers and herbs had meanings and if you wanted to send a message to someone who had passed on, a way of doing it was to drop a flower into the sea.

'What flower do you suggest?' Beth asked quietly.

'That's up to you. I 'ave taught you the meaning of each flower.'

Beth was too tired to try and remember; the day had been long and she still had a mile to walk before she reached home. Instead she just nodded in agreement and stepped out into the little road. Martha, content with her advice, waved her off.

Martha leant against the doorframe with folded arms, taking a moment to watch Beth's receding figure pushing her barrow along the street. She heard Tom begin to wail inside. She sighed and shut the door, and in doing so shut the sunshine of the day out. She followed the sound of her son's distress and found him standing in front of the kitchen table, his collection of sticks laid out in rows, all straight and the same length except for the one Beth had given him. Tears ran down his cheeks and he slapped the top of his head, rocking in agitation. Martha was not upset by his distress. She had seen it all before.

'Oh lad, what will become of ya,' she said quietly to herself as she picked up the offending stick. Taking a knife, she cut off the end and laid it back on the table, its length now the same as the rest. Tom's features relaxed and he stopped rocking; all was well in his world and his smile returned.

'Beth brought me a stick,' he repeated, his voice still choked from his crying.

'That's because Beth likes ya, Tom,' his mother replied kindly.

'Tom likes Beth.' Tom's smile brightened.

'Tom does,' Martha answered, a worried frown forming on her brow. Tom may have the mind of a child but he had the body of a man. 'Don't like 'er too much, Tom. She is not a stick. She cannot fit into your world as you would wish.'

Tom ignored his mother, gathered his sticks together and placed them in his bag. Content, he placed the handle over his shoulder, as he always did, and sat in his favourite chair.

Martha sat down opposite him. She knew that her son did not understand what she had just said to him. He often thought she talked in riddles. She could almost see the confusion in his eyes. Of course Beth was not a stick, Tom would think to himself. Martha often found it difficult to talk to Tom and make him understand the world about him. As far as Tom understood, he liked Beth and Beth liked Tom, and he could see no problems ahead. Martha, on the other hand, could not help but feel a little worried.

Chapter Five

Joss woke late. It did not surprise him that he had slept in as he had lain awake until the early hours trying to remember the woman he had married. The name was familiar, yet any memory of a woman called Charlotte continued to elude him. Exhausted, he had finally fallen into a tormented sleep where his dreams played with him and mirrored his worries. He raked his hand through his hair and sat for a moment remembering his dream. He had dreamt he was standing at an altar with his bride by his side, yet he could not move his head to look at her. It was as if he was paralysed, yet despite his internal struggle the vicar did not seem to notice and continued his blessing, his voice monotonous and indifferent to his distress.

At the end of the short ceremony his bride gracefully turned and walked down the aisle. He followed, still desperate to see her face, which remained obscured to him – until, that is, he noticed his surroundings for the first time. Dead bodies of men sat in the pews, their blood seeping out of weeping wounds and onto the wooden floor, which felt sticky beneath his soles. As he looked down at his feet, he noticed for the first time that his hands were covered in blood. In disbelief he looked up to his bride to see her reaction to the carnage about them but she could not see him. She continued to walk ahead without him, her back straight, her path unhindered, and as he watched her walk out of his life he realised that despite walking in the blood at her feet, her wedding dress remained unstained. With a sickening feeling he realised that the blood and bodies that haunted him were for his eyes only, and no one else.

Joss shook his head as if to clear his thoughts and got out of bed. He looked around the shed that was now his bedroom.

Being a man of leisure did not sit well with him. He must find something useful to do. He had watched Beth prepare her mending for delivery the evening before and could not help but admire her for her independence and hard work. Reluctantly she had left him alone in the house she so prized, and he did not want her to find he had done nothing all day while she had been out working. She would need wood to burn over the winter, and there were several fallen trees covered with moss, waiting to be chopped.

He stepped over his makeshift bed and searched her grandfather's workbench, laden with tools, which lined the back wall. He soon found an axe and a saw. However they were not the tools he needed. He had found a trunk of a tree, already sawn into sections, and he had a plan to split them. Instinctually he knew the axe and saw would not work. Finally, he found what he wanted: three small wedge shaped metal objects and a long handled hammer. He didn't know how he had gained such knowledge, but he knew that if a man wanted to split wood it was these tools he needed.

Moments later he was outside. He lined the wedges up along the large sawn trunk and began hammering each wedge deep into the wood until it split in two with ease along the line. The satisfaction he felt from achieving such a minor task seemed ridiculous but he needed something useful to spend his frustration on.

Joss lined the wedges up again and again and each blow from his hammer felt good to him. He swung the hammer and it hit its target. Against his will, his thoughts turned to Beth as they so often did. He had spoken sharply to her yesterday, and he hated himself for doing so. He had already known about the scar on his chest before she had discovered it, having found it by accident shortly after his arrival. He had not known about the one on his back, though, and he had recoiled at the discovery of further evidence to his violent past. Joss wondered if the perpetrator of his injury had survived the encounter between them. If his dreams were anything to go by, he had not. He had stood there, his mind reeling from this new discovery, when Beth touched him. An innocent touch with no other intent meant, but it had stirred something in him. On the very day he had discovered he might be married, Beth Jago had touched his bare skin with her soft hand and looked up at him with wide eyes, filled with a mixture of fear and sympathy. It was too much to take, too many discoveries to make in one day, and he stepped away in order to put some distance between them.

Joss lifted the hammer and hit a wedge deep into the wood. He hit another one, again and again until the wood split in two at his feet. His frustration remained, and shouting in anger he flung the hammer away from him, the heavy head producing momentum for it to swing wildly away. He watched it crash into the trunk of a tree. He had enough complications in his life without discovering that she stirred feelings in him that a man should have for his wife and no other.

Beth stood before the row of fish cellars that lined the harbour. Today they were empty but it would not be long before they were being filled with pilchards when the season began in earnest. Kept separate from her deliveries, in her wheelbarrow lay two neatly wrapped fresh fish, which had just been given to her by an old friend of her grandfather's. Beth could not afford to refuse the gift so it had been gratefully received. She now stood alone. Her visit to Port Carrek was at an end and she took a moment to admire the working port. She read the inscription carved into the stone lintel above the centre fish cellar. Her grandfather had shown it to her when she was a little girl. Now, each time she read the foreign words, they made her feel close to him again. *Lucri Dulcis Odor* it said, and for years Beth had wondered what it meant. As if reading her thoughts, a man's voice from behind her translated the words.

'It's Latin and means *profit smells sweet*.'

Beth spun around, delighted. She recognised the voice immediately although it had been a long time since she had last heard it.

'Sam Pratt!' she cried. She had only rarely seen her childhood friend since he had received a patronage from his spinster aunt. This good fortune enabled him to leave Port Carrek's Wesleyan Methodist School to attend a boarding school. Whereas Beth's education had ended at the age of twelve, Sam's had continued to a level Beth could only imagine. He was smiling at her, and then he laughed as Beth gave him a big hug.

'Only Beth Jago would hug a man in the street,' he teased.

'Sam, what are you doing here?' Beth stepped back, unable to conceal her happiness at seeing him again. His sandy brown hair blew in the sea breeze and his smart clothes seemed at odds with the harbour surroundings, but she saw appreciation in his eyes as he looked at her and her happiness increased.

'I have been back for a month. I have a position in Kernow Bank and if I do well I hope to become manager one day.'

'A month?' Beth said disappointed. 'Why didn't you visit me?'

Sam had the good grace to look embarrassed.

'I meant to, but I didn't know what to say. I had heard about your grandfather and I thought you may be grieving.'

'I consider you a friend, Sam. You should not feel uneasy about visiting me at such a time. It is at such a time we need our friends the most.'

'It is good to see you again. It has been too long.' He smiled again and looked at the woman standing before him. 'You look as pretty as a picture. When did you turn into a lady?'

Beth self-consciously touched her hair. 'I put my hair up and my best dress on to look professional when I'm working. I even have my best boots on.' She lifted her hem slightly to show them off and realised they were still a little muddy from her riverside walk that morning. She quickly covered them again.

'You were always so independent.' He picked up the handles of her barrow and they walked side by side, their strides matching one another's. 'I remember the first time I saw you at school,' he said smiling. 'You were fighting, I recall, and punching Betty Jolif on the nose.'

'It was the first time I fought back. There is only so much taunting a girl can take.'

Sam was enjoying reminiscing, unaware of Beth's discomfort.

'Oh yes, what was it they used to call you?'

'I would rather not remember,' she said quietly, but Sam continued on.

'I know it wasn't nice. What was it?'

'The bastard from Benedict's,' she said simply, coming to a stop.

Sam frowned, aware for the first time the memories were not happy for her.

'I forgot your arrival to Port Carrek was difficult.'

'I am illegitimate, I came from Benedict's Workhouse and I knew no one. Children can be cruel without really understanding the effect their words have. You befriending me helped a lot. Having the most popular boy in school take my side put a stop to the bullying.'

'Perhaps, but their parents had also learnt who you were by then. Will Jago was well liked in the town and being his granddaughter helped the villagers accept you.'

Beth smiled and started to walk again; she liked talking about her grandfather.

'My grandfather was well liked, wasn't he? I miss him so much.'

'He would be so proud to know how well you are coping without him. You will make a fine wife one day.'

Beth reddened. 'Now you are teasing me, Sam,' she said with a laugh. 'Your aunt and mother would not consider me fine enough, especially now that you can speak Latin.' She was teasing him too, but there was a hint of truth in her words. A tense silence fell between them until Sam spoke again.

'It is good to see you again after so many years. I mean it when I say you have grown into quite a lady, and a lady of property too. I assume Kynance Cottage is now yours.'

Beth nodded. She didn't want to speak about her troubles with Sam and spoil their walk. They had come to the edge of the town and the mile of country road stretched out in front of them. It was time to part.

'Can I walk you home, Beth?' asked Sam.

It was a simple question but it meant so much more and they both knew it. Since the day Sam had stepped in to break up the fight with Betty Jolif, he had been a hero in Beth's eyes. His expressive green eyes, which were like windows to his sensitive soul, had turned the young Beth into his lovesick follower. Now she was a young woman of twenty-two and he an educated man of twenty-four, yet his smile could still melt her within. While Beth's position in life had not changed, Sam was on the path to a managerial position and success, and yet her childhood friend still offered her his company and had asked to walk her home. She straightened her shoulders and spoke in a voice she hoped would be acceptable for a bank manager's wife.

'I would like that very much,' she said politely and in all seriousness.

Sam laughed at her attempt to sound ladylike, unaware he was hurting her feelings.

'Only you can make me laugh, Beth Jago,' he said fondly. 'Come along, you can show me your cottage. I have not seen the little house for years.'

Beth followed on behind as he pushed her barrow, much as she had done as a child. Realising her folly she caught him up and walked quietly beside him. As Sam spoke of his time away, the friends he had made and the lessons he had taken, Beth took pleasure in the thought that to a passer-by they would look like a courting couple. As they neared the entrance to the track that led down to the valley, Beth's mind turned to her little cottage. Remembering that it was no longer empty, she began to regret accepting Sam's offer to accompany her home. What would Sam think if he discovered that she, a single woman, was living with a man she did not know? It didn't help that the man in question was only a few years older, good-looking and more powerfully built than Sam.

'Perhaps now is not a good time to see River Valley,' she said anxiously, taking her barrow from his hands. Sam frowned at her change in behaviour and she realised she must seem very rude. 'I'm sorry, Sam, perhaps another day ... when I have a chance to tidy the house.'

'Beth, you were never untidy and I don't believe you are now. Let me take the barrow.' Sam tried to grasp the handles but Beth would not let him.

'You are behaving very strangely,' said Sam, giving up and a little annoyed. 'Why don't you want me to come to River Valley?'

'Because,' said a man's voice, 'she doesn't want you to meet me.'

They both turned to see Joss standing amongst the shadows of the trees watching them. His handsome features did not diminish his threatening presence and Beth became instantly concerned for Sam's welfare. Sam was not a fighter and Joss had the body of one.

'I think you'd better leave, Sam.'

Sam did not move. 'Who is he?'

'His name is Joss.'

'And what is he to you?'

Beth was lost for words. What was he to her? She knew instinctively that Sam, his spinster aunt and snobbish mother would not think it was suitable that a young, single woman should have a man staying with her. She gave Joss a pleading look. An unspoken message passed between them and she knew he understood her dilemma. Joss studied them both as he considered his next words. From his expression she could tell that he had taken an instant dislike to Sam. His next words could sully her reputation and this power he possessed concerned and angered her.

Joss saw the fear in her eyes and the tension in her lips. *She likes this boy and she does not want me to come between them.* He looked at Sam's clothes, and although his jacket was too long in the sleeve, it was worn with pride and a swagger. The boy strived to be a gentleman, but he lacked the breeding and experience of life. Joss found he disliked Sam and he wondered if it was in his nature to have an aversion to those who believed they were someone they were not. Or was it just Sam who made him feel like this? He had the urge to tell him that he had slept in the cottage with Beth, just so he could see his face fall. However, this admission would damage Beth's reputation, which he did not want to do. His shoulders relaxed and his voice softened.

'Miss Jago is paying me to make some repairs to her cottage. It has deteriorated in recent years. It is understandable that she would wish you to see it when it is at its best.' Sam did not move, but nor did Joss. 'It would be poor manners to embarrass the lady by insisting,' he added.

Joss's suggestion that it would not be gentlemanly to insist upon his visit unsettled Sam. 'Perhaps another day, then,' Sam said hesitantly. He dragged his eyes away from Joss. 'It is time I returned to Port Carrek. It was good to see you again, Beth. Goodbye.' Sam threw Joss an angry glance before striding quickly away.

Joss sensed Beth's anger as they watched Sam leave and he had a feeling that it was directed at him rather than Sam.

'If he really cares about you he will be back.' He lifted the handles of her barrow and began to push it along the track to her house. Beth followed.

'How do you know? You don't even know him,' she grumbled. 'You come out of the woods, strutting like a cockerel over a hen. I'm surprised you didn't cock your leg to mark your territory! Who gave you the right to interrupt us? You should have kept out of sight.'

Joss did not reply at first. The truth of it was, he didn't know himself why he had interfered. Seeing her so angry told him it was not a good time to remind her that cockerels did not cock their legs.

'Sam is a good man. I knew him when I was a child. I have not seen him for years and you have ruined it for me.' Joss let her continue her tirade; it would do her good to vent her anger on him. 'He has only been back in the village a month. He was educated at Eton. He has mixed with the sons of Members of Parliament, doctors and gentry.'

They arrived at her cottage and quickly entered it. She started to unpack her mending, walking angrily to and fro. He had not seen her like this before. He hated that she was so upset over the puffed-up boy. Joss had had enough.

'So this boy, barely out of his adolescence, returns to Port Carrek so he can play the big fish in a little pond,' he retorted back at her as he helped her to unload. He picked up a package and hesitated. It felt soft and moist.

'Fish for supper,' Beth stated simply, pushing past him. For want of something to do he took the package to the table, opened it and grabbed a knife.

'So he has been back in Port Carrek for some time but you have not seen him. He is no friend if he does not visit you to offer his help when you are bereaved.' Beth winced at his words and he knew he had voiced her thoughts. 'No,' Joss continued, waving his knife at the window and the road beyond to indicate who he was talking about. 'Sam waits until some time has passed and it seems more appropriate before he comes calling, but it is not *you* he wishes to see but your *house*.' With a single slice he decapitated the fish. 'A beautiful, single woman,' he ranted, 'with property, is a catch indeed to a man who has outgrown his humble beginnings.'

Expertly, he sliced the fish along its belly and deboned it without hesitation. 'Did he attend your grandfather's funeral?' he asked.

Beth did not answer but stared stubbornly at the fish. Joss realised his words had hit close to home and hurt her. He would say no more. He casually threw the knife down on the table and allowed the tension in his shoulders to seep away. He looked at his hands covered with streaks of fish blood and quickly crossed the room to plunge them in a bucket of cold water. He scrubbed his hands clean, eager to be rid of the blood.

'You can gut fish,' Beth said in surprise.

'So?'

'It could be a clue to who you are.'

'I can also repair a slipped slate on a roof and split wood for firewood,' Joss said, wiping his hands dry. 'This is how I have filled my day.'

'You must be a labourer. A man with means would not do those types of jobs. He would employ someone.' Beth could not hide her excitement and she came to his side.

Joss looked down into her intriguing, dark blue eyes. 'Yet the watch is of good quality, as are my boots.'

Beth would not be put off. 'But you may have stolen the boots and watch, which would mean you may not be married at all.'

Joss smiled at her childlike excitement. 'You would rather I am a labourer who steals, than a man of means with a wife?'

Beth's mouth opened then shut. She turned abruptly and busied herself cooking the fish.

'Perhaps,' she said finally, aware he was waiting for her

answer. 'But it is because I have no respect for the rich.' She placed the pan over the fire and watched the fish cook. 'My father was rich. He was also married to a woman who was not my mother, so I have little reason to respect him or the class he came from. He took advantage of my mother, a miner's daughter, and when he was done with her he cast her aside.'

She crouched before the fire and turned the pan on the trivet. 'So yes, Joss Whoever-you-are.' She looked up at him. 'I would rather you were a labourer who had stolen but had no wish to steal again than a rich man married to another woman.' She turned the fish over and its aroma began to fill the room.

Joss did not know how to reply. Whether rich or poor, married or single, he was at the mercy of his past – a past he could not remember.

'Joss,' Beth said sadly as he made to leave to put the barrow back in the shed. He turned back to listen. 'Don't be like my father. He did not treat my mother well.'

'I don't know what you mean,' he replied quietly, confused at her words.

'Don't call me beautiful again, for there is a woman out there that will be missing you, and that thought alone is enough to break a person's heart.'

They had eaten their meal in silence and for once Beth's mood matched Joss's sullen one. His possessive behaviour towards Beth when Sam was there, and his slip of the tongue, hinted at his growing attraction to her, an attraction that must be stopped until he could discover his marital status. He despised adultery as much as Beth did, and at the moment he felt he was being unfaithful in thought if not in deed. An overwhelming urgency to discover his identity engulfed him as he watched her settle by the fire with her sewing. The summer evening meant there were several hours of light left and the sun shone in through the window and cast shadows of her lashes on her cheek. The delicate shadows and the homely chore that occupied her just added to her femininity. Joss stood up abruptly, making her jump.

'I am going to Port Carrek for a few hours. Perhaps someone will recognise me,' he announced, half to himself and half to Beth. Before Beth could reply, Joss was gone, banging the door behind him.

A lone figure of a man sat on the cliff edge above River Valley. The only grass that he had flattened lay beneath him, a sign he had not moved for some time. Motionless, the man seemed content to wait and watch. Only when he saw Joss go did his eyes leave the cottage and follow his figure through the trees towards the road above. When Joss disappeared amongst the canopy of leaves and thick gnarled trunks, the man's focus returned to his main interest and the reason he was there – Kynance Cottage and the woman inside.

Port Carrek did not seem familiar to Joss at all. This complete absence of any feeling or emotion made him acknowledge that River Valley had felt different when he had first seen it. He did not remember either place, but there was a tangible difference none the less. He walked the streets for several hours. The shops were shut and he had no money to visit the local inn, The Hevva Hevva, so he wandered aimlessly around the harbour and narrow streets that formed the town. He had hoped the smell of the nets and lobster pots that lined the harbour wall, or the sound of the water as it lapped the fishing boats, would trigger something within him – but he felt nothing.

He made his way along the coastal path, passing whitewashed fishermen's cottages and noisy children as they chased one another, screaming and shouting in pure joy and fun. Their sun-kissed skin had a healthy glow due in part to their fish-rich diet. It meant their parents' occupation not only allowed them to enjoy the health few city children had, but also the freedom to play in a place of beauty.

Joss sat and watched the harbour below and he began to smile to himself as he remembered Beth's words. *Strutting like a cockerel around a hen. You might as well have cocked your leg and marked your territory.* He started to laugh at her astute observation at his petty jealousy. Only Beth would be forthright enough to make such a remark to him. He laughed again, enjoying the warm summer evening, and he noticed again how strange it felt to laugh. If he were married, he realised, the match could not be a happy one, for his facial muscles told him that it had been a very long time since he had laughed so much.

The sun began to set and he slowly made his way back to Beth, despondent that not one person had greeted him as a friend or an acquaintance. On several occasions he noticed someone look at him and his spirit would lift for them to only look away or through him. He was not a person they recognised, and they were strangers to him. By the time he approached Kynance Cottage the light had almost faded. A great shadow from the rocky banks of River Valley cast an eerie darkness on the gorge as the sun set on the ocean's horizon. Each tree and every contour of its rock face became unnerving to see, and Joss's senses were already heightened before he saw the bent figure of a man standing at one of the cottage windows.

His outrage that someone appeared to be up to no good made him shout before his brain had a chance to advise caution. This slip in judgement was enough for the man to see him, straighten and take flight. The speed and agility of the dark figure took Joss by surprise but he immediately gave chase. Running, and at times stumbling, he followed him along a narrow track, where tangled roots and small rocks lay as traps to trip him.

The man reached the river's edge but did not follow the course of the river to cross at the footbridge. Instead he made his way to an area where the water ran shallow and crossed it in several well-aimed leaps, each foot hitting a large stepping stone that was barely visible in the fading light. Joss followed shortly behind, but he did not know this river and one foot slipped, delaying him and making him lose his stride and momentum. He glanced up to see the figure jogging up the winding, precarious track out of River Valley. Joss was able to match his speed, but he could not match his knowledge of the area, and as he watched him disappear into the dark he wondered who the man was and what he had been doing. His agility was almost unnatural, his knowledge of the area complete and, Joss believed, his intention was to cause mischief.

The valley now seemed empty, silent and peaceful, and as Joss caught his breath, he questioned what he had seen. Had there really been a man standing before Kynance Cottage before disappearing into the darkness with an unnatural gait to his run, or had Joss's nightmares come to haunt him in the day? It had been difficult to tell how tall the man was; perhaps there was some truth in the folklore that piskies roamed the county – strange fairies, small in stature, that liked to cause mischief and often led travellers astray.

To make sense of what had occurred, Joss retraced his steps until he stood in the same spot as the apparition he had chased. He placed his feet in the footprints he found and crouched as the man had done. As he lowered his line of sight the glow of the oil lamp within the cottage shone out through the chink in the curtain. Directly in his line of vision was the rim of a metal bathtub. Sitting in it, bare shoulders and knees glistening in the light reflecting on her wet skin, was Beth.

Oblivious to being watched, she washed her shapely calf with a flannel cloth. Strands of her hair had fallen loose from her pins, and lay damp against her neck, gently stroking her smooth skin as she turned her head. Joss's mouth went dry and his heart began to thump. He had no right to see her like this and his growing desire to touch her wet, clean skin with his lips made him no better than the man he had just chased off. He closed his eyes and withdrew a step, but the vision of her bathing still remained behind his lids.

Joss turned away and marched to the shed in the hope of finding a weapon. Whether she knew it or not, Beth needed protecting and next time he wanted to be ready. After a little rummaging, he found a broken wooden handle that had once been a shovel or hoe. No more than three foot in length, the weight and diameter felt good in his hand as he held it. He swiped a figure of eight in the air, as if he was hacking at an enemy with a sword. He tested it against his bent knee to see if it would break, but it held fast. Satisfied with his find he strode back to the front of the cottage and hid in the shadows of nearby trees to lay in wait, his weapon by his side. He would not tell Beth someone was watching her, it would unnerve her and dampen her sunny, although naive, disposition. He would, however, check the locks on her door and fit wooden shutters to her windows.

It was some time before he heard the inside bolts slide across and Beth come out to empty the water away. Eventually, when all was quiet again, he came out from the shadows and entered the cottage.

All signs of her bathing had been tidied away and Beth sat in the corner, hard at work, mending. Joss quietly placed his wooden weapon in the corner of the room, slid the bolts across the door and sat down opposite her.

Beth looked up. 'Did anyone know you? Did you see anyone?'

Joss shook his head, unable to meet her gaze.

Beth returned her attention to her sewing, blissfully unaware of what had just played out. It was best it stayed that way, thought Joss. She would be afraid if she knew that a stranger had watched her bathing – and that he had too. The delicious vision still teased his mind and threatened to remain there well into the night. Joss massaged his brow, as if to wipe it away. He must remain focused.

The evening finally came to a close. Joss watched Beth pack away her sewing in readiness for bed. He was reluctant to leave her alone, but he knew she would not allow him to sleep under her roof unless he told her why he wanted to stay. He wasn't sure if it was a good idea himself. He certainly wouldn't get much sleep knowing she slept in the room above him, especially after what he had seen through the window today.

He slipped his makeshift weapon beneath his shirt while she wasn't looking and went to the door. He opened it, but paused on the threshold.

'Goodnight, Beth. Don't forget to lock the door.' He closed it behind him, before she questioned why he felt the need to remind her. He waited outside until he heard the familiar sound of Beth sliding the locks across the door. Moments later, her shadow passed from room to room, extinguishing each light in preparation for bed. Her bedroom was the last. Finally the cottage was in darkness, but for the eerie light cast by the high crescent moon. Only then did Joss go to her grandfather's shed and his makeshift bed.

Chapter Six

Beth watched Joss with her hands on her hips. He was like a man possessed, as if there was something on his mind that troubled him. He had been busy all morning making shutters for the windows and fixing a padlock to the door so they could lock it when they went out. She was glad of the changes. Little did he know just how much she needed the extra security. However, working like this, with no rest, was not good for him and she decided, there and then, that he needed to relax and enjoy life a little more. And she knew just what would help him to do it.

'You want to show me River Valley?' Joss asked as he carried the ladder to the shed.

Beth nodded as she followed him.

'All of it? Every track and every hiding place, so I would know as much about the valley as a local man?'

Beth nodded. 'Yes, although I was thinking more of a gentle walk—'

'No, I want you to show me all of it.' He put the ladder in the shed by his bed and shut the door. 'Now is a good time.'

Beth was surprised. She had expected a rebuff, as he had never taken an interest in nature before.

'I'm serious. Show me the secrets of this valley and why you love it so much.'

Beth tilted her head as she looked at him. He appeared genuine.

'When I'm finished with you,' she said, smiling as she walked away, 'you will fall in love with it, too. Everyone falls in love with River Valley and you will be no exception.' She glanced over her shoulder at him. 'Come on.'

Joss followed her along the earth track. The tangled roots, which helped form worn steps in the earth as the path descended, were easier to see in the sunlight. At the bottom was the river's edge. Beth led him south to where the Trevillet River entered the valley. The roar of the waterfall, as it cascaded down onto the rounded stones at its base, could be heard long before they saw it. Its power and beauty, together with the rising mist and vibrant arc of a rainbow, momentarily brought them to a halt and stole their next breath.

'St Piran's Fall,' shouted Beth above the noise. 'Named after the patron saint of Cornwall. Follow me.'

Beth made her way to the side of the fall. Joss followed. The vibrant colours were so close it felt they could almost touch them. Beth looked up at Joss and was glad to see his frown had already faded away.

'Come.' She gave his hand a gentle tug and led him along the narrow path that took them behind the curtain of white water. Strangely, the roar of the waterfall was quieter here. With a rocky recess behind them and a cascading river in front, they were hidden from the world. Droplets of fresh water settled on their skin, hair and lashes, adorning them with fine beads of transparent jewels. Beth breathed in deeply and exhaled with a soft sigh.

'Years ago, people would travel for miles to come here. They believed the water was blessed by a wood nymph called Morzelah who had healing powers.' Beth encouraged Joss to breathe in too. 'The moisture and sweet smell of the lichen have special properties. My grandfather often came here to help with his breathing. Try it.'

Joss closed his eyes and breathed in, and as he held the sweet air in his lungs, Beth took advantage of the moment to gaze at his handsome face. How his wife must miss him.

Joss exhaled with a sigh. 'Why did the nymph bless the water?' he asked as he looked down on her. Beth blinked. She had been caught staring. It took a moment for her to understand what he had just said.

'Oh! The river saved the life of the man she loved.' Beth

felt her cheeks burn at the mention of love. She quickly turned away and continued on the path out from behind the waterfall.

Joss followed. 'What happened to them?' he shouted as he competed with the roar of the water on the other side.

'He left her,' Beth shouted back, 'and she almost died from a broken heart. She wanted no one else to suffer as she had, so she ensured that her blessing would continue and heal the suffering of others.'

Away from the noise they paused again to watch the waterfall from a distance. Beth looked up at Joss. This time it was she who had caught him gazing at her. Despite his hair and skin remaining damp from the mist, he had a gentle shine in his eyes.

'Perhaps it will heal what ails you, Joss.'

'Perhaps it will.' A sweet message passed between them, one of hope and acceptance. It was fleeting, but it was magical all the same. 'Why did he leave her?'

'I don't know. When she heard he had died, she spent many years searching for his spirit. When she found it she used her magical powers to bring him back to life.'

Joss pulled back his shoulders, lifted his chin and looked up the valley. 'Is that what you would have done?'

'I could not remain in love with a man who had left me. Such a man does not deserve to be loved.'

'Even if the man had lost his memory and did not know how to return?'

'I am sorry. I did not mean—'

'I know you did not. I just wish ... no matter. Show me more.'

She continued with her tour and led him away from the river onto another trail. The fragile spell between them had been broken, if it ever existed at all. After some moments they arrived at a glade where the sweet smelling lichen and mosses grew in abundance. It clung to the rocky walls and formed a soft carpet underfoot, yet soon their muted colours gave way to a blaze of colour as sea campions and pink thrift took their place. Beth indicated for Joss to stay still and she carefully stepped forward until she stood amongst the wild flowers that grew rampant in the sheltered clearing.

'This is Butterfly Glade,' whispered Beth. Satisfied the stage was set, she opened her arms and began to slowly spin. Copious numbers of butterflies, of all colours, took flight and fluttered haphazardly in the air around her. They flew in all directions, their ungainly flight making them appear like puppets suspended from strings. Gradually, one by one, they began to settle again.

'Lovely, isn't it?' asked Beth. Her smile was infectious and Joss could not help but return it.

'Magical and beautiful. Are you sure you are not Morzelah?' he asked, without thinking.

'Follow me,' Beth said, secretly pleased with the compliment. 'I want to show you where there really is magic.'

Joss followed, taking note of each track she showed him. As he walked, he tested the firmness of the ground beneath his feet and tried to memorise the area, particularly where emerging roots and rock ledges could trip a man giving chase. He was concentrating so hard on the trails that when they finally arrived at their destination he stared in disbelief. Before them stood an ancient tree, its growth stunted and twisted by the Atlantic winds. Countless coloured ribbons and strips of cloth were tied on every branch, lifting and curling in the breeze like paper streamers. They varied in length and thickness. Some were bright, others more faded and frayed, the degree of their vibrancy a sure sign of the length of time they had been tied there.

Joss stepped forward, awed by the sight. 'What is this?'

'It's a wishing tree. People have come here to tie a ribbon on the tree and make a wish for centuries. If they could not afford a ribbon they brought a small strip of cloth.' She pointed to a pale blue piece of cloth, now faded and stained. It hung on one of the lowest branches, at the level of her waist. 'When I first came here I tied this one and made my first wish. I wished I could stay here with my grandfather.' She searched for a moment then pointed to another at shoulder height. 'I tied this one when I was twelve. I wished Sam would return when he finished his schooling. This wish has now come true too.'

Joss braced himself but Beth did not notice. She lifted her sleeve and tied to her wrist were two scarlet ribbons. They looked new and unused.

'I bought them on a whim.' Beth ran the ribbons through her fingers. 'When I was a child I saw a man wearing a bright red coat with beautiful gold buttons. The ribbons reminded me of that day, but I soon realised their colour is far too bright for me to wear. I have kept them in a drawer until now.'

Joss looked at the blood red colour of the ribbons. He had seen their colour before. The memory was elusive and quickly floated away, like gossamer caught on the wind.

'Now we can both make a wish,' Beth said, smiling and holding out her wrist to him.

Surprised and touched at her suggestion, Joss hesitated only briefly before untying them. His fingers grazed the inside of her wrist, causing a delightful tingling sensation to race up both their arms. They stepped back from each other, ashamed. He was married and they had no right to feel such things.

Silently they tied their ribbons to the tree, both choosing the same branch so they blew in the wind side by side. They watched the ribbons curling and twisting in the breeze like dancers in the sky, neither asking the other what they had wished for nor offering to tell.

Eventually, they began to make their way out of River Valley to Kellis Cove, leaving the wishing tree alone with its colourful swaying wishes of hope. Something was changing between them, and it was something that should not be.

It was not long before the valley opened up. The golden sand of Kellis Cove lay before them, framed by rock formations jutting out of the sand. They spent the next hour walking over limpet-encrusted rocks and searching the rock pools that had been captured at high tide. Like carefree, inquisitive children, they delighted in discovering their secrets. Red tentacles of anemones waved at them beneath the waters, while starfish and hermit crabs attempted to hide. Finger-like seaweed lay limply on the rocks, waiting for the tide to reclaim it and carry it back out to sea.

Although Beth had played in the cove most of her childhood, sharing the experience with Joss made it feel as if she too was seeing it all anew. Their time together, as they explored, laughed and made footprints in the sand, was made all the more precious because they were alone. New experiences waited for them in the future, old ones lay captured in their past, but none of them mattered. Only the present felt real and true, worthy of a memory that would be forever cherished, yet also sadly mourned.

The inside of the cave was blacker than they had expected. Beth had dared Joss to enter it and he only agreed on the condition that she would come, too. Now they both stood in its inky depths listening to the eerie silence around them.

'Why is it called Sailor's Rest?' Joss's voice broke into Beth's sombre thoughts. She was glad to know he was still standing next to her. It was one thing to agree to enter when the sun was shining on your back; it was another to be standing inside. She hoped her voice did not betray how scared she felt.

'That is not its real name. Its real name is Pepper Hole, but fifty years ago a Spanish ship was wrecked on Gull Rock and thirty sailors lost their lives. Their bodies were brought here until they were all recovered and the parish could decide what to do with them. No one knew the name of the ship or how to contact the families of the dead.'

Sadness emanated from every wall of the cave. It was easy to imagine the harrowing sight of the dead bodies lined up in the light of a flickering oil lamp. Today they had no lamp. Beth was sure she could still feel their spirits about them.

'What happened to them?' Joss asked.

'The local vicar donated a plot in his graveyard and they are buried at Lanmeneth Church. The villagers from Port Carrek did not like to think of the sailors not having a stone so they raised enough money for a monument. It is sad to think that their relatives do not know where they are.'

'I must have relatives who do not know where I am.'

Joss's words made Beth's heart ache. The mixture of pain and fear of the darkness was too much for Beth and she had to leave. She turned abruptly and walked straight into Joss, who had been standing behind her, rather than next to her, in the pitch black.

It was a fleeting, clumsy moment as her body slammed into the full length of his, yet she had felt all of him more intimately than any man she had ever met. She had felt his chest, his waist, his hips and his thighs, and in turn she knew he had felt hers. Images of them entwined flashed in her mind. She stumbled back, shaken, as his hands came to rest on her elbows to steady her. The desire to step back into his arms and feel his body against hers again was all consuming and in her panic she roughly pushed his helping hands away.

'It's getting late, we need to go home,' she mumbled. 'I have mending to do.'

She brushed past him out into the sunlight.

Joss followed her. 'You go back to the cottage.' He stood for a moment as he looked about him. 'I would like to stay here for a bit longer.'

Glad of the chance to be away from him for a while so she could gather her thoughts, Beth nodded and left to return to the safety of Kynance Cottage. The brief escape from their troubles, and the magical moments they had shared, had come to an end and it was time to return to reality.

Joss watched Beth walk away, leaving a trail of small footprints in the fine sand. When he could no longer see her, he turned his head and looked along the coastline and the beach. He breathed in deeply before letting the air out in one long, controlled breath. She had been embarrassed at bumping into him and had wanted to leave. He could understand her need to put distance between them. Lord knows he needed it, too. He wanted time to think and to try and remember. He had not told Beth, but as he had entered the mouth of the cave, and again when he had walked out and seen the view of the beach, he knew, without a doubt, that he had seen this cove before. The memory was delicate and he was afraid to force it in case it should disintegrate as quickly as it had arrived. It presented as a deep feeling and vivid snapshots on which he could not elaborate, and it gave him a fragmented knowledge of the cove that he did not remember obtaining. Yet it was there none the less. He felt that he had been here many times – which raised the question: did Beth actually know him, and had she been lying to him all this time?

A figure of a man near the cliff edge caught his attention. The same man, he felt sure, who had been watching Beth the evening before. Had he been watching them throughout the afternoon? Joss was determined to find out. He ran towards him, jumping with ease over rock formations, sandy banks and tufts of wild grass that sprouted through its windswept grains. Soon he was following one of the many tracks that led up to the cliff edge. In places it was so steep that he had to use his hands to help him climb the gradient. His fitness and agility, together with the good light, aided his speed and he soon reached the top where the man had sat. But he was too late. He had gone.

Joss swore. All that remained were five sticks, all the same length and neatly lined up on the flattened grass. Angry and frustrated, Joss grabbed them up and threw them over the cliff. They rose high in the air, sending screeching seagulls flying in all directions, before falling silently onto the sand below. As the birds' cries died away, Joss noticed for the first time another sound coming from the depths of the valley. It was Beth – and she was screaming.

Chapter Seven

Beth screamed as she felt herself propelled through the cottage door. The force of the push from behind her was so abrupt and strong that she had no time to brace herself. She hit the corner of the table with a sickening thud before sprawling onto the floor. Dazed, she looked up to see two towering men standing over her. She stared blankly at them, confused and in shock, until she realised they were throwing her belongings out of the door. She scrambled to her feet and grabbed a pan.

'Who are you and what are you doing with my things?'

The men ignored her and continued rummaging through her cupboards, emptying shelves and throwing everything that was not nailed down outside. She attempted to rescue a chair from one of them.

'Get out of my house! Get out!'

The larger man, already sweaty from exertion, grabbed her pan and threw it out the window with ease.

'You,' he said, pointing a grimy finger at her, "ave to leave. This isn't your 'ouse and you're trespassin'.'

Beth shook her head. 'That's not true. There's been a terrible mistake.' She hated the uncertainty in her voice. He must be wrong. 'My grandfather owned this house. He died a few months back. I am his next of kin so it passes to me.'

The large man approached her. He stood so close that she could smell stale sweat and cheap ale as his breath fanned her face.

'We 'ave been ordered to get you out by Mr Nankervis and that is what we intend to do.'

When she shook her head, he grabbed her around the waist, lifted her off the floor and threw her out of the door.

Beth fell forwards onto the stony earth. It tore into her palms as she landed. As she lay there, catching her breath, she noticed her mending lying discarded in the dirt next to her. It was too much to bear. She scrambled to her feet and ran back in, jumping on the back of the thinner man and hitting him with her clenched fists. Irritated by her interference, the two men grabbed her arms and started to carry Beth to the door. She continued to struggle, fighting and kicking, as their fingers bit into her flesh.

'I will not leave my home!' she shouted. 'Let me go!'

The room fell into shadow. Someone was standing in the door and blocking the light.

'You heard the lady,' said a man's calm voice.

The men halted and looked at the interloper standing squarely in the doorway. Beth sagged with relief. Joss had arrived.

They let her go as they squared up to Joss, enabling her to run to his side. He surveyed the scene slowly, tapping a broken hoe hard against his open palm to a slow beat.

'Who are you and what are you doing here?' he asked, remaining unruffled.

The larger man answered. 'We are on business. We 'ave been employed to evict this trespasser. She 'as no right to stay 'ere.'

'Who is your employer?'

'Mr Nankervis.'

'Who is this Mr Nankervis?' asked Joss patiently. His weapon seemed at odds with his calm tone.

The larger man hesitated. ''E ... 'e is a gentleman.'

'Where does he live?'

'I ... we don't know.'

'But you have met him?' continued Joss.

'Well, no. We were told what 'e wanted done.' By way of explanation he added, ''E knows someone who knows us. We 'ave not met 'im face to face.'

His explanation did not surprise Beth. Thugs often got their jobs by word of mouth.

'Show me the proof the house is not hers,' said Joss. 'I assume you insisted on some proof before you acted on his demands?'

The thinner man fingered his collar and edged towards the door.

'I 'ave a job to do and that's what I'm goin' to do,' said the larger man. 'I ain't afraid of the likes of you wavin' your stick about. Don't you know who I am?'

Joss raised an eyebrow to indicate he did not, and did not really care.

'I'm Jorey Jose. I was a champion wrestler in my day.'

Joss was unimpressed by his boast. 'Well, Jorey Jose, your day has come and gone. Get out and take your weasel of a friend with you.'

Jorey was beside himself with anger at the snub and picked up a fire poker. Yelling, he ran towards Joss as he swung it in the air. Joss blocked the attack with his homemade weapon as expertly as if it were a sword. Swinging it again, he sliced it through the air and hit Jorey between the neck and shoulder. Jorey dropped his poker but almost immediately lunged again. He took a fistful of Joss's shirt and attempted to perform a wrestling move and bring him to the ground, but Joss was ready for him. He parried, swung the wooden handle over his head and grabbed both ends, effectively pinning Jorey by the neck. Jorey could do nothing but fall to his knees and gasp for breath as Joss stood behind him. Pulling hard on the wooden handle, he forced the ex-wrestler's face upwards.

'Look at me, Jorey Jose,' he demanded.

Jorey stubbornly refused. Joss gave him a shake. Jorey began to struggle for breath. 'I said look at me!'

Jorey slowly obeyed.

'Listen to me, Jorey Jose, one-time Cornish Wrestling Champion, who is now nothing more than a paid thug. You have made your message clear and you have terrified this woman. Now leave and don't ever come back or next time you will see just what I am capable of doing.'

Jorey nodded his head like a child. Beth suspected he had seen something in Joss's eyes that she had never seen, and it had frightened him. Joss suddenly smiled and released him. Jorey scrambled to his feet and stumbled from the room.

'Where is the other one?' Joss asked her.

'He's already gone,' Beth said quietly.

She eased herself down onto a chair as her legs had begun to tremble and would no longer support her. She looked about her. The room was a shambles and she dreaded his next question. Joss had rescued her and fought on her behalf, but now he would want to know the truth – and that was hard to tell as she herself did not know it. He waited for an explanation. As none was forthcoming, he asked for one.

'What the hell was that about? Who is Nankervis and what is he to you?'

Beth picked up her sewing box from the floor and attempted to sort its contents.

'Tell me! How can I protect you if you don't tell me what is happening?'

'No one has asked you to protect me!' Beth put the box aside and got up. She felt stronger now.

'If there is a problem then I need to know. You cannot hide from it.'

'I've never needed anyone to protect me before. I can look after myself.' She attempted to pass him.

Joss caught her arm and swung her to face him. 'Not against thugs who are three times as heavy as you.'

'I will have to be more careful.' She shook him off. 'I have lived on my wits before now.'

Joss scoffed. 'What would you know about living on your wits when you live in this idyllic place?'

He was angry with her. The day had started so well. She

had felt so close to him, almost too close, but now he was shouting at her. Angry and frustrated, she turned on him too.

'You know nothing of my life!' She turned to leave but Joss barred her way.

'Tell me.'

Beth shook her head. 'No.'

'How strange life is,' he said quietly. 'Here you are, not wishing to talk of your past or face up to your troubles and here I am, desperate to know my past so I can put an end to whatever troubles I might have.'

'We are very different,' said Beth. How she wanted to rest her head against his shoulder and share her troubles. The light was fading. Soon they must light the candles.

'We are both alone, with no family that we can call our own,' he replied. 'I can't help you if you don't tell me the truth.'

'And I can't help you unless you tell *me* the truth,' replied Beth. 'Perhaps,' she continued, 'we are not so very different after all.'

Joss frowned. 'What do you mean?'

'I have heard your nightmares. I have seen the look of uncertainty in your eyes, as if you feel you are not a good man. I have now seen you fight. You threatened to kill him, Joss.'

Joss turned away from her, unable to meet her gaze. 'I don't know my past, but you do. Tell me about it, Beth. Then perhaps we can work on the present together. For without both there will be no future.'

Beth watched Joss light the candles. They had just finished putting the cottage in order and their warm glow was the final touch it needed to make the room feel cosy and safe. Everything was peaceful as a home should be. The only thing missing was her grandfather. She had felt so alone since his death. Joss had spoken the truth when he had said she had no family she could call her own. She had tried to make ends meet, but her meagre earnings no longer seemed to stretch as they had done when her grandfather brought his wages home each week. When he could no longer work, he always had something under the mattress to tide them over. Now it all seemed such a struggle. To the outside world she was coping, but inside her grief for her grandfather was ever present. Then there were the solicitor's letters that confused and frightened her. They threatened to take away the one thing that belonged to her, and their legal terminology was intimidating. She didn't know Joss well, yet he was offering his help and speaking words of kindness. Until now it had been possible to carry on with life. People were content to believe that she was coping. They accepted without question the image she portrayed to the world and in doing so it allowed her grief not to be stirred. However, when words of kindness were spoken they had a habit of unlocking fragile emotions deep within.

'You have injured your hands.' The sound of his voice brought her back to the present and she realised he had taken her hands in his own. 'Let me see,' he said softly, turning them over to look at her palms. Small stones were embedded in tiny bruised indentations, and in places her flesh was torn. 'Does it hurt?' he asked.

She looked at his bowed head, now so close to hers, and nodded. The concern in his voice and his gentle touch made her mute, as she felt unable to form words to speak her thoughts. He blew gently onto her skin, cooling it and taking away the pain. His unexpected gesture was full of kindness, and the caress of his breath felt like ghostly kisses on her upturned hands. No one had shown her such gentleness since her grandfather had died, and suddenly it was all too much for her. His image blurred behind a film of tears, her legs buckled and she heard a woman's anguished sobbing. She felt Joss's arms wrap about her and his hushed, soothing tones whispered into her hair. She tried to catch her breath. The sobbing quietened and only then did she realise the sound of the tormented woman was coming from her. She felt his warm body supporting her, and, taking strength from him, she finally allowed herself to be comforted. She leaned into him and he held her tight before gently lowering her to the ground so she could rest.

Joss sat on the floor, his knees bent, his back against the cottage wall. Lying between his legs, with her tear-stained face on his chest, lay Beth. His arms held her in a comforting embrace and he felt each steady rise and fall as her body took a breath.

They had remained silent, since he had sat her down, listening to the sizzling sap of the wood as it burned in the fire. He had not pressed her again for information, but in the comfort of his arms, she slowly began to share it with him.

'I don't know who Nankervis is or why he wants me out. This is *my* house, I know it is.'

Joss did not reply, but simply stroked her hair as if she were a child.

'I told you that my grandfather was once a miner, didn't I?' He nodded against her hair. 'He worked at Penarth Mine and lived in one of the mining cottages that went with the job. One day a tin-bearing rock pillar gave way below ground. Women and girls were on the surface breaking and sorting ore when the ground gave away beneath them. They managed to leap to safety but it left a thirty-foot hole in the ground. At the same time ore dressing slimes began to cascade down into the mine, dragging anyone who was near with it. The owner had been visiting with his son and his son was knocked off his feet and carried down into the mine, along with six men. My grandfather was able to catch the boy's arm and drag him to safety but the others died. The boy was about seven at the time.' Beth teased a fold on his shirt with her fingers. 'It was a tragedy that no one could have foreseen but as a reward for his quick thinking, the mine owner gave Kynance Cottage to my grandfather. At the time my grandfather was beginning to suffer from miners' lung. It meant that he could leave the mine and recover his health, but still have a home to live in.'

'Tin-bearing pillar rocks rarely give way,' remarked Joss.

Beth smiled. 'You sound like you know about mining. You know how to gut fish, do general labouring, ride a horse. You are a jack of all trades—'

'—and master of none,' he finished for her with a smile.

'Penarth Mine is closed now. It was forced to close when it could no longer produce enough tin to make it profitable as the tin prices had begun to drop. Penarth Mine was just one of many mines to have closed over the years.'

'How old was your grandfather at the time?'

'In his late thirties. He brought my grandmother and my mother to live in River Valley when he gave up mining, and took on general labouring jobs. My mother was a young woman and only lived here for two years, but she lived on those memories for the rest of her short life.'

'What happened to her?'

Beth looked up at him with her wide, sapphire blue eyes. 'She fell in love with a man far above her station, ran away with him to a boarding house, and became pregnant with me.' She rested her cheek against his chest again. She felt so right there, as if his body was made to hold her like this. 'When she told him that she was pregnant he told her that he was married and would not leave his wife. She was devastated but it was too late. He returned to his wife and abandoned her. My mother didn't return to River Valley. She didn't want to bring shame on her parents. She was also afraid that her aunt Amy, who was unable to bear children, would take me away from her and bring me up as her own. She lived on a farm on the edge of Bodmin Moor and my mother knew she would not get to see me very much if I lived so far away. My aunt Amy and uncle Zachariah eventually adopted a runaway boy.

He was quite a handful and caused them no end of trouble. My uncle and aunt have both passed on now.'

'What happened?'

'My mother struggled for some years but eventually there was only one option left to her: the workhouse. I was three when we went there. I have no memories of my life before Benedict's Workhouse. I lived there until I was eight years old.'

'Your mother should have let your aunt care for you. Better to live on Bodmin Moor than in a workhouse.'

'I would have refused to go. I would have found my way back to her.'

'Then you are as stubborn as your mother.'

Beth smiled. It was good to smile again and she had him to thank for that.

'I was allowed to remain with my mother in the female section until I was seven. We shared a bed in a ward of fourteen, but the guardians were reasonable and she was allowed access to me throughout the day. I was one of the lucky children. I had three hours of schooling from the age of five, so I can read and write. My mother would often sign herself out of the workhouse to find work or do odd jobs and then sign herself back in during the evening. They expected her back so they never gave our bed away.

'When I was seven I was moved and sent to a ward where I was meant to stay until I was sixteen. I was permitted to see my mother at a daily interview but it was never the same as living in the same ward as her. What is there to say when your day is no different from the one before? The last time I saw her she looked pale and I think she knew it would be the last time she would see me. When she was asked to leave she clung to me and sobbed so much that it frightened me. I wish I had understood and had hugged her back, but I didn't and I will regret it for the rest of my life.'

Beth sniffed loudly and roughly wiped a tear away. 'The first time I knew my mother had died was two weeks after the fact. The warden found me and gave me some matching boots. I had never had matching boots before and at first I was delighted. As she gave them to me I recognised the style and the ink-stained leather tongue. They were my mother's. I found out that she had died during the winter diphtheria outbreak. The wardens had forgotten that she had a child in the same workhouse so I was not informed of her death. By chance and nothing more, it was me who had received her boots to wear. She was already in a pauper's grave and to this day I do not know where she is. I felt so angry that I had not been told. I am still angry that the man who was my father could discard my mother and his own child so easily.' Beth shook her head in disbelief at her father's lack of responsibility. 'He had a life of luxury, and a wife; he did not want me as a reminder of his past mistake,' she added bitterly.

'How did you end up here?' asked Joss.

'My mother used to tell me about River Valley and her parents. It sounded so wonderful. Before I was eight I had never left the workhouse grounds. My meals were adequate but my life was drudgery. I learned to sew which kept me away from sack making and oakum picking. I lived by a rigid timetable with paupers who snored, fought and swore. When I learned my mother was dead there was no reason for me to stay. I had the confidence of an eight-year-old who does not understand that the outside world could be a bad place, too, and one morning I simply walked out. I was taken aback by how easy it had been. Finding my way to River Valley was a little more difficult but as luck would have it I was introduced to Bill, the farmer who looked after the loan horse, and he brought me here.'

'So one day you turned up at your grandfather's door,' said Joss. 'Did he know you existed?'

Beth laughed. 'No. He was taken aback at first. I had disturbed him as he had a guest. He was delighted and confused all at the same time. He ushered me into the kitchen and asked me to wait while he said goodbye to his visitor. I couldn't quite believe I had found him and could not help but follow him to see who his guest was. I peeked through the door and saw him talking to a man in a splendid scarlet coat with buttons made of gold.'

'Is this the man you spoke of when we tied the red ribbons on the wishing tree?' asked Joss.

Beth nodded. 'I never saw the man in the red coat again, but that was the day I met my grandfather and he was everything I had hoped he would be. My grandmother had already died by then. I miss him so much. He told me about how he came to River Valley and my mother's story was the same as his. He always said that I had nothing to fear after he died. He told me that I would be looked after, that he would see to that.'

She looked up at him again. They had been lying together as a father would comfort a child, as a friend would comfort a friend, yet the simple act of her lifting her head again, with her story now told, changed it all. The tilt of her head and the way their bodies moulded into one another made them appear to an observer like lovers. She wondered if Joss desired her as much as she desired him. Did he want to touch her lips with his, to hold her body against his as a lover would rather than a friend? In this magical moment, did he want her to the exclusion of all others – including his wife? Was this how her mother had felt when she had met her father, before she found herself with child, before he ruined her? As if coming to her senses Beth withdrew and broke free of Joss's comforting embrace. She knelt before him trying to sound matter-of-fact.

'Now you know about me, what is your truth?' she asked. 'Tell me what you dream about. Is it of your life before River Valley?'

He thought for a moment and chose his words carefully as if he did not want to frighten her.

'I have dreams that just add to my confusion,' he said finally. 'They may mean nothing, or they may mean everything. My memory is just as confusing. Today I thought I knew the beach, but I may have seen it when I arrived here. Sometimes I feel that it has been a long time since I have been happy. Today, when I was on the beach, I felt as if it was the first time I had been at peace in a very long time.'

Beth smiled. 'I'm glad you felt some peace.'

'But there is no clarity or sense to it all. I don't know why I came to your cottage, but wonder if you know why I was there. I have even wondered if you know who I am.'

Beth's smile faded. 'Do you think I would lie to you, when I have done everything in my power to help you regain your memory?' Joss's accusation had hurt her.

'I have to ask you. Do you know me?'

Beth stood. 'How can you ask me that?'

Joss remained calm. He leant his head back against the wall and casually rested his arm on his knee as he looked up at her. 'Sometimes, when I look at you, Beth, I feel like we have met before. I look at your blue eyes and your raven hair and I feel something, it's like a knowledge that will not translate in my head.'

Beth's heart softened. Slowly, she knelt down in front of him again. 'Go on.'

'When I saw the beach I felt sure that I'd been there before. Many times. Which would mean you might know me too. Yet, in an instant, the feeling was gone. So I thought I would ask you for the truth.'

'We have never met before,' said Beth. 'That is the truth.'

Joss took out the watch from his pocket and looked at the worn engraving.

'I thought that is what you would say, and I think it must be true.'

Beth raised an eyebrow. 'How can you be so sure?' She was still a little annoyed he should question her on such a thing.

Joss rubbed the engraving that bore his wife's name. 'Because if I had met you first, this inscription would bear a different name.' He lifted the watch by its chain. It slowly turned in the firelight and brought them both under its spell. If things were different—

Beth escaped its enchantment first. 'Well, you didn't, and we must live with those consequences.' She looked at the night sky through the window. 'It's getting late,' she said, standing. She quickly crossed the room and carefully closed the shutters. It had been easy to lie in his arms. How long had it been? Long enough for the day to have come to an end without either of them noticing.

Beth stretched her arms and gave an exaggerated yawn. 'I'm tired and need my sleep.' She gave him a furtive glance. The message she was sending was clear.

Joss snatched the watch in mid-air and slipped it into his pocket.

'You are right, it is getting late, and I am tired, too.' He stood up and looked down on her. She was barely an arm's length away, but for all the right he had to touch her, she may as well have been on the other side of the valley.

Beth turned away. 'Goodnight, Joss,' she said as she left the room.

'Goodnight, Beth.' Joss left the cottage to sleep on his bed in the shed. She slid the locks across the door and went to bed herself, but it was another hour before she finally fell into a fitful sleep. An hour spent wondering if Joss's thoughts were troubled by the same woman that filled hers. A woman neither of them knew, a woman who called herself his wife.

Martha sat looking at her son. His windswept hair stood up at peculiar angles, a sure sign that he had been walking the cliffs again. This habit did not worry Martha, as his wanderings gave her a break from his strange ways. He would disappear for hours but eventually come home when he was hungry, happy and tired, which was always good to see. No, it wasn't where he had been that concerned her, or the way

102

he sat staring into the fire. What did worry her was that his bag, normally full of sticks, was empty. He obsessed over his sticks and went everywhere with them, yet today he had lost them and showed no concern at all. She would rather see his normal reaction of stress and agitation than this attitude of indifference. Indifference was not like her Tom – unless his fixation had changed to something else.

'Where 'ave you been, Tom?' she asked him gently.

Tom ignored her and continued to stare into the fire. She asked again.

'River Valley,' he replied, without taking his eyes from the dancing flames.

'You will be careful, Tom. Don't want you fallin' off the cliff.'

'Saw Beth. She was 'appy.'

Martha felt relief flood her. He had been with Beth. That was good, as she would have looked after him.

'She was 'appy with the man who fell. He lives in 'er 'ouse. At night 'e sleeps in 'er shed. I saw them running and laughing on the beach together.'

Martha couldn't hide her surprise.

'The one you fetched me for? I thought 'e would be long gone before now.' She put a log on the fire, easing her creaking joints and stiff back with some tentative stretches. 'Beth should be careful,' she muttered. 'She can't 'ave a well man living with her in the valley. 'Tis different when he was ill, but not a fit an' 'andsome one as 'e is. She will get a name for 'erself.'

'She 'as a name. 'Er name is Beth,' replied Tom, confused.

'I mean people will call 'er *loose*.'

Tom's confusion remained, so Martha tried to explain again. It was good to have a conversation with Tom; it did not happen very often.

'Folk may call a woman *loose* if she lives with a man before she is wed to 'im. If a man likes a woman, and a woman likes a man, then they should wed.'

Tom thought for a moment then returned his attention to the fire. Martha realised that, as far as Tom was concerned, the conversation was over and he did not wish to speak again. What was going on in her son's head? He looked confused, almost sullen. She wished she could help him, but she knew better than to push him. She watched him staring intensely into the fire, his pale complexion growing pink from the heat of its flames. She wished her son had friends but he did not seem to want them. His odd behaviour confused people his own age and they had no patience for him. Martha sat down in the chair beside him and before long her eyelids began to close. Tom was safely home and that was all that mattered for now.

Tom continued to watch the fire late into the night until the flames had dwindled to no more than ash and glowing embers. Only when the last red spark, which had glowed and burned like a beating heart in the hearth, was finally extinguished did Tom's concentration cease. Leaving his sleeping mother and his empty bag by the mound of ash in the fireplace, he got up and went to bed. Sadness weighted heavily in his heart, his mind full of images of his Beth as she laughed and smiled with another.

Chapter Eight

For the past few days, Joss had busied himself fixing the shed. He worked like a man possessed, as if he wanted to keep his thoughts occupied and tire out his body. Beth recognised the need. She had also immersed herself in work, resulting in her finishing her mending long before she expected to. Yet several times Beth caught herself idling away the time just watching Joss through the window, wasting her minutes when she should be sewing and earning money. She had often watched her grandfather working, but that was different. Watching Joss at work stirred unfamiliar feelings inside her and as much as she wanted to stop watching him, time and time again she found herself back at the window under the pretext of cleaning or looking for something. He appeared almost driven to put the shed to rights. She wondered if he was doing it for his own comfort, as he had his bed there, or to fulfil a need of being of some use. She needed his strength and skills, they were useful to her. Yet she could not ignore the fact that he was a fine-looking man, and it was an even more basic need that drew her back to the window each time. In fact, she had been so occupied with watching Joss work that she didn't notice the washing had fallen from the line at the front of the house. Frustrated that it would have to be washed again, Beth went outside, picked up the clothes and carried them back indoors. She needed to take a walk and put some distance between herself and Joss, she decided. Leaving the dirty washing, she picked up two packages of finished mending, told Joss where she was going and left for Port Carrek.

After delivering her sewing, she had hoped to have a long chat with Martha and confide in her about Joss, but Martha was not at home so she found herself walking around Port Carrek with no deliveries to make and no Martha to talk to. Just when Beth made up her mind to return to River Valley with a renewed vow to stop falling for Joss, she heard someone call her name. Before she had a chance to turn round, she felt a hand touch her arm. It was Sam and, from the look of him, he had run out of Kernow Bank to speak to her. He stood smiling down at her, a little breathless. She could tell from his face that he was as pleased to see her as she was to see him. Their awkward parting in front of Joss the other day felt like a distant memory.

He was well dressed in a suit made of good cloth. He looked smart and Beth told him so. Sam's smile broadened, pleased that she had noticed.

'Mother says it's good enough to be buried in,' he said, brushing invisible dust off his sleeve.

'Your mother always likes to plan ahead,' replied Beth, smiling proudly at him. She thought about apologising for Joss's behaviour, but then she would have to explain her own.

'Speaking of planning ahead ...' said Sam as he guided her to the side of the road. He then proceeded to launch into a subject Beth knew nothing about. She watched his lips move and felt his enthusiasm but she understood very little, if any at all. Why was he talking to her about bank accounts? People walked past them, but Sam did not seem to notice. Was this the reason he wanted to say hello? To talk about money? Her smile faded. Finally it dawned on Sam that she knew nothing of what he spoke about.

'Beth,' he said, 'I know all about it. It was one of my first jobs at the bank. There is no need to be so secretive. Mr Goode would like to speak to you about your intentions. Come with me.' He proffered his arm, but Beth did not take it.

'I don't know what you are talking about, Sam. Who is Mr Goode?'

Sam laughed and Beth suddenly felt very silly in her ignorance. He proffered his arm to her again and this time she took it.

'He is the manager of Kernow Bank. Mr Bolitho, the owner, has many branches now. You don't expect him to be able to manage each one, do you? Mr Goode is the manager of Port Carrek's branch. One day I will have my own branch to manage, and he has taken me under his wing. If you bank with one of Mr Bolitho's banks it will look good for me. Come, Beth. I will look after you.'

Beth did not move. She would not be railroaded into following him, no matter how much she liked Sam.

'Sam, I have no money to put into a bank. I have never set foot in one before. A customer like me would do nothing for your job prospects.'

Sam would not take no for an answer. Placing his free hand firmly on hers, he led her to the large, wooden, double doors of the bank. Beth realised that she could not pull away without appearing rude. Sam patted her hand to comfort her.

'Don't worry, Beth. I know it can be daunting to step inside the first time, but I am by your side and will not leave ... unless Mr Goode wishes me to.'

Beth looked up at the grandest building in Port Carrek. Its symmetry and neat, tan coloured brickwork, so very different from the cottages of the fishing port, boasted its Georgian heritage. Bewildered, Beth found herself walking past its fluted pillars.

With a flourish, Sam opened the seasoned oak double doors and proudly escorted her through them. Ornate cornices, covings and a large ceiling rose looked down upon her, making her feel small and out of place. She had never seen plastered mouldings before, but even they were not as beautiful as the tiled floor. Highly polished and dramatic in pattern, it spread away from her and tempted her forward. Sam walked proudly beside her, as he led her past a long, tall, wooden counter where a customer was speaking to an employee who was holding some paper money in his hand – more money than she had ever seen before. Sam encouraged her onwards towards the manager's office at the far end. Just before he knocked, Beth stopped him.

'Sam, please stop. This place is not for me. I want to help you in your profession, but I don't think my presence will help you at all.'

'Mr Goode wants to see you. My part is only that I know you and have brought you here. Come,' said Sam, gently patting her hand again to reassure her. Content he had done so, Sam knocked and a voice answered. Within minutes Beth found herself sitting before the manager of Kernow Bank, but just as confused as ever.

Mr Goode sat opposite her behind a large mahogany desk littered with papers, an inkpot, ink-stained blotting paper and a number of fountain pens. However, directly in front of the thin, middle-aged man, the desk was completely clear except for his neatly clasped hands. Even more disconcerting was the fact that he was smiling at her.

'Miss Jago, we finally meet. Forgive me for not being in touch sooner. Now that your grandfather is no longer with us I feel it is my duty to offer help and guide you with regard to your financial situation.'

Beth looked anxiously across at Sam, who had remained in the room after obtaining Mr Goode's agreement. His reassuring nod helped her to find her voice again.

'Mr Goode, it is very kind of you to think of me and offer me support but I do not see what you can help me with. I am not in debt and I do not have money to spare to invest in your bank. I'm sorry if this has been a waste of your time.'

Mr Goode threaded his fingers into a steeple and tested his chin on them while he thought for a moment.

'Miss Jago, I must satisfy myself that you are not being foolish. It is not good financial sense to use teapots or jars to hold money. An account at Kernow Bank is the safest place to deposit your money.'

'I agree, Mr Goode, but I do not have any money to deposit.'

'I apologise for any mistake, Miss Jago. The last thing I would wish to do would be to cause you embarrassment.' He stood, and Beth stood also, glad the short meeting was over. 'I was sorry to hear of your loss, Miss Jago. Your grandfather was quite a character and often brightened our Monday mornings when he would visit us to take out his money.'

He offered his hand for Beth to shake. Beth stared at him and did not see it.

'Mr Goode, I think you must have my grandfather confused with someone else. My grandfather was a miner until a poor chest meant he had to work above ground. Granted, he earned a small wage as a general labourer, despite his increasing ill health, but he did not have enough to deposit in a bank. I can assure you that my grandfather has never set foot in here.'

There was a short silence.

'Oh dear, this is all rather awkward,' said Mr Goode. 'I understood that you and your grandfather were very close as he often spoke of you. I had no idea you were not aware of his visits. I would never have mentioned them if I had known.'

Beth frowned. 'I think you have the wrong man.'

Mr Goode's gaze wandered away to the objects on his desk.

'He had no reason to come here,' she insisted, aware that her tone held less conviction than before. 'He always brought the money he earned home to me.' She turned to Sam for help, reassurance, anything.

'Your grandfather did have an account at Kernow Bank, Beth ... Miss Jago.' Beth shook her head. 'He did. I know he did, as it was my first job to close it when he died.'

Beth believed him. Sam knew her grandfather; he would not mistake him. Yet why didn't her grandfather tell her this? The news shocked her. Nothing around her seemed real.

'It is true, Miss Jago. I thought you would know this. Your grandfather had a substantial sum paid into his bank each year. Every week Mr Jago would arrive at the bank and take out a small amount. At the end of the twelve months the account would be empty and another sum would be deposited.'

'How long had this been going on?'

'Eight years.'

Eight years? Beth tried to think. She had been fourteen when it had started. It was around the time that her grandfather's health had deteriorated; yet he continued to bring money into the home. Her grandfather had told her it was his earnings from his labouring jobs. Beth suddenly felt foolish for believing his tale. To make matters worse, Sam voiced her thoughts.

'I understand that Will Jago had a chronic death rattle in his lungs. He could do the odd job but not earn enough to keep two people in food and clothes.'

Beth pursed her lips. She wanted Sam's support, not this.

'As a child you do not question such things.'

Mr Goode indicated that she took her seat again. Beth reluctantly did so and he sat back down behind his desk.

'Eight years of wages for doing nothing?' Beth shook her head in disbelief. 'Are you telling me his benefactor knew he was unable to earn enough and stepped in to help?'

Mr Goode looked at her solemnly through his brows. 'It is not our business to know such things.'

'Is there any money left?'

The bank manager shook his head. 'Your grandfather died a week before the next deposit was to be made. We were duty bound to inform the benefactor that his beneficiary had died, so of course that put an end to the transactions.'

Beth turned to Sam. 'Who gave my grandfather money, Sam? I want to know.'

'I do not know, Miss Jago,' he replied, using her title to put distance between them. 'It was a confidential transaction. But if I did know, I would not be allowed to tell you.'

Mr Goode nodded in agreement. 'In fact, Miss Jago, I fear we have divulged too much already. We thought, and it seems wrongly now, that the benefactor may have transferred the gift of money to you and we were concerned you may be keeping the equivalent of a year's wages under your mattress.'

'If I had a year's wages, I would not be pushing a barrow around the hills of Port Carrek delivering mending!' snapped Beth, hurt that her grandfather would keep such a secret from her. She rubbed her temple to ease the knot of tension forming. 'I'm sorry, Mr Goode. It's just a lot to take in.'

'I can see that, Miss Jago.' He gave Sam a worried look. 'Perhaps Sam could take you out for some air. You have had a bad shock.'

Sam took her arm. 'Come with me, Miss Jago,' he said in a businesslike manner. 'We can stroll down to the harbour and take in the sea air.'

Beth stood and took Sam's arm, nodding absently. She needed to get out of the imposing building. Though it intimidated her, it seemed that it was a place her grandfather had frequently visited. It was Will Jago's second home and he had kept it from her. Suddenly the air choked her and she wanted to be gone.

Sam sat beside Beth on the harbour wall. They dangled their legs over the side as if they were children again. His banking persona had been left at Kernow Bank's door and once again he was her old school friend. She was grateful for that, as now more than ever she needed a friend to talk to. Sam listened as she voiced her disbelief at her grandfather's secretive life. It tested everything she knew about him, and she wanted to hate him for it. The trouble was that she couldn't. Whenever she thought of her grandfather he was nothing but kind, funny and loving. Beth angrily threw a stone into the water.

'I'm sorry, Beth. Really I am. No wonder you looked so confused when I first spoke to you about opening an account. I assumed that if you were paying a labourer to make repairs to your cottage, you had money from somewhere. You must have thought I was mad.'

'Not mad, just enthusiastic. Oh, Sam, I feel so miserable,' Beth grumbled. 'I must look like a fool.' Sam shook his head to protest but Beth would not be comforted. 'I bet Mr Goode thinks I am. How can a grown woman not question how her ill grandfather can still bring home a wage as good as any fit man can earn?'

'For the most part you were a child,' replied Sam.

'But when I was older, Sam,' Beth said, angrily throwing another stone into the water. 'I should have questioned him.'

Having run out of stones within easy reach, they sat in silence and watched the gulls crying and swooping over the jagged rocks of the cliff opposite. Their frantic battle to search for food in order to feed their young mirrored the struggle that many of the local families had.

'Why do you think they choose to build their nests on the rock face like that?' asked Sam. 'It is such a precarious place to build.'

'This is where they were born, a place they know where there is food. They would not build there if their nests could not survive.'

Sam shook his head. 'I see no reason to stay in a place just because you were born there.' He nodded towards a well-to-do family walking along the harbour. 'That is the life I want to have. And I can. I will.'

He turned to Beth. 'There are great opportunities for men with skills and motivation to succeed as never before. A man can challenge the landed privileged, and gain rewards that are based on merit and not where or who you are born to. Children have opportunities for education as never before—'

'Some do, not all,' interrupted Beth.

Sam dismissed her observation with a wave of his hand.

'—and industry is expanding. There are more opportunities for people like me. We all must take responsibility for ourselves, our families and our future. The establishment is changing, and I want to take advantage of that.'

'I believe you will, Sam. I really do.' Beth lifted a foot and looked at her boot, twisting it in the sunshine so the polished leather caught the sun. Today it was clean as any lady would wear, with no evidence of river mud on it. She had nothing more she could say to Sam. Each time he spoke of his plans she felt as if he was slipping away from her.

'They have finally set a new date for Golowan Feast Day which was postponed due to the fishing tragedy. It is to be next week. Can I take you?'

Beth stopped twisting her foot and let it drop. She had not expected Sam to ask her, especially after voicing his plans for the future. She had no money and she was illegitimate. If he knew of the trouble she was having with Kynance Cottage he may not have even asked her at all.

'I know what you are thinking. Why should I ask you, as an illegitimate woman would not make a suitable wife for a bank manager.' Beth winced at his words. He was right of course but it still hurt to hear it. 'However, Port Carrek has accepted you and you are well liked, so your illegitimacy is not an issue for me.'

'Yet you mentioned it,' replied Beth warily.

Sam playfully nudged her with his shoulder. 'I voiced your thoughts, no more.'

'I am also thinking your suit will get dirty from sitting on the harbour wall,' she quipped.

Sam scrambled to his feet and attempted to brush himself clean. Beth began to laugh at his absurd panic.

'I'm glad I have put a smile on your face,' grumbled Sam. He threw her an irritated glance, but was soon smiling too. 'Beth, you have a way of making me forget my plans. I shall have to ask Mother to brush it clean for me. Lord knows what Mr Goode will say.'

Beth laughed. 'Tell him I fainted from the shock he gave

me and you dirtied your suit coming to my aid.' Beth thought of Joss, who was still troubled with amnesia and needed her help. She wondered what he was doing and if he was missing her company today. In comparison Sam seemed like a boy. Beth grew serious. She must not think of Joss like this. She must not compare him to Sam.

'Sam,' she said suddenly. 'I would be delighted for you to take me to Golowan Feast.'

'You have no prior engagement?'

'None,' said Beth, 'and I can think of no one who I would rather spend the evening with.' She reached for Sam's outstretched hand and pulled herself to standing.

'Good. I will look forward to it.' Sam's eyes darted over her shoulder. 'Oh no, your shadow is here.'

Beth's heart skipped a beat. Had Joss missed her and come looking for her at Port Carrek? She turned, surprised at the excitement she felt, but it soon died away when she saw the young man approaching. Walking towards them, with a childlike gait, yet tall as any man and with hair the colour of polished copper, was Tom Kitto. He was excited to see her. Beth pasted on a smile, but it soon turned to a genuine one when she saw his infectious feeling of joy shine through his pale blue eyes.

'I'd better return to the bank,' Sam said under his breath. After a quick goodbye and a hasty retreat, he left her alone with Tom.

'Hello, Tom,' greeted Beth.

Tom's smile grew bigger. He fell into step with her as she walked towards home.

'I thought I would not see you today. Your mother was out. How are you, Tom?'

''Appy,' replied Tom.

They both fell silent as they walked along the road together. Even after all these years Beth did not find it easy to have a conversation with Tom. Sometimes he would speak of things that had no bearing on the previous conversation, making it confusing to understand his train of thought. Today, however, he surprised her.

'You like Sam?' he asked suddenly, in all seriousness.

'Yes, Tom, I do. He has asked me to accompany him to Golowan Feast Day.'

'Tom will take you,' he replied hopefully.

'I'm sorry, Tom. Sam has asked me and unless he changes his mind I will be going with him.'

Tom thought for a moment. 'You like the man on the beach.' Beth's steps slowed. 'The man who 'urt 'is 'ead. I saw you laughing on the beach.'

'I like the man on the beach,' she replied warily. 'Tom, please don't tell people about the man on the beach. Sam may not want to take me to Golowan if he knows about the man on the beach.' Tom looked a little confused. Beth squeezed his arm gently. 'Please, Tom, don't tell anyone about the man on the beach.'

Tom looked at her hand on his arm. 'Tom not tell,' he said quietly, tolerating her touch. Beth realised she was making him feel uneasy and withdrew her hand. He looked up at her, expectantly, and quickly fell into step beside her again.

'Tom likes Beth,' he said, smiling crookedly.

'And Beth likes Tom,' she replied fondly. 'Beth likes Tom very much. Now you better run home or your mother will wonder where you are.'

'Tom and Beth will marry one day,' Tom exclaimed. He had started to become overexcited and dance around her. Beth knew she must calm him.

'Hush, Tom. Calm down or you will get too excited.' Beth held out her hands and lowered them to give him a visual cue to lower his voice, as she knew that when Tom became too excited he would not listen to the spoken word. 'We cannot marry, but I will always be your friend. You are very special to me and always will be.'

'Special, is not *like*?' stated Tom.

'It is far better than *like*,' Beth said, in an attempt to reassure him. Tom shook his head.

'You like Sam. You want to marry Sam. You like the man on the beach. You laugh with the man on the beach. You want to marry the man on the beach. You want to marry everyone but Tom.' Tom gave a shuddering sigh, his mood had swung again and his happiness had deserted him. He looked as if he was about to cry.

'I'm sorry, Tom. I cannot marry you,' Beth said softly, touching his arm again. She had to tell him the truth, it would be cruel not to.

Tom did not want to listen. He jerked his arm away and shouted in anger, startling Beth. She stepped back, hating to see his distress. His shoulders had rounded and his pain appeared almost physical.

'Tom,' Beth soothed. 'Find your mother. Speak to her. She will explain.'

Tom looked up and, for the first time in his life, more by chance than design, he looked into Beth's eyes. It was an instant, no more. His pale blue eyes were the windows to his soul and for a brief moment she saw a tortured person, whose deep feelings were hurt as surely as any normal man's could be. She saw that the unmistakeable pain he felt came from unrequited love and, to her horror, she realised she was the cause.

Beth tried to comfort him but it was too late. Crying out again, Tom turned and fled, his uncoordinated gait, with its unusual speed, soon darting out from Beth's sight.

Chapter Nine

All week Beth had felt troubled and worried for Tom, but she had been too afraid to visit him in case she upset him further. Not knowing if he was still distressed weighed heavily on her mind. The day had not started well either. Her barrow wheel had become loose and she had to ask Joss to mend it. To make her day worse, the letter carrier had visited again and handed her another letter.

Beth looked at it in her hand. Neatly written, in elegant handwriting, was her address. She was relieved Joss was out chopping wood. He was prepared to protect her from thugs employed by a man named Nankervis, but if Joss knew that a solicitor also wanted her gone she may lose him as an ally. She stood holding it in her hand, but this time, unlike the second letter, she had the courage to open it.

It was as she thought. The letter was also from Tremayne and Goldsmith Solicitors and their message was clear and direct.

As previously instructed, the lease for life on Kynance Cottage, River Valley, Port Carrek, terminated with the death of Mr William Jago. This indenture, made on the seventeenth day of January in the year 1837 between my client (the lessor) and Mr William Jago (the lessee) is now terminated and the property known as Kynance Cottage is now lawfully and completely the property of my client. We are writing again, on behalf of our client, to inform you that unless you make contact with our Truro Office forthwith, we will have no option but to take further action to remove you and all your possessions from the said property. Remaining in the property is a criminal offence and I have advised my client that if no contact is made by you to our office we will consider reporting the matter to Truro Borough Police. May I take this opportunity to advise you that an act of omission is no form of defence. Contact and vacation of the property by yourself is of paramount importance to avoid the commencement of further action.

The letter shook in her hand. It was fragile, she could easily destroy it like the others, but it would not stop Tremayne and Goldsmith's plan to remove her. She remained convinced that there had been some terrible misunderstanding. She knew nothing of a landlord, and she had never seen her grandfather pay rent. Yet recently she had discovered things about her grandfather that she had not known before. Perhaps there was some truth in the letter after all. Tom's sad eyes had played on her mind for days and now this letter had arrived to torment her. It was all too much. Spending her formative years in a workhouse had taught her it was best to avoid trouble, or at least block it out of your mind, if you wanted to survive. When she heard Joss's footsteps on the path to the house, she did just that. She slipped the letter back into the small envelope, and, reaching up on tiptoe, she placed it on the highest shelf of the dresser, out of sight. She would deal with it tomorrow or perhaps the next day, but not now.

At first the strange happenings were put down to bad luck and nothing more. Beth's washing line had broken, tools had gone missing and her barrow wheel kept working loose. Joss became suspicious but did not voice his concern lest it should cause Beth to worry. However, when they found a dead rat at her door, its bloated, foul-smelling body polluting the air, he finally voiced his suspicions. He had questioned Beth again about the man named Nankervis, but she remained adamant that she had never heard of him. Yet he could not help but feel that she was keeping something from him.

He sat alone at the table eating the broth that Beth had made, mulling over his concerns as he tore at a thick slice of bread. He was convinced that the thugs – who had taken the trouble to appoint a lookout high on the cliff – would not be easily put off by one beating. It was very probable that they had returned to do mischief and show they were still determined to frighten her and make her leave. He would like to know who Nankervis was and throttle him. Joss looked at a piece of bread floating on the surface of his broth. Irritated, he moved it around with a spoon, his agitation and frustration clear for anyone who cared to watch him. However, he was alone, as Beth had spent the last hour in her room preparing to go out.

Despite the broth's tempting aroma, Joss had lost his appetite. The truth of the matter was that the recent pranks were only responsible for half of his bad mood. The woman upstairs was responsible for the other half. Today, after a week of feeling that she was hiding something from him, she had told him about Golowan Feast Day and that Sam had asked her to accompany him. This confession had explained everything to him, and if he had not known what jealousy felt like before he lost his memory, he knew what it felt like now. Sam, the skinny boy who had just escaped puberty, with overly large hands and sticky-out ears, had asked Beth to the celebrations and she had accepted. He placed his spoon over the lump of bread and held it under the surface. He did not release it again until all the air bubbles had found their way to the surface. It began to disintegrate into the broth, turning into a limp sludge beneath the metal of his spoon. This act of destruction did not make him feel any better. Still irritated, Joss dropped his spoon on the table and pushed the broth away. The longer Beth took in her preparations the more frustrated he became. Did women take their time, he thought, in order to torment a man and fill his head with images of them in a state of undress? He heard the stairs creak and he stood, bracing himself for her entrance. He hoped that seeing her would dispel the knots of jealousy in his stomach so he could be happy for her and her fledgling courtship with her childhood friend. He was wrong.

Her polished boots, peeping out beneath a blue hem, came into view as she stepped carefully down the steep, narrow stairs of the cottage. He recognised the blue fabric. It was the dress she had been making and had recently stayed up late into the night in order to finish. It draped from her waist in even folds, following the movement of her body and trailing from step to step behind her like a train. Yet when she reached the bottom the train disappeared and the hem was even like any serviceable dress. Despite it not being overly fussy or wide, it fitted her from neck to waist like a second skin and his breath caught in his throat as he looked at her. Why had he not questioned her reason for staying up late to work upon it? Why had he not guessed that she wanted it completed for a reason? He should have known, he should have asked. If he had known, at least he would have had time to prepare, so the hurt was not felt as keenly as he had felt it today when she finally confessed.

'Do you like it, Joss?' Beth asked apprehensively as she stood before him.

He watched her shaking her skirts to even out the folds. She looked like a genteel lady preparing to take a leisurely stroll, except for the tremble in her fingers that gave away her excitement.

'If I owned a sewing machine I would have been able to make it within days. One day I must buy one as my customers will not be prepared to wait for a hand-stitched garment in the future.'

She was nervous, he realised, and she had no idea just how beautiful she looked.

'How do I look? Will I do?' she added, with a nervous smile.

He wanted to reach for her and slide his hands about her waist. He wanted to kiss her – Lord have mercy, he wanted to have her right here, right now. He blinked. She was expecting an answer, but the fob watch and chain in his pocket was as strong and as inescapable as any shackle and it restrained his response.

'You will do,' he said simply, nodding an approval. 'Sam is a lucky man.'

Beth was content. She did not push him for further reassurance and he was glad. If she had, his resolve to not touch her and show her just how beautiful he thought she looked may have left him as quickly as it took for him to reach for her.

When Sam knocked on the door moments later, Joss stepped back into the shadows by the fire so he could not be seen. He nodded encouragement to Beth as she glanced over to him. Taking courage, she slid back the bolts and opened the door.

Like a voyeur watching a tragedy unfold, Joss did not move away. He could see Beth clearly, the evening sun casting a warm glow onto her smiling face. He was glad he could not see Sam, who remained at her doorstep, for to see the pleasure on his face as he cast his eyes on her would have been too much to tolerate. As a man, Joss would recognise the look and know his thoughts, and to see it on Sam's face would twist him inside.

'Hello, Elizabeth,' said Sam softly.

Joss snorted his annoyance. Did Sam not know Beth preferred her name shortened? Of course he knew. It was just Sam's priggish attitude and attempt to change her into a suitable wife for the gentleman he supposed himself to be.

'Hello, Sam,' replied Beth. 'The evening is warm. Perhaps I need not bring a shawl.'

Sam answered but Joss missed his reply. Despite not wanting to hear their words of courtship, he held his breath and strained his ears to listen. There was a silence and he looked up to see Beth no longer smiling. Her back was ramrod straight and she remained as still as a statue. Something was wrong.

'I'm sorry,' Sam continued, his voice a little clearer. 'I should have told you this morning, but I felt it was best I came and told you face-to-face. It took time to muster up the courage to do it.' Do what, thought Joss? What has he told her?

'May I ask why?' asked Beth quietly.

'There is talk in Port Carrek that you are living with a man. I can only assume it was the man I met here.'

'Who has told you this?'

'Mrs Knight, Mark Smith, even Tom Kitto has been telling anyone that cares to listen.' Beth looked away. 'My mother heard you had been seen riding in a wagon of hay with him. Is it the same man I saw? Is it true he is living under your roof?' Sam asked.

'The man you met is called Joss. He was injured and lost his memory. While he recovers I have given him a bed in the shed. There is nothing more to it.'

'He is not a lodger?'

'He is not. A Good Samaritan does not charge rent,' answered Beth pointedly.

'A woman who allows a stranger to stay with her, who is not his housekeeper, his wife or landlady, risks her reputation,' Sam replied. 'There is talk that you have loose morals and that you take after your mother.'

Joss took a step forward. He had heard enough. Hearing Joss move and knowing his intent, Beth lifted her right hand to stop him. He halted mid step.

'You have known me since I was eight years old, when I first came to Port Carrek. You know that I am a good woman.' Beth's anger flared when he did not reply. 'You know me, Sam! How can you believe such things?'

Sam shuffled his feet. 'I do not believe them, but others

do. Mother says I will not be able to hold my head high if I marry a woman who courts gossip. She says it will affect my prospects. How can I court a woman who is considered to be free with her favours? She will never accept you into the family.'

Beth clenched her teeth in attempt to remain calm. 'Yet you are prepared to ruin my reputation in order to protect your own. Don't you see? By cancelling our assignation you are lending credence to the rumours. You are leaving me unprotected against them. You are sending out the message that the lies are true.'

'But they are not lies,' said Sam sadly. 'You are living with a man under your roof, and what sort of man would I be if I allowed it?'

'You would be a better man than you are now,' Beth said simply. 'Do you value our friendship? In your haste to become a gentleman, you have acted in a most ungentlemanly manner. You believe that the people of Port Carrek would be as unforgiving as you. You might be wrong. Perhaps if they knew the truth they would not be so judgemental. Yet you do not want to run that risk. I wish you well for your future, Sam. I hope the sacrifice of our friendship was worth it.'

Joss heard Sam walking away. Beth's bottom lip trembled as she watched him go. Coming to her senses she closed the door carefully and slid the bolts across, shutting out the sunshine and the beauty of River Valley.

Joss walked towards her, but she turned away. He could see that she felt humiliated and wanted to return to her bedroom, take off her dress and probably throw it in a dark corner. How foolish Sam was not to consider her a suitable match for him in his future. He needed someone like her more than she needed someone like him.

Joss stepped in front of her, blocking her way. 'I will take you.'

Beth shook her head. 'There is no need.'

He held her shoulders so she could not step past him. 'There is every need. My presence has caused you trouble. We will go to Golowan Feast Day and I will explain to everyone who will listen that I injured my head from a fall, lost my memory and you are allowing me to stay in the outbuilding until I recover. I will make it clear that there is nothing more to the story.'

Beth shook her head again. 'No, I can't let you do that.'

'Why not?' Frowning, Joss tilted her chin with a finger. Her beautiful blue eyes, glistening with unshed tears, lifted to meet his. He could so easily drown in those eyes. 'It would stop the rumours about you.'

'Since Killygrew you have walked the streets of Port Carrek only once in the hope of someone knowing you. You have made no other enquiries anywhere else. I believe it is because, in your heart, you don't want to be found.'

Joss shook his head in denial. 'That is a foolish thing to say.'

Beth smiled sadly. 'Although they are less frequent now, when you first arrived here you had nightmares. I heard you in the night and I heard your cries. You spoke of killing, Joss. You talked of death.'

Joss's hand fell away. How long had she known?

'I have seen you hate to have blood on your hands and I have seen the scars on your body. I believe you are worried you may be a wanted man. If you go to Golowan Feast, where there will be hundreds of people celebrating midsummer, you run the risk of being seen and someone knowing you. I cannot allow you to run that risk, not before your memory has returned and you know who you are. Only then will you know if there is any truth in your fears.'

'You allowed me to stay here despite knowing this?' Each day she intrigued him more. Was it her kindness, her guilt at causing the injury, or something more that prevented her from sending him away?

Beth turned away from him, but he caught her elbow and held her still.

'I will take you to Golowan Feast and we will tell everyone the truth. There is no shame in it. Your reputation is more important to me than discovering who I am and finding out I have done wrong.'

'But what if you are a wanted man? They will take you away,' replied Beth. Her concern touched him and made him all the more determined to help her.

'For you,' he said calmly, 'it is a risk I am willing to take.'

Joss and Beth looked down on the harbour of Port Carrek as the evening sun warmed their skin. The reflection of the clear blue sky turned the sea turquoise. The vibrant colour seemed almost unnatural against the grey cliffs that framed the port's entrance. The town folk had already gathered in the harbour and their jovial laughter and banter wafted up to them on the summer breeze.

'Golowan Feast is late this year,' said Beth softly. 'It was postponed in respect for the families of the fishermen who lost their lives in a storm on St Peter's Eve. Normally bonfires would be lit all along the headland, but today it will be just Port Carrek celebrating.'

From their vantage point they looked down on the people as they mingled around the stalls, screamed with delight on the self-propelled, wooden swing boats and bought food from the vendors vying for their custom. A fishing boat entered the harbour. Laden down with people, it precariously tilted in the water and laboured its way to the quay. A great cheer went up as the spectators recognised the human cargo. Fiddlers, pipers and a drummer jumped from the deck to the quayside, to the laughter and cheers of their friends. Their instruments soon followed, thrown across the water to be caught by waiting hands. Within minutes they were ready and the pagan beat of their music started in earnest. The vibration of the drum pulsated through the air and could be heard for miles around.

'This is Golowan Feast?' asked Joss, amused at the antics of the people who appeared dressed in their Sunday best on a weekday. Beth began to walk down the steep street towards the harbour, as if drawn to the festivities by the music alone.

'No, this is just the beginning,' she answered, looking at him over her shoulder. 'Golowan is about light and rejoicing, but it is when the sun goes down that the celebrations really begin.'

Despite her excitement, Beth could not help but feel nervous about how the day would go. She had told Sam that the people of Port Carrek would be more understanding than him, but she had her doubts. After all, had she been so sure of their response she would never have felt the need to pretend that Joss was a labourer doing some work for her. One untruth leads to another, and she wished for the hundredth time that she had not been so hasty to pick up a pan to defend herself on that day. If only she had asked Joss who he was first, she would not find herself in this situation now.

Joss fell into step beside her as they made their way down to the quayside. Soon they were swallowed up in the moving crowd, and whenever an opportunity arose, Joss was as good as his word and introduced himself, seamlessly offering an explanation for his presence at River Valley. Beth saw a side of Joss she had not seen before. He was not fazed by the crowds. Blending amongst them he conversed easily with strangers and was soon accepted by them. He had a way with him that caught their interest, yet he also showed an interest in them, making them feel listened to and their opinion valued. On hearing about his memory loss, although initially surprised, the people of Port Carrek showed their interest, their concern, and more importantly, their understanding. Beth was praised for her kindness in helping him, and apologies were given that her character had been judged poorly. After each conversation, whether it was long or in passing, Joss was wished well and Beth congratulated before he was introduced to someone else. Joss went from person to person and Beth saw that although he had a purpose for his interactions, he also appeared relaxed and happy, as though he genuinely liked the people of Port Carrek. Finally, she found herself relaxing, and for the first time since Joss had offered to escort her she felt she could actually enjoy the celebrations.

Walking side by side, they browsed the stalls by the quayside, pausing now and then to touch a bolt of fabric, taste a sample of food or listen to the music. The atmosphere was jolly, and laughter and chat filled the air. Beth saw Jacca in the crowd. He was proudly escorting the spinster, Amy, on his arm. Beth was pleased to see him smiling affectionately at her and listening carefully to what she had to say. The other hand he used to carry one of his younger children on his hip and behind them followed four others. Beth wondered where the baby was, but when Amy turned to speak to Jacca, she noticed his small body was strapped to her chest with a shawl. Jacca caught Beth's eye. He smiled broadly and Beth nodded back in approval. She was glad to see Jacca was trying his best to treat the spinster well, even if it meant they were surrounded by some of his brood.

Beth saw Tom walking through the crowd, his shoulders hunched and his face solemn. In the past she would have gone to him and exchanged some words, but she was concerned she would be encouraging him. She thought it best to pretend not to see him, but she could not help hating herself for doing so. Changing her mind at the last moment she looked for him again, but Tom was nowhere to be seen.

Joss took a turn at throwing a ball at a hoop. The first two bounced off the hoop's edge, but the third hit its mark. His prize was an apple dipped in toffee and he handed it to Beth. Not wanting to eat alone, she purchased one for him.

'You must be careful,' she said as she handed it to him

laughing, glad to have her thoughts diverted from Tom. 'You are becoming a Carrekan. That honour is usually for people who have lived in Port Carrek for two generations.'

Although the light was fading and dark shadows had begun to lengthen in the town, Beth was in high spirits. She took a bite and the toffee cracked beneath her teeth and the juices from the apple flowed and dribbled down her chin. She rubbed her chin dry with her arm but stopped in mid wipe. Another man had caught her eye. With a steady gaze, Sam looked back at her through the crowd. Beside him was his mother, Gladys Pratt. Beth lowered her arm, embarrassed that she had been caught, but it was too late, he had seen her poor manners and was already turning and escorting his mother away from the harbour. His walk slow and steady, his chin proudly tilted, he looked ill placed amongst the carefree crowd.

'I like Port Carrek people,' Joss was saying as he looked about him. 'But I know I am not one of them. Not one person has recognised me, which confirms to me I am not from these parts.'

Before Beth could reply, the crowd began to part. A man, carrying a flaming stick that had been tarred and pitched, was lighting a bonfire at the far end of the harbour. Its scorching flames grew quickly, dancing and twisting, stretching to the sky and lighting up the upturned faces nearby.

'It has begun,' Beth said, forgetting Sam and clutching Joss's arm. 'Golowan celebrations have truly begun.'

To Joss's surprise, young men began to run through the streets, carrying flaming barrels filled with tar on their backs and leaving a trail of golden, hot embers in the wind. Other men carried torches of fire, which they swung before them. Several other bonfires were also set alight. The flames from the torches and bonfires illuminated the town, while the loud bangs from the black-devils and serpent firecrackers showered the ground causing excited young men and women to run for safety. A drumbeat began again and the crowds started to dance to the beat in twisting snake-like lines. Beth grabbed Joss's hand and led him towards it. Man, woman and child held hands in a long line, moving through the crowds to form convoluted loops and shapes. Beth broke into the line and encouraged Joss to do the same. Together they followed the beat of the drum, and wound their way through the streets of Port Carrek. When they got to the top of the hill, Joss and Beth broke free, preferring to stay by the warmth of a bonfire at the top of the town. They stood in silence as they watched the dancing trail of people turn and make their way back down the hill. Each time they came to a discarded tar barrel, two people from the chain broke free and held their hands up high while the chain of people passed beneath. Young men and women, silhouetted against the torch flames, jumped over the dying embers of the tar barrel itself before holding hands once more and continuing their journey.

At some point, while Beth and Joss watched the ritual, their hands touched by accident, yet neither had the strength nor wish to withdraw. Both felt the other's touch, both felt the other's warmth, yet both pretended not to notice for fear the other would break away. Although they watched the crowd receding into the distance, neither really saw it. Their minds and thoughts were too consumed with their touch of intimacy no one else could see. Eventually, Beth felt Joss's fingers move. It was only a slight movement, but it was there all the same. Her heart missed a beat when she felt two of his fingers hook hers. She didn't remember turning towards him, or how they came to be holding both of each other's hands, but suddenly she was facing him and did not want to turn away. Their fingers threaded between each other's, as if they were meant to be like this, entwined and connected as close as any touch could be. Beth looked at his darkening eyes and smiled.

'The town people like you. They believe you are a man of

good character,' whispered Beth, enjoying the warmth of the bonfire beside them and the feel of his touch against her skin.

'When I look at you like this,' said Joss hoarsely, 'with the glow of the fire dancing on your skin, I want to be anything but a good man. Lord knows I have struggled not to touch you.' He brought her hand to his cheek and turned into it, kissing its soft palm. 'But I cannot go on like this. Tomorrow I will go to Truro Borough Police.' Beth tried to protest but he touched her lips with his finger to silence her. 'I must. I will hand myself in,' he said, letting his hand fall. 'At least then I will know if I am a wanted man or a married one. I want you, Beth Jago. I must find my past, as my past is not finding me.'

Tom remained rooted to the spot, staring at the flames of the bonfire. They twisted and turned, engulfing the silhouettes of Beth and the man from the beach as they stood alone on the far side in a lovers' tryst. He had seen him kiss her hand. Tom's chin dimpled as he held back his tears. He hated them for excluding him like this. Beth was his friend but she wasn't behaving like a friend. He liked Beth, but Beth did not seem to like him any more. Tom hated change at the best of times, and this change made him feel even more unsettled and angry.

'Come away from the fire, Tom.'

His mother's words did not register with him at first, and it was only when he felt a tug on his coat that he knew his mother was by his side.

'Tom, come away from the flames. You know a Cornish wind can turn on a penny. It is dangerous to be so close to a fire. If the wind changes the flames will set you alight.'

Martha tugged him again and made Tom turn to her. 'Tom, listen to me. Don't start fixating on fire. Fire is dangerous. Fire can 'urt. Go 'ome, boy. Go 'ome! It is too dangerous for you out 'ere tonight.'

Tom pulled away and started to run. He ran and ran, dodging people, jumping discarded burnt barrels and popping firecrackers, but it was not towards his home that he ran. He ran towards the source of his pain. He ran as fast as his legs would carry him, across street, along road and down track. His lone figure disappeared into the night, leaving behind him the noisy celebrations of Golowan Feast. Despite gasping for air, he did not stop running until he reached his destination, an isolated building in the secluded River Valley.

Beth and Joss walked home together under a starlit sky. The bright summer moon, its craters and tracks visible to the naked eye, illuminated the slow passing clouds. Their footsteps echoed along the quiet narrow country road. Each step they took brought them to her home where they could shut out the world and be alone. Deep in thought, neither spoke. Joss's gentle fireside kiss on her hand had drawn a line in their relationship, yet they did not know if they were prepared to step over it.

Beth glanced across at Joss in the moonlight to gauge his thoughts. He was looking ahead, his mind elsewhere but his strides measured. He looked so handsome, and Beth realised that she had been fooling herself to think it was Sam she had wanted. She had fooled no one, leastways Sam himself. Perhaps that was why Sam was not prepared to stand up for her. Yet Joss was prepared to speak to a constable, despite the risk he ran. Tomorrow I may lose him, she thought. A wife might claim him or he could be under arrest. She should feel pleasure that he was prepared to do this in the hope of a future with her, yet all Beth could feel was dread. The realisation that tonight may be the last time he laid his head in River Valley ignited a wanton desire to tempt him and claim him as hers for just one night – this night.

She looked away horrified. How could she have such thoughts? That she should contemplate tempting a man away from his wife so he could be hers was unfamiliar to her and jarred against all her beliefs. Yet, she thought as she looked at him in the moonlight struggling with his own demons, she wanted him more than any other man she had ever met. If it was just the scraps of one night before reality demolished her dreams, so be it.

As Beth walked, struggling with the discovery that she was prepared to behave like a mistress, she began to think of her mother. For the first time she wondered if her mother had known all along that her father had been married, but was prepared to risk her reputation for love. Was it really her shame at being content to be a man's mistress that had stopped her from returning to Beth's loving and forgiving grandfather? Beth didn't want to end up like her mother. As much as she had a need for Joss, as much as she wanted him, she would not risk bringing a child into this world for the sake of her own selfish desire.

They arrived at the track that would take them away from the road and through the shelter of the trees. They were now hidden from the outside world and all its complications. Beth looked across at Joss again, concerned that he had not spoken a word since they had started their journey home.

'Joss?' she asked quietly. 'What ails you?'

Joss finally looked across at her. 'Tonight could be my last night with you, Beth.'

To hear him say it made it seem all the more real. Her resolve, her determination not to make the same mistake as her mother, dissolved in that instant as the reality of the situation sank in. She wanted him, and in her madness she did not care who she might hurt. All she could think of was being in his arms and taking what she could before it was lost to her. She stepped into his arms and he held her tight. Their heartbeats raced furiously against one another as their breath mingled in the chilling air.

'Beth ...' he said in a broken voice. 'You fit so well in my arms.' His lips sought hers in the moonlight and, despite her earlier reservations, she gladly responded. Their first feverish kiss filled both her mind and body with intoxicating pleasure and a thirst for more. Shaken, he pulled away slightly and she knew, in that moment, he had felt it too. He threaded his fingers into her hair and studied her face. 'I have never felt such a strong feeling as this before. Feeling that this is right, and it is how it should be. Tomorrow I may lose you.'

For once Beth ignored her inner voice and followed an instinct that was primal and self-seeking. An instinct that before today she had never realised she possessed. Perhaps it was the magic of Golowan that made her behave like this, or the illusion of seclusion from the world by the tall trees that surrounded them. Perhaps it was because she felt that should Joss be taken from her, she would never meet another man like him. Whatever the reason, she had suddenly decided that she wanted him to be her first love, and damn the consequences.

'Then have me,' she whispered back. Joss looked at her in disbelief. She nodded to reassure him. 'I am yours for the taking.'

The tight control he had held on his emotions up to that moment shattered at her words. There was no need for more words; they had made a pact with the devil and they would deal with the repercussions another time.

Joss's kisses rained down on her cheeks and neck, as if he were a starving man presented with a feast. Overwhelmed with his need for her she almost laughed in delight. He quietened her with a heartfelt kiss on her lips that took her breath from her and rendered her thoughts into confusion. She could not think, she could not speak – all she could do was feel. Inwardly her body melted, as she felt an aching need, almost a pain, deep inside her. Holding tight to his coat, she clung to him as she returned his kiss, matching his desire, each shared breath, touch and caress. Her need for him overtook her, and she found herself wanting to tear at his clothing in order to feel his skin underneath. She wanted him to remember her and this moment, and to leave him with a memory that made him want her again.

She felt his body leave her as he pulled her towards the cottage, but it was still too far away and he needed to touch her again. Pulling her towards him he reached for the trunk of a tree. It gave their shaking bodies support and he caged her against it with his arms. She became still so he could kiss her and touch her at will. Beth savoured it and gloried in it, allowing it to burn into her memory so she could relive it again and again. She could not remain still for long; her body would not allow it as her need for him was too great. In their haste for one another, they fumbled. Buttons became impossible, cloth became a barrier and hooks became chains, but their frustration only heightened their desire. Joss pulled away, his speech ragged, his body breathless.

'Not here. Hell knows I want you, but not here. Not your first time. Come,' he said, taking her hand. 'Before I am forced to carry you.' They half ran, half slipped down the slippery track, occasionally falling into each other's arms and laughing at their unruly behaviour. Like children up to mischief, their spirits were high, only matched by their feeling of lust born from a newly discovered love. It was heady stuff they were feeding on. During those few moments, as they made their way along the track from the road to the cottage, they believed that it might just be possible that no one would be hurt.

They could just make out the cottage through the trees. They were nearly there. Beth almost tripped on a tree root and without thinking Joss scooped her up in his arms to prevent her from falling, laughing as he did so. He stopped to look at her in his arms, his eyes dark with excitement, slowly turning troubled as he gazed at her. Beth could read his thoughts as if he had written them down on a page. She feels light, soft and warm, he is thinking. A woman made of flesh and bone, with deep feelings and complicated emotions. And her deep feelings would be hurt, should a wife come to claim him. His face turned solemn as he met her gaze and realised Beth's thoughts mirrored his.

Their rapid breathing and heartbeats slowed and quietened, so only the rustle of the leaves in the wind could be heard. Carefully he lowered her feet to the ground and embraced her. His heart was heavy and so was hers. They stood together in a tight embrace and in silence. This time there were no kisses or lustful thoughts. The real world had returned, and it hurt. They were playing at being people who in reality they were not. Joss and Beth had a strong sense of loyalty and morality, and they knew their make-believe game was already coming to an end. Although their desire remained and their love still burned, they would not act on their lust for one another, not when there might be a wife or children who bore his name. They did not need to tell each other this, or explain their unspoken decision. They broke from their embrace and continued their walk to the cottage. The rhythm of their breathing had returned to normal, and their steps had slowed. There would be no lovemaking tonight. Each knew how the other felt, for they had seen the joy leave each other's face.

'We can't,' he said finally, confirming the change in how they both felt.

'I know,' she replied.

Beth felt as if she had lost something and it hurt. She wondered if Joss felt the same ache. Even their hands had fallen away from each other. It was almost too painful to touch him; better not to touch him at all. They continued their journey to the cottage, but now walked at a sedate pace, both deep in thought, both with a memory they hoped they would never forget. It was a shared memory of their kisses and embraces, and thoughts of what would have happened if things had been different.

Joss was speaking and his words dragged her from her

painful thoughts. They had arrived at Kynance Cottage and he was staring at the building made of granite.

'Someone has been here,' he said, picking up a stick for a weapon and signalling for her to stay behind him. 'And a pretty mess they have left behind.'

At first Beth could see nothing amiss, as all appeared calm. They were alone and it was quiet but for the comforting sound of the river in the distance. Yet Joss had sensed something and remained on guard until the moon's light broke forth from behind a cloud. What had appeared normal became sinister and threatening in its light. Its brightness illuminated the white lime wash that had been thrown over the granite walls, the frantic damage to her front door and the metal head of her grandfather's axe buried in its wood. The logs Joss had cut to provide heat for the winter lay scattered about. Some were charred, evidence that someone had attempted a fire, while others lay in the river beyond. The crunch of brittle glass beneath their feet made them aware of a broken window. The shutters inside, which Joss had made, had prevented access to the house and forced the glass to fall outside rather than in. The damage remained confined to the outside of the house, but as they entered the cottage it still felt violated by the attacker's visit.

Beth felt shaken that someone would target her with such hatred. She remained in the kitchen, while Joss searched the rooms to ensure the attackers were gone. She listened to him searching each room. His anger gave him energy, his measured steps had no fear. She was not anxious for Joss. It was the attacker who was in danger, for she had no doubt that at this moment Joss wanted to make them pay for what they had done.

'They have gone,' Joss said angrily. 'We must report this as soon as it is daylight. This man, Nankervis, cannot send his bully men to intimidate you like this!' Joss began to pace the floor, his frustration at not catching the culprits clear for Beth to see. 'We will report it to a constable and they will be arrested. Nankervis and his men can hang from a rope for all I care.'

'No, you cannot report them,' Beth blurted out.

Joss halted and stared at her. 'Why not? Damage such as this is breaking the law.'

Beth began to wring her hands. Realising this was the time to be truthful she took courage and braced herself.

'The reason I don't want you to report them is because I fear that it is I who is breaking the law, not them.'

Joss watched Beth struggling to reach the letter on the top of the dresser; despite being on tiptoe and stretching every fibre, she was still unable to grasp it. He was angry with her for keeping something like this from him, yet her ineffectiveness at trying to reach the letter brought out the need in him to help her. He placed the oil lamp he had just lit on a table nearby, stood behind her and reached for the letter. For a moment he did not want to move away, preferring to cage her against the dresser to ensure she saw the disappointment in his eyes.

'I know,' said Beth irritably. 'I am a coward, but I was afraid. I *am* afraid. I can read, but what do I know of the law? Don't judge me too harshly. I am not the only one in this world who has not confronted a problem.'

She broke free, sat down at the table and waited for him to read it. Joss quickly opened the letter and read, his eyes darting across the page several times as he took in its content.

'If this is true, Kynance Cottage is not yours and you have no right to be here.'

Beth covered her ears. It was not what she wanted him to say, but he would not lie to her. He sat down beside her and pulled her hands away, but he did not let them go. 'You say that your grandfather did not pay rent, this may be true, but it does not mean that the house was his. He may have only had to pay a peppercorn rent.'

Beth frowned. 'I don't know what you mean.'

'It is a small amount of rent to seal the contract, so nominal that even one peppercorn would suffice for the lease.'

'You seem to know a lot about leases and rents,' said Beth, staring miserably at the ground.

Joss let her hands go and sat back in his chair. 'I cannot choose what I remember, Beth.'

The atmosphere had changed so much from just a few moments ago. There had been so much promise, so much temptation, and now everything was ruined. Yet seeing her so troubled tugged at that need in every man to make things better.

'There is hope,' Joss said. Beth looked up at him expectantly. 'If I remember rightly, a lease for life often includes three people, and in this case it could be your grandfather, your mother and you. Failing that, perhaps there will be room for negotiation to put your name on the lease.'

Beth's smile lit up the room. Without thinking she stood up abruptly and flung her arms about his neck, almost knocking him from his chair. As she buried her face in his neck, Joss held her tightly. For a brief moment, he pretended that this was how it might always be, if he was not a married man.

Joss eased her away and got up. 'It is late,' he said gruffly, putting some distance between them. 'Tomorrow we will both confront our demons. Now go to bed, Beth. Before I take you to mine.'

Chapter Ten

Truro had once been a small village situated at the source of the Truro River. Over the centuries it had grown steadily into the stannary town of Cornwall. It was here that the tin and copper mined from the surrounding land was brought to have its quality tested and verified before being distributed to purchasers from the port. Over the centuries the town continued to grow. The profitable wool trade overtook mining, resulting in the port of Truro flourishing and the population growing to more than ten thousand. Now it was the centre of Cornish administration, retail and trade, but alongside the growing population came the problems of overcrowding and unsanitary living conditions for poor residents. Truro had two faces, and which one you became familiar with depended on the amount of money in your pocket.

Beth watched two carriages pass by, full of passengers and overloaded with tightly strapped trunks and chests. Excitable, thin horses pulled the precariously stacked cargo, the adrenaline in their bodies causing them to lift their tails high and drop steaming dung onto the street. Pedestrians mingled with the carriages and wheelbarrow traders, darting out of the way when another horse trotted by.

Joss took her arm and escorted her safely across the busy main street. 'This is Pendor Street,' he shouted above the noise. Initially surprised that he knew this, Beth then saw the cast iron sign bearing the street's name. 'Tremayne and Goldsmith Solicitors is the building with the green doors,' Joss added taking her towards it.

Beth looked at the large building and halted.

'I want to go in alone,' she said.

'You don't have to. I will go with you.' He seemed a little hurt by her rejection but Beth would not change her mind.

'I have been a coward about all of this and I will be a coward no more. This is something I want to do – on my own.'

Joss pulled her aside into a narrow alcove and away from the crowd walking around them. 'Is there nothing I can say to make you change your mind?' he asked.

Beth shook her head. She was determined to do this her way.

'So this is the point where we part,' he replied, resigned to her decision. 'I will go north to the police station and you will go to the solicitor.' He touched her cheek with the back of his fingers. 'We will meet at the Town Hall clock in Brunel's Square at the top of Moresk Street in one hour,' he said softly, taking a loose strand of her hair and feeling its softness between his fingers before dropping his hand. 'If I am not there by ten minutes past two, come to the police station to find me. If I have not met you it will be because I am in the cells down below.'

Realising that this may be the last time she would see him as a free man she opened her mouth to speak, to plead with him not to hand himself in, but it was too late. He had already left her side and was striding through the crowds away from her and, perhaps, out of her life. There was no chance to say a heartfelt goodbye, or to be held by him in a loving embrace. Perhaps that was to the good. The former would bring the realisation that she may not speak freely with him again, the latter she had no right to enjoy. In that moment his parting filled her mind – so full that she did not question how he would know the names of the square and street they had yet to visit.

'Mr Tremayne will see you now,' said the clerk.

Beth nodded and took a deep breath. She had been waiting patiently for only ten minutes, yet she was relieved the wait had come to an end. The sombre atmosphere of the office, the daunting and dark interior, all added to her feelings of inferiority and criminality. Yet Mr Tremayne was not as she had expected, and his polite greeting momentarily took her off guard.

As if echoing her thoughts he said, 'At last we meet, although you are not quite what I expected.' He indicated to a chair with a wave of his hand. 'Please, take a seat.'

Beth lifted her chin in defiance. 'I would rather stand, sir,' she replied in a clear voice. She had come to do battle, or at least plead her case. She was prepared to do what needed to be done in order to keep her home. Mr Tremayne made his way slowly around the desk and back to his seat.

'My knees think they are older than I and tell me so with every movement I make. Standing for a long period of time is not an activity I like to partake in.' Preparing to sit, he added, 'Please do not make me feel uncomfortable by having me sit in a lady's presence.'

He waited by his chair and Beth could see that he was in considerable discomfort. Grudgingly she took a seat opposite him. Smiling, Mr Tremayne eased himself down into his favourite wooden chair. His features relaxed as he sat back to study her.

Not wishing to be unnerved, Beth matched his gaze. She had met people before who showed a face like a friend, but underneath their heart was still one of stone. He was in his late fifties, with a rounded belly and large grey sideburns. The hair on top of his head was wiry and thin and had been swept across a receding hairline in a poor attempt at vanity. Yet there was no other sign of arrogance or conceit; in fact if he had been half his weight and three inches shorter he would look very similar to her grandfather – but for his clothes. Perhaps it was this similarity, or the gentle softness in his eyes, which gave Beth reason to hope for a positive outcome.

'Clarkson has told me you are the present occupier of Kynance Cottage.'

Beth nodded. 'I am.'

'I was expecting someone a little larger. Mr Nankervis advised me that he had made an attempt to discuss the situation with you but you resisted and became violent.'

'There was no attempt at discussion, Mr Tremayne. Mr Nankervis has been spare with the truth.'

Mr Tremayne tapped his lips with a single finger as he considered her words. 'So it seems. You do not seem the sort to be able to remove a Cornish wrestler.'

'He was an ex-Cornish wrestler who had eaten more pies of late than won fights.'

Mr Tremayne started to laugh. 'I was not happy when I heard about the exchange,' he said finally. 'It is not how I like to do business. However, Miss ...'

'Miss Jago.'

'... Jago, you have no legal right to live in Kynance Cottage. As I explained in my letter, the lease ended with Mr William Jago.'

'Who was my grandfather.'

Mr Tremayne agreed. 'I do not doubt it. But now my client wishes to have the cottage back.'

Beth sat forward. 'I have been told that life leases are commonly made for three people. I had hoped there was a mistake and my name was on the lease.'

A look of sympathy passed across his face and he reached for a large roll of paper from a desk drawer.

'Mistakes are rarely so accommodating,' he said as he moved some items from his desk to make room. The red seal, and his careful handling of it, told her that this was the legal document that took away her right to live there. She watched as his thick-fingered hands untied the lease ribbon and unrolled it for her eyes. Neatly written words covered the paper. They were penned along tightly placed lines, too numerous to read quickly, too complicated to understand. She followed his finger as he trailed a line of writing and read from the document.

'... during the natural lives of the said William Jago, aged thirty-eight years, Elizabeth Jago, aged forty-two years ...' He looked up at Beth.

'She was my grandmother. She is now dead,' Beth answered his enquiring look as any hope she might have had begun to fade.

'... and Anne Jago, aged sixteen years in this year of our Lord eighteen-thirty-seven. I assume Anne is your mother?'

Beth nodded miserably, and as if those words were not painful enough, she noticed for the first time her grandfather's signature. Although carefully written, its childlike execution indicated his poor literacy in stark contrast to the complicated legal document he had signed. Seeing her beloved grandfather's simple, poorly crafted signature in ink was painful. His scrawl had provided her with security until his death, but now it helped to dismantle her secure world. Yes, it was painful to see. As painful as a dagger in her heart.

'Perhaps I can arrange for a new lease, with my name upon it. Would Mr Nankervis be open to this arrangement?' There were many signatures at the bottom of the document and words she did not understand. All were beautifully written and difficult to read, but just as Mr Tremayne removed the document from the table she saw what she was hoping to find. Yet, she was confused by it. 'Mr Roscarrock is the owner of Kynance Cottage? Mr Tremayne, please explain to me who Mr Roscarrock is, and what is his connection with Mr Nankervis?'

Mr Tremayne carefully put the document away and settled himself back in his seat. Many years in the legal profession had hardened him to the pleas of people who were not his clients. However, for once he felt disposed to act kindly towards the young woman who was about to lose her home.

'The lessor of this document, named Mr Roscarrock, was a mine owner. He owns, or rather owned, River Valley and Kynance Cottage.'

'Which gives truth to the tale that my mother and grandfather told me. My grandfather was *given* Kynance Cottage as a reward for saving a mine owner's son,' Beth replied excitedly. Perhaps there was hope after all.

'No, Mr Roscarrock senior *leased* the cottage to your grandfather for the term of his life, which is a different situation altogether. It would have been explained to your grandfather at the time, I am sure.'

'I will talk to Mr Roscarrock. If he was kind enough to do this for my grandfather then there is a strong possibility he would do the same for me.'

'Perhaps, Miss Jago. However Mr Roscarrock senior has since died, and his son, the present Mr Roscarrock, now owns River Valley and Kynance Cottage. The terms of the lease were also inherited. I am afraid you have no legal claim.'

'Is the present Mr Roscarrock the boy my grandfather saved?'

The solicitor nodded.

'Would he not have an obligation, or at least a moral obligation, to help Will Jago's granddaughter?'

Mr Tremayne interlocked the fingers of his hands and held them against his lips while he considered his next words carefully. 'Miss Jago, I like you. I think you are a fine woman with a bright future. I would not like to see a beautiful butterfly, such as you, be damaged by going too close to a thorn bush.'

'You speak in riddles, Mr Tremayne. I am not of your class. My class speak plainly, so please do so with me,' Beth replied in a clipped tone. She saw admiration in his eyes.

'The present Mr Roscarrock is my client and I work for him. However I see no harm in providing you with some advice. Mr Nankervis is his friend and is also employed by him. Mr Nankervis has no power; he only carries out Mr Roscarrock's instructions. Mr Roscarrock is powerful but he is also ruthless. Business and money come first with him. If a mine is unprofitable he will close it with no concern for the destruction and deprivation of the community that relies upon it. If a miner is injured and can no longer work, he shows no concern for their welfare or that of their family. He has no qualms about turning them out of their cottage, and if he sees a profit is to be made, he cares little for the countryside he will destroy. He has plans for River Valley.' He shrugged. 'I do not know what they are.' He leaned forward on his desk and fixed her with his gaze. 'I do know that a girl, who happens to be the granddaughter of an old man who once saved him ... an incident he barely remembers ... will mean little to him now. He considers that the debt to your grandfather has been well paid and he is free of any further obligation.'

'Then there is no more to be said,' said Beth, standing abruptly. 'May I have a few days to pack?'

Taken aback by her sudden change in stance, Mr Tremayne nodded and struggled to stand. 'I will advise my client that perhaps one month would allow you some time to find alternative lodgings.'

'My grandfather was not an educated man, sir. He was given a house that required no rent and could be passed on to his daughter on his death. I believe he did not fully understand what he had signed and he thought the house was his. He told me I had no need to worry about our home. I loved him and trusted him.'

'I understand your reasoning, especially if he has given you no other reason not to trust him in the past. But I would have not done my duty if I had not explained it fully to him at the time, and I can assure you, my partner or I would have undertaken our duties fully.'

Beth felt uneasy. She had trusted her grandfather, but he had also not told her about his mysterious benefactor.

'I am an old man, Miss Jago, and my profession is a constant battle to ensure that people who make promises do not break them. I have come to the conclusion that there is no one you can trust in this world, not even yourself.' He waved a finger at her. '*Especially* yourself, when love is involved. I have seen many unhappy spouses walk through our doors to bring me to that conclusion.'

Beth considered his words solemnly.

'I thank you for your help, Mr Tremayne ... and your counsel. Do I have your reassurance that the harassment will stop in the meantime?'

Mr Tremayne nodded. 'The harassment should never have happened and I will voice my disapproval to my client. It is always better to use a carrot than a stick.'

Beth liked his wisdom and respected it.

'I assume Mr Roscarrock, the son, inherited all the property his father once owned.'

'Indeed, Miss Jago, he did, but I would not advise you to find out where he lives and visit him. He will not entertain you.'

'I hear what you say, Mr Tremayne. I will not make any attempts to discover his address,' she said politely, offering her hand as if she was a lady.

The solicitor took her hand and gave a stiff bow over it. She smiled in return and with renewed confidence swept from the room, leaving Mr Tremayne looking slightly bemused at her quick exit.

Stepping out into the street and the bright sunlight, Beth shielded her eyes from the bright light to look about her.

'No, Mr Tremayne,' she said quietly to herself as she straightened her modest hat. 'I will not attempt to find the address for the simple reason that I already have it.'

Beth may not have had the education or knowledge to understand legal jargon, but she could recognise the words *address of lessor* and had quickly memorised the details. Mr Roscarrock may not seek to speak to her directly, but that did not mean she would not attempt to speak to him.

Joss stood on the pavement watching the bustling pedestrians and carriages filling the street. He had just left Beth to face the solicitor without him. It was not how he had wanted it to be but despite spending much of the journey to Truro trying to persuade her otherwise, she had remained stubborn and wanted to speak to them alone. She had felt embarrassed that she had chosen to ignore such important correspondence and keep it secret from him, and now she wanted to claw back her self-respect. Joss felt that she was being too hard on herself, yet he understood her feelings on the matter.

The Town Hall clock chimed the hour and Joss could not shake off the fact that the sounds of horses' hooves and footsteps around him seemed familiar. He had walked these streets and heard the noise of Truro town before, but this did not surprise him. Truro was one of the main towns in Cornwall, and if he came from Cornwall – and there was no evidence to suggest he did not – then it would not be unusual for him to have walked on its streets at some point in his life. As each day passed, more and more images and feelings had entered his mind and soul. It was difficult to know what was real and what was imagined, brought to life from wishful thinking or a dream. With no person who knew who he really was, he had no one to confirm which memories were false and which true. He stood at the end of the street. To his right was Truro Borough Police Station, with its recently renovated sign above an imposing door. Very soon I will walk through that door, he thought, but first I have another task to undertake. He spotted a gentleman, who was similar to himself in age, and stopped him in the street.

'Sir,' Joss said. 'I was wondering if you could help me.' The man, unaccustomed to being accosted by a stranger, eyed him suspiciously. Joss reassured him with a smile. 'I have a pocket watch and fob on my person.' He took it out from his pocket and placed it on his palm so the man could see. 'I would like to buy something similar as a gift for a friend. Where, in Cornwall, would you recommend I could purchase such a gift and have it engraved?'

The man bent over his hand to examine it more closely, then straightened, confident he could help.

'There is only one place in Cornwall that I would trust and you are in luck, sir.' He lifted his cane and pointed to the opposite street. 'Take the narrow street to the left, and you will find Merryweather and Son. They have been selling clocks and watches for seventy years and there is none better. Ask for Music Merryweather.'

'How will I know him?' asked Joss, delighted.

'He walks on the twist, you won't miss him,' was the man's reply.

Joss thanked him and followed his directions with purposeful strides, moving easily between the traffic until he found the shop he had been looking for. He had expected a large shop, built on the profits of a successful business over many generations, but the shop he found was quite small and inconsequential. Its painted window frames were peeling and cracked. An overstocked interior gave the appearance of cluttered disorganisation and as he entered, the relentless ticking of numerous clocks crowded him from all quarters. Yet despite all this, a family of good fortune had just exited the shop and Joss realised that the stranger had spoken the truth. This odd little shop had a solid reputation, and people from far and wide sought the Merryweather family out for advice and to purchase their timepieces.

As the bell above the door chimed to mark his entrance, a man emerged from a door behind the counter. His shortened, withered right leg gave him a rocking gait and Joss immediately understood what the stranger had meant. His disability had resulted in a twisting of his spine, forcing one shoulder higher than the other and giving the appearance of a crooked neck. Joss felt sorry for the man, yet Mr Merryweather had no sorrow for himself. He had lived with the affliction since he was a child and he did not let it defeat him.

'May I help you, sir?' he asked, lifting his head as much as his limited flexibility allowed him.

'I have a pocket watch in my possession and I would like to learn about it. I hope you can help me, Mr Merryweather.' Joss placed the watch on the counter and Music picked it up in his surprisingly dainty hands.

'You wish me to value it?' he asked, turning it over and feeling its metal under the slide of his thumb.

'It is not the value that interests me, it is the watch itself and the engraving inside.'

Music brought out his glasses, placed them on his nose and lifted the timepiece upwards so the light from the window made it clearer to his eye. He opened its case and the covering to admire the workings inside; his examination continued as he spoke.

'It's a fine pocket watch, sir, made by Desbois and Wheeler of London. The sign, number and date it was made are engraved next to the working, confirming it was made in 1834. The fob often has the family seal of its owner, or the organisation it represents. This watch has a bird, more precisely a chough which is, I'm sure you know, a sign of Cornwall.' He turned the watch over in his fingers and back again. 'It has a fine verge movement, beautiful engraving, with diamond endstone and blued screws. The hinged gilt curvette is in good condition, nice gold serpentine hands. There is a little wearing on the engine turning but in all it is an excellent pocket watch and fob.'

'You think it was sold in London?'

'It was made in London, but the chough tells me it was sold to someone who came from this county. It may well have been purchased from here, but I do not keep records of my customers, sir. Looking at the engraving I suggest that a lady called Charlotte bought it for her husband, a man called Joss.'

Joss was disappointed with his reply, yet what had he expected? He should have known he was on a fool's errand.

'You look disappointed, sir,' said the man.

Joss decided to tell him the truth. 'I believe it to be mine, Mr Merryweather. I had it in my possession but I have lost my memory. If the inscription is to be believed, my name is Joss and I am married. However, I had hoped that by discovering more information from the watch I would find ...' Joss swallowed; the next words did not sit well with him. '... my wife.'

Music chuckled. 'There is many a man I know who would like to lose his wife,' he said, looking at the watch again and reading the engraving. He picked up his magnifying glass and examined it more closely. A broad smile grew on his face. Finally, he put it down again and looked up at Joss. 'But the truth is, you are not one of them. This watch was engraved by my father. My father took pride in his work and on each engraving he undertook he left his signature.' Music showed Joss a mark in the shape of an M which was hidden amongst the decorative pattern on the watch. 'Now, you look around thirty, perhaps thirty-two. Whether or not you are called Joss I could not say but you do not have a wife called Charlotte. I know this for a fact, as my father stopped engraving in the year eighteen thirty-seven.'

'Is this a fact?' asked Joss, not quite believing his ears.

'Absolutely, unless there is a call for engraving in heaven, as he died that same year.'

'Which means this watch was engraved,' Joss said, making some mental calculations, 'when I was a young child.'

'Which is too young to be wed,' finished Music, breaking into a smile as he saw the relief on Joss's face.

'Mr Merryweather,' he said, shaking his hand with gratitude, 'you have just made one man very happy!'

'I have just told you that you might not be called the name you thought you were called and you are not married to this Charlotte. You may well be married, and you have yet to discover your name.'

'True, but at least I am in a better position than I was before. I now know something of the watch I carry and in turn something more about myself. The name, Joss, will do for now in the absence of any other. Good day to you, Mr Merryweather. You have been a very great help to me.'

Adrenaline pumped through Joss's veins – Charlotte was not his wife. Now for his final task, which was not so easy. Retracing his footsteps he returned to the main street and set out for the police station. He took a deep breath to steady his nerves. Inside its walls he would discover if he was a wanted criminal or if anyone had reported him missing. Stepping inside was not easy for him, as he wasn't sure if he would be stepping out again. Striding through the main door he felt a sense of unease. A constable stood at the desk, and on his entrance he looked up from his ledger. His uniform, military in style but for the colour blue, churned Joss's stomach. He felt, deep down, that he had a disastrous connection with it, yet he would not turn back. If he had any hope for a future with Beth, then the truth about his past must be faced. Bracing himself, he entered and announced himself to the waiting constable before hearing the door slam shut behind him.

Chapter Eleven

The Town Hall clock had chimed the hour ten minutes ago and still there was no sign of Joss. Beth paced anxiously at the top of the granite steps, which fanned out beneath the clock tower. The square bustled with people going about their lives, all unaware of Beth's mounting anxiety. She took no pleasure in watching the couples strolling leisurely by, the children as they dipped their hands in the modest fountain or the smooth-feathered pigeons as they scrambled for discarded crusts of pie. Beth was searching for Joss and Joss alone. Suddenly she saw him. Standing tall, he easily stood out from the ordinary folk about him. He was watching her and when he saw the recognition in her face, a sign that she had seen him too, he broke into a smile.

Joss swiftly strode towards her, his eyes never leaving her face. Later, Beth could not recall running towards him at all, yet she would always remember his first true loving embrace. It was strong, unwavering and heartfelt and mirrored her feelings for him. She wrapped her arms about his neck, as he lifted her from the ground, and buried her smile into his shoulder. His embrace was not as a friend, nor was it born from lust. It was given with love, and it filled her with pure contentment. It was like coming home.

'You are here,' she said simply, filled with relief.

'I am here,' he replied. He breathed in deeply. 'You smell of the sea breeze and fresh flowers. Only the devil knows how long I have wanted to be this close to you. To be able to touch you and to hold you, and feel no shame or fear of the judgement of others.' He lowered her to the floor and cupped her face.

Beth pulled away laughing. 'You can't kiss me here, not in public!'

'You are right,' Joss said, grabbing her hand and leading her across the square. 'But I know somewhere I can!'

Joss's speed and determination forced Beth to run to keep up with his strides. It did not take long for Joss to find a secluded spot: one turn down a narrow footpath and they were by a river and footbridge with a quiet garden beyond. Joss swung her around to face him, drew her forward and gently framed her jawline with his fingers. Gazing at her face for the briefest of moments, as if she was the most beautiful woman he had ever seen, he kissed her. The kiss was no chaste kiss from a boy to a girl, eager to please but not knowing how to. His kiss, a mixture of tenderness and demand, blocked out the world about her. His kiss had the power to satisfy, yet create the desire for more. It unlocked primal feelings of lust and need. But most of all, his kiss touched her heart.

She was still drowning in the sensations it had evoked when he broke free and hugged her tight.

'Charlotte is not my wife,' he said softly into her ear. Her heart skipped a beat at the revelation. 'I have spoken to the son of the man who engraved the watch, and it was done when I was a boy. It is impossible the engraving relates to me.' He stepped back to look at her. 'Of course, this could also mean I am not called Joss, but at this moment I do not care.'

Beth had never seen him so happy and full of hope. His mood was infectious.

'I thought I had lost you,' was all she could say.

'And I have more news.' Joss began to pace as if filled with energy that demanded release. 'I went to Truro Borough Police Station. I feared the worst and expected to discover something bad about myself.' He almost laughed at the absurdity of it all. 'I told them of my circumstances and I was informed, after looking through a lot of files and posters, that I am not a wanted man. The constable also told me no one had reported me missing.'

Beth frowned. 'No one?'

Joss stopped his pacing, came to her and cupped her face.

'Not a single soul.' He attempted to give her another kiss, but she stopped him.

'But it's awful that no one has missed you.'

Joss released her and became serious. 'Not at all, it sets me free. It stands to reason that if I were a married man my wife would report me missing. My memory may never come back fully, Beth. Am I to live the remainder of my life fretting about who I am if no one else cares?'

He threaded his fingers through hers, just as he had done when they stood in the glow of the bonfire at Golowan Feast Day. 'We could start a life together, as man and wife. We could not be wed legally without knowing my real name, but we could call ourselves by the same last name. We could move away where no one knows us. No one would ever know. There are many couples who live their lives as man and wife but have never married due to the fact that they cannot do so legally. Perhaps one of them is married to someone else, or their spouse is locked away in an asylum. I want you in my life, Beth, as my wife.'

'You want me to move away from Kynance Cottage and River Valley?'

'We would have to. We will take lodgings and I will find work. We can start a new life together.'

Beth wanted to feel excited at the prospect of spending the rest of her life with Joss, yet there was something stopping her and she did not know what it was. Was it the fact that he could desert her at any time, leaving her with no claim and perhaps a brood of children to look after?

'You spoke of your memory never fully coming back. Do you remember anything, other than your dreams?'

Joss let her hand go and dismissed her words with a wave of a hand. 'I have no memories I can trust.'

'Yet you remember the streets of Truro, and this place.' Beth indicated the gardens. 'This *secluded* place. You easily found the solicitors and who to speak to regarding your watch.'

Joss frowned. He did not like the turn in conversation.

'I asked a passer-by, I remembered nothing.'

'It was a miraculous incident that you happened to speak to the son of the engraver.'

Joss's frowned deepened. 'Are you suggesting I am lying so I can take you as my wife?'

Beth stepped onto the footbridge and rested her hands on the railing. She looked at the narrow minor river below her. She did not think Joss was lying, but she could not help but feel a sense of unease. He wanted them to move away from the only place she had loved and called home.

'I saw Mr Tremayne and I now know who owns Kynance Cottage,' she replied simply. 'I want to speak to the owner and ask for an extension of the lease.'

'There is no need to do that,' said Joss, coming to stand beside her. 'For us to live as man and wife we would need to move to a place where no one knows us.' With a single finger Joss tilted her chin towards him so she was forced to look into his eyes. 'Do you not want to be with me?'

'I do, but I want security. As a child I never had it, and living with you in name only would not give that to me.' She straightened her shoulders and lifted her chin from his touch. 'I want to speak to Mr Roscarrock.'

As Beth said the name she saw a flash of recognition in Joss's eyes. The atmosphere between them changed as if a black cloud had cast a shadow over them. He knew the name, and although he instantly tried to hide the fact, she had seen his reaction and it turned her stomach. 'You know him? Did he send you, too?'

Joss shook his head and stepped back from her. 'I told you, I do not know what is real or what is not. I do not know the name. I do not know the man.'

Mr Tremayne's words came back to haunt her and she

wondered if Joss had hoped a life with him would be the carrot to entice her out of River Valley. After all, once they were in lodgings he could just leave her.

'Tell me the truth, Joss. Do you know who Roscarrock is?'

Joss's jaw tightened. 'No.' He stared off into the distance, too angry to look at her. Neither spoke for some minutes, the only sound coming from the running water racing beneath their feet. Finally Joss pushed himself away from the railings. 'Let us go home. I find no pleasure in this town any more.'

Chapter Twelve

Beth stared at her reflection in the mirror. The mirror was small and she could only see her face, but it was all she needed to check her hair appeared neat and her hat was straight. She was not a vain woman, but she wanted to be taken seriously, and appearing tidy and smart would be an advantage. It had rained heavily in the night, but dawn had just broken and the first rays of sunshine began to filter through her thin curtains and light up her bedroom, making it easier for her to see. She picked up her purse, which had little in it, made her way quietly down the wooden stairs, left a note for Joss and carefully slid back the bolts on the door.

On the way out of the valley, she paused at the shed. Joss had taken to leaving the door open so he could hear any disturbance caused by a return of Nankervis's thugs, but the wind direction must have driven the rain in, for his hair was wet and his bedding a little damp. However, her visit offered Beth the view that she hoped for: his sleeping body on the makeshift bed. If they had not argued Joss might well have spent the night in hers. But they had argued and she had tried, but failed, to fight the urge to see him before she left.

Joss lay in a deep sleep, naked to the waist. The soft morning light touched his body, highlighting parts and casting shadows on others, defining his muscles and emphasising his strength. Yet he was at peace and his face, free of stress or worry, appeared relaxed and content. For a moment Beth's resolve faltered as she watched the rise and fall of his chest. It was so tempting to remove her hat and dress, slide beneath his blankets and mould her body against his. To hell with the consequences and that he might abandon her. It would be worth taking the risk just so she could experience being his wife in all ways but legally.

157

Joss turned over in his bed and she watched the blanket slide a little lower on his hip. She dragged her eyes away before temptation overtook her. The fact was she knew less of Joss than she did before. His name might not even be Joss. Despite her heart falling for him, her mind was telling her to beware. There were too many things gnawing at her and she could no longer ignore them. Why had he entered her cottage without knocking? How did he know his way around Truro? Just as she was about to discover the owner's name, and ask for an extension of the lease, Joss spoke with the son of the watch engraver and had discovered he may not be married. Now he offered her a future with him away from River Valley. If she went with him, her fight to stay would come to an end. It sounded all too convenient. Mr Tremayne had said Roscarrock was ruthless. Mr Tremayne had said a carrot works better than a stick. The more she thought about it, the more she felt that Joss had been sent by Roscarrock to remove her. If she had any doubts about this, they were crushed when she saw in Joss's eyes that he knew the name Roscarrock. His memory was returning – that is, if he had ever lost it in the first place.

Beth quickly made her way along the track to the road. Waiting patiently for her was her neighbour, Bill, in his cart. Without a word she climbed up beside him.

'It's not like you to be so secretive when you ask me for a lift. Do you want me to take you all the way?' asked the farmer.

Beth nodded solemnly.

'I won't ask you what this is all about, maid, but from the look on your face it's not something you are looking forward to.'

Beth looked straight ahead. 'I may not be looking forward to it, but it is something that must be done.'

Bill raised an eyebrow, and then flicked the reins of his horse. The wheels of his cart began to turn. They were on their way, and by the time Joss woke she would already be at her destination.

Beth looked up at the Elizabethan manor. Designed by master masons, Bras-stenack House was an imposing stone building and, much like its owner, a contradiction. Despite being saved as a boy by her grandfather, Mr Roscarrock now cared nothing for Will Jago's granddaughter. However, where she disliked its owner, she couldn't help liking his home. Windows, larger and more plentiful than Beth had ever seen before in a building, allowed natural light to flood into the spacious rooms. Yet the building had touches of gothic architecture, adding an air of mystery and danger. The sombre grey walls provided a climbing frame for the beautiful, purple flowers of the wisteria plant that hung down and swayed in the gentle breeze. The landscaped gardens, quiet, peaceful and not overly pretentious, appeared natural with no hint of their contrived planning. The flowering shrubs, which attracted a variety of butterflies, reminded Beth of River Valley and for a moment she wished she were home and not standing before Roscarrock's residence.

A few weeks ago Beth would not have had the courage to knock on such a grand door. Today, however, things were different. She felt sure she would find the answers to her questions, and if Mr Roscarrock agreed to extend the lease it would mean that her grandfather had also spoken the truth. He had told her she need not worry about living in Kynance Cottage. If Beth had her name on a new lease, he would have been proved right. Beth looked at the door and braced herself. Without hesitating further she walked towards it.

A middle-aged woman with a flushed face and a starched uniform answered Beth's knock. Her smile was warm, but after glancing at Beth's clothes her greeting words were not.

'The trade door is to the side.' Already prepared for the rebuff, Beth stood her ground and put out her hand to prevent the woman shutting the heavy door.

'I'm not selling anything or looking for work. I have come here to speak with Mr Roscarrock on a matter of urgency.'

Taken by surprise, the housekeeper slowly reopened the door and looked more closely at the visitor. 'I'm afraid that won't be possible. Perhaps you can leave a message. Can you write?'

Beth couldn't help but feel hurt. She was wearing her new blue dress, yet she was still considered lacking.

'I can read and write, but I do not wish to leave a message. I must speak with Mr Roscarrock. I woke early and travelled several miles to be here before he had a chance to be about his business. I would be grateful if you could inform him that the occupier of Kynance Cottage in River Valley is here and wants to speak to him.'

The housekeeper smiled and Beth realised that her polite insistence had won a little respect from the woman who, on closer inspection, did not appear at all well. Whether she was too ill to argue or she felt Beth had a good reason for her visit, the housekeeper relented.

'I will see what I can do,' she said finally, stepping back to allow her to pass. 'Wait here in the hall until I fetch you,' she added over her shoulder, before slowly walking away.

Beth did not have to wait long. There was just enough time for her to admire the high ceilings and the ornate cornices of the hall, and feel envious of the sweeping staircase that dominated it. She could not help but feel a growing resentment and anger at the gulf between the rich and the poor.

'Are you ready?' asked the housekeeper.

Beth hadn't noticed the housekeeper had returned. She tucked a loose hair behind her ear.

'Oh yes, I'm ready,' she said clearly. 'I've never been more ready in my life.'

Beth stood in front of the closed oak door to the study and hesitated.

The housekeeper raised an eyebrow. 'Has your courage deserted you?' she croaked.

Beth realised her first impression of the housekeeper had been right: she was not at all well.

'I'm just gathering my thoughts. You don't sound well, Mrs ...'

'Mrs May,' replied the housekeeper. 'I have a troublesome cold and my throat is sore.'

'You should put your feet up,' Beth said, momentarily diverted from her task by her concern for the older woman. The housekeeper was touched by her kind words.

'I know I should, and I will. Mr Roscarrock does not like a large number of people about him, so there is not the staff to delegate tasks to, unlike in other large houses.'

'You must rest in order to recover. My friend, Martha, knows a great deal about remedies for all sorts of ailments. For a cold she recommends mixing two teaspoons of cider vinegar and two teaspoons of honey in a glass of water. To make a gargle, double the cider and honey and add a strong infusion of sage. Gargle four times a day and it will relieve your sore throat. I believe she adds a tot of whisky to the gargle ... or perhaps it is the drink, I'm not sure.'

The housekeeper was delighted with the advice. 'I have all of those ingredients in the kitchen. I will try them straight away. Are you ready?'

Beth nodded nervously.

'Mr Roscarrock is not at home today, but Mr Nankervis has agreed to see you instead. He is in charge while Mr Roscarrock is away.'

Beth was about to protest, as it was Roscarrock she wanted to see, but it was already too late – the housekeeper had opened the door and was announcing her. Beth saw a man standing inside the room waiting. She realised she had no choice but to follow Mrs May in.

Nankervis was tall and his feet were set squarely with his

shoulders, a stance Joss had a habit of adopting. But where Joss was dark, this man was fair, with narrow eyes and a straight, sharp nose that Beth did not find attractive. Although he had not uttered a word, Beth felt there was a devil-may-care attitude about him. This was the man responsible for sending Jorey Jose and his thug to her house. Beth took an instant dislike to him.

If she had any doubt in her gut reaction to this man, it was set aside when his eyes swept up and down her body as if to envisage what she looked like beneath her clothes. The gesture was impolite at best, but for him to consider it acceptable told her that he thought she was beneath him and warranted no better treatment. Beth waited for the housekeeper to leave before she spoke.

'I came to see Mr Roscarrock, not you.'

'It is me you see or no one at all.' He waved to a chair. 'Sit down, Miss ...'

'Miss Beth Jago. I live in Kynance Cottage and I do not want to sit down.'

Mr Nankervis pulled out a chair, sat down and stretched out his legs. He rested his elbow on the arm and allowed his other to dangle lazily by his side.

'Well, I *do* want to sit down. I know some may consider it impolite to sit while a lady remains standing, but I do not see a lady. You have been living in a property that you do not have a right to live in. On this basis I do not feel you deserve the same respect as a lady.' He helped himself to a cigar from a silver box on the desk and turned it in his fingers while he examined it. 'Although I must admit, you are not quite what I expected.'

'You are not the only one to have said that to me.'

Beth was not impressed by his study or his cigar. They were nothing to her but symbols of his wealth and power, neither of which she gave one fig for.

'My grandfather was given a lease for life for the cottage.

The lease was to pass to his wife and daughter. They are all dead and I have come here today to respectfully ask for my name to be placed on the lease. I will pay rent and I promise to be a good tenant.'

Without taking his eyes away from her, Mr Nankervis smiled and cut the end of his cigar with a slicer. The end fell onto the desk and would lie there, discarded, until it was cleared away later by a member of his staff.

'That is not possible,' he said simply. He waited as if he expected her to leave. Beth did not move.

'I would like to see Mr Roscarrock. He is the owner of Kynance Cottage and it is up to him if I stay or leave.'

As if he found Beth amusing, Mr Nankervis continued to smile. 'Mr Roscarrock is in London visiting friends, but he will not change his mind. He has plans for River Valley that do not include that cottage.'

'What plans?' Beth asked.

She had not expected this turn of events. Her frustration gave her courage and she made up her mind that she would not leave until she found out more. Impatiently she waited while Mr Nankervis rotated the rolled tobacco in the flame whilst making slow gentle puffs to encourage it to burn. Satisfied it was evenly lit, he sat back and took his first draw. He swirled the fragrant smoke around his mouth, as he looked at her, before exhaling from his mouth and nose. They both watched the smoke coil and rise from the end of his cigar to hover between them.

'The banks and cliffs of River Valley are made of slate, and Mr Roscarrock plans to take advantage of this.'

'In what way?'

'He has plans to quarry the valley, extract the slate and sell it.' Mr Nankervis took another draw on his cigar and savoured its flavour in his mouth. Beth was not impressed by the action.

'It will destroy the valley and the coastline. He cannot do that.'

'On the contrary, he owns the valley and can do whatever he likes.'

'But he is a prosperous mine owner. Why would he quarry for slate?' Beth moved around the chair he had offered earlier and ungraciously sat down. She leaned forward to add weight to her pleading. 'Please, Mr Nankervis, don't let him destroy the valley when he already has so much.'

Mr Nankervis was unmoved. He studied the end of his cigar. 'It is no secret that Cornish mines are struggling to compete with the prices from overseas tin production. Penarth Mine, where your grandfather worked, was the first mine owned by the Roscarrock family to close. It is only thanks to the present Mr Roscarrock that Bodannock Mine is still working. It is a difficult time, Miss Jago, and we all have to adapt.' His eyes lifted to hers and he smiled. 'I'm sure a pretty thing like you can find a live-in position. You may not have the skills for a country house, but there are many farms in the vicinity that require servants.'

Beth was unsure if he was trying to be kind or insulting. She stood. 'I would like to speak with Mr Roscarrock.'

Mr Nankervis's smile faded. 'I told you,' he said, getting up and summoning the housekeeper. 'He is away and has left me to run his business affairs.'

'I'm sure he would be interested to find out that the man who he has trusted his affairs to has employed thugs in his name to break the law by using violence on a woman.'

Mr Nankervis was about to respond when the door opened and Mrs May came in. The sight of the housekeeper gave Beth further courage.

'He would also be interested to learn why you have not given Mrs May a day to recover from her illness. Any sensible person would see that this woman is feverish and at risk of pneumonia.'

Mr Nankervis stubbed out his cigar in annoyance. Burning ash scattered onto his fingers and he flinched as he hastily brushed it away.

'I think you had better leave, Miss Jago. The lease will not be renewed and you are to vacate the property forthwith.' He glanced at his housekeeper, adding irritably, 'Mrs May, for God's sake, go to bed before you drop down dead. You will not be required again today.'

Joss opened his eyes and stretched. He had experienced another night free of nightmares and, from the position of the sun, it must be about nine in the morning, much later than he intended to sleep.

He placed his hands behind his head and thought about the events of the day before. He had felt a great sense of relief when he had discovered that he was not married to a woman called Charlotte, or a wanted criminal. The possibility that he could start afresh with Beth had been overwhelming, and never more so than when he saw her waiting anxiously on the Town Hall steps. She had looked beautiful and vulnerable, a free spirit who enjoyed the gift of life and made him feel at peace. Before yesterday he knew that he wanted her and had felt jealous of any man that took her affection, but in that moment in the square, he realised he wanted to spend the rest of his life with her. It was probably something he had wanted for a long time, but had not dared to hope for. He could see now that he had overwhelmed Beth with his plans.

Then things had changed. When she had started to talk of a man called Roscarrock, he knew he had heard the name before. Yet, if the man had sent him to remove her from the cottage, what did it matter now? He no longer worked for him, if he ever had in the first place. He did not want his possible connection with Roscarrock to spoil their plans. If they were to have a future together, it would be better if they moved away.

Joss thought of Beth's reaction to his plans. He had become frustrated by her lack of enthusiasm. He had hoped that she would be as excited as he was, yet she appeared to be choosing

River Valley over their future as a couple. But the passage of time can soothe frayed emotions, and on returning to River Valley he could empathise with her reaction. It was a new day and he now realised she needed time to consider what he was asking her to do – to move away, live in sin and pretend to the world that they were married. She also had a deep-rooted fear that he would abandon her with children to care for alone. It was understandable, and he must be patient, however much he wanted to be anything but patient. He wanted to start living his life, and he wanted to do it with her by his side.

He got up, dressed and went to find her. The cottage was not locked and it seemed unusually quiet inside. He could not hear Beth in her bedroom above and she was not downstairs. Joss felt wary that something may have happened, yet everything appeared in order and there were no signs of a struggle. On the table lay her mending, untouched from the night before. The only signs that Beth had passed through were that the inside bolts had been pulled back and there was a note on the table written in her hand.

Joss picked up the letter and read it. With a growing sense of disappointment he realised that she had chosen the fight to remain in the valley over a new future with him.

> *My grandfather always told me that courage is not when a man fights without fear, but when a man fights despite feeling fear. I must speak with Mr Roscarrock, despite being afraid of what I might discover.*

She was gone, and would probably discover that he did have a connection to Roscarrock. He crumpled the letter up in his hand. Her grandfather had spoken to her about courage. What did he know about courage? What does anyone know about courage? He could almost hear her grandfather speaking the words, as though he had said the same thing to him in the past.

Courage is not when a man fights without fear, but when a man fights despite feeling fear.

Joss dropped the letter and watched it fall to the ground. He *had* heard her grandfather speak those words, and it was to him he had said them. His past, as though prodded into momentum, began to return with a vengeance. It presented memories like spectres from the darkness, to settle in front of him before they took up their place inside his mind once more. As each memory formed, a sickening feeling of betrayal, guilt and anger descended to weigh heavily on him, as he began to remember his former life and who he was.

Mrs May showed Beth out of the room. Beth felt miserable. She had achieved nothing. A strong smell of whisky emanated from the housekeeper.

'Mrs May, how much whisky did you add?' whispered Beth as she followed her into the hall.

'A glass full, just as you said, and I have never tasted anything so vile.'

'I said add a tot to a glass full of water, with honey and cider vinegar, not the vinegar and honey to a glass of whisky!'

'You have turned me into a toper,' replied the housekeeper. 'But I thank you for arranging for me to have the rest of the day to recover. Mr Nankervis is not a sympathetic man, much like Mr Roscarrock.'

'I am no better off,' said Beth miserably. A painting of a man and a woman caught her eye and she came to stand before it. 'I wanted to speak with Mr Roscarrock. Where can I find him, Mrs May?'

The housekeeper stood next to her and admired the painting too. 'He is in London staying with friends. This is Mr Jocelyn Roscarrock and his wife Charlotte. He died some years ago and his wife lives with her eldest daughter in Devon. He preferred to be called Joss and named his son after him.'

She moved on to the next painting and waited for Beth to

follow, yet Beth hesitated as realisation dawned on her. Her stomach flipped as she guessed who would be staring down at her from the next painting. She forced herself to look.

'This is the present Mr Joss Roscarrock, in his army uniform,' said Mrs May proudly. 'We are unsure when he will return from London.'

Dressed in the scarlet uniform of the 46th Regiment of Foot, with an expression of confidence and pride, was her Joss. Beth visibly paled as Mrs May, her tongue loosened by alcohol, gave a short history of her present employer. As Beth listened, muted in her surprise, she realised it was not only Joss she recognised. The military uniform, decorated with gold buttons, was similar in style to the one worn by the young man she had seen speaking to her grandfather all those years ago. To her eight-year-old eyes he had been a man. He had been almost magical in his splendour, yet in fact he had been no more than a youth of eighteen, an enthusiastic junior departing for Royal Military College at Hull. The man who claimed to have no memory and who wanted her to leave Kynance Cottage to live as his wife was the ruthless businessman Joss Roscarrock. He had known her grandfather, he owned River Valley, and now he wanted her gone. His returning memory, which seemed selective and often hinted at his previous life when it suited him, appeared nothing more than a ruse. The more she thought about it, the more she doubted him and whether he had lost his memory at all. He had achieved his goal, entry to Kynance Cottage, and had almost persuaded her to leave when all he wanted was to destroy the valley for monetary gain.

Beth came to her senses and realised it was her turn to speak.

'He will return by the end of the day, Mrs May,' said Beth through gritted teeth. 'On that I will stake my life.'

'Are you all right, Miss Jago?' asked the concerned housekeeper. 'You look like you have seen a ghost.'

Beth gave her a weak smile and made her excuses to leave. After all, how could she tell this woman that she had lost everything? She had lost her home, her valley and the man she had fallen in love with. For the truth was, the man she had grown to love had never existed at all.

Chapter Thirteen

Three months earlier
Spring 1861

Before Mrs May could announce Mr Nankervis's arrival, Edward swept into the room.

'Joss! How are you?' he asked, dropping a parcel onto the desk. The two men roughly shook hands, as only old friends do.

'You are back,' Joss replied solemnly. 'How were the lakes? Your parents are in good health, I hope?' He indicated to a chair, inviting Edward to sit down. 'A drink?' he asked, lifting a decanter and tilting it in his friend's direction.

'My parents are in rude health and will outlive me, but it is good to be back.' Edward sat down, but immediately got up again, remembering his parcel. 'I have brought you a gift,' he said, and without waiting for Joss, he opened the box that he had placed on the desk. Joss gave his friend a glass of whisky in the hope it would calm him, before looking inside it. Edward did not usually bear gifts and Joss was wary.

'Cigars,' Joss said. It was as he thought. 'I don't smoke cigars.'

'No, but I do,' said Edward, laughing. He polished the silver cigar box with his sleeve before placing it in the centre of Joss's desk.

'You are my right hand man, Edward, but this is still my desk,' said Joss, pushing the box towards his friend.

Edward laughed again, before raising his glass. Their glasses chinked and both men drank the amber spirit in one gulp, just as they used to as young men. The banter and trick-playing was nothing new between them. They had been friends since they were ensigns in the regiment and it was often a man's dark humour that helped him through difficult times. This habit, born of comradeship, brought thoughts of war to both the men's minds.

'Have you heard the news from America? The war of the states is escalating,' said Edward, settling himself back in his chair.

'Yes, I have. War is never good. It is even sadder to know that the blood that is spilt and the lives that are lost are between countrymen. Yet their cause is just. Slavery is abhorrent and needs to be brought to an end. If it cannot be done over a table, it has to be done in the field.'

Joss sat quietly for a moment, deep in thought. Talk of war always did this to him, and the war of the states in America had brought the old memories back to the forefront of his mind. His memory of the Crimea was not good, unlike his friend's.

'I miss the comradeship of war, marching to battle, the nervous tension, seeing your enemy for the first time and fighting side by side with your fellow soldiers,' mused Edward.

'Your memories are few. A few days after arriving you were injured.' Joss poured another drink for the both of them.

'And I have you to thank that I am still here to raise a glass. The care I received afterwards was a battlefield in itself, I will have you know.'

'I know that more people died of illness than from wounds. At least our ship did not suffer cholera as many of the others. It's a sad state of affairs to lose half your regiment from illness before you set foot on land. I heard tales that the sea was littered with their bodies. They tried to tie weights to them but they still managed to float to the surface like corks.'

'I caught dysentery and was glad when I was shipped home.' Edward admired the contents of his glass. It was a good quality whisky, just as he expected from Joss.

'After you left we discarded the Alberts.'

'That does not surprise me. Whoever designed the shako

and uniform had never been to war. Impractical and heavy ... more suited to ceremony than battle.'

The men sat in silence for a moment. They rarely talked of their experiences, but when they did, it was only to each other. Only together could they pick this particular scab.

'Do you remember using our bayonets to kill the rats?'

Joss nodded that he did. 'There were plenty of them, and it was not difficult to do.'

'Do you remember the first Russian I killed?' Edward smiled. 'It was by accident; the musket went off by mistake and I shot him in the chest. I had no idea he was so near to us. He must have been lost.'

'I think he was surrendering,' replied Joss quietly.

'Really? Poor man. I took a button from his uniform as a memento. It does not have the same value now. I lost touch with many in our regiment. What happened to Curly?'

'He died.'

'What about the one with the big moustache? I think he was called Kent.'

'Typhoid.'

'MacKenzie?'

'He had frostbite. He lost both his feet to it and then his life.'

'Davidson?'

'Died of starvation at Sebastopol when the food supplies did not arrive during the winter.'

Edward moved uneasily in his seat. He had never bothered to ask about them before now. It had never seemed the right time somehow.

'What about Digger?'

'I don't know. He disappeared,' said Joss, standing up to look out of the window.

'He ran away?' asked Edward. 'I don't believe he would have done that.'

'I wish he had, but I don't believe he did. Digger was a

brave man. I can only assume there was not much left of him after the cannon bombardment.' Joss watched the light reflect on his glass. He turned abruptly. 'Enough of this talk of war. It takes me down a dark path I am tired of following. I have asked you here to talk to you about my new venture.'

He prepared to pour them both another glass but decided against it. Drink did not numb his memories, although it was tempting to view the world through the bottom of a crystal cut glass. It blurred and distorted life, and provided a black hole of oblivion to hide in. He had tried it on a number of occasions but the result was always the same: to wake and find that nothing had changed. Work was his salvation now.

'Why a new venture, Joss? Since taking over your father's mining business after selling your commission, you have worked hard to keep it going.'

Joss took a map from a drawer and unrolled it on his desk. Edward snatched up his whisky glass just in time to make room for it.

'I have only managed to survive because I am quick to close a mine and reinvest when it is no longer profitable. It is common knowledge that Cornwall is finding it hard to compete with other countries. Even our miners, the best in the world, are leaving Cornwall to find work in mines overseas. It is said that there is a Cornishman at the bottom of every mine in the world. Bodannock Mine is running out of tin and I will have to close it in the near future, so I am looking for a new venture.'

'As you closed Tredeaver and Penarth mines. The men from the nearby villages relied heavily on them for work. Their closures devastated the area.'

'I employed the men when there was work. When there is no more work they are no longer my concern,' said Joss abruptly.

'Well, I have to admire you for your ruthlessness,' Edward said as he helped himself to another drink. He offered one to

Joss who shook his head. 'You are well suited to business,' continued Edward. 'Although I don't remember you being quite so callous when we first met. I hope I have not influenced you to change your ways.'

'No. Not you, Edward. Your influence does not have that much power. It was the war and returning home to find nothing here had changed. The sacrifices that were made seemed a waste and it left a bitter taste in my mouth. Only war has the power to change a man.'

'It has certainly changed you. Although, I have to disagree with you,' said Edward, smiling. Joss suspected Edward wanted to lighten the mood. Edward's experience of the war had not been as long as his own, or as barbaric, yet even Edward's memories were not the sort that his friend would want to dwell on for too long. 'War is not the only thing that can change a man,' Edward continued. 'A woman can, too.'

'A man will not change for a woman,' replied Joss, looking down at the map. 'Unless he wants to, of course.'

Edward joined Joss and looked down at the map, too. 'So what is this new venture you have in mind?'

'This is a map of the North Cornish coast. I own this area ...' Joss pointed to two headlands. 'And this valley. I inherited it from my father. As a boy I often stayed with an aunt during the summer. An elderly aunt is not an entertaining playmate for a boy, so this beach and River Valley became my playground. Now it will be my new business venture. These cliffs are made of slate and I plan to extract it.'

Edward was not convinced and told him so. 'How do you know this?'

'An old miner, called Will Jago, lived in the valley and he told me so. He knew all there was to know about mining and he could recognise the quality of any mining material. I have been informed that the man has recently died, so now is a good time to exploit this fact.'

'Why now? Why have you not dug a quarry there before?'

'The man's home was there, and I did not want him to lose it.'

Edward laughed. 'Great God, you do have a heart! You do not care for a village full of people but you cared for this old man. Why?'

Joss gave a shrug. He tolerated Edward's teasing because they were friends, but both knew that no other man would have that privilege.

'He saved my life when I was a child. During those summers when I visited my aunt, he treated me as if I was his grandson. He taught me to fish, mend things, cut wood ... all manner of skills that I did not need. Yet it was one of the happiest times of my life. Now my aunt and Will Jago are dead, only the land remains.'

Joss decided to pour himself a drink after all. Edward watched him as he took his glass to stand and stare out of the window.

'Yet you want to destroy the place that brought you happiness,' said his friend.

Joss tipped his head back and finished his glass in one.

'Like I said,' he replied solemnly. 'War changes a man, and it changed me.'

Bodannock mine, one of the largest in Cornwall, was in fact made up of three engine houses. There was a rare beauty to the mine. Unusually, the steam engines were built upon protruding rocky stacks at the base of the cliff, with the sea lapping close to their foundations. Though constructed by man, they were part of the fabric of the coastline. Their eighty-foot towers, with the sea and cliffs as their backdrop, would have resembled castle towers in a fairy tale, but for the deafening noise, dirt and mine labourers on the cliff above. The mine employed up to four hundred people, women above ground and men below, in a network of complicated tunnels, which led out under the seabed. Unlike other mine owners in the county, Joss refused to employ anyone below the age of fourteen. Although it would have been cheaper, they were not as strong and he did not want a child's death on his hands.

Joss and Edward sat on horseback looking down on the mine workings and watching the bal maidens breaking the ore with their hammers. They were hardworking women, plain-spoken and coarse in their language. They spent their days breaking up the ore into smaller pieces before loading it onto trolleys and pushing it to the ore-crushing machine. Although their work was hard, they were paid well and preferred working at the mine to domestic service. Their large hoods protected them from the sun and flying debris. Their dresses, unusually short and showing their ankles in order not to hinder their work, did nothing for their appearance. Steadying his agitated horse, Edward saw a woman wipe her nose on her sleeve.

'They are an uncouth lot,' Edward said. He watched two of them converse using their own sign language, as the noise from the steam engine and tin stamp machinery made talking difficult.

'They are honest and reliable, Edward,' replied Joss. 'And they would have a few choice words with you if they thought you were disrespecting them.'

Edward nodded thoughtfully. 'Of that I have no doubt. Do they know that in a year only half of them will still have employment, and within two the mine will be closed?'

'No, not yet.' Joss looked down at his muddied boots. 'I have just been down Piper's shaft. I wanted to check the ladders are still sound and I spoke with Jacob, the mine captain. He says he can sniff more tin and he wants me to dig another shaft, but he has said this before and it came to nothing.'

Edward looked at him. 'You do not want to take a chance?'

Joss shook his head. 'No; if you take a chance and it does not work, you are considered a fool. I have not told Jacob I plan to close the mine, but he has been a mine captain since I was a boy and he knows the lie of the land. I can see it in his eyes that he knows that closure is on the cards, and it is the reason he is trying to persuade me to dig further. He is desperate.'

'Desperate to find tin?'

'Desperate to save the livelihoods of the surrounding villages.'

Impatient, their horses began to prance beneath them. They had been standing too long while they waited for Joss at the mine and now he was back they were eager to return home.

'You do not sound regretful that it will all be silent here, Joss. This is one of your largest mines. You are well known, well respected, even feared. Do you not enjoy your standing in the community?'

'Edward, I am only well known in the mining community. Cornish people stand united against the world, but within it there are different communities that do not mix. If I were to walk about the farm markets, the farmers would not know me. If I were to walk through the fishing communities, I would be a stranger to them. They would treat me no different, or perhaps even with a bit of contempt, as no work is harder than the one they were born into.'

Edward was satisfied with the answer; it was as he thought too. Changing the subject, he said, 'I have the costs for the purchase of mules and track lines for River Valley.'

Joss and Edward turned their horses for home.

'Good, I will look at them when we get back. However I have been notified of a fly in the ointment since I last saw you. Smoke and signs of life have been seen at Will Jago's cottage. Someone has moved into it before his dead body has turned cold. I was tempted to go there and beat them to a pulp, but violence is not the way and I refuse to use those means. I instructed my solicitor to deal with it but as yet he has had no response.'

He took out his father's fob watch and flicked it over in his fingers to look at the time, before encouraging his horse into a trot. Edward followed his lead. 'It is getting late,' Joss said. 'Karenza will wonder where we are.'

'I assume her husband is away again?' asked Edward, catching him up to ride beside him.

'Indeed. She is tired that her husband's job takes him away so much, but he was a captain of a ship when she met him and it goes with the territory. She gets lonely and wants company when he is away.'

'I look forward to seeing her again.'

'As do I. She is the only woman whose company I enjoy.'

A thought occurred to Edward and he frowned. 'When was the last time you visited River Valley?' he asked shrewdly. Perhaps there was another reason he wanted a solicitor to deal with his unwelcome guest, and had asked Edward to prepare the estimates for the quarry.

'Not since the day I said goodbye to Will Jago, when I was about to enter the army. I was eighteen.'

'Don't you want to see it again before it is destroyed?'

'No, I do not,' Joss said firmly as he dug his heels into his horse's side. It lurched forward into a gallop and Edward, unaware of his friend's tension, eagerly followed in hot pursuit.

The sleek horses and their riders left the dust and noise of the mine far behind them as they raced across the fields in the sunshine. However, the ride soon began to bore the former soldiers, so they headed for the muddy bridle paths that snaked through the woods, skirted ploughed fields and weed entangled riverbanks.

When they finally reached Joss's home, both men were splattered with mud from the waist down. A stable boy ran to greet them and took charge of their horses. Joss and Edward briskly entered the hall, saw a pair of women's gloves on the hall table and headed straight for the drawing room. They were both as breathless as their horses, but whereas Edward felt exhilarated, Joss remained solemn. A fact the woman who greeted them did not miss.

'You both look a mess,' she stated simply, looking them up and down with a raised eyebrow as they entered the drawing room. 'Joss, have you been down a mine? You look no better than a labourer. Have you been racing your horses again? You will break your necks one day.'

Karenza allowed her hand to be kissed by Edward, as Joss poured his friend a drink. She wrinkled her nose when Joss lifted an empty glass in her direction.

'You know I do not drink alcohol so early in the day. A cup of tea will suffice. I have already spoken to Mrs May.' She turned to Edward. 'How are your parents, Edward?'

'Very well, Karenza. How is your mother?'

'Spoilt rotten by Catherine.'

'What part of the world is William sailing to at the moment?'

'Canada. He sailed from Padstow last week. I hate it when he is away for so long.'

Mrs May came in and placed a tray before them. Out of courtesy to Karenza, Joss accepted a cup of tea rather than pouring himself a drink.

'The emigration trade from Cornwall and Devon to Canada is a lucrative one,' said Joss to Edward. 'William's ship will return in a few months with Canadian timber. Of course, with the demise of mining, many of our most skilled miners are using these routes to find work overseas. Padstow harbour has grown significantly from this trade.'

Karenza sighed. 'I wish there were something for William to do here.' She waved her hand at Joss to prevent him from speaking. 'I know ... he will never give up the sea, but perhaps there is something on land that still involves shipping in some way. Joss, you are well informed regarding business. Isn't there something you can do for your brother-in-law?'

Joss looked at his older sister's pleading eyes. 'Let me

think on it,' he said finally. 'But I do not promise anything. I know little of the maritime trade and it will need thoughtful consideration.'

'He spends his time teaching me about mining,' said Edward with a rueful smile. 'He thinks it will keep me out of mischief making.'

'You flatter me as I am no tutor,' said Joss. 'You happened to be by my side and watched as I struggled to make my father's business profitable. You know as much as I do now and need no lessons from me.'

'Now you flatter me, as my knowledge is not so great.' Edward turned to Karenza. 'However, if my help with the mine allows Joss time to consider how he might best offer help to you, than I am happy for you both.'

'It is all I ask,' Karenza said, smiling, before taking a sip of her tea. She looked about her. 'You should have more staff, Joss,' she chided. 'Mrs May runs the house, greets guests and brings the tea. You do have a cook, I hope.'

Joss knew it would not be long before his sister began to offer advice.

'Most of the time I am alone here, which is how I like it. It is not at my invitation Edward and you decide to stay for several days at a time.'

Edward and Karenza did not take offence; what he said was the truth.

'If we did not come to stay you would become a recluse.'

'The life of a recluse sounds favourable to being bullied into attending dinner parties with people I do not care for, and being matched with women who do not interest me.'

Karenza watched him get up and stand before the window. 'I know you do not feel like you fit in with those sorts of people, but they cannot help inheriting their wealth. You inherited your mines.'

'Not all were profitable at the time. But it is nothing to do with money. I just don't enjoy it.'

Karenza made a signal to Edward and Edward took his cue.

'If you will excuse me,' he said, standing abruptly. 'I really need to get out of these muddy clothes. You will still be here when I return, Karenza?'

Karenza nodded. 'Yes, Edward, I will.' She waited for him to leave before she joined her brother. 'You enjoy looking at the garden,' she said quietly as she slipped her arm through his.

'It gives me peace.'

Karenza had an idea, and perhaps the garden would be an ideal setting to broach it. 'I would like to take a turn in it. Walk with me,' she said.

Brother and sister walked in silence through the garden. Modest in size, its flowers, shrubs and trees provided a peaceful oasis from Joss's busy life. Butterflies and bees flew from flower to flower, while cheerful birdsong filtered down to them through the branches of the trees. After a while, Karenza could see Joss relax and finally she felt it was time to talk to him about her thoughts.

She gave his arm a squeeze. 'I worry for you, Joss. Each time I visit, you look a little more tired. Have the nightmares returned?'

Joss did not answer straight away but finally relented. 'I don't think they have ever really gone away.'

'Yet I feel that there is a greater sadness in your eyes, a burden that seems to weigh heavier and heavier on you. Has the war of the states brought back old memories?'

'My memories have never left me. I wish they would, but I confess that they have come to the forefront of my mind when before I could lock them away for most of the day.'

They continued to walk in silence, their footsteps rhythmic and as one.

'Perhaps you should take a holiday, Joss. Edward returned quite refreshed from his time away, and you might, too.'

'I did not know you had seen Edward since he returned. He did not mention it.'

Karenza realised she had said more than she should, but decided that she could not lie to Joss.

'I wrote to Edward to ask how you were.'

'Spying?'

Karenza looked at him sheepishly. 'I think that is a little harsh. We are both concerned for you. You know Edward thinks the world of you and I'm sure he would be happy to look after your businesses while you have a break of a month or so.'

Joss laughed, but his laughter was hollow.

'I am serious, Joss. I am worried about you. We all are.'

'All?'

'Mother, Catherine and William,' Karenza replied. Joss swore. 'It is only because we love you,' insisted his sister. 'We have left it too long to mention anything before. We thought by encouraging you to go to functions—'

'—you would cheer me up?' Joss finished for her. 'You thought parading women past me with nothing in their heads but finding a suitable husband with money would cheer me up?'

Karenza gave his arm a little shake. 'It may not have been the best tactic to use, but my intentions were good. You work from dawn to dusk and you have no interest in finding a wife. Soon you will be an old man with no children to inherit all that you have built up. There is more to life than work, Joss. Please, just think about it.'

Joss halted and looked at Karenza. She was his favourite of his two sisters, as they shared the same humour, wit, and intellect. He cared deeply for her and normally would do anything for her, but he did not feel that taking a holiday was a good idea. He looked into his sister's pained eyes. He saw the concern for his welfare etched on her face and he wanted to take that anxiety away.

I do not deserve to feel happy, but Karenza does and she cannot while she worries for me.

Joss turned away from her to study the horizon. He felt responsible, even a bit betrayed. He did not like the idea that the two most important people in his life discussed him as if he were a fragile invalid. Perhaps going away would put an end to their discussions.

For the first time he began to seriously consider her suggestion. If he went away, when should he go? If he waited it would coincide with the extraction of slate from the valley and the announcement of the imminent closure of the mine. If he were to go away it must be soon. Yet, what about leaving his businesses? Edward was well informed regarding the mine and valley. He could leave them in his care. There were no excuses to delay and the more he thought about leaving it all behind him, the more enticing it seemed. It would not cure him of his nightmares, but it would stop them plotting behind his back.

He was not a man who acted on impulse. Yet a strange sensation now pulsed through his veins, and he had the desire to shock them all by leaving today. The sooner he left, the sooner he would return. It would make them happy, although he knew that in reality it would change nothing.

'You win. I will go and visit friends in London.' He turned abruptly and began to walk back to Bras-stenack House.

Startled that he had agreed, Karenza belatedly ran after him.

'You will?'

'It is what you wanted. I will leave tonight. No ... I will leave this very minute.'

'There is no need to rush, tomorrow will suffice. It will give Mrs May time to pack your trunk.'

Joss shook his head. 'No, one bag will be enough. I will leave as I am and the sooner the better.'

Edward was waiting for them in the hall as Joss entered with Karenza in hot pursuit.

'He has gone quite mad.' Karenza looked at Edward.

'I suggested a holiday and he wants to leave now, this very minute!'

Joss walked straight to his bedroom and began to pack a small bag. Encouraged by Karenza, Edward followed him.

'Joss, old friend, there is no hurry. What about your mines? What about River Valley?'

'You can keep an eye on the mines, and there is no rush with starting the slate quarry. I will leave you in charge of evicting the hoodlum who has moved into Will Jago's house. Do what you need to do to sort that problem out and when I return we will be in a position to begin setting up the slate extraction facilities.'

'I'm honoured that you trust me with this. But are you sure, Joss?'

Joss straightened, picked up his bag and shrugged. 'It is what you both want. I know you have conspired together to have me go away, and now you look surprised I have taken you up on your suggestion.'

Edward followed Joss down the stairs where Karenza was waiting for him in the hall.

'There is no conspiracy,' Edward argued. Joss threw him a doubtful look. 'Well, perhaps a little, although I did not know Karenza was going to suggest a holiday.'

'It is true. I saw the pleasure you got from looking at your garden. It is no secret you based it on the valley where you spent your summer holidays exploring, so I thought that another holiday would do you some good.' She looked disapprovingly at his single, small bag. 'I did not expect you to travel like a tramp with muddied clothes and no belongings! You are behaving like this to prove some point or other, to make me persuade you to stay.'

Joss softened. 'No, Karenza, I am not,' he said reassuringly. 'You are right. A break will do me good and I have not been to London for a long time. I may travel a little after my visit ... Scotland has always fascinated me. I will be back in a month or so, no more.' He kissed her cheek and shook Edward's hand. 'Thank you, Edward, for looking after things for me. Treat my home as if it were your own. I would trust no one but you to manage things while I am away.'

Edward smiled. 'I need no encouragement in that, my friend. Go away and enjoy yourself and when you are ready, come home.'

Joss nodded. 'I will take a coach to the station and from there catch a train to London. There is no need to worry, Karenza,' he said as he looked at his sister's worried expression. 'I will be there before nightfall and your plan will be in action. I will come back a changed man.'

'We don't want you to change, Joss,' Karenza said softly. 'We just want the old Joss back again. The one I remember fondly.'

'I cannot promise I will find him,' he teased before leaving to find the stable boy.

Edward watched him go. 'Karenza,' he said quietly as he came to stand beside her. 'You hope for too much. The Joss you remember will never return. He died on the battlefield of Sebastopol.'

Deep in thought, Joss stood on the station platform and looked down on the track. Despite the crowd, and the usual hustle and bustle of people waiting for their train, Joss felt quite alone. As alone as the tramp he had seen earlier, who had furtively looked about before searching a bin for something to eat. The smell of oil, coal and damp brick lingered in the air and infiltrated Joss's nostrils, dampening what little appetite he had. The squeaking of a trolley's wheels grated on his nerves and the incessant chatter of the waiting people provided a constant noise that pierced his temples and stabbed at his brain. Only the stationmaster's announcement concerning the arrival of a train on the opposite platform claimed his interest. Joss looked up.

'The train will be stopping at Pelbury, Downtor, Killygrew, Castlecorn ...' Joss recognised Killygrew. He smiled inwardly at the thought of the small town. As if to tease him further, an old man with a young boy walked past him. The old man reminded Joss of Will Jago, the old miner who had once saved his life as a child, and he wondered if the child was his grandson. Joss had been an only son and had felt his own father's emotional distance keenly. Will Jago had filled that void all those years ago.

He had spent each summer with his aunt, but was left to wander and entertain himself on the beach leading to River Valley. One day he had plucked up the courage to thank the old miner who he knew now lived in the cottage by the trees. That day was the beginning of a firm friendship between them. As each year passed, and Joss grew taller, their friendship continued as if there had never been a break. Will had treated him like the son he never had and told Joss that his only child, a daughter, had run away and had later died in a workhouse. When Joss was eighteen, his father had bought him a commission in the 46th Regiment of Foot. The last time Joss had seen Will Jago was on the day he bid him farewell. He had arrived at Will's cottage dressed in his uniform, keen for the old man to see the man he had become. He wanted the old miner to be proud of him, and strangely that mattered more to him than what his own father felt. And Will Jago was proud; apart from a knock on the door momentarily disturbing the old miner, it had been a good farewell between them.

Joss had promised to write, but he was young and did not. His new life and friends kept him busy and soon his time with Will Jago became a distant memory – and then the war started. After the war, and on the death of his father, Joss inherited River Valley. He sold his commission and returned to take over the mines, but by then his experience of battle had made him bitter. He could not face visiting the valley or the old man. He did not want the miner to see the change in him and wanted him to remember him as he once was. However, he had heard ill health meant he was struggling to support himself and maintain the cottage. To make up for his lack of contact, he arranged for a payment to be sent to Will each year. It was a generous sum, equivalent to a miner's wage. The same amount he would have earned had his lungs not been damaged by his time down his family's mines. It was a salve on a wound that Joss dared not see. Instead he buried himself in his father's mining business, determined to make it profitable. But what good had it done? His father was dead, and so was Will Jago; yet strangely it was Will Jago's death that he felt the most grief for. It angered him that someone would move into his cottage with no respect for the man.

Joss watched the train arrive on the opposite platform in a cloud of steam. The doors opened and people spilled out onto the platform on the other side of the train. He could just see them between the remaining passengers as they gazed out of the windows, read their papers or talked. They were heading in the opposite direction to the journey he was about to make, yet he envied them. Suddenly his own train arrived and its doors swung open. Passengers exited the train and pooled in groups about him blocking his view of the one bound for Killygrew. He felt a sense of loss that he could no longer see it. It felt as if the only connection he had with Killygrew had been severed. Now he could only glimpse it through the carriage windows. He felt himself jostled by someone. Rooted to the spot, he was in the way and people around him were becoming impatient. He heard doors beginning to close and he knew that soon the other train would be leaving.

Suddenly, he wanted to see River Valley again. He ran along the length of the platform to the footbridge that would take him to the other side, dodging couples, jumping over bags and almost crashing into a trolley as he went. He climbed the wooden steps two at a time and ran across the wooden planks, his footfalls echoing surprisingly loudly in the enclosed passageway that took him over the tracks. He skidded at the corner before descending down the stairs to the platform almost falling in his haste. Most of the train doors had already been slammed shut by the platform guard. Only two remained open and, as luck would have it, they were near to Joss. He jumped across the gap between platform and carriage onto the train heading south to Killygrew. He sat down in a vacant seat feeling a mixture of exhilaration, confusion and surprise at his sudden change in plans.

It was only as the train moved away, and he watched the platform opposite being left behind, that he realised he had left his bag and most of his money on the platform unattended. No matter, he would hire a horse and have the bill sent to his home. If he had any plans they were only to visit River Valley once more, confront the man who had moved into the cottage and return the next day to continue his journey to London. Joss settled himself back into his seat. The corners of his lips lifted ruefully as he imagined the tramp picking up his bag and carrying it to the nearest public convenience. Joss knew that within a few minutes the bag would be empty and discarded in a bin, its contents made use of by a man with nothing to call his own. Joss closed his eyes to block the world out. Not a single soul who knew him would know where he was or where he was going. He was quite alone, free, with no plans he had to adhere to. And for those few minutes it felt good.

Joss sat on his hired horse and looked down on the valley. He had been watching the little house for some time and it was as he had been informed: there were clear signs it was inhabited. Gulls screeched in the distance and a cool breeze from the Atlantic chilled his skin, yet neither distracted him from watching the old building nestled amongst the trees of the beautiful River Valley. From his vantage point high on the cliff, he could see the full length of the valley, and despite his lengthy scrutiny of the area, he had seen no one. Suddenly, a young woman emerged from the cottage to peg a garment on the washing line. Her long black hair and skirts lifted and tossed in the breeze as she did so, before she disappeared again behind the old cottage door. So this was the person who had taken Will's home and claimed it as her own.

Joss had had enough, and without taking his eyes off the cottage he gradually rode down the earthy track. Although narrow and ancient, it held firm beneath him. He did not fear falling as he had travelled the track many times as a boy and he knew it well. As he neared his destination, the gurgling of the river welcomed his arrival, but the sound of the water did not give him the pleasure he thought it would. He had been numb for too long and any hope that the sight and sounds of this coastline would unlock any emotions from their dormant state had already been dashed.

After tying up his horse, he approached the door of the cottage. It was closed, yet that did not deter him in his goal. He wanted to confront the person inside and throw them out himself. The door gave way easily to his pressure. He entered with no announcement or greeting. Within seconds a cloak of painful blackness engulfed him.

Chapter Fourteen

Present Day
Summer 1861

'There is a storm coming,' said Bill, nodding to the clouds that had infiltrated the sky and cast a dark ominous shadow over the valley. 'I knew there would be one. When the birds stop singing and go to their nests, you know they have sensed it on the wind.'

Beth looked up at the vast grey clouds edged in white light, as the sun tried in vain to break through the insidious invasion. The power of nature, together with an impending sense of doom that only an approaching storm emanates, felt oppressive to Beth. It was as if God was sending a message of sorrow, anger and revenge to match Beth's mood. Deprived of the sunshine, the valley appeared bleak and neglected. Beth wondered if she was now seeing it in its true colours, or if Joss Roscarrock had robbed her of its joy by his betrayal – the extent of which she would learn when she knew the truth about his memory loss. It was time she found it out. She climbed down from the cart.

'Thank you for taking me, Bill,' she said.

'Do you want me to come with you?'

Beth shook her head. 'No, I will be fine.'

She waited for Bill to leave before turning and making her way down the track towards the valley. It gave her precious minutes to be alone with her thoughts. Discovering that her grandfather had received money from a benefactor had shocked Beth. Her grandfather was a proud man, and it was probably for this reason that he did not tell Beth that he was living on charity. Yet Beth's ability to trust had been surely damaged by this omission. When she recognised Joss in the painting, she felt she had been lied to again. Her heart had felt raw, her anger rivalled only by the bitterness deep inside her. The long ride home, and the rhythmic beat of the horses' hooves on the track, had calmed the emotions arising from the new discovery. Her ability to reason had gradually returned. It was possible that she was judging Joss too harshly and there was no ruse. Perhaps Joss did not know he was Roscarrack. She hoped he did not. Yet, if he did not, should she tell him? If she did he would return to his home and continue with his plans for River Valley. She would lose her home and Joss. What if she did *not* tell him who he was? They would move away and live as man and wife. However, Beth would know that they were living a lie, and would dread the day that he discovered she had known all the time. As if to torment her, her thoughts came full circle and she began to wonder again if Joss knew who he was. She was getting nearer to home. She knew she must choose her words carefully if she wanted to discover the truth.

Beth heard the cottage door open and looked up. Joss stepped out and was watching her approach. His timely appearance told her he had been waiting for her. He stood in the doorway as if ready for battle, a stance she had seen many times before. She could see his connection to the army and wondered how she had missed it. Was he waiting for her, or standing guard to stop her from entering? The man who had laughed, smiled and kissed her was gone. In his place was a man with a solemn expression – of disappointment.

'You did not wake me.' Beth tried to pass him but he barred her way. 'Why?'

Beth looked into his eyes. The same hazel eyes that had mesmerised her before and still did each time she allowed herself the pleasure of looking into them. She looked away.

'Am I not allowed in?' she asked.

A momentary tense silence descended between them until a sudden gust of wind dusted them with leaves and broken twigs. Joss stepped aside and Beth entered the cottage. It was late afternoon, but the storm had already sucked the light from the day. Joss lit a lamp, its warm glow casting a soft light about the room and onto the straw weave of her hat, which she had taken off and placed carefully on the table. It was her best hat, and she had worn it to give the impression that she was a responsible woman who could take on a lease. Now that she had glimpsed Joss's world it looked cheap and labelled her as a poor country girl. As if to remove further traces of her earlier intentions, she unpinned her hair and placed the pins neatly beside it. Her black hair lay loose about her shoulders, and despite still wearing her best dress her appearance had now subtly changed to how she had looked when he had first met her.

'What did you learn?' he asked.

She touched her hat with her fingertips. 'I have learnt that the valley is to be quarried for slate.'

Beth shot him a glance, looking for any signs of awareness. His face remained unchanged; his steely gaze did not waver. She pushed her hat away from her.

'I learnt that the owner of this valley lives in opulence and he cares nothing for the community, let alone me.'

Joss lifted his chin but said nothing.

'I learnt that I cannot extend the lease, and that I must leave.' She frowned, unsure how to proceed. He had given nothing away. Did he really not know who he was? Had he still no memory of his past at all?

'Who told you this?' he asked finally.

'Mr Nankervis. He is managing things while Mr Roscarrock is away. He took great delight in telling me this.'

Joss considered her reply. Distant lightning flashed, followed by a low grumble of thunder, the only sound to break the silence.

Joss spoke, his words decisive and clear. 'Edward is only doing what I asked him to do.'

Beth's mouth went dry. He had confessed and yet she could not quite believe what he had said. It was as if he had reached across the room, grabbed her heart and wrenched it from her chest. The pain of her heart's destruction, and the vacant hole it left behind, was too much to bear. She clutched her chest in shock, before turning into a feral cat and launching herself at him.

'You bastard!' she cried, hitting and grabbing at his clothes. 'You lied! You have always known who you were. You have tried to worm your way into my affections to persuade me to leave, while your thugs and solicitor make me fearful for my life and my rights!' She wanted to tear him apart, to scratch him, to kill him. 'I wish I had killed you! What a fool I was, to feel guilty about protecting myself from a man like you. A man who works his miners until they can hardly draw breath.'

Joss had taken her hits, but he would tolerate them no longer. He grabbed her wrists, turned her around and wrapped his arms about her from behind. She struggled to be free of him but he held her tight.

'A man who desires profit over the health and the future of his workers,' she continued breathlessly. 'A man who works his miners until their lungs become so diseased they cannot work again!' She slipped free from him and smacked his face. 'A man who cares nothing for anyone but himself. No wonder they call you ruthless!'

Joss grabbed her wrists again and pinned her against the wall. His grip shackled her wrists, but did not hurt her.

'A businessman has to be ruthless to earn profit, and without profit there would be no work for your precious community. So stop the recriminations about something you know nothing about, especially where your grandfather was concerned. Will was like a father to me and I paid him a wage until he died. I did not know you existed!'

Beth struggled to free herself, so Joss pressed his firm body against her, forcing her to stop. She felt his warm breath against her hair.

'It is true that I came with the intention to remove you from the house. I *did* lose my memory and I have only recently regained it. I did not know who you were. Everything is different now.'

Beth turned her head away, reluctant to let her guard down, too fearful to trust him again.

'You are unwilling to forgive me?' The pressure of Joss's body lessened. She had hurt him by her rebuff. 'I have been out of my mind waiting for your return so I could explain. But instead of understanding you turn away?'

Beth continued to avert her gaze, too angry or too stubborn to believe him so easily.

'You are not the only one hurting,' said Joss, his lips touching the top of her head as he spoke. 'You left and did not wake me. Why didn't you tell me where you were going?'

'For you to tell me more lies?'

'I have not lied to you.'

Beth tried to shake him off but he would not have it. 'You are lying to me now!' she shouted close to his ear. Momentarily he loosened his grip and she tried to escape but he grabbed her around the waist from behind and held her arms tight across her body. Once again her body was encased in his arms.

'I have never lied to you,' he said, holding her tighter than before. 'What has happened to us? Yesterday we were a hair's breadth away from becoming lovers and today we fight as cat and dog. Damn it woman, I demand to know!'

Suddenly the fighting instinct that had taken hold of her left her body and she relaxed.

'When I mentioned the name Roscarrock at Truro, I saw the recognition in your eyes. You knew the name, yet you did not tell me.'

'I recognised it, but I did not know it was me.'

'Yet, magically your memory has returned today, on the very day I discover your identity.' Joss had relaxed his grip and she pushed his hands aside and walked free. 'How convenient.' She began to pace the room. 'I have been such a fool. So many times you have given yourself away, yet I was too foolish to be suspicious. Your knowledge of support pillars in mining, knowing the meaning of Kynance Cottage, knowing your way around Truro ...' She turned to him. 'You have taken me for a fool and I did not prove you otherwise.'

Joss reached for her but she stepped away as if he had the plague.

He let his hand fall to his side. 'I have never lied to you. I have told you that sometimes I remember things, but that I do not know which are true memories and which are false. When I read your note it all came back to me.'

Beth laughed in disbelief. 'In one fell swoop.'

'I know it must sound strange,' Joss conceded, 'but it was like a floodgate had been opened and everything fell into place.'

'At the same time I found you out.'

'Yes.'

'As I said ... how convenient. It sounds to me more like a poorly written play!' she scoffed.

Joss's hurt changed to anger and he reached for her. Cupping her face in his hands so she could not look away, he said, 'I have not lied to you about who I am, or my feelings for you.' His hazel eyes captured hers once again, their centres almost black as they took in her image. 'But you have lied to me. You led me to believe that my feelings for you were returned. Yet when you had a choice to leave this place and start a new life where no one knows us, a new life with me, as my wife, you did not choose it. Like a coward you slipped out of the cottage without waking me, and sought out Roscarrock. You chose a cottage over a life with me. I am Joss Roscarrock, but I am also the man who hugged and kissed you at Truro, the man who wanted to spend the rest of his life with you.'

As if he could not bear to only look at her any longer, he kissed her. It was passionate, short-lived and almost painful in its intensity. From the look in his eyes, she believed it was only a token of what he really wanted from her. She had shown him only her hatred and anger, yet he had done it all the same.

His kiss began to work its magic, softening her anger towards him and leaving her wanting more, but she quickly regained her senses. It was just an opportunity to show his power and dominance over her, and like a selfish man he had taken it.

'The man who wanted me never existed,' Beth said coldly as he withdrew from her lips.

Joss frowned as if he did not recognise her and said as much.

Arching her eyebrow, and as coolly as she could manage, she replied, 'I have not changed, I have just had my eyes opened.'

Joss stepped away from her. 'Keep Kynance Cottage, it is yours,' he said suddenly. 'Live a lonely existence here. You made it clear that there is nothing more important to you than this house when you did not wake me this morning. You would rather secure a longer lease here, knowing that we could not live as man and wife amongst a community who knew that we were not married. Any marriage between us would have been void until the day I could truly prove my marital status and I could only do that when I knew my true identity. There was a way for us to be together, a new start, a new home, but you preferred to stay here where we could not be together. I was willing to leave everything to be with you. I gambled that I would prefer a life with you over any other life I might have had. I was willing to leave it all for you, but you were not willing to do the same for me. I would not have left you as your father did.' Joss saw the doubt in her face.

'You do not believe anything I say. If I had known who I was, and planned to take the cottage from you, why would I spend these last few weeks repairing it?'

'To deceive me.'

Joss's anger rose sharply at the injustice of her accusations. 'I can think of less tiring ways to do that. Why would I not throw your belongings out of the house when you were doing your rounds at Port Carrek? Or today? I had plenty of time on my own here to empty it.'

Beth's confidence began to wane. She turned away from him, but he would not let her. With his hands on her shoulders, he forced her to face him. His anger faded as he looked into her eyes.

'Is this the end of something that never really had a chance to start? I have struggled to remain loyal to a wife that I didn't remember. I nearly did not succeed. It is not easy for a man to live with a pretty woman such as you and not want her.' He stroked her jawline with a single finger. 'Now I see that you do not want me. So how do we part, Beth? As friends? As lovers? Or perhaps as enemies? If I were to kiss you goodbye, would it be our last?'

She remained still, bracing herself for him to do as he wanted. Now the truth was discovered, and bitter words between them spoken, their relationship would never be the same again. If he kissed her now, it was very likely that it would be their last.

'You look as if you are waiting to be sacrificed,' he said sadly. He rested his forehead against hers. She saw his struggle in his eyes and felt his fevered brow. The repercussions of their fight struck her; how could their wounds ever heal? A basic need to experience one last passionate kiss with him took hold of her. As if in a trance, she allowed her body to respond to him, and without knowing what she was doing, she leaned towards him, tilted her face upwards and parted her lips slightly. Joss pulled away, leaving her feeling humiliated at his rejection. She silently berated herself for giving in so easily to his presence and was glad he was no longer looking at her.

'I will not give you a farewell kiss, Miss Jago. We do not part on such good terms. You sought out Roscarrock and now you have found him. Roscarrock is back, and God help you, as God will not help him.'

He left her swaying for support as he went to the door and swung it open.

'Where are you going?' asked Beth. He stood on the threshold and looked at the flash of lightning illuminating the dark grey clouds in the sky.

'I'm going home.'

'What are you going to do?' It seemed such a feeble question, even to her own ears, but his plans for the future meant everything to her.

He turned his head to the side, but would not look at her.

'Joss. What are you going to do with the cottage?'

'The cottage?' He turned one final time to look at her, his dark frame silhouetted in the door frame as thunder rumbled around the valley. 'Keep it. Enjoy it on your own. It can burn to the ground for all I care.'

He watched Beth's horrified face, but it appeared to give him no pleasure. Instead, as if he despised his own words and could stomach no more, he turned and walked out into the swirling wind and heavy rain of the storm. Beth stood alone with her prize of the cottage, yet with the overwhelming feeling that she had lost everything she held dear.

Chapter Fifteen

Beth sat by the fire. Like a wounded animal gone to ground she had sought Martha out at the end of her deliveries and now took comfort in her surroundings. The small room, cluttered with things that Martha had collected over the years, wrapped her in a blanket of normality and security. Dimly lit by one small window, the room smelt of herbs, flowers and a faint odour of fish, a sign that Martha had spent the morning packing fresh pilchards from the latest fishing catch.

'Ow long 'as it been since 'e left?' Martha asked her as she handed Beth a dish of mugwort tea. She pointed a bent gnarled finger at the brew. 'I've added mint and St John's wort to 'elp relax you. You look as if you 'ave not slept well these past few days.'

Beth gratefully took it in her cupped hands. 'Eight days come this evening.'

Martha looked shrewdly at her as she lifted her own dish to her lips. 'Not just *about a week*, but exactly *eight days*,' she said, before taking a noisy sip.

Beth looked away and hid herself behind her cup.

'I 'ad 'eard the gossip that 'e was still living under your roof. I expected you to 'ave sent 'im on 'is way as soon as 'e was better.' She took another noisy sip to cool the steaming liquid. ''Ard to send packing, was 'e? I expect 'is good looks 'ad something to do with it.'

Beth sunk lower in her chair. Martha noticed.

'Are you 'iding something from me, girl? You 'aven't let 'im 'ave 'is way with you?'

'No! I'm not so foolish as my mother, Martha.'

Martha smiled, relieved. 'Tempted though, weren't you?'

Beth sighed. 'It's all such a mess, Martha.' Beth explained what had happened.

'You wonder if it was all a trick?'

Beth nodded sullenly.

'You thought 'e was falling in love with you and now you think 'e wasn't?' Beth looked up surprised. 'You can try to look innocent but you were seen looking into each other's eyes at the bonfire. I saw you, my Tom saw you and a few others too, no doubt. Sounds like you 'ave 'ad your pride 'urt.'

'He claims to feel the same. He believed I was falling in love with him but now he feels I was not.' In an attempt to explain further she added, 'Before his memory returned he wanted me to move away with him and live as man and wife. He says he would never have left me, even if his memory had returned after we had set up house together. But how can a man promise that? What if he was already married? Even if he was single, my children would be illegitimate because they were not born in wedlock. If I had run away with him, I would have been as foolish as my mother. So I refused.'

'Very wise, maid,' said Martha.

'Oh, Martha. Now we both know who he is, things are no better. He lives in a house that is bigger than any I have ever seen before! He *owns* mines. Even his garden is larger than the biggest park. His hall is bigger than all the rooms put together in many cottages hereabouts. I am a *nobody* compared to the people he must meet on a daily basis. Brought up in a workhouse and illegitimate. Would a man of means really want to be tied to someone like me? I would be an embarrassment to him. He made plans for us to be together when he was not fully recovered. What sort of woman would I be to take advantage of that? Some women would stake their claim to him by ensuring they had his son in their belly. I am not one of those women.'

'Seems to me, you think you are not good enough for 'im. You question if a man of 'is standing in society could fall in love with you. I believe you find it easier to think 'e lied about 'is feelings in order to 'ave you removed. The fact that you 'ave always 'ad a bad opinion of the rich made it very easy for you to believe this. You are quick to doubt their word and you are quick to judge.' Martha waved a finger at her. 'I can understand you feeling that way, girl. Your parents made a mess of things and you are frightened of doing the same.'

Beth placed her dish on the floor by her chair. 'I've had plenty of time to think about the mistakes my parents made and how to avoid making them myself. It is what occupied my mind as a child while I tried to keep warm in the workhouse, on a hard bed and surrounded by noises from other inmates.'

'Yet you 'ave fallen in love with the owner of Kynance Cottage, and the cottage remains a link between you, whether you like it or not.' Martha heard a noise in the next room. 'We must talk no more,' she whispered. 'That must be Tom coming 'ome and 'e 'as a liking for you, Beth. Talking about your affection for another man will confuse him.'

Martha eased herself up from the chair and left the room to greet him, but soon returned.

'Strange, I thought I 'eard the door open. I thought it was Tom. I will check 'is room.'

Beth watched the older woman leave and listened to the floorboards of the house creak as she moved about the rooms above her. The search did not take long as it was not a big house, boasting no more than four rooms. ''E is not 'ere, I must 'ave mis'eard.'

'Perhaps it was the wind?' suggested Beth helpfully. 'When is he due home?'

Martha settled herself down in her chair but it was obvious she remained troubled.

''E comes and goes as 'e pleases. Sometimes 'e is gone so long I barely see 'im. I wonder what 'e does, where 'e spends 'is day, but when 'e comes 'ome 'e seems content – most of the time.' Martha glanced to the window and bit her lip. 'I do worry for 'im though, and what will become of 'im when I am gone.'

'Would you like me to care for him, Martha? I would if it would ease your mind.'

Martha shook her head. 'No dear, it's not easy caring for someone special like my Tom. 'E is a darling most of the time, but sometimes 'e gets confused and distressed. 'E don't understand the ways of the world as normal folk. Sometimes I just want to wrap my arms about 'im to comfort 'im when 'e is upset, but you know my Tom, 'e doesn't like that sort of thing. Makes 'im feel boxed in, I suppose, as 'e wants to break free.' Martha collected the empty dishes. 'This talk is depressing. What about you? What will you do now?'

'Joss says I can stay in the cottage, but I suspect he will do as he pleases with the valley. We parted on bad terms. He is angry with me for not believing him, and I would not be surprised if he wants to seek his revenge on me. He has taken all the joy of living in the cottage. I no longer feel any contentment when I am inside it. It feels empty, cold and quiet. The silence is at times deafening. It seems worse than the first few weeks after grandfather died. It is as though he has put a curse on it. It feels like bricks and mortar, without the heart of a home.'

'Perhaps 'e 'as already 'eard the same silence as you do now,' said Martha wisely. Beth looked up questioningly. 'Perhaps 'e 'eard it when you left 'im to search for Roscarrock. There is nothing worse than the pain of rejection, Beth, and it makes you say cruel things. It's understandable. It cannot be easy to discover that despite offering your 'eart to someone, they 'ave chosen to turn elsewhere. The pain in your 'eart is as real as if they stepped upon it as they left.'

'Martha, you sound like you know what it feels like.'

'I 'ave felt it every day since Tom was born, Beth. I love 'im and I want to show my love for 'im, but 'e accepts none of it and gives nothing in return. I offer 'im my 'eart every day, since the day 'e was born, and each time 'e rejects me.'

'Martha, he does love you. He just doesn't know how to show it.'

Martha nodded. 'I know, but it still 'urts, although I comfort myself that 'e does not do it on purpose. One day 'e will let me 'ug 'im and that will be a 'appy day for us both. I just 'ope I get the chance before I die.' She went to the door, opened it and glanced up and down the narrow road looking for her son. 'I 'ope 'e won't be long. I know 'e is a young man now and watched over by the villagers, but I still 'ave a 'aunting fear that 'e will run into trouble. It is a worry I 'ave 'ad for a long time now.'

She came back into the house and smiled at Beth who was collecting her things to leave. 'My grandmother used to say that if you think too much about something that is worrying you, it will 'appen. As a young woman, not blessed with good looks, I often worried that I would not find a man to love me.'

Beth gave her a hug goodbye. 'Well, that did not happen, Martha.'

Martha patted Beth's cheek with a sad smile on her face. 'Yes it did, child. I married a man who was cold, and I 'ave a son like Tom. My grandmother was a wise woman and I should 'ave taken 'eed of 'er words.'

Beth opened the door and was about to step into the street, when Martha suddenly grasped her wrist to stop her.

'Look after yourself, Beth. I want you to know that you are as dear to me as if you were my own daughter.'

Beth smiled reassuringly. 'I know, Martha. Don't fret over Tom. I'm sure he will be home soon.'

Martha's grip tightened, and suddenly she grew fearful. It was if she had had a glimpse into the future and it had worried her.

'I love you, Beth,' she said urgently. 'Whatever 'appens in the future remember that I love you.'

Beth nodded. Confused by her words, she stepped out into the narrow road of Port Carrek. The sudden brightness of the sunlight, after the dark cottage, blinded her for a moment. When her eyes had become accustomed to the outside world, she turned to question Martha further only to find that her door was already shut. Beth felt shaken. Had Martha had a premonition? Her friend was not prone to them, but if she did Beth wasn't sure she wanted to know. She had enough bad thoughts to weigh her down, namely Joss's parting words and absence. The man never left her thoughts. Joss Roscarrock, the man she hated to love.

Tom watched the flames of the fire as they twisted and turned, their red glow reflecting in his wide excited eyes. Some of the flames were small and fragile, like children, yet others grew tall and strong. Their movement always mesmerised Tom, and for a time he forgot about the confusing world about him.

He had heard his mother talking to Beth about the man from the valley. Tom had stood silently in the next room, listening to their words through the crack in the door. He had heard it all, as they talked of love and the cottage he owned. He heard Beth's sadness – and then he could listen no more.

Gradually the fire merged to form orange sheets of heat that spread from the log pile to devour the wooden door. Their appetite became insatiable as the animal of flame moved onwards to devour the contents, belching black smoke to send a message to the world it was here. Tom watched the angry flames lick the evening sky through the roof and felt uneasy that the fire was taking over the cottage. Soon all the wooden rafters had ignited and a sheet of flame ran like a river across the roof, fed by the bitumen that had been used to seal the roof in days gone by.

Tom became frightened. Fires had always remained tame, not like this wild beast. He had never seen a river of fire like the one that had begun to devour Beth's cottage. It was as though the devil was clutching the little house in its hand and crushing it. Tom attempted to put it out by blowing on it with puffed cheeks. The heat was too much so he ran for a bucket.

He had not meant to cause so much damage. He had wanted to burn the woodpile the man had collected, not the cottage itself.

Grasping a bucket, Tom headed for the river. He dipped the bucket into the fast flowing water and made his way back up the bank. He had watched Joss chop wood for Beth for weeks, and his frustration and jealousy had grown. Tom slipped and fell. Precious water spilled from his bucket, but he did not have the sense to return and refill it. He climbed back up the muddy riverbank with the half full bucket of water carried lopsidedly in his hand. Water seeped over the edge to leave a trail behind him. Out of breath, and satisfied all would be well in the end, he finally came to stand before the flames. Feeling confident he could stop the fire, he mustered all his strength and threw the now empty bucket into the fire. The heat scorched his skin and he took a step back. His effort had done nothing to help and he realised that his mother would be angry with him when she found out what he had done. Beth's home was being destroyed before his eyes. She would have to live with him. He smiled. The thought of Beth living with him and his mother was nice. He watched the flames rise tall into the night sky and felt the wind at his back. He could not help but admire the power and noise a large fire could make. The sight took hold of him again and gave him comfort, something he had difficulty finding elsewhere. As Tom watched the flames destroy Kynance Cottage, he retreated into a world that made him feel at peace. In his world he forgot about the dangers of the Cornish wind, for the Cornish wind can turn on a penny and now howled at his back. On its haphazard journey up the valley, the wind suddenly changed direction. It whipped up the flames that had been leaning eastwards, and in its frenzied dance twisted them on their stalks to turn westwards and towards Tom. Their fingerlike touch ignited his clothes in a blink of an eye, and like a human torch he ran screaming for the river. The wind and the flames took no pity on the boy, and while the flames scorched his body, the wind captured his cries in its clutches and took them out to sea.

Beth made her way home on the road she had walked a hundred times before. The barrow, full of clothes she had collected to mend, shuddered rhythmically with each step, indicating that there was something wrong with the wheel again. It was yet another reminder that Joss would not be waiting for her when she returned home, as he would have mended it. In recent weeks she had walked this journey with a happy step, knowing that the mysterious man with no past would be waiting for her. Any energy or happiness she had felt before had now left her and each step that took her back to her empty cottage felt like walking through thick mud.

She missed the man who had waited for her return, who had spent the day putting her house to rights despite having troubles of his own. She had heard his nightmares, she had heard him speak his fears in his dreams, yet she had felt no fear of him herself. However, the man she had fallen in love with had gone. Now she knew who he really was, and she felt fearful of what he might do. The valley was still his and he could do what he liked with it.

Beth smelt the smoke long before she saw it. At first she thought someone had lit a bonfire, but as she neared the valley, the source of the smoke that polluted the sky became more obvious. Like a black spirit escaping from the valley, it spiralled into the sky to send a message that it was her home that was on fire. She dropped the handles of her barrow. *It can burn to hell for all I care*, Joss had told her.

'Please not this,' Beth cried, abandoning her barrow, picking up her skirts and running towards her home. Soon she was leaving the road and running down the track through the trees. She did not hear Bill call out to warn her to take care, or feel the fiery embers that rained down from the sky as she reached her little cottage. The sight of it shocked her.

The cottage that had been her home since the age of eight, of which she knew every nook, every cranny, was engulfed with wild flames. It did not look like her home any more. It looked like a gateway filled with fire; it looked like the entrance to hell.

With a sweeping movement of her hand, Martha gathered the cut stems from the table and placed them into her mortar. Picking up a pestle in her large hand, she carefully began to grind them with practised precision. Their distinctive purple spotted stems, thought to resemble Christ's blood upon his crucifixion, were soon split and crushed to form a fibrous pulp and release a distinctive, mousey smell. Martha continued the rhythmic grinding, the sound of which echoed around her silent kitchen and gave her a sense of peace at a time she needed it most.

As she worked Martha thought of Beth. She hoped she had not unsettled Beth too much by her unexpected declaration of fondness for her as they parted. However, the need to tell her that she loved her had been sudden, strong and could not be ignored. She was glad she had given way to the feeling and spoken the words that needed to be said.

Martha's peace was soon disturbed by hurried footsteps in the street and the sound of people shouting. The task Martha had been so focused on until now was momentarily and reluctantly abandoned.

Martha stood behind her door and tilted her head in the hope of making out the reason for the commotion. There had been no cry of 'Hevva! Hevva!' to announce the sight of a pilchard shoal off the coast and she knew that they were not fishermen running to their boats as they had already left. No, these cries were different and the footsteps were running away from the harbour, not towards it. Martha opened the door and looked out. She saw several men and women collecting buckets from neighbouring houses and carrying them to a waiting cart. Others, eager to lend a hand and help, climbed aboard and shouted to make haste. Yet despite their good intentions, the crisis was causing confusion and panic in what was usually a quiet little fishing port.

Martha spotted Jacca. "Ey, Jacca, what's 'appening?'

Jacca came over, a little out of breath, with a child in his arms.

'A fire has been seen in River Valley and they think it is Beth's house.'

'Oh no, not our Beth!' cried Martha, retreating backwards in shock to the safety of her little house. She clung to the door frame for support.

Jacca reassured her. 'Oh, Martha, this must be a shock for you, but be sure we will bring Beth home. She was seen walking the road not long since. She couldn't have been inside when it started.'

Martha remained visibly shaken by the news, and muttered a prayer to herself.

'You stay here, Martha. I would go and help but I have the children to see to. She will need a place to stay, so I am going to sort that out for her. Can she stay here, Martha? You know some womenfolk will be reluctant to have her for fear of their menfolk, and you have always been a good friend—'

'No!' Martha closed the door so only her face showed through the crack.

Jacca frowned at her.

'I can't 'ave 'er 'ere. Tom is ill with something. The doctor says it is catching. 'E is mortally ill and I need to look after 'im. I don't 'ave the room for Beth. What about your lady friend? 'As she a spare room?'

Jacca moved his child onto his other hip. 'I could ask her, but it will only be for a day or two. We are to be wed next week and there is already a tenant waiting to move in. However it will do for now. I must be going, I have a houseful of frightened children needing their pa.' He hesitated before adding, 'I hope Tom feels better soon. I'm sure Beth will understand.'

Martha retreated still further behind the door, ashamed she was unwilling to offer her home.

'Don't worry, Martha. You can't help not being able to take care of Beth. I know you would if you could.'

Jacca turned and made his way back up the hill to his home and Martha carefully shut the door. Her hands were shaking. She leant her forehead against it, feeling the hard, splintered surface against her weathered skin. She paused for a moment to gather her strength, before taking a deep breath, straightening her rounded shoulders and returning to her task.

Martha gathered her pestle and mortar, and tested the consistency of the pulp. Satisfied it was now ready, she spooned out the crushed hemlock into a jug and added some sloe gin she had made the year before. She stirred it and watched the two mingle together. It was enough to kill two dogs, but she wanted to make sure. Opening a cupboard, she searched her array of homemade herbal medicines. Crushed root of the aconite plant and the bottle of laudanum, which had been left over after her husband had died from an illness, would all serve a purpose this night. She collected them all and mixed them together, adding some milk to turn it into a milky drink. Finally she was satisfied and a sense of relief flooded through her veins. She had always known this time would come, but not today, and not under these circumstances. Yet, now the time was here there was a sense of peace. There was no longer any fear of the unknown, as the unknown was here and known to her. She picked up her jug of poison, enough to kill a horse, and carried it carefully through her cluttered kitchen, up her narrow stairs and to Tom's bedroom.

Lying on his bed and trembling with pain and fear, was Tom. Martha could smell the bitter, dry smell of his burnt clothes mingle with the aroma of the drink as she poured it into his glass. She was careful not to spill a drop. She wanted every drop to release him from his distress.

Tom looked up at her with a worried expression born from confusion as to why he should be in such pain. To Martha's eyes, there was no confusion. Tom's lower body was burnt so badly that clothes and skin had fallen away to leave weeping wounds that covered his limbs, chest and stomach. How he had managed to run home, Martha did not know, but home he had come and Martha couldn't help but feel pleased that it was her he had thought of in his time of need. Tom was looking into her eyes. Martha had dreamt and prayed for him to look into her eyes and see her for the first time. Yet now he was doing it and it was not what she wanted to see. She saw nothing but pain, pleading and fear. Martha looked away first.

'Tom, my dear boy,' she said brightly, lifting his wounded body into a sitting position. 'I told you not to play with fire. I was worried this would 'appen. But don't fret, you are not in any trouble. I 'ave a drink for you that will take the pain away.' She lifted the glass to his lips and obediently he began to drink. 'That's my boy. You were always good with eating and drinking what I gave you.'

He lay down and Martha pulled the sheets up to cover his wounded body and tuck him in as if he was a child. She lay down beside him. 'Soon you will fall asleep, my 'andsome boy,' she said, stroking his copper hair away from his fevered brow. 'So 'andsome you are, so clever. Folk don't know you like I do. You mean no 'arm to anyone. I blame myself. I should not have eaten those unripe berries. I didn't know, you see. I was a young foolish woman that knew no better.'

Tom's trembling body relaxed and his breathing slowed.

'I'll not let you 'ang, Tom. It was a mistake. I know you love Beth in your own way. I know you never meant to 'arm 'er, but others won't understand, so this is 'ow it 'as to be.'

Minutes ticked by and Tom's breathing became slower.

Finally it ceased. Martha remained next to him and continued to stroke his forehead for another hour to ensure that he was gone. She wanted this time to be alone with him and ponder to herself how things would be if he had not suffered from his affliction. She spoke softly to him, musing on what his life may have been. Perhaps he would have himself a wife, children, a well-paid job. 'And, of course, your wife would 'ave been a very pretty girl, because I am sure all the young ladies would 'ave considered you a good catch. I know you would 'ave taken care of me too, and I would look after your children and they would call me Granny Kitto.'

Martha wiped away a tear. Time had passed quickly and he had not stirred; she knew he was truly gone now. Reaching across to the bedside table, she reached for the second glass. With determined gulps, she emptied it and carefully placed the milk-filmed glass back onto the table. Content it had not tasted as bad as she had feared, she settled herself down to lie next to her son, but this time was different. Now he was still she could do the one thing she had always wanted to do, but he had never welcomed. She reached across and held his body in a comforting hug, closed her eyes, and with a smile on her face, waited for death to take her.

Chapter Sixteen

'It's not over yet. There must be a way.' Joss placed his empty glass on the centre of a map which illustrated Bodannock Mine's shafts and tunnels. 'I am not ready to give up on it yet.'

'You have given up on mines before.'

'Yes, and left miners without work and their wives weeping. I do not have the stomach for it now.'

'They will drown their sorrows in their cups at the Cat and Fiddle, no doubt. You cannot help how and when they spill their tears.' Edward and Joss circled the map on the table. 'You can't continue to put money into a mine that is not profitable, Joss,' argued Edward. 'The miners will find work elsewhere.'

'I fear they will not. Mines are closing everywhere. They are struggling as it is.'

Edward glanced up at him. 'How do you know what their struggles are, Joss?'

Joss stared at his glass on the map. The markings of the mine were clearly visible beneath its base, albeit distorted and blurred.

'Since my return I have been visiting their villages. They have dedicated their lives, and generation after generation of their families, to mining. They will see the closure of the mine as a betrayal. In their eyes I will be robbing them of their only means of putting food on the table.'

Edward shook his head. 'You are thinking too deeply. You have provided them with work longer than many others have. Are you considering offering them work in the slate mine?'

Joss lifted his glass and looked at the map beneath it. 'No.'

Edward was relieved to hear it. 'No, of course not. That would be a foolish idea. They are miners of tin and copper. Quarrying for slate is different and we need experienced men to start it off.'

'It is not that. They would soon learn. No, it is because the valley is too far from their families and homes. If the men leave, the women will follow and the mining villages will die.'

Unable to settle, Joss picked up a pile of papers and looked through them. Each page had lists of equipment and estimates for labour neatly written on them.

'What is this?'

Edward glanced over his shoulder. 'It is the estimates for quarrying River Valley. I collected the information while you were away. I think we should draft in workers from a slate quarry in the north. The owner owes you money and he can repay you with his labour force for the time being. His slate is all but worked out and we could take advantage of that.'

Joss's gaze raked the figures. It was difficult to reconcile the cold calculations with the distant land where ribbons, representing wishes, blew in the breeze.

'The valley is beautiful this time of year. Quarrying the slate will destroy it.'

Edward laughed. 'Don't get sentimental, Joss. It does not suit you. That is something your dear sister would say. She is visiting this afternoon, isn't she?'

'She is.' Joss put aside the papers and stood up. The map of Bodannock Mine lay on the table, taunting him. He stepped closer and noticed his glass had left a circular mark between the mine and the sea. He stared at it, his brows drawn in deep thought.

'What about the other woman in your life? She is expecting the braying of mules and the coarse language of slate workers to arrive at her door. You will disappoint her if you do not go ahead with your plans.'

Joss lifted his chin. 'She is disappointed in me already. I don't want to talk about her, Edward. She has got what she wanted and I must continue my life in the way I see fit.'

'Are you thinking of backing out from a profitable venture

so she can stay in the valley and cook on her trivet, or whatever these country people cook on?'

Joss winced. He did not like his friend to talk of Beth in that way. In fact, he did not like him to talk of her at all. It hurt too much to think of her.

'Edward, we are friends, but watch your tongue. Don't talk so glibly about a woman you know nothing about.'

'I'm sorry. I meant no offence.'

'I know. I'm sorry too. My temper has a short fuse these days. I just know how much the valley means to Beth.'

Edward settled back in his chair and brushed off a speck of dust from his trouser leg with a flip of his hand. 'Go on.'

Joss looked down at the map of Bodannock. 'She ran away to the valley as a child. It became her haven. It also became mine. I no longer have the motivation to destroy it.'

'Destroy what?' A woman's voice interrupted their conversation and both men turned their heads to see Karenza entering the room. 'And who is *she*? Have I missed something?'

She allowed Edward to kiss her cheek, before glancing casually at the map and papers on the table. She wrinkled her nose then looked up expectantly to Joss.

'*She* is no one of importance. We were talking business, nothing more.' Joss picked up his empty glass and poured himself a drink, belatedly offering the others in the room one.

Karenza shook her head. 'As usual I have already arranged my beverage. I see you have taken on extra staff since my last visit. I swear I have seen at least two new faces just walking from the hall.' Karenza moved a cushion from her favourite seat and sat herself down, arranging her dress neatly in her usual efficient manner.

Joss looked pointedly at Edward. 'It was brought to my attention that although I wished to live modestly with little fuss, a house of this size still warranted a certain level of staff to run it.'

Karenza arched an eyebrow. 'As much as I am very fond of Edward, I don't think he would offer such advice as he has absolutely no idea what a house of this size requires.'

Edward clutched his heart, pretending her words cut him deep, but the glint in his eye showed he was not in the least bit hurt by them. 'I confess, I was the one that passed on the words of wisdom, but it was a woman who advised me to do so.'

'Which woman?'

Edward winked at Karenza. '*The* woman we are not allowed to mention.'

Joss took Edward's glass from him and placed it on a tray. 'Tread carefully, my friend,' he muttered under his breath.

Edward smiled. They had spent years sparring with words and banter, and this subject was no different to Edward. However, Karenza *had* heard and she was prepared to tread more softly.

'How was London?' she asked, hoping to change the subject. Joss was about to reply when Edward interrupted him.

'There is no point asking him that, Karenza, for the simple truth is he never arrived. While we all thought he was visiting his friends in the big city, he was but twenty miles away and had not left the county.'

Joss saw the look of concern on his sister's face. 'I changed my plans on a whim,' he reassured her. 'I did not plan to spend so long there. It was to be one night, no more. I wanted to see who was occupying Kynance Cottage and throw them out.'

Karenza sighed in exasperation. 'Could you not leave your work and go away as planned? Why did you stay in Cornwall? I wanted you to have a rest and forget about your businesses.'

Much to Joss's building irritation, Edward could not hold his tongue and answered for him. 'Oh, he forgot about his businesses. In fact he forgot everything, even who he was. It was only when his memory returned that he came home.'

Joss waved his sister's concern aside. 'I am well now. In fact, I think the whole episode did me the world of good, in a strange sort of way.'

'But how did it happen? Did you fall ill? Were you injured?'

Edward mimed being hit on the head.

Joss grunted. 'I am glad you are enjoying yourself, Edward. Remind me to return the favour one day.' He looked at his sister. 'It was an accident. She did not mean to hurt me so badly.'

'The same *she* you spoke of before?' Karenza was becoming more intrigued as time went on.

Edward collected his confiscated glass. 'The very same. She is also the woman who has been illegally occupying his cottage in River Valley and nursed him back to health. She may not have been so generous with her ministrations if she had known who he was.'

'If I had known about this I would have visited you sooner,' said Karenza.

The conversation was temporarily halted as a maid brought in a tray of tea and biscuits. The room was unusually silent, which unnerved the new girl and she quickly made her exit. As soon as she had gone Karenza turned to her brother and the interrogation continued.

'Who is this woman? What is she like?' To her surprise, Edward answered.

'A pretty little thing, although rather brazen. I have met her but the once. She marched in here—'

'Beth does not march,' Joss muttered.

Karenza lifted an eyebrow. He had spoken her name with a tenderness that he had not used for a woman before. She returned her attention to Edward to learn more about her.

'—demanded to speak to Mr Roscarrock and I had the task of speaking to her in his absence.' Edward poured himself a whisky and picked up a biscuit on his way back to his chair. 'She was polite enough, although a little too assertive for someone of her background. She wanted to extend the lease, which I would not do. Then she proceeded to tell me that Joss's housekeeper was ill and that she was worked too hard. During her very short visit she somehow managed to persuade Mrs May to drink a glass full of spirit for a chill she was suffering. I had to send her to bed smelling like a brewery.'

'Send this woman to bed?'

'No, Mrs May.'

'But Mrs May is a staunch Methodist. I thought they did not drink alcohol. This *Beth* is quite persuasive, it seems.'

'Indeed she is, for she has managed to persuade Joss not to remove her from the cottage and now he is reconsidering his slate mining venture.'

Karenza took a sip of her tea but her eyes did not leave Joss.

'I have been persuaded to do nothing I did not wish to do myself.' He returned to study the map of Bodannock.

Karenza recounted the story to ensure she had all the facts straight. 'So this woman accidently injured you, which caused you to lose your memory and these past few weeks you have been living with her while she has nursed you back to health. Now you are considering changing your mind about the future of River Valley. The latter I am rather pleased about as I understand it is rather beautiful. Did this woman change your mind?'

Joss fingered his collar. 'She believes me to be a ruthless man. I have no wish to prove her right by behaving as one.'

Karenza's eyes widened with interest. 'My goodness. Do you care for this woman?'

Joss cleared his throat. His sister could always see through him. He chose to ignore her last remark. Besides, a thought, much more interesting than his sister's teasing, had just struck him. He picked up the map of the mine, placed it on Edward's lap and pointed to the area circled by the stain from his glass.

'See here, Edward.'

Edward placed his glass of precious whisky on the side table out of harm's way and looked at the map balanced precariously on his knees.

Karenza watched their bowed heads. 'Do you find it painful to talk of her, Joss?'

'Not now, Karenza.' Joss circled the area he wanted Edward to study with a swirl of his glass. 'The deepest shaft is two hundred and fifty fathoms below sea level and we have not hit any new reserves in this area for some time.' He straightened himself. 'We cannot go further as the miners tell us they can hear the sea above them. We cannot risk digging nearer to the surface of the seabed.' Joss paced around to the other side of Edward and indicated to the map again. 'But look here. If we dig a diagonal shaft along there, it will allow us access to deeper ore deposits and open up a new area to search.'

Edward frowned. 'I thought you did not want to plough more money into this mine.'

'I will if there is a chance of profit and to keep the mining community thriving.'

Edward looked at the map. 'Could this work? I have never heard of diagonal shafts before.'

'It could. We will make it work.'

'We will be very busy these coming months, what with this new shaft and starting the slate quarry.'

'I told you I am not going ahead with the slate quarry. I want to concentrate on Bodannock Mine.' Joss helped himself to a cup of tea. Karenza offered him a biscuit.

'I would like to meet this persuasive woman called Beth,' she teased.

Joss's expression remained serious. 'This has nothing to do with Miss Jago. It is a business decision, no more than that.'

Karenza bit into a biscuit. 'But it is fortunate, nonetheless, that a good business decision will mean that local miners will keep their jobs and a beautiful valley will survive another day.' She indulged herself by dipping her biscuit into her tea, a habit her mother would be mortified to see if she had been present. 'It is fortunate indeed that a ruthless man such as you, brother, will not be as bad as this woman first thought.'

'Read nothing into it, sister dearest,' Joss replied. 'She has been terrorised enough these past weeks. Thanks, in part, to Edward's overzealous orders.'

Edward looked up from the map. 'I did no more than you asked. I arranged for further letters from the solicitor and one visit to persuade her to leave.'

'I was there, Edward. You sent ex-wrestlers to manhandle her.'

'I paid two men to remove her belongings. I did not know it was a lone woman. If I had, a different tactic would have been employed.'

'You employed men who rejoiced in their power over her.'

'She was occupying a house she had no right to be in,' argued Edward. 'I was acting on your behalf.'

'I did not give you leave to step beyond the boundaries of the law.'

'They overstepped the mark, I agree. When I found that out I told them no more visits.'

'Yet they did continue, spying on her, dead animals at her door, lime wash thrown over the house, tools broken—'

'No!' Edward stood up to accentuate his denial. 'I ordered none of those things, and paid for no further pressure on her. Whoever undertook such mischief was nothing to do with me.'

Joss put down his cup and met Edward's eyes. He had known Edward for years. He was a cheerful, loyal friend and his only flaw was that he never took life too seriously. The Crimean War had a lot to answer for. Yet, Joss knew for certain Edward was no liar.

'If you did not order it, then it is the work of someone else,' Joss said getting up and making for the door.

'Where are you going?' asked his sister, surprised at his sudden intention to depart.

'I am leaving for River Valley. I must speak to Beth and warn her that there is someone who wishes her harm. She is in danger, and for the first time it is not from me.'

Within minutes of his instructions, Joss's horse was saddled and attempts were being made by the stable boy and head groom to hold him steady for Joss to mount. The horse had sensed the urgency and it had unnerved him. Sidestepping and shaking his head, he fought them for control of his bridle and would not stand still.

'Leave him,' Joss commanded the men, before taking the reins of his wide-eyed horse. Joss mounted quickly, and on his command the black horse obediently leapt forward into a gallop. With a twist of his body and a twitch of a rein, Joss turned his horse for the main drive that led out of the estate just as Karenza came to stand in the doorway to watch him leave. She saw the horse's black mane flying in the wind, and she saw the look of determination on her brother's face. Edward came to stand beside her.

'I have never seen him like this before,' said Karenza thoughtfully. 'How has he been, Edward, since his return?'

'He looked well, although perhaps distracted. Do you think this woman could be a problem?'

Karenza bit her lip. 'I don't know. All I know is that any woman would love to think a man would ride twenty miles to come to her aid, and for the man to be so focused on saving her, that he would quite forget to take a coat, his riding crop or to say goodbye to those he has left behind.'

They stood in silence for a moment, shoulder to shoulder, gazing at the trail of hoof prints in the normally neat gravel. Karenza smiled at the mild destruction. It was a sign that Joss cared about someone else, and it intrigued her.

'I don't know if she is a problem, but I do know she has

reached him in a way that we have failed to do since he returned from the war.' She touched Edward's shoulder before leaving his side to return to her cup of tea.

Edward did not join her immediately, but looked towards the now empty and quiet drive. Up to this point he had thought Beth Jago an amusing hindrance and nothing more, but perhaps he had been wrong. Perhaps she was not quite as amusing as he had first thought as she appeared to wield more power than even she knew herself. Joss was his friend and already Edward had witnessed Joss make decisions based on this woman's opinions. He had only met her once, yet he felt Joss held her opinion in higher regard than his own. He was probably being irrational, even immature, but he felt it all the same. He would need to watch out for this woman, whose appearance of a modest country girl hid her true strength. He had underestimated her. He would not make the same mistake again.

Chapter Seventeen

Despite his speedy departure, Joss knew that his horse would not make the twenty miles unscathed if he did not pace his ride. Alternating between a trot and a steady canter, he headed south towards River Valley, secretly glad that he finally had the excuse he needed to see Beth again.

They had parted on bad terms, and although he had wanted to hurt her for not believing him, his need to see her again was more powerful. He had never known the torture of addiction before. Even when he drank heavily to drown out his memories and help him sleep, he had never craved it. Yet Beth had remained in his thoughts every hour of every day since his return and her image tormented his thoughts at night. He needed to see her again, even if only to prove that she was not as special as he remembered. He hoped she was not. At least then he would be rid of her spell and cured of his craving for her. Yet, the anticipation of achieving what he wanted gave him a dull, twisting ache in his gut and made his mind race. All thoughts of his surroundings, his responsibilities and his plans had become insignificant. The thought of seeing her again was as heady and as strong as the drive of an addict reaching for an opium pipe. He spurred his horse on and gritted his teeth. She was doing it again, filling his mind with fanciful thoughts. Was he addicted to her? As addicted as a man could be to the woman he loved, said a voice in his head.

Wishing to avoid the roads, he took a shortcut across the mine-infested countryside. Each stage of his journey was marked by abandoned engine houses towering to the dull sky. In years gone by their noise gave an industrial heartbeat to the landscape, but now many were just silent monuments to an age when tin and copper mining had been a lucrative trade for the county.

222

After several miles he turned towards the coast, crossing lush grassy fields and causing clods of sodden turf to be tossed in the air by his horse's hurried stride. He could smell the fresh sea air long before he could see the grey Atlantic Ocean, its steady rise and fall resembling a gigantic sleeping animal lying beyond the dramatic cliff edge. As he followed the cliff path, inexplicable feelings of peace and contentment descended upon him. His shoulders relaxed and he rocked in unison with the steady canter of his tiring horse. He was almost there. Soon he would see her again.

Joss stared in disbelief at the black, skeletal remains of Kynance Cottage. Its stone walls, now blackened by soot, were the only sign that a house had once stood on the site. With slow, careful steps he walked towards it and onto the carpet of brittle, scorched grass that snapped beneath his feet and crumbled to dust. With an outstretched hand, he carefully eased open the remnants of the door. He noted that the lock he had fitted now lay useless on the floor. The timber that had survived was as black as coal and so dry that fissures, resembling the scales of a reptile, had been burnt into the wood. He looked at his hand and saw the charcoal dust on his skin. Feeling its smoothness against his fingertips, it confirmed to him what he had feared. That this was no illusion, it was real.

He ventured further inside. Like a voyeur of a tragedy he looked about him. The floor was covered in thick, grey ash and remnants of collapsed roof rafters lay about him. The floorboards, upstairs floor and roof no longer existed. The grey clouds above him were visible through the few charred rafters that remained. Joss looked around the room and found little that he could recognise. The furniture Beth owned had been made of wood and had all been consumed by the fire, so that the room now appeared empty, as if it had been looted. There were only three things that had survived that he could recognise, despite their blackened state. The triangular shaped trivet that she had cooked on lay upturned by the fire grate. The kettle she had boiled water in to brew cheap tea sat on the floor. It was as if someone had placed it carefully there and would soon return to collect it. Lastly, he recognised the battered frying pan she had used to hit him with. Feeling like a child left abandoned in a barren landscape, Joss's feelings of shock and despair rooted him to the spot. He stared at the old pan – an insignificant object to everyone but the two of them – until it blurred before his eyes and he could see it no more.

It was the gentle sound of rustling leaves that brought Joss to his senses again. At first he did not recognise the fluttering colours before him, but as they came into focus and he returned to reality, he realised he was standing before the wishing tree again. His eyes were focused on two ribbons, tied side by side. Although he had felt numb during his walk through the valley, now a lump formed in his throat as he recognised them. They were the ribbons Beth had with her when she had shown him the valley. They had tied them onto the tree and had each made a wish. His wish had not come true. He had wished Beth would live a long and happy life. His arrival had brought her nothing but unhappiness, and at that moment he did not even know if she was alive at all. He noticed his skin and hair felt slightly damp and he realised that, in his trance-like state, he must have followed the same trail that Beth had shown him all those weeks ago. Even in his state of shock and grief, she had led his mind and body here, but enough was enough.

He raked a hand through his hair. He had things he must do. He needed to know if Beth had survived and if she was well. He wanted to know who was to blame, for although he had killed as a soldier in the name of his country, he had never had the desire to kill as he did now.

Joss retraced his steps back to the charred cottage. His horse was where he had left it, grazing on some grass that had escaped the fire. He caught the trailing reins, but before he could mount, a man's words halted him.

'What are you doing here?'

Joss recognised Bill's voice instantly. Speaking to him was a good place to start his search. He let go of the reins.

'Where is she?' Joss asked.

The farmer's gaze was steady, as if he was considering his answer, or whether to answer at all. Joss had no patience to wait.

'Damn it! Is Beth alive?'

Bill spat on the ground and looked at him. 'She lives.'

Joss glanced back at the burnt shell of Kynance Cottage. 'Who did this?' he demanded.

'Until now, I thought it was you.'

'I did not do this. Why would I do something like this and risk Beth's life?'

The farmer began to pick up bits of twisted metal and place them against the wall. It was an ineffectual attempt to tidy up, but it gave him something to do as he considered his words.

'I have wondered the same thing myself these past two weeks. I would not have considered you at all. However, on the night it happened I heard Beth crying out your name and asking why you would do something like this. When I asked her about it she refused to say more. She said she was in shock, but I heard it all the same.' He straightened and turned to Joss. 'We both know this fire was not an accident. There was no one home, no oil lamps or fire burning in the grate.'

'Tell me what happened, Bill.'

The old man said nothing.

'Bill?'

The farmer looked at him and narrowed his eyes. 'I didn't recognise you when you arrived,' he mused. 'The first time I saw you, you were just a young boy. Yet on the day Beth introduced us I couldn't help thinking I had seen your eyes

225

before, even if the face and body were different. It made no sense at the time so I didn't speak about it, but then Beth told me who you were and I understood. You know that Will Jago enjoyed your visits, don't you? He said you were a good lad. Do you remember me now that your memory has returned to you?'

'Perhaps. I remember a day Will was chatting to his neighbour over a gate, and the man he was talking to allowed me to climb his gate and play with his dog in his field.'

Bill smiled. 'That was me. Bess is long gone now.' He scratched his whiskery chin. 'Will Jago thought you were a good lad, so I didn't believe you would grow up to do something like this.'

'Although Beth thinks I did.'

'She was in shock. She's told no one else.'

'Tell me about it, Bill. I need to know.'

'I was heading for home when I saw the smoke and Beth running into the valley. Concerned, I followed to help.' He scratched his head through his untidy grey hair. 'I had never seen a fire like it. The heat was so strong that I could feel my skin burning. I heard Beth accuse you as she approached. Embers rained down on us, some no more than sparks, others much larger. Bits of cloth caught on fire and caught up in the wind, I suppose. One caught at her hem and took light, so I pushed her to the ground and covered it with dirt to put it out. There was nothing we could do for the cottage, as there was nothing to carry water, nothing to beat out the flames. Then some people from Port Carrek arrived. They had come to help. It was too late, but they tried their best. They made a chain and carried pails of water up from the stream. A lot of shouting at first, but when they realised their efforts were having little effect they became silent. Eerie it was ... so many people here and yet no one saying a word.' He shook his head. 'Poor Beth. After her initial efforts all she could do was just stand and stare. She had not uttered another word. Can see her standing where you are now, the front of her dress scorched, with tears in her eyes. Suddenly, she started to sob and her legs gave way. Two women from the village came over and helped her to walk back up the track. The villagers took her home with them and I've not seen her since.'

Bill came to stand beside him and they looked at the ruin. 'It wasn't just a home, Mr Roscarrock. This little cottage was the only link she had to her grandfather and her mother.' He dug the heel of his boot into the burnt grass. 'I feel sorry for the maid. Now she has nothing. Now she has no one.'

Joss had heard all he needed to hear. He had reacted badly to her decision to fight for an extension to the lease rather than play at living happily as man and wife with him. He finally understood how important the cottage was to her. He had been a fool. It was badly done, he told himself, badly done. Grabbing the reins of his horse, he mounted him with ease.

'Where are you going?' asked Bill.

'I am going to find her.'

The farmer barred his way. 'I hope you find her, but she won't welcome you. She thinks you did it.'

Joss moved his horse to the side. 'I did not and I will tell her that when I see her.'

Bill's thick fingers grabbed the reins. He showed no fear of Joss's horse. As a farmer he had worked all his life with horses; one young gelding did not scare him.

'She may not want to see you.'

Joss remained determined. 'I will convince her otherwise.' The two men stood their ground, neither moving, neither giving way. 'I mean her no harm,' Joss said quietly. 'I promise.'

Bill considered his assurance and finally nodded acceptance. He let go of the reins.

'There is a field to the right of Port Carrek's village sign,' he said. 'It is a field that I rent. Put your horse in there to rest when you get to the village. He is in need of food and water and you will need him for your return journey.'

The offer of the field would allow his horse time to recover. Joss appreciated his help and thanked him. He turned his horse towards the track and looked down on the farmer who stood watching him.

'You believe that Beth has no one in her life, Bill, but you are wrong,' Joss said, steadying his skittish horse. 'She has me.'

Joss only knew two people in Port Carrek who might know of Beth's whereabouts. Martha and Sam. He did not know where Martha lived, but he knew where to find Sam. He looked up at the prestigious bank sign. It was highly polished and overly large for such a small bank, but it was the only one in this small coastal town so its status among the local families remained unchallenged. They may feel in awe of its fine architecture and the employees within, but Joss felt no such thing. He swung open the door and strode in.

He walked the length of the long wooden counter but could not see Sam. He wasted no time and asked a young man who was employed there.

'I wish to speak to Sam on some urgency.'

The young man looked up and over the rim of his round glasses. 'I'm afraid I know of no Sam. Perhaps, if you could offer me his surname?'

'I have no surname, but I know he works here. I want to see him, now.'

The man left him and whispered to his colleague.

'Could the man be Mr Pratt?' he asked Joss when he returned.

Before Joss could answer, Sam spoke from an open door. 'It is me he is looking for and I know what he wants.' He lifted an arm to welcome Joss into the empty room behind him. 'I will give you three minutes.'

Joss marched passed him. 'I will be gone in two.'

Both men assessed one another, neither taking a seat.

'I want to find Beth. Do you know where she is?'

Sam smiled. 'As much as I would like to infuriate you and say that she is staying with me, she is not.'

Joss released the breath he had been holding. 'I should be glad that she is not living with you. However, I can't help but think you did not offer her a place to stay more to prevent damage to your own reputation than to hers.'

Sam sat down behind the desk and allowed his forearms to rest lightly on the arms of his chair. He did not offer Joss a seat.

'Your opinion of me is very low. I hate to disappoint you, but at the time I did not need to. She already had a place to stay.'

Joss inclined his head. 'I apologise. My comment was uncalled for. How is she?'

'That I don't know. I was away on the night of the fire and I have not seen her since.'

Joss leant forward over the desk towards him. 'You have not called on her to see how she is?'

Sam moved back in his chair. 'I have not. I am courting the daughter of the bank manager. It would not be seemly for me to visit a single woman.'

Joss's laugh was hollow. 'I was right after all. I don't know whether to despise you or thank you. If she had any feelings for you at all, your lack of concern and support will have destroyed them. If you cannot help me, perhaps you can tell me where Martha lives.'

'If you remove your hands from my desk I may consider it.'

Joss grabbed his collar and pulled him to standing.

Sam shook him off and straightened his shirt with trembling fingers. 'She lives in the cottage at the bottom of Princess Street. It is the one with blue window frames and window boxes full of herbs.' Joss turned away and left the room. As he walked through the bank, Sam called after him, 'When you see Beth, tell her I wish her well.'

Joss stopped briefly, but did not turn round. Customers paused to listen around him.

'No, I will not. I am not your lackey to deliver messages you are too cowardly to deliver yourself.' He looked at the customers around them. 'Be wary entrusting your money to someone who thinks more about himself than the people he serves.'

Joss banged loudly against Martha's door with the side of his fist again and waited, but to his frustration the house remained silent. He wondered if Beth was inside and hiding from him. He stepped back and looked up at the window but saw no one. The curtains were open, but there were no faces at any of the windows. He tried again, a rhythmic thud that this time he would not let up until someone opened the door.

'Martha has not been seen for two weeks now. Her son is ill and she wants to keep folk away. She said he has something contagious.'

Joss stopped his knocking and looked at the old woman from next door.

'Two weeks, you say?' The old woman nodded. Joss stepped back again to look at the windows. 'No one has seen Martha or her son for two weeks? Not even to get food?' Joss noticed a movement in the top bedroom window as a constable approached.

'Sir, I have been told you are disturbing the peace with your knocking. What is going on here?'

'This woman, Martha, might have some information on the whereabouts of a friend of mine, Beth Jago.'

'Well, it appears she is not in, so I suggest you call another time,' said the constable.

Joss ignored him and continued to stare at the bedroom window. 'Martha and her son have not been seen for two weeks. A little unusual, do you not think? Look there. Can you see movement behind that glass?'

The young constable looked up, squinting in the midday sun. 'I do. It looks like a swarm of flies. How strange. I have never seen so many in one area before.'

'I have,' said Joss. 'I fear it is not a good sign and we need to take a look inside.'

Without waiting for a reply, Joss kicked at the door. It swung open, ricocheted against the wall and began to shut again. Joss stopped it with an outstretched hand and stepped inside over the splinters of wood that littered the ground.

The constable signalled to a gathering crowd to wait outside and, with some trepidation, followed Joss inside. 'You had no right to do that, sir,' he said, following cautiously in his footsteps.

'If I am proved wrong, I will pay for it.' Joss looked about the room. It felt cold and smelt stale as if it had not been aired for some time. Although cluttered, there was nothing unusual about it. The fire had gone out a long time ago and there were no signs of recent human activity. Joss carefully picked his way through the clutter and headed for what he believed to be the small back kitchen. As he entered it he noticed some sticks lying neatly by the door. To find sticks in a room with a grate was not unusual, but these were straight and all the same length. He had tossed similar shaped sticks into the sea. They had been left by the man with the copper coloured hair who he had seen sitting on the cliff watching River Valley. The very same man who had been watching Beth bathe. What had started out as a search for Beth's whereabouts was taking a more sinister turn.

The kitchen was small. Mould in the dishes showed it had not been in use for some time. Joss noticed some plants and a pestle and mortar on the table. He lifted the pestle and smelt it. He knew little of plants and herbs, but he recognised the hemlock plant. He lifted the small glass bottle beside it and read the label.

'What have you found?' asked the constable at his side.

'A preparation of some kind.' Joss put down the bottle. 'I think we will find the answer upstairs, in the room with the flies.' Joss led the way. 'What do you know of the people who live here?' he asked the young constable. 'I have met Martha once myself, but I was unwell at the time.'

'Martha Kitto is a widow and a good-hearted soul. Her son, Tom, is simple and has strange ways but she thinks the world of him. I have not long been posted here so that is all that I know.' The stench hit them as they reached the top stair. 'Great God, what is that smell?' asked the constable, reaching for a handkerchief and covering his nose.

'I know what it is. As a former soldier I have smelt it many times. It is the smell of death. Follow me.'

Joss signalled for him to follow, but the young constable could not enter the room. Joss left him to his retching and went straight for the window. With little difficulty, he opened it to allow the flies out and the sea breeze in. The disturbance sent the flies into a noisy frenzy, before they found their escape and dissipated into the early evening sky. Joss filled his lungs with fresh air, before he turned to the dresser beside him. Two glasses caught his eye, each with remnants of fibrous tissue from the hemlock plant staining their sides. He selected one and smelt the contents: a mixture of spirit and, no doubt, laudanum from the bottle downstairs, but it was difficult to tell. The stench behind him was too strong and was becoming too much. He returned the glass and reached for a handkerchief to cover his own nose before finally turning to look at the bed. Lying side by side, in a comforting embrace, were the bodies of Martha and her son. Their decomposing bodies were still recognisable but only just. Martha's hair was a silvery grey, befitting a woman of her age, whilst her son's, caught in the beam of sunshine through the open window, shone like polished copper. Its beauty, mixed with the horror of his decomposition, was difficult to take in. So this is Tom Kitto, thought Joss as he pulled back the sheet and saw the boy's blackened, charred clothes and worn, white lime-wash splattered boots. Joss recognised it as the same paint that had been thrown over Kynance Cottage on the night of the Golowan celebrations.

'What have you found, sir?' asked the constable, who had finally been able to enter the room.

'I have found the perpetrator who burnt down Kynance Cottage in River Valley,' said Joss quietly, replacing the sheet over the two bodies. 'And strangely, the discovery gives me no joy.'

Joss and the constable stood in the front doorway of the house, shoulder to shoulder, and watched the gathering crowd. They filled their lungs with fresh air as they considered their next move.

'You will need my details, of course. There will be an inquest.'

The young constable fumbled for his notebook. 'Yes, yes of course.'

Joss noticed his hand shaking as he tried to hold his pencil and took pity on him. 'Give me the book,' he said, taking it from him and writing down his name. 'How long have you been a constable?'

'One month. I have never experienced this situation before.'

Joss flipped the book shut. He wanted to look for Beth but he felt sympathy for the constable. He had worn a uniform once. He understood that once a uniform is put on the public expected you to know what to do, whether you had the experience or not. The uniform makes you stand out and acts like a target. It screams the message, *This man has experience. This man has no fear. This man will do what no one else will do. Look to him, he will solve our problems.* Joss had felt the same when he was a new soldier. It did not matter how you felt inside. It did not matter at all.

Joss lowered his voice so no one else could hear. 'The

deaths appear unnatural. There is hemlock, laudanum and a spirit of some sort in the kitchen and in the bedroom. I believe Martha's son committed an offence and she killed him to protect him and then committed suicide. I have witnessed this Tom Kitto watching Kynance Cottage. The burnt clothing, the paint on his boots is further evidence of his mischief.' He paused, waiting for the constable's pencil to stop scribbling to indicate that he had caught up with his note taking.

'This crowd is growing,' Joss said, looking at the sea of faces in front of him. 'As macabre as it may sound, they hope to have a look for themselves. Post someone at the door to stop them from entering the house. Fetch a doctor to bear witness and confirm their deaths. Inform the coroner, and arrange for another constable to advise and support you. There is no shame in asking for help.' Joss frowned at his own words, recognising the truth in them.

The constable looked at Joss's details in his notebook. 'Thank you, Mr Roscarrock. You have been most helpful.'

'It is nothing,' he said, brushing off his help as of no importance. He was about to leave when the constable stopped him by catching his arm and offering his hand.

'I mean what I say, sir. How well I handle this situation will form my reputation. The townspeople will judge me on this act and I feel they will judge me well thanks to you.'

Joss took his hand and they shook briefly. 'I was glad to help.' To his surprise Joss realised that this too was true. Helping this stranger made him feel good, as if he had done something worthwhile for once in his life. 'Good luck,' he said. 'Do not hesitate in contacting me and I will be happy to provide what information I can.'

He left him and entered the crowd. It felt as if he was wading against the strong current of a river, as he made his way through the jostling people. Those nearest to the house watched him pass but as he went deeper into them, he was largely ignored. Everyone's upturned face was now fixed upon the new constable and the sound of the constable's rattle as he called for attention. They hushed obediently and Joss smiled to himself as the young man took charge and asked for volunteers to help.

Joss broke through the crowd on the other side of the street and was able to turn briefly to look back at the young man. They exchanged nods and an unspoken message passed between them. They had shared a gruesome discovery that would remain with them forever.

'What brought you to Martha's house and to break down her door?' asked a man beside him.

Joss looked at the man who had a young child beside him. 'I am looking for Beth Jago and I was told Martha might know where she is.'

'She's not in Port Carrek any more. She stayed with my wife for a few days, before we were wed. She refused to stay longer as she did not want to trouble us at the start of our marriage. Martha wasn't answering. We thought it was because Tom was ill. And the women of the village were unwilling to take in a pretty girl as they don't trust their menfolk. So in the end she left.'

Joss's hope at finding Beth rose. 'Where did she go?'

The man became wary. He lifted the child onto his hip. 'Why do you want to find her?'

'I am a friend. I found out today that her house has been destroyed and I want to offer help.'

The man considered his reply. 'A friend you say? Were you with Beth at Golowan Feast? I believe I saw you together by the harbour.'

Joss nodded. 'I was.'

'Then I am glad you can help her, for she is in need of it just now. You will find her at Benedict's, four miles from here.' The name sounded familiar, yet Joss could not place it. The man saw his confusion. 'It's a workhouse. She grew up there. She thought she would never have to go back.'

Joss remembered the name. 'If I have my way, she will not be in there for very long.' He shook the man's hand. 'Thank you for your help. With whom do I have the pleasure of speaking?'

'My name is Jacca, and I am happy to help if it means that Beth has some good luck for a change.'

'She will come to no harm and I will offer her help. Whether she accepts it is another matter altogether.'

Joss wasted no more time and headed out of Port Carrek. His horse had eaten and rested, and now it was time to continue his journey and find Beth.

Chapter Eighteen

Beth lay curled up into a tight ball beneath her blanket in a vain attempt to keep warm. The north-facing ward saw no sunshine, resulting in a permanent chill in the room no matter the time of year. She feigned sleep in an attempt to make her problems disappear, if not herself. All the memories of her formative years had turned into reality once more. She felt like a child again and all the insecurities and despair she had felt then had come back with a vengeance. She felt so alone, despite sharing the ward with thirteen other women between the ages of fourteen and sixty. It was past eight o'clock in the evening and they were all meant to be asleep, yet she could still hear some of them cursing and arguing around her, while others snored and slept. She kept her eyes firmly shut to block her surroundings out. She had been awake since five o'clock and had worked a ten-hour shift with the other able-bodied women. Despite being tired, the noise and cold conspired to stop her from sleeping. Even the meagre cheese and bread supper lay heavy in her stomach. She hated Benedict's, but not as much as she hated the man who was responsible for her downfall.

With one single sweep, her blanket was torn away from her grip and the cold air chilled her body. She opened her eyes to see a candle shining in her face and Matron Haynes looking down on her.

'Get up. You have a visitor.' The Matron threw her clothes at her. 'Make haste, before the others wake.'

Beth obediently put them on, as it was against the workhouse rules to disobey the master and matron, and followed her through the ward to the spiral staircase at the end. They descended the steps that led them away from the segregated male and female wards to the ground floor.

'Is it a woman called Martha?' Beth asked hopefully as Matron hurried on ahead.

'No, it is a man called Mr Roscarrock.'

Beth stopped. 'I don't want to see him.'

'He said you would refuse.' Matron turned and looked up to Beth from the lower step. 'Now you listen to me, my girl. It did not please me to see you fall on hard times again. I had hoped you would never come back here, but you are here now so you must make the best of it. If a gentleman wants to see you then that is what you do. He might just be a way for you to get out of here.'

'I don't care. I don't want to see him.'

The Matron would have none of it. 'You have to. He said that if I brought you to him he would make a donation to Benedict's. If an interview with Mr Roscarrock is a way of raising money for Benedict's, then you will see him, whether you like it or not.' She began making her way down the stairs again. Beth followed. 'No one wants to come here, but if it weren't for this place you would all be starving in the gutter. Now make haste. We have kept him waiting long enough.'

They reached the ground floor, passed Master Piper's office, the head of the workhouse, the female day room and the dining room. A long narrow corridor, which segregated the male and female outdoor courtyards, led them towards the doors of the receiving wards, where paupers were admitted to wait for medical inspection upon arrival. Finally they arrived at the committee room door. It was the only room that Beth had not been in, apart from the male facilities. Matron turned to her and took out a comb from her pocket. She handed it to Beth.

'Here, tidy your hair. I want the best for you, Jago ... and I want the donation for Benedict's.'

Beth looked at the broken comb. As much as she wanted to show Joss the realities of the workhouse existence, she also had her feminine pride. She reached for the comb and dragged it through her hair.

Beth entered the large committee room. She did not need to see his tall figure waiting for her arrival to know that he was there. She could feel his presence, but her pride would not let her look at him. The truth of it was that she was afraid of what she might see. She would know in an instant if he had ordered the cottage she had chosen over him to be torched. She would see it in his eyes and in the tilt of his chin. She was also fearful that, despite everything, she would still love his face – if not his soul. Uncharacteristically, Matron left them alone without saying a word. Did he nod for her to leave? Did he make it plain he wanted her gone?

Beth stood proudly and focused on a patch of peeling paint. Normally the committee room was used for meetings of the rich patrons of Benedict's and parish representatives. It was meant to be the best room in the workhouse, yet its walls were in need of decoration. At least his donation would mean some good would come out of her humiliation, she thought.

He did not speak at first. She could feel his assessment of her take in her oversized blue and white pinstriped dress made of coarse cloth. She could sense his disgust as he noted her stained white smock and large blue stockings that wrinkled at her ankles. Even the length of her workhouse uniform, which was shorter by several inches compared to any dress a woman in his circle would wear, indicated how far she had fallen. No lady of quality, no modest woman, no country girl living in a cottage by the sea, would wear such a dress. Only a pauper, only the unfortunates of this world would be in such need – only someone like her. The heat of embarrassment rushed up to her cheeks and she reddened. She tilted her chin higher and continued to stare at the flaking paint on the wall that curled like a lock of hair on a privileged child's head. And then he spoke. Just the one word, yet she knew that everything she had sensed in that minute of silence had been true. He had looked her over and saw how far she had fallen.

'Beth.' His voice was tender and full of kindness.

Beth pinched her lips together to stop them trembling. He was showing pity. No, that was harsh. He was showing concern and it could be the undoing of her.

'I did not do it, Beth,' he added.

She could not stop herself from looking at him.

'I did not burn your house down, or order anyone to do it. I swear on my life.'

She saw the concern in his face. He was not the composed, smartly dressed man she had been expecting; in fact he looked slightly dishevelled and she was grateful for that. It narrowed the distance between them very slightly, and that was all to the good.

'It was Martha's son, Tom Kitto. He was also responsible for the broken tools, the dead animal and the paint.'

'Tom? No, you are wrong.'

'It is true.'

'It can't be. You don't even know Tom. It is easy for the villagers to use him as a scapegoat and blame him, but he would not do such things.'

'I have just come from his home. I thought Edward had been overzealous in his orders, but he denied any involvement. This meant that someone else was to blame, so I came back to warn you. When I discovered what had happened to your cottage I went to Port Carrek to look for you. I thought you might be with Martha, and it was there that I found him.' Joss took a step towards her. 'He had lime wash on his boots, Beth, the same that had been thrown over the cottage. He had also suffered severe burns from setting it on fire.'

Beth felt unable to move. 'Tom isn't capable of such acts. What does Martha say?'

'I am sorry to have to be the one to tell you, but Martha is dead. So is her son.'

'Dead? No, that can't be true.'

'I speak the truth.'

Beth covered her ears and turned away. 'No. I don't believe it.'

It was hard to believe what he was saying. Tom did it, and now they were both dead? He'd told her just like that, as though he was remarking on the weather. It did not seem real. Was she in a nightmare? Yet, her numb thoughts conjured up her last visit to Martha, her heartfelt goodbye and that look in her eyes – had she known what was about to occur?

Martha had once claimed to have the gift of second sight, but when she had said it Beth had seen a twinkle in her eye. A pedlar who visited Port Carrek each Lady's Day claimed to have the gift, too. He also had a twinkle in his eye – a look that made one wonder if he spoke in jest or told the truth. The pedlar would give away lucky heather and tell your fortune for a copper farthing. Beth had asked him once why he charged a farthing. He had winked at her and explained that the rich sometimes gave him half a sovereign by mistake on account that they looked so similar. Beth had laughed. What fools the rich were, to give away so much by mistake—

Joss came across the room, turned her to face him and took her hands. She found herself back in the room with Joss. The pedlar's cheeky face was gone.

'It is true, Beth. There is evidence that Martha poisoned her son and took her own life. His body was so badly burnt that he would have died anyway. She knew he would not survive and that she would be arrested for ending his suffering, so she took her own life.'

Beth shook her head. 'No, Martha took her own life to be with him. She did not care for herself.'

'I'm sorry to have brought you this news. I did not want to upset you like this, but I needed you to know it was not of my doing.' Joss looked down at her fingers in his cupped hands. 'Your hands ... they are blistered.'

'Picking rope. My hands have not yet hardened to the oakum.'

She had forgotten about the soreness of her fingers. What did she care about the pain when she had just heard about the death of her friend? She had so badly wanted to speak to her after the fire but Martha would not answer her door. Jacca had said Tom was ill and she wanted no visitors. Yet this turned out to have been a falsehood that Martha had spread to keep people at bay. Her mind continued to try and sort her jumbled thoughts, but there were too many questions, too much to make sense of. Her brain ached with it all.

She watched Joss smooth her palms with his thumbs. He was gentle and tender and she was in need of some tenderness in this harsh world she found herself in. She felt herself relax as his caress soothed her. The apprehension she had felt about seeing him again had melted away on the tide of bad news. Gently, he blew on each palm, just as he had done after fighting the thugs when they had tried to remove her from Kynance Cottage. He had fought to protect her. He would not have done that if he had known he was Roscarrock, she realised. He would have helped them.

She watched him bow his head and kiss each of her fingers. His soft lips sent a shiver of sensations down her arms. It felt good, but she felt guilty to experience such pleasure at this time. Her friend was dead, poor Tom too, and she felt dowdy and dirty. It was all so at odds at what he was doing. She eased her hands away from his.

'They will harden soon,' she added solemnly.

Beth stepped away from him. She wanted to be alone with her grief and find a dark corner – perhaps the toilet block – where she could weep her sorrow in private and retch the contents of her stomach down the drain under the seat. Retch until her throat and heart were sore, hear it fall and smell the stench. Yes, it would fit in well with how she felt and it would ease the sickness that was rising inside her.

Joss saw her misery. 'You have cared for me, and now it is my turn to care for you.'

'You don't owe me anything. You need not feel any responsibility for my wellbeing. It was kind of you to visit and tell me about Martha and Tom, Mr Roscarrock.'

'I'm not offering you help out of a misguided sense of responsibility. I am offering you marriage.'

Beth almost laughed. 'You do not mean that. You don't need me.' She wanted to leave and hide beneath her covers, in the dark, all alone, to absorb the bad news.

Joss stood in her way. She could see that he was losing his patience.

'Have you ever thought I might *want* you in my life? I existed before I met you, but I did not enjoy living.'

This time Beth did laugh at the absurdity of what he was saying. He was a mine owner and lived in a grand house while she had nothing and had just heard of the death of her closest friend. His impatience with her was due to the fact he did not like being rejected and nothing more.

'Yes, your life must be hell,' she scoffed.

Joss's temper snapped. 'I have ridden for more than twenty miles and seen two lives wasted. Forgive me if I have lost patience with your silly prejudices.' She tried to pass him but he barred her way again. 'Don't talk to me about hell.' He thumped his chest. '*I* have seen hell. Hell smells of cannon and artillery smoke. It smells of rotting flesh and gangrene and tastes of mud. The images remain in your mind forever. I will tell you about hell. It sounds like the explosion of firearms, it sounds like men crying out in pain. I have been to hell and its colour is blood red!'

His anger had been sudden. Her words had been the spark to ignite this explosion of hidden, tortured memories and Beth realised her folly. She had spoken glibly about his troubles when she knew nothing about them. Yet it all became clear in that moment. His scars and his nightmares had hinted that he had his own demons, which until now he had not acknowledged to her.

As quickly as it had erupted, his temper left. They stood quietly facing each other and somehow Beth knew it was the first time he had opened the door on his innermost feelings regarding the war. He had dropped his guard and spoken without thought but with candour, and now he was unsure how to proceed. Yet he wanted to speak more, she could tell.

Why he felt safe to do so now, she did not know. Perhaps it was because they were shut away from the world, within a building that people from normal society did not enter. Away from everyone who would not understand. Beth saw an escape from her own pain – by listening to his.

'You speak of the Crimean War?'

He did not answer at first. Beth waited and did not press him further. Finally he spoke.

'Yes, although I feel no honour or pride. Our involvement in the Crimea will go down as the most mismanaged and unnecessary campaign in British history. More men died of disease than from war wounds. Where is the honour in that? Yet they sacrificed their lives and did not return, each one as brave as the next, however they met their maker.'

Beth remained silent, so he continued. 'I was in the 46th Regiment of the Foot. I was a lieutenant and then second captain. Our regiment took part in the siege of Sebastopol.' He was watching her, as if assessing her reaction, perhaps her consent to continue further.

'Tell me about it,' Beth encouraged.

Joss raked a hand through his hair. 'Do you really want to know?'

Beth realised she did. She had thought it would be a diversion, but now she found herself wanting to understand what he had experienced and how it had sculpted his character.

'Yes, tell me. Tell me the truth of it.'

He frowned and looked away.

'I remember all the battles I took part in. They were all played out in a cesspit of confusion, but it is the memories of Sebastopol that won't let me go. So many brave soldiers died unnecessarily and it was not the hero's death they had expected.'

Joss had made a start. The rest came easier to him. Like a confessor, his words spilled from his lips. 'It was the main naval base of the Russians. The siege lasted eleven months. Their defences were good but it was the weather and poor decisions made by our incompetent leaders that cost lives and lengthened the siege. We lacked heavy artillery to smash the defences and there was no provision for a winter campaign. What little we had was destroyed in a storm. Supplies were often late and not distributed until they had already rotted. During the winter their incompetency brought our soldiers to the brink of starvation.'

He walked over to the window and looked out onto the grey courtyard beyond. He stared into the distance, but she suspected it was the battlefield in his head that he saw. His innermost feelings on the war had finally found a voice. His tone was quiet, but his words were clear.

'It was a war like no other,' he said. 'Cavalry charges had no place in a war fought in manmade trenches and defences. Our soldiers were cannon fodder and thousands died needlessly. If the war did not kill them, the cold, starvation and disease did. Their dead bodies rise up in my dreams and try to claim me too. Yet the Russians fared no better. A dead Russian soldier is the same as a British or French one, but for the uniform. The blood that seeps from their wounds is the same colour as ours. The last words of the dying are the same no matter what side they are on.' He paused and looked at her. 'They still call for their mother or whisper their wife's name. It is always the same, every man, every death. It is always a woman's name on their lips as they die. No matter how brave they have been, it is a woman they cry for.'

Joss looked back at the window, and then turned away as if he could not bear the sight of it any longer.

'War changes a man, Beth, as it should. War has changed me. No man should see the horrors of war and be unmoved as it would be a betrayal of those who died. Yet victory is a hollow feeling. After eleven months of death and destruction, I walked through the remains of the siege. Despite having won, I felt no feeling of victory. Their dead are like our dead, and amongst the ruins are the ordinary people of Sebastopol.

'You say I have a reputation for being ruthless.' Joss gave a bitter laugh. 'Being ruthless is killing a mule to feed your men despite the fact that it bravely carried loads for you throughout the war. Ruthlessness is choosing to leave men to die in no man's land because it would risk others to fetch them. What is the point of risking another life for the wounded when you have no provisions to care for them? Yet you still carry the guilt of your decision. We had no dressings, no medicine, no food. Ruthlessness is asking your men to advance, when the risk of their dying is overwhelming.

'Yet when I returned to Cornwall I saw no change. People were still going about their lives, working, laughing and having children. What do they know of a war in a country they do not know, against people they have not met? Most Cornish men have never left the county, let alone understand a foreign war. I have been to hell and the experience tainted my enjoyment of life.'

Beth was horrified to hear the truth. She was only fourteen at the start of the war, and it was as foreign to her as the land it was fought in. Yet her lack of understanding had been like that of many others, and to hear that this ignorance had added to his burden and pain was a surprise. Their ignorance was not born out of malice; it was not intended to harm him further.

'I know little about war,' Beth said. 'And I'm afraid that

any words of kindness I might say may sound superficial, but I want you to know that I wish I could take your pain away.'

'Not many people do know what it feels like to have been there,' Joss acknowledged.

'And it is for that reason that you cannot blame people for continuing to live their lives. You cannot blame them for not understanding what it is like to fight a war.'

'I do not blame them. I question why one man should be able to live his life when so many more deserving men have died ... better men who have fought in the name of their country.'

'You sound as if you wish you had died too. As if you feel guilty that you were lucky enough to have come home.'

Joss did not answer. He did not need to. She could see from his face that she had spoken the truth. Beth went to him and gently touched his cheek, feeling the fine growth of his stubble beneath her fingertips. All thoughts of Martha and Tom were put aside for the moment.

'You must not feel bad that you are still living. There are enough families grieving for lost ones without the desire that you should be among them.' She took his hand in hers. 'If you had died too what good would that bring, except grief to another family? Our presence touches people's lives, no matter how insignificant it may seem. Even a smile can brighten someone else's day and if you are not there to give it, that moment never happens.'

He covered her hand with his own and smiled. 'So if I touch people's lives in a good way I will find a purpose for my own. How simply you view life.'

He was mocking her. Gently, she pulled her hand away.

'I may see life simply, but it is the best way to live when you own little.'

'You assume I am making fun of you but I am not. You believe that if someone is rich they must be self-serving. Perhaps it is because of your father's abandonment, and I know that my own actions in the past have done nothing to alter your belief. However, you have opened my eyes to this flaw in me as surely as if you have held up a mirror and forced me to look upon it. It is true, in the past I have not cared about my workers as I should. However, I can rectify this, and perhaps I will feel the better for it. What about you, Beth? Do you have the desire to change your prejudices regarding people with money?'

'I am in a house full of paupers while others buy dresses with money that would feed a family for several months.'

Joss thrust out his chin. 'I have worked hard to build up my father's business. I am not ashamed of my accomplishments. There is no shame in improving yourself, Beth. Is this why you will not marry me? Do you feel that you would be betraying your community if you marry me?'

Beth turned and looked at him, surprised by his hurt tone. She felt her own heart ache for him. Joss deserved to be happy, but he would not find happiness with her. He needed a wife from his own class, one who knew how to behave in polite society and would be accepted by his friends and family. He deserved a woman he could be proud of, not one who would be an embarrassment to him and a subject of gossip. If she accepted his proposal he would come to regret their marriage and see it for what it was, a proposal made in haste. At first she had been frightened to look upon his face in case she might discover that she still loved it. She knew now that she did. Yet love did not conquer all. Morzelah would not cast her magic here.

'No, it is not about that.'

'You do not love me.'

'If it were about love, Joss,' Beth said softly, 'I would marry you today. But a marriage is a journey and it goes through good times and bad. If we married now, whenever we rowed I would always wonder if you had married me out of sympathy or a misplaced sense of responsibility.'

Joss shook his head and was about to speak but Beth stopped him with an outstretched hand.

'And I would wonder if I only married you to be rescued from here. If we were more equal, we would have no doubt.'

'I have no doubt. The doubt is on your side and your side alone. I believe that your own insecurities cloud your judgement.' Joss straightened his shoulders. 'Let me give you some money to start afresh.' Beth shook her head. 'You see it as charity? How do you plan to get out of here?'

'I will work my way out. Find work mending.'

'Difficult when you own nothing.'

'Life is difficult. I hide from difficulties too often, but now I must face them. It will do me good. What will happen to Martha and Tom's bodies?'

'Do they have relatives or money?'

Beth shook her head. It would be an unmarked, communal, pauper's grave for them.

'I will arrange a plot for them and provide a headstone, so those who loved them will have a place to mourn.'

Beth felt the tears sting her eyes. He was doing this for her and her alone. Joss walked towards her and touched her hair. This time she did not move away. She leaned into his caress. She had made the ultimate rejection of him for the good of them both, but it had come at a price. He was hurting and so was she. She closed her eyes and felt his fingers thread through her hair, determined to savour his last touch.

'You thought your grandfather lied to you when he said that you would be well taken care of,' said Joss quietly. 'I do not believe he lied. He knew I would make contact on his death. He knew I owned the lease and that we would meet.'

Beth felt relief at his words. Joss could well be right.

'He just did not imagine that you would refuse my help and reject me.' Joss let his hand fall from her hair and turned to leave. He hesitated. 'Has it not occurred to you that I do not feel comfortable in my own life? I do not enjoy the company of frivolous people with more money than sense and no purpose to their lives. I thought that with you by my side we could laugh at their absurdities together.' He looked at her with his golden brown eyes, flecked with green. 'However, I will not do my class an injustice, Beth. Not everyone is like that and not anyone that I would count as my friend. I can see my proposal of marriage has come at the wrong time. You have just learnt about the death of a friend and you do not trust my motivations, or your own. I will not believe that you do not love me enough to enter my world. When the time is right and you change your mind, come to me. You know where I live.'

He waited for her response, but Beth found she could not find the right words to say. Time stood still for the briefest of moments, until he came towards her, cupped her face in his hands and looked deep into her eyes. His sudden closeness ignited a feeling of pleasure that spiralled deep down inside of her and made her legs tremble. His eyes darkened and she recognised her own primal response reflected in his. She had told him, without words, that she wanted him as much as he wanted her. He brushed a thumb over her soft bottom lip and instinctively her lips parted in invitation. It was what he had hoped for.

At first his kiss was soft and gentle, as if he was still afraid she would retreat from him, but as she allowed herself to respond, so did his desire and need for her increase. He broke free to look into her eyes, but he wanted more. To see his need for her, his desire for her, heightened her own. It was as if they were already lovers – what pleased one pleased the other, and Beth knew that his kisses would remain with her for the rest of her life. All too soon their kissing came to an end. It had to. It could certainly go no further – even if there was the desire to. Not in this damp, cold room, with peeling paint on the walls.

Joss held her in his arms and whispered into her hair. 'I

started my journey this morning to warn you that you might be in danger, but it was too late. I had also hoped that by seeing you again I would purge you from my heart, yet I ended up wanting to make you my wife. I have failed on every single aim I set out to achieve ... every single one. And now we are to part. Your valley is safe, Beth. I will not destroy it. Call it my parting gift to you.'

He kissed her one more time, a tender soft kiss that lingered and left as gently as it had begun. Finally, when she allowed herself to breathe again and open her eyes, he was gone. The pain of loss clawed at her all over again, but this time it was not for the dead that she grieved. This time it was for herself.

Chapter Nineteen

Beth looked at her hands. The memory of Joss's kiss upon them two days earlier made her smile. She had had pretty hands once, but now the nails were torn and her skin was stained with black tar. She realised that she would not make her quota of oakum today. Her sore fingers had meant she had to adapt how she worked to avoid her blisters. Although more experienced inmates had shown her how to roll the strands of the tarred ropes on her knees to extract the oakum, it was still a skill Beth had yet to master.

She looked at her pile of oakum on the floor, which would soon be bundled up with the others and sold to make decking on ships. The monotonous recycling of tarred rope helped to waterproof the joints between the planks, and also provided an occupation for the paupers and an income for the workhouse. Beth's elbow was nudged and she looked up. The jostling of elbows was a common occurrence and it meant nothing. It was bound to happen when a large number of women were so tightly packed on a bench to work. Beth looked at her fellow inmates. They each had a tale of sorrow etched on their faces in the guise of deep wrinkles, dark shadows and hunched shoulders. She had been too proud to accept Joss's help, and now she was at risk of becoming like the women about her: defeated and with no hope for the future.

'Jago, you are wanted by Master Piper,' said an orderly standing in front of her.

Beth looked up, surprised. She had not heard her approach.

'Be quick and follow me,' the middle-aged woman ordered before turning away.

Her fellow inmates watched as she slowly rose to her feet. No one was ever summoned to see Master Piper, unless it was bad news. With trepidation Beth followed her, just as she had followed Matron Haynes two days before.

She had rarely seen the master of the workhouse, just glimpses as he walked along a corridor or spoke to the staff. Now he was talking to her as if she were an equal, inviting her to his office as though she were important. What had brought about this change?

Beth looked at the two brown packages on the master's desk and the letter in his hand. She had a feeling that she would soon find out and it had something to do with the letter, which he now held out to her. Tentatively she reached for it, but before she could open it, it became clear why he was treating her differently.

'Mr Roscarrock has kept his promise and made a generous donation to the workhouse and you are lucky to have him as a benefactor.' Master Piper stroked one of the packages in front of him. 'He has informed me of what is in the letter and we have come to an agreement. The committee room is yours for one month and you are relieved from your oakum duties on condition you use the committee room as instructed.'

Beth frowned. So it was Joss's donation that elevated her standing, and the master hoped to have more. However, he was talking in riddles and it still made little sense. The master encouraged her to open the letter with a nod of his head and a flap of his hand. Carefully, Beth did.

It was written in a neat, masculine hand, and although she did not know Joss's handwriting, his name at the bottom confirmed it was from him. Her heart began to thud in her chest as she read its contents.

Dear Miss Jago,
Following our meeting and your subsequent refusal
to accept my help, I am writing to reassure you that I
understand your decision. You made it quite clear that you

do not wish to feel in debt to me. I also understand that the acceptance of money, or my offer of marriage, would be difficult for you to separate from feelings of sympathy or responsibility on my part. I acknowledge and accept your decision. Rest assured these offers are withdrawn.

Beth swallowed. It hurt to read his businesslike tone, and he had not even addressed her as Beth. Had their kiss meant nothing? She could not bear to read more, yet she could not stop herself from reading on.

I also hold the same conviction to not be in debt to others. It is a good philosophy to live by and I commend your stance. With this in mind I have itemised all the services and purchases that I have incurred during my stay at Kynance Cottage (see enclosed invoice) and, to the best of my ability, calculated the amount that I owe you. With the aforementioned obstacle (your refusal to accept money) I have taken the liberty of giving you two items and rented the committee room for a period of one month. This I have done to the value of the amount I owe you. This arrangement has repaid any debts on my side. I hope you will find a use for these items and that they will provide a means for you to leave the workhouse.

You owe me nothing and I owe you nothing. We are as equals.

> *Yours sincerely,*
> *Joss Roscarrock*

Frowning, Beth looked at the second sheet and quickly read the items.

Full bed and board, hiring of her grandfather's clothes, nursing services …

Beth found herself beginning to smile.

... purchase of one toffee apple at Golowan Feast and one wishing ribbon. Purchasing the services of a cleaner, a mender, a ...

Beth began to laugh.

... tour guide, fighter, advisor...

He was being ridiculous, of course. He need not pay her for any of these things, but it seemed he was determined that she accept his help. He had tried to disguise it in the form of a business transaction, but she saw it for what it was. However, this time she was grateful.

Under the silent glare of Master Piper, Beth began to undo the two large packages. When the purchases were exposed, she stood back to look at them with tears in her eyes. She had mentioned her desire to have one of them only once to Joss, yet he had remembered. She was touched by his kindness and thoughtfulness. He had found a means of helping her that allowed her to keep her pride. Sitting amongst the crumpled brown wrapping paper and string was a black and gold sewing machine that far surpassed the one she had seen in Mrs Tilly's fabric shop. Its highly polished surface bounced light into the room and its intricate engineering was a mixture of elegance, strength and speed. Beside it was a bolt of fabric, matching cotton and buttons. It would be enough for her to make a sample dress to advertise her work. Her smile broadened as she imagined Joss seeking advice in a haberdashery. She knew that he would not know what a dressmaker would require, yet he had gone out of his way to make sure the right purchases were made. To an onlooker the purchases might seem strange, yet to Beth they were as clear as if he had handed her a key to unlock a prison door. Joss was persistent in his desire to help her and would have his way. She loved him for it and she would not let him down.

Chapter Twenty

One year later
Summer, 1862

The much-anticipated Red Feathers' Charity Ball had begun. A heavy shower of rain, which fortunately finished just an hour before the doors were opened, had left the road wet. Yet even the glistening cobbles, as their wet surfaces reflected the light of the oil lamps, added to the glamour of the occasion. The shimmering soft light flattered the ladies' complexions and put everyone in a jovial mood. The downpour, it seemed, had done little to dampen the excitement of the guests or diminish the fairy tale atmosphere that balls of this size always managed to capture.

A line of carriages slowly filed past the main entrance of the Guild Hall Assembly Rooms, each one pausing momentarily at the bottom of the steps for its occupants to descend onto the pavement, whilst another waited patiently behind for its turn to move forward. Once descended, the ladies, dressed in elegant gowns, gathered themselves before being accompanied by their escorts up the stone steps to the grand entrance.

It was *the* ball that everyone had wanted to attend. A ticket to the Red Feathers' Charity Ball was expensive, yet everyone who was anyone wanted one. To be in possession of a ticket would not only demonstrate one's charity, but also indicate affluence and good connections. The growing excitement surrounding the occasion, and the desire by many to obtain such a sought-after ticket, could only be orchestrated by an experienced businessman. A businessman who also had the skills to form the charity itself, and who had chosen to name it after the nickname of the regiment in which he had served. However, it was not only for charitable reasons that many of the young ladies attended tonight. If the gossip was to be believed, this same businessman happened to be one of the wealthiest and most eligible bachelors in Cornwall – and quite handsome too.

The rumour was that he had always been moderately wealthy, but according to the news-sheets he had hit a profitable load of tin by using a unique diagonal shaft. This method of mining was so unusual that it was at the forefront of engineering. It was even reported that Prince Albert himself had expressed an interest in visiting his mine. The load was so large, it was reported, that it would provide enough work for the local miners and their families for the next twenty years, despite the competitive prices of tin from abroad.

The chance to meet this wealthy mine owner added to the popularity of the ball, as in the past he had been inclined to keep himself to himself. Yet since the establishment of the Red Feathers' Fund, he was making himself more visible to the public for the good of his charity. This grand occasion would be a chance to satisfy curious minds, and for parents to introduce their daughters. As the businessman watched the guests arrive, he knew that his ball had already been a success. The tickets had made more money than he had dared to hope for, but he was under no illusion regarding the reason they were coming. Curiosity and a desire to catch a man of means, not an understanding of poverty, had fuelled the popularity of the ball tonight, and no one knew this better than the businessman himself.

Joss Roscarrock welcomed each guest like a long lost friend. Some may have hoped he would take an interest in their daughters, however he had no desire to look for a wife. His aim was to raise money for his charity, and each guest was important to him for buying a ticket and helping his cause. He had discovered that helping a family at a time of crisis through his charity brought him a deep feeling of satisfaction. It finally gave him a reason why he had survived the hell of war when so many others had not. He was relaxed and content as he greeted each guest. His pleasure at seeing them was genuine and he welcomed them to the ball as though he hosted such events every day of the week.

The ball had been in full swing for an hour. Couples began to disperse from the floor as the orchestra came to the end of their sheet of music. Smiling, and a little out of breath, Karenza was escorted from the dance floor by her dance partner and back to her husband. She politely thanked the gentleman for the dance and, after a short bow to her husband, Karenza watched him depart and gave a little sigh.

'From the look on your face, you enjoyed the waltz,' her husband said to her as they surveyed the room.

'It was wonderful. I feel five years younger. You must ask someone.' Karenza looked up at him with a mischievous glint in her eye. 'But only someone I approve of.' She gave him her brightest smile. 'I'm so glad you are home, William. Your recent voyage was much too long.'

'It was too long for me too.' William looked down at his wife's face. She was radiant, in a gown of moiré, trimmed with light tulle. 'And I feel you will make me suffer for leaving you so long with your choice of dance partner for me.'

Karenza looked around the room at the ladies present. It had been such a long time since she had attended a ball, and this one was all she had hoped it to be.

William watched Joss as he conversed with a group of men. 'Your brother looks well,' he said. Karenza nodded in agreement. 'And I swear Edward is attempting to dance with every lady in the room. He and Joss have been friends for a long time.'

'Yes. Edward is very loyal to Joss. Joss saved his life in the Crimea. He was shot and Joss stopped the bleeding and got him to safety. I think Edward will never forget that.'

As if Joss had heard them, he said his goodbyes to the men

he had been talking to and began to make his way towards them. He does look well, thought Karenza, and handsome in his black superfine evening dress-coat, well-fitting trousers and white silk waistcoat. She noticed a few of the ladies turn their heads to watch him move across the room as they hid shyly behind their mother-of pearl and ivory fans.

'Joss has not danced with anyone,' Karenza said quietly to her husband, her smile fading a little.

William noticed the sadness in her tone. Wanting to cheer her he bent his head and whispered into her ear. 'I wish I could dance with you.'

Karenza's smile returned and she playfully hit him on the arm with her own fan.

'You know it would be the height of bad manners for a husband and wife to dance together. We must circulate. At least you can choose who you ask, whereas I cannot refuse anyone who asks me unless I have a good excuse, which I do not.' She looked at her dance card. 'I have to dance with Francis Goldsworthy on my fourth dance.'

As William laughed, Joss arrived and it was plain he had heard their conversation.

'If I was married, I would insist on dancing with my wife at least twice.'

Karenza tutted. 'That does not surprise me. Even as a child you were never conventional.' Both men laughed at her exasperation with them. 'Why have you not danced, Joss?' his sister asked him suddenly. His laughter died.

'I am the host. My role is to ensure everyone is enjoying themselves and encourage the gentlemen to ask the ladies for a dance. It is my job to make sure that there are no wallflowers. I have no time for dancing.' Joss changed the subject. 'How are you, William?'

'Glad to be on dry land again, Joss,' his brother-in-law replied.

'I might be able to help there. I have a proposition for you. Can we talk more tomorrow?'

Karenza did not attempt to conceal her excitement and insisted he tell them more.

Joss relented. 'It is in the early stages yet, but I am on the committee of a new business venture. We hope to take advantage of the development of Falmouth docks and buy a composite ship. We plan to start using a maritime route across the North Atlantic to North America, but we have a problem. We need someone who can manage our new enterprise, but they must have experience of maritime trade, ships and navigation. I told them I might know someone. What do you say, William?'

At first William could not believe his ears, but after a nudge from his wife he found his tongue. 'I'd be delighted, but aren't you too busy with the mine and The Red Feathers?'

'The mine is profitable and stable. Edward manages it for me now, and I hope you will manage the maritime business for its shareholders. We need someone who is knowledgeable and in whom we can place our trust. It will mean that you will need to spend more time on land, of course.'

It was something his sister and brother-in-law had wanted for a very long time now.

'It sounds perfect,' said Karenza.

Joss was pleased to see that her smile had returned.

'What about you?' asked William, his mind already racing at what this opportunity would mean – more time with his wife, perhaps even a family.

'I have a large share in it, but I plan to concentrate on raising more funds for The Red Feathers. The mine provides my living but a large proportion of my profits from the maritime trade will go directly into The Red Feathers' Fund.'

William was intrigued. Karenza had told him a little about Joss's fund, but not in great detail. 'Tell me about this charity.'

'I do not like to call it a charity. It is more akin to a benevolent fund. Money is made available to its members who have lost their main breadwinner through injury or death whilst carrying out their duty or work. The membership is open to three of the main occupations in Cornwall: fishermen, miners and soldiers. When a member's family is in need, they are given funding for a period of three months until they get back on their feet again. It will help them pay rent and feed their families until they can support themselves. In the event of a death, the fund will also pay for the funeral and headstone. This will mean that no member will have a pauper's unmarked grave and the family will have a headstone where they can go to mourn.'

'And how do they become a member?'

'It is on the same lines as a peppercorn rent. It is a one-off token amount and they can choose how much. It can be as little or as much as they please. People are proud, and can feel reluctant to accept charity. This way they feel ownership, they feel that as members they are able to accept the help without shame.'

Karenza and William could hear the enthusiasm in Joss's voice and how important it was to him.

'Surprisingly I have found that my fellow mine owners have been willing to donate to the cause, and an added benefit has been that they have also increased safety in their mines as a result.' Joss lowered his voice so only William and Karenza could hear his next words. 'They do not want to be seen as owning a mine with a high death or injury rate.'

William was impressed. Karenza had told him little about the details, other than it was a fund to help poor people. However, Joss's explanation showed that he had put great thought into not only how to raise funds, but also how to distribute it without causing offence. He had never seen this side of Joss before.

'Admirable,' William replied. 'It sounds like an insurance policy for the poor. I also hear that you have the healthiest miners in Cornwall. Karenza tells me you pay for their medical fees.'

'If they are mine-related, yes I do. Mining will always be dangerous, but I have found that if wounds or illnesses are treated quickly, the miners soon return to work. They are happier, too, knowing they do not have to worry about the cost of treatment. I suppose you can call it an insurance policy for the poor, however I make no profit from their time of crisis. I pay out far more than I will ever make, which is why I need to raise the funds.'

Much as Karenza admired her brother's charitable works, she was getting bored. This was a ball and no place to talk business. She had also noticed Joss had been watching the guests throughout their conversation and to her disappointment it was not the women he was studying. Her brother's eyes sought out gentlemen of means, with the intention of persuading them to donate further to his cause.

Exasperated, she slammed her fan shut and changed the subject. 'Is there not one lady here who takes your fancy?'

Joss answered a little too quickly, 'None.'

Karenza turned to her husband. 'I would like to have some time alone with my brother so I have found the perfect partner for you. Mrs Bell is over there by the large green plant. I'm sure she would like a dance.'

William followed his wife's gaze to the middle-aged woman who sat alone on the other side of the hall. 'But isn't she in mourning?'

'Yes she is, but she is not wearing scarlet or black and her dress is trimmed with mauve, which means she is open to dances.'

William gave his wife a short bow. 'Your wish is my command,' he said, before leaving her side and making his way across the room.

Joss watched him walk away. 'The widow can be an outrageous flirt. I'm surprised you trust her,' he teased.

'I don't, but I do trust William.' Karenza looked up at Joss and leant towards him so only he could hear her next words.

'Besides, her breath has the most terrible odour and it will probably be the only dance she will have all night. Her late husband suffered from a chronic blocked nose, which is just as well.'

They stood in companionable silence for a moment and watched the new set of couples begin to dance the quadrille. The music filled the hall and it was difficult not to sway to the tune. Eventually Karenza could not hold her tongue any longer.

'You still think of Beth, don't you?'

Joss looked down at one of his sleeve-links and rubbed it with a single stroke of his thumb. Finally, he lifted his chin and stood tall, his hands tightly clasped behind his back as he surveyed the scene. It was as if she had not spoken, so she tried again.

'Edward is your closest friend. Does he know how you feel?'

'Men do not talk of the affairs of the heart,' said Joss. His voice, although quiet, held a sadness she had not heard for a while, but then he had become good at hiding this side of him.

'Yet you talk to me.'

'Correction: you incessantly question me and I answer.'

'It is what sisters do. We would learn nothing of our brothers unless we asked.'

'So I have learned to my cost,' said Joss, looking down at her fondly.

'You have told me much about your time with her, but what has become of this woman?' For the first time that evening, Karenza was no longer interested in the ball.

'She rents some respectable rooms above a fabric shop in Killygrew. She is a seamstress and is doing very well.' Karenza could hear pride in his voice.

'You have spied on her?' she teased.

'I made enquiries once. I needed to know that she was safe, well and happy.'

'Have you spoken to her?'

'No.'

'Seen her?'

'Only the once and by accident.' Joss fell silent as he remembered the moment he had seen her in the street. He was unaware that Karenza watched his face in fascination as it softened at his memories.

It had been on a market day in late autumn when he had seen her walking along the bustling streets of Killygrew. He had been visiting the town on business, and his thoughts were elsewhere and his time limited. Suddenly he saw her through the crowd, walking alone with a basket on her arm. Her appearance was so sudden and unexpected that he stepped into the recess of a door to watch her pass. He could see now that it had been a selfish and cowardly act on his part, but he had wanted to see her face and watch her move without being observed. Feeling ill-prepared, he did not want anything to spoil the short precious moments of seeing her again, and so he had hidden in the shadows like a thief in the night. Had he spoken to her, he would not have known what to say. That day he had been struck dumb – like an inexperienced youth meeting a great beauty.

Karenza watched him in silence. She had not realised, until that moment, that his feelings for this woman remained so fresh.

'You still love her,' she said, unable to hide the surprise in her voice. The softness in Joss's face left, but she would not be put off. 'You must ask her to marry you again. It has been almost a year … she may have had a change of heart.'

'She rejected me twice,' Joss said abruptly. 'How many times must a man ask before he is considered a fool or a pest?'

'The timings of the proposals were not your best decisions, Joss,' she replied curtly. 'From what you have told me the first time neither of you knew who *you* really were. The second time you had just informed her that two people she knew had died and one of them was responsible for burning her house down. Besides, what woman would accept a marriage proposal if it meant that for the rest of her life she would be labelled as the woman you rescued from the workhouse? You know what people would say, that you only married her because you felt responsible for her.'

'Why would they say that?'

'Because it was her grandfather who saved your life when you were a child.'

'If you love someone, then the circumstances need not matter.'

'And if you love someone enough the circumstances would mean a great deal. For an intelligent man, Joss, you do say the most foolish things sometimes. Why do men have to see everything in such black and white terms?'

'Why do women have to be so complicated?'

'Because we see life in colour.'

Only his sister could speak to him in such a way. Joss found the argument frustrating yet refreshing at the same time. It shook things up and gave a different perspective. Just like two fighters, they stopped to rest from their sparring. In a companionable silence, they watched the dancers move about the floor in front of them. William danced past with Mrs Bell.

'Poor William,' Karenza said as she acknowledged them. 'He thinks he is a good dancer but he is not. He dances as if he is on the deck of a ship navigating rough seas. I do not have the heart to remind him that the floor beneath his feet is still. Secretly I am glad it would be in poor taste to dance as a married couple.'

Karenza and Joss exchanged glances and she smiled at him. He could not help but return her smile. No more words were needed.

Yet, as Joss returned his attention to his guests, Karenza noticed how quickly his smile left his face. She would not broach the subject of Beth Jago again. She did not have to voice her name, she realised, to bring this woman to the forefront of his mind.

The music stopped and William returned to them. 'Now I understand why I have been the only one to request a dance from Mrs Bell.'

'Her breath has not improved, I take it.'

'I should have known you already knew. You are enough to drive a man back out to sea. Nevertheless, the dancing has made me hungry.'

'There is a refreshment room over there with a table full of food that would satisfy any sailor's appetite,' said Joss. 'And, more importantly, there are glasses of claret and port to drink.'

William took his wife's arm. 'Let us have a look, Karenza. I am quite starved.'

Karenza resisted; she did not want to leave Joss alone. 'In a minute. Let's stay with Joss.'

Joss would have none of it. 'Don't concern yourself with me. I have seen a lady in the room who needs my attention.'

Karenza was delighted. Eagerly she turned to see which lady had caught her brother's eye.

'Who is it? I want to see her,' she asked.

'Mrs Bell, of course,' Joss replied, knowing it would frustrate her. He raised an eyebrow at her accusing look. 'You don't think I would be happy for her to have only one dance this evening, do you?'

Karenza and William watched him stride across the floor, as couples took up their places and waited for the orchestra to strike up again.

'I look forward to speaking to him about this new job. It is a very exciting proposition. I would be home more often and perhaps we will be fortunate enough to start a family this time.'

William realised Karenza was not listening, as her thoughts and mind were on her brother. He stroked her arm. 'What will you do while Joss and I talk about the new maritime venture tomorrow?' he asked.

Karenza watched Joss's tall frame as he escorted Mrs Bell onto the dance floor. 'If I tell you, you must promise not to tell Joss.'

William agreed he would not. Karenza smiled, as she watched the dance begin.

'I have a fancy for a new dress,' she said, opening her fan and waving it with quiet determination. 'And I know just the dressmaker to see about it.'

Chapter Twenty-One

Karenza stepped down from her carriage and looked up at the shop sign. Harper's was one of the largest shops in Killygrew and Beth Jago had done well to have her dressmaking services linked to the premises, despite never having undergone an apprenticeship. It was reassuring to see that the shop was of a good standard. Karenza understood Joss's desire to make enquiries about her welfare. She had heard that needlewomen often resorted to finding employment in sweatshops where they undertook exhausting work whilst earning a poor wage. It was not uncommon to read terrible tales of such women being taken advantage of by unscrupulous employers, yet Beth Jago had managed to avoid this. She had found a respectable shop owner whose patronage had allowed her to work privately on the site. This connection had immediately elevated her position to a much sought-after dressmaker who could reproduce fashionable designs for a cheaper price. She had managed all this with just the help of a sewing contraption and a single bolt of material given to her by Joss in payment for his stay.

As her carriage moved away, Karenza's gaze was drawn to the large display window. Swathes of material, in an assortment of colours, were draped across a chaise longue and spilled from an ornately carved wooden trunk. The window looked like a painting of a lady's private room. Any woman passing by could not help but stop and compare the display with her own bedroom at home. Mr Harper certainly knew how to entice a lady into his shop. Like a moth to a flame, Karenza was drawn to the entrance to view the delights within. It was an added bonus that she was about to meet the woman who had captured her brother's heart.

The inside of the shop was a little disappointing, although

Karenza did not really know what she was expecting. The interior contained numerous rolls of material displayed neatly on shelves, along with button jars, boxes of samples and rolls of ribbons. Mr Harper himself welcomed her from behind a counter.

With the obligatory greetings out of the way, Karenza took out an illustration of a day dress she had taken from her copy of *Ladies' Fashion Journal*, and showed it to the shop owner.

'I would like to have this dress made and I understand you have a dressmaker who may be able to undertake this.'

Mr Harper took the illustration from her. 'Indeed I do. I have two, Mrs Peabody and Miss Jago. Both are quite capable of making this for you. Do you have a preference in the material to be used?'

Karenza looked at the abundance of samples and rolls. 'Perhaps I should take advice on the colour and type from the dressmaker. I have had Miss Jago recommended to me. Is she available?'

Mr Harper handed back the illustration. 'Miss Jago is on an errand at the moment, but she has rooms here where she undertakes her work and she will be back shortly. Mrs Peabody works from home so if you wish to discuss your needs today, Miss Jago would be the most suitable. She is highly trained and skilled.'

Karenza took the illustration. She knew that Beth had no such training but she understood it was in Mr Harper's interests to promote her. The dressmaker who rented rooms from him would be more obliged to recommend his fabrics.

'Perfect. I shall wait,' said Karenza.

Pleased, Mr Harper showed her into a room at the back. 'Miss Jago will not be long. Would you like some tea while you wait?'

Karenza nodded regally and while he was gone she looked about Beth's fitting and sewing room. It was of a moderate size, with only one window. Fortunately, it was a south-facing room, which allowed the sun's rays to shine directly through the window for most of the day. The first thing she saw was the sewing machine, which was placed carefully by the window to make the most of the good light. It was a neat room, with a large table at the side. The worn, wooden tabletop was covered in silk, which was in the process of being cut into shapes ready for sewing. On another table were three dresses – a day dress, a simple evening dress and a ball gown. They were miniature versions and not more than three feet long, yet the detail and workmanship were exquisite. Each style was unique and finely tailored, yet they all had one thing in common: they were all made from the same roll of material. Karenza could not help but be impressed at her ability to design, make and present such different items from the same cloth. Is this what Beth had chosen to do with the material that Joss had given her? Had she chosen to make samples of her work to show prospective employers her skill? If she had then no wonder Mr Harper had wanted to link his name with her, as she had more skill than any seamstress Karenza had used in the past. Perhaps she would have a dress made after all.

The doorbell rang. Karenza heard Mr Harper's lowered tones and a woman's voice reply. Karenza moved away from the samples and stood in the centre of the room. Strangely she felt herself stiffen as she heard Beth's footsteps approach. Soon she would meet the woman she knew so much about and who knew nothing about her. She was intrigued to see what sort of woman could render a former soldier unconscious and steal his heart, only to reject him – twice. Did every sister feel as she did, curious to see the sort of woman her brother would want as a wife? For the first time she questioned why she was here. Was it to tell Beth to write to Joss and tell him she was happy, so that he could move on with his life? Or was it to matchmake?

Karenza heard Beth in the narrow hall outside. She

positioned herself so she could see Beth's reflection in a mirror on the wall. She watched her remove her hat and gloves and place them on a small table. She was finally meeting the woman who she had heard so much about, thanks to her incessant questioning of Joss. Karenza had expected a woman with an aura of a hard life, a tough woman who would be hard to relate to, yet she did not see this in the woman's reflection in the mirror. One should never underestimate the strength of a woman, Karenza thought to herself. Beth was smaller than she had anticipated, quite delicate in fact, and did not appear the sort to hit anyone at all.

Karenza watched Beth pat her hair into place in preparation for their meeting. Her hair was neatly dressed and was as black as Joss had described, yet despite her preparation, she did not appear fazed to be meeting a woman from Karenza's social standing. Joss had said she despised rich people, yet she did not appear to have this attitude now. Perhaps her work as a dressmaker had brought her into contact with more women who had money, Karenza thought. Perhaps she now realised they were no different from her when their clothes were removed for fitting.

Beth looked up and their eyes met; she had caught Karenza watching her in the mirror. Beth smiled and Karenza had no choice but to return it. They had finally met, and it was not the way Karenza had planned. Beth left the table and entered the room.

'Good morning, Mrs Fitzpatrick. Mr Harper has told me you would like to see me.'

'Good morning,' replied Karenza. 'Yes, I am in need of a dressmaker.'

There was an awkward silence as the two women looked at each other. Unusually, Karenza was lost for words, for she had discovered that there was one thing that Joss had not told her about Beth Jago. Something he had kept secret, so that he still had a memory of her that he alone owned. Beth's eyes were a beautiful deep blue colour. Some months ago Joss had purchased a pair of sleeve-links with a single gem set in each one. Karenza had thought it was odd at the time. He was not the sort of man who wore gems. Even stranger, he had taken to having them displayed in their open box on his desk as he worked. Now she understood why, and it brought a lump to her throat. Those sleeve-links, with their deep blue sapphire stones, reminded him of this woman's eyes.

'Mrs Fitzpatrick, are you all right?'

Karenza came to her senses at the sound of Beth's gentle Cornish accent. She sounded concerned, but not uncouth in the way she spoke. That was promising, thought Karenza, and in that moment she realised what her aim in coming here had been: to ascertain Beth Jago's suitability for her brother.

'Yes, thank you,' she replied briskly, and handed Beth the illustration. 'I would like to have this dress made for me.'

Tentatively Beth took it and looked at the drawing. She glanced up at Karenza and back at the picture, frowning slightly. Mr Harper came in with a tray of tea and left immediately. In the absence of a reply, Karenza sat herself down and poured herself a cup.

'Do you think you can manage it?'

Beth sat down beside her. 'I can make it for you but I don't think you will like it.'

Karenza paused, her teacup held in mid-air. 'You don't believe you have the skill?'

'I have the skill. May I speak plainly to you, Mrs Fitzpatrick? I only ask this as I want you to have a dress that you will love and want to wear, and I don't think you will love this dress.'

Karenza was baffled and unsure if she really wanted her to. She lifted her cup again. 'Speak plainly.' She watched her over the rim of her cup as she took a sip of tea.

'You have a big bust.'

Karenza almost choked on her drink. There was a difference between speaking plainly and being downright rude. This woman was not suitable and it did not take long to find that out. Beth, however, did not see her annoyance; she had taken a sheet of paper and was quickly redrawing the illustration.

'I suspect that you prefer your evening gowns to your day dresses.' Beth worked her pencil furiously as she drew. 'And you probably wonder why your day dresses make you feel matronly and make your bosom look bigger than it actually is.'

This time Karenza did not take offence at her intimate choice of words. Normally a dressmaker would fawn over her and make anything that she asked for. They would never utter the crude word *bosom* in her presence, as Beth had done. Yet Beth had voiced something Karenza had always felt, as if she had seen into her mind. She did indeed feel matronly, too big on top, and preferred her evening gowns to her day dresses. Beth had brought clarity to how she felt, and she hardly knew her. Curiosity overtook her shock at her plain speaking and she looked at Beth's drawings.

'The difference with many evening gowns is that their neckline is often low.' With a sweep of her pencil she drew some evening necklines. 'What that does is cut the appearance of a full, large bust by at least a third.'

Karenza did see, although until now she had not realised why those necklines had suited her better. They just did.

'You cannot expect me to have such a neckline for a day dress. I will look like a strumpet.'

Beth smiled at her use of the word. 'No, I would not. It is the fashion for high necklines and it is more modest ... just as ladies prefer. I do suggest, though, the area that is normally flesh on a low neckline could be made in a lighter material, or lace. This would give the impression of a smaller bust, yet keep your modesty.'

Karenza took the drawings from her and looked at them. For a brief moment Joss was forgotten. Her hand shook a little with emotion as she looked at the sketches. Since leaving her childhood behind her she had been embarrassed by her large breasts. They made her look larger than she felt and her day dresses always disappointed her. She never understood why until now. Beth Jago was the only dressmaker who had recognised the problem and chose to offer advice, even if it meant losing the order.

'How did you know that I prefer my evening gowns?' asked Karenza, her voice thick with emotion.

'I didn't know for sure,' said Beth softly. 'Until now.'

'You took a chance by speaking so plainly. I may have taken offence.'

'If I had not spoken, and I had made the dress you wanted, we would both have taken offence by the garment.'

Karenza smiled; she felt as if she had been given a sacred piece of information that had eluded her until now.

'I think I would prefer a dress that you have styled,' she said, picking up the teapot again. 'But first let me pour *you* a cup while we discuss the best material to use.'

Beth brought another cup. 'I will have to take your measurements. It will mean several visits for dress fittings.'

Karenza poured the tea and handed her a cup. 'Several visits?' Her smile broadened. 'That sounds perfect to me. It will give us a chance to get to know one another.'

Beth returned the smile and took her cup from her.

Over the next few weeks Mrs Fitzpatrick visited every other day. So many visits were not necessary, yet this particular customer would insist on dropping by for a chat, if not for an organised fitting. Beth did not have the heart to tell her to leave – in fact she found that she quite enjoyed having someone to talk to while she worked. Over the past year Beth had become used to speaking to her affluent customers, and she had come to realise they often had the same issues, insecurities and thoughts as her own. Beth no longer felt ill at ease with or inferior to these women. Although the dressmaker and customer relationship remained defined, and there was no confusion about who was paying whom, it was not unusual for an intimate relationship between dressmaker and customer to form. However, her relationship with Mrs Fitzpatrick had quickly become quite different from that she shared with any customer she had had before.

Beth was unsure when the change in their relationship had occurred. She had put the frequency of her visits down to Mrs Fitzpatrick feeling lonely, as she had mentioned her husband often worked away. Perhaps it was because of their first meeting. Mrs Fitzpatrick had not hidden the relief she felt when it had become clear why certain garments suited her and some did not. Beth felt her advice had earned Mrs Fitzpatrick's respect and confidence far quicker than anything else she may have offered. Whatever the reason for the ease of their conversations, this relationship had an indefinable difference that Beth could not quite put her finger on.

By the fourth visit, they were chatting as if they had always known each other, and it was then that Mrs Fitzpatrick first insisted that Beth use her first name. It felt a little strange, to call a woman of her class by her Christian name, yet soon it became second nature and Beth wondered what all the fuss had been about.

While Beth was unsure of the reason for so many visits, Karenza was not. She wanted to find out more about the seamstress and had made excuses to visit and engage her in conversation. Beth had been guarded at first and she could see the distrust in her eyes, yet she remained pleasant and polite to her face. At first their conversations felt stilted, with Karenza often taking the lead, but during one particular visit their relationship shifted and was never quite the same again. Karenza had remarked on something and for the first time showed a flash of her caustic wit. Normally her sense of humour received a disapproving frown from the company she kept as they would miss the irony. Beth, on the other hand, smiled, and their glances had held briefly. After that moment of shared humour, their conversations flowed more easily. It was as if they understood the barriers between them and found there were none there at all.

All too soon it would be time for the last fitting. With some surprise, both women realised that they would miss the visits, which had not only given them both pleasure, but also blurred the distinction between customer and friend.

Karenza marvelled at her reflection as Beth straightened the skirts of her new dress. She was delighted with the dress, but also unsure how to proceed next. She felt as if she had discovered a fragile butterfly and if she made her presence felt, the butterfly would fly away. The more she met with Beth, the more she began to like her, and she could see what Joss had seen in her, too. She was hardworking and plain speaking, as he was. If something was on her mind, she would say it, yet she did not share her burdens or troubles easily with people she did not know well. Only those she trusted had that particular privilege. The similarities in their characters were numerous, yet where Joss had a quick temper, Beth did not. Karenza believed that she would be the calming balm he needed.

She had not disclosed that she was Joss's sister, and she had never mentioned his name. In fact she was unsure how Beth felt about him at all. During their chats, Karenza had once steered the conversation to love, but Beth had remained guarded, only saying that she had been in love just once but it had not ended well. Yet time was running out, and Karenza had to think of a way for them to meet again.

After changing back into her clothes, she watched as Beth carefully wrapped the finished dress in brown paper. There was an air of sadness that they would not meet so often now, if at all. Karenza went to the dress samples that remained displayed on the table and touched the sleeve of one. She had not asked Beth about them during her many visits, but it was easy to guess what they were and how she had come by the material to make them. Now was the time to test how Beth felt about her brother.

'These are exquisite, Beth. Can I buy them?' she asked in a matter-of-fact way.

Beth was quick to answer. 'No, I'm sorry, Karenza, they are not for sale.'

Karenza touched the fabric as she chose her next words carefully.

'Why not? They are just samples of your work. You have others now.'

'The material was given to me by a very dear friend. The samples helped me find employment at a time I needed it most. I will never sell them.'

Karenza played ignorant. 'A dear friend? Is this the love you lost?'

Beth nodded but did not utter a word. Karenza sensed a change in Beth and looked back at her. Her eyes were filled with emotion and Karenza realised she had not spoken because, in that moment, she could not. *She does have feelings for Joss after all. It was time to confess.*

'Beth, I am about to tell you something. I do not want you to be angry with me, just remember my intentions were good and he does not know I am here.'

Beth became wary. Her task of wrapping the garment slowed.

Karenza took a deep breath. 'My name *is* Karenza Fitzpatrick, I *am* married to a captain, just as I have told you. What I have not told you is that I have a brother and his name is Joss Roscarrock.'

Beth looked up from her task.

'I *did* want a dress made for me, but I sought you out to be the one to do it. I usually go to a dressmaker in Truro, who has made my dresses for years.'

'You came to spy on me?'

'No,' said Karenza. 'Well, perhaps I did. I wanted to meet the woman who had rendered my brother unconscious.' Karenza tried to make light of the awkward confession. Confessions were never an easy thing to do, and Karenza had a habit of having to make them often.

She waited for Beth to be angry with her.

Beth stopped wrapping the dress. The brown paper slowly unwound from the fabric. 'How is he?'

Karenza felt a little relieved that Beth's reaction was not one of anger. 'He is very well. He has been very busy this past year. He has set up a charity called The Red Feathers.'

'I have read as much in the news-sheets.'

Beth's interest in his life was a good sign. Karenza felt more confident that she had been right to visit her after all.

'He has also improved the working conditions of his mines.'

'I had read that, too.' Beth rested her hands on the table. Only the slight tremor of the paper showed how the confession was affecting her.

'And he has arranged a position for my husband so he can spend more time on land. It is something we have wanted for a very long time.'

'That was very kind of him.'

'He has also hit a large load of tin in one of his mines. Edward manages it now so Joss can concentrate on The Red Feathers' Fund.' Karenza felt she was rambling. She must not talk quite so much. She needed to know how Beth felt about him.

'But how is *he*?' asked Beth again.

'Happier than when he came back from the war, but not as happy as he could be. I don't know what happened in River Valley, but he came back a changed man. No, that is not quite right. He returned to the Joss I used to know before he went to war. I can only put that down to you.'

Beth returned to her wrapping. 'No, I was not responsible. He has worked hard to start his charitable foundation when so many thought he was mad at the beginning.'

Karenza was encouraged by Beth's knowledge. She had followed the news of his venture and knew of the obstacles Joss had to breach before The Red Feathers' Fund could function how he had wanted it to. She watched Beth carefully, as she wrapped and rewrapped the same part of the dress. Karenza crossed the room and took over the chore.

'You should visit him. He would like to see you again,' she said, smiling.

'I couldn't. It would be too embarrassing.' Beth stood back and watched Karenza efficiently wrap the dress. 'Did you know he proposed to me? I was too proud to accept. I turned him down.'

'I think he admired you for your stance.'

Beth glanced sheepishly at Karenza. 'He shouldn't.' Unable to hold her gaze, she walked to the window and looked through the bull's-eye pane framed in lead. The wavy glass distorted the view of the narrow, cobbled footpath beyond, and in doing so blurred the weeds sprouting through the inhospitable stony terrain. 'I was also too afraid to accept,' she finally confessed. 'I would make him a laughing stock amongst his friends. They would say, "Did you know that Captain Joss Roscarrock, war veteran of the Crimean War and one of the richest men in Cornwall, has an illegitimate workhouse slut for a wife? Who does she think she is fooling, acting with airs and graces and trying to mix with gentlefolk?"'

'Joss does not think that way.'

'They would snigger behind their hands.' Beth turned away from the window and looked at Karenza. 'I would look such a fool if I turned up at his door.'

Karenza wanted to knock their heads together. They were both too scared they might look foolish in each other's eyes. If only they realised by not taking a chance they were already being foolish. Joss had said there was only one thing that Beth was prepared to fight for and that was River Valley. Karenza had an idea.

'William and Joss are having a meeting tomorrow. I hear Joss has some major plans for River Valley.' Karenza enjoyed seeing the dismay on Beth's face. It was a glimmer of hope that her plan might just work.

'He promised me he would not destroy it,' Beth said softly, the tremor in her voice a hint at the hurt she felt from his betrayal.

Karenza tried to remain nonchalant. 'I do not know what his plans are, but they seem quite big. Joss is determined to go ahead.'

'He mustn't. Karenza, please persuade him not to.'

Karenza placed the parcel containing her dress under her arm. 'Keep me out of it. If River Valley means so much to you I suggest you tell him yourself. As I said, he will be home tomorrow morning having a meeting with my husband. It may be your only chance to speak to him and tell him to stop whatever he plans to do with it.'

It was time to leave, before Beth's stricken face caused her to relent and tell her it was a partial lie. 'Send the bill on to me, Beth. It has been lovely meeting you. I will miss my visits.' Karenza made a quick exit, leaving a confused and anxious Beth alone in the room.

Karenza quickly made her way through the shop, not stopping to acknowledge Mr Harper. She hoped Beth still had enough passion for River Valley to march into Joss's house tomorrow and confront him. She would not be there to see it, but she hoped that Joss and Beth would come to their senses.

Karenza stepped outside into the light drizzle and took a deep breath. She felt she had just left Beth in the midst of a dilemma. Feelings of doubt started to build as she realised her plan was based on nothing more than flimsy hope. She would have to confess to William. Confessions were never easy, yet it somehow shared the responsibility of what she had done. He would be annoyed at her for what she had just orchestrated, but he would understand her reasons for it – wouldn't he?

She hurried across the street to her waiting carriage and climbed in. There was one person she was not prepared to confess to. She would have to make her husband swear not to reveal her plan to Joss. It was best he did not know anything about it, just in case Beth chose not to pay a call. She bit nervously onto her bottom lip and tasted the rain. She hoped they did meet and everything turned out well, but just in case she offered a little prayer for good measure.

Karenza looked out of the window as the carriage pulled away. She saw Beth's figure walk past a small upstairs window and realised she had retreated to the sanctity of her bedroom to recover. Karenza suddenly felt a pang of sympathy for the young woman inside as she contemplated her next move. She hoped she would not let fear hold her back.

Karenza sat back in her seat, a worried frown upon her brow. She hoped she had not made matters worse. Perhaps she would not confess to her husband tonight. It was best if he did not know about it, as William was an honourable man and would feel compelled to warn Joss.

Karenza sank deeper into her seat. The role of cupid was complex. She had a dreadful aim and often missed her target. Yet she could not ignore the nervous frisson deep in her stomach as she thought of what she had just done. The feeling was not unpleasant, although it was cultivated by the risk she had taken. The feeling grew inside her and strained at any forms of control. Karenza could stop it no longer. Unleashed, it sent a shoot of excitement up through her body to blossom on her face in the form of a guilty, but contented smile.

Chapter Twenty-Two

Beth paced her little bedroom. It only took a few steps before she had to turn, but the rhythm on the wooden floor helped her to think. Nervously, she pressed the seams of her neat gloves into the crook of each finger. She had awoken far too early and although she had been dressed in her smartest dress for almost an hour, she was still undecided on what to do. A mixture of emotions churned in her stomach. Anger and betrayal that he had gone back on his word, frustration that the mere sound of his name still evoked excitement – and nervousness at the prospect of seeing him again after all this time.

On the one hand she relished this opportunity. His last image of her was when she was dressed in a workhouse uniform, grubby and shabby with no future. To speak to him about River Valley gave her an excuse to erase that image and present herself as she was now: smart, clean and successful in her own little business. She was no longer in need of his help and she certainly no longer wanted him to feel pity for her. This situation gave her the perfect opportunity to regain her reputation in his eyes.

Yet on the other hand he had betrayed her. He had promised her he would not destroy River Valley, and now it seemed his promise meant nothing. She meant nothing. The speed of her pacing quickened. How could he destroy a place that was so beautiful, where people went to make their wishes and walk on the sand? Had he not enjoyed his time there with her? If he had chosen to ruin it for future generations, he obviously had not. The thought hurt more than she cared to admit.

Beth stopped pacing and looked out of the window onto the busy streets of Killygrew. She suddenly felt small in a town full of people. Who was she to march into his house and dictate what he did with his own land? Why would he take any notice of her? She was nothing but a woman who had nearly killed him and let him stay until he was better. They had become close in those last few days and he had fancied that he had loved her, but that was then. Almost a year had passed and it was quite probable that he no longer thought of her at all. He may even have fallen in love with another woman. Perhaps Karenza did not like this other woman and wanted to stir things up. Perhaps Karenza was not as nice as she appeared and was up to mischief. Beth's legs felt weak and she sat herself down. Perhaps it would be best if she did not go after all.

Joss laid out a set of papers and a map he required for his meeting when he heard a soft knock. The door opened. He glanced up to see Edward's head peeping around the door.

'William has arrived. I have just seen his carriage pull up. Is everything ready?'

Joss straightened. 'Yes, I think everything is prepared.'

Edward came in and closed the door with one hand. 'I am glad everything is going well for you now, Joss. It has been a long time coming.'

Joss nodded solemnly.

'While we are alone, I want to thank you for the trust you have placed in me. Giving me the responsibility to run Bodannock Mine has done me the world of good.'

Joss allowed himself a slight smile. 'You needed something to focus on. I just happened to have something suitable.'

He went back to his task. It was not often Edward spoke like this, preferring to cover up his feelings with laughter and banter. It was far easier to chat of other things, however this time Edward would not be put off.

'I mean it. Only you knew my light-heartedness and banter was a cover. Only you saw that I was starting to drink too much.'

'I knew because I had tried that route. I had tried blocking out memories in the bottom of a glass once. It does not work.'

'I feel you have saved my life for the second time. I owe you ... again.'

Joss shook his head. 'You owe me nothing, Edward. Your friendship is enough.'

Edward nodded solemnly. His voice thick with emotion, he added, 'If you want me I will be in your office. Good luck with the meeting, Joss. It is good to see that your life is going well now and that you are happy. If you need anything, just ask. No, there is no need to ask, I will be there anyway. You can count on me.' Edward left and Joss was alone once more, but his heart felt heavy.

Edward looked up to him like an older brother and a hero. True, he had saved his life in the war, but Edward should not feel in debt to him. Being a hero in someone's eyes could feel like a burden, and the weight of that burden was sometimes uncomfortable to bear.

Beth looked up at the door knocker and grabbed it in her hand. With a firmness and loudness resulting from nervous determination, the knocking of brass on brass shook the door and echoed through the hall. Beth took a deep breath to calm her nerves. Already she had started to make a fool of herself, slamming on the door like someone demanding admission, rather than requesting it. She almost turned and fled but, to her relief, when the door opened Mrs May was smiling at her.

'Miss Jago, what a pleasant surprise. It has been a while since your last visit. Come in, come in.' She opened the door wider to allow her to enter.

Beth, a little shocked that the housekeeper remembered her, nervously glanced about to see if she had been seen and then slipped inside. Already she felt frustrated with herself for not behaving like a lady of quality but instead as a woman more suitable for domestic service. Perhaps she should have used the trade entrance after all. Joss would soon see her for what she was and he would realise what a fool he had been to ask such a woman for her hand in marriage.

What do I care what he thinks? Beth argued with herself. *I am here because of River Valley.*

'Mr Roscarrock is having a meeting with Mr Fitzpatrick, and I am here to see them,' she said, trying to sound casual and businesslike herself. To her surprise, Mrs May did not question her.

'Follow me. I don't think the meeting has started yet, so you won't have missed much.'

Beth quietly followed the housekeeper through the hall. A maid carrying a tray crossed their path. As if to explain the new member of staff since her last visit, the housekeeper said, 'When Mr Roscarrock came home and heard about the suggestion you made that the house needed more staff, he immediately gave me leave to employ as many as I required. My life is much easier now, Miss Jago.' Beth followed her along another wide passage, a part of the house she had not yet seen. 'I had mentioned my difficulties to him before but it had fallen on deaf ears. Mr Roscarrock always had other things on his mind to worry about. The house was not at the top of his list.'

Beth saw an oil painting hanging on a wall. It was of a tall mine engine house at the edge of a cliff, with frenzied waves crashing against the rocks at its base. She wondered if her visit would be as fruitless as the waves' attempts to reach the stone building in the painting. Given time, even those waves would wear the rock away, but Beth did not have time on her side. She would have liked to stop and admire it but Mrs May had already surged ahead. She was certainly much healthier than when Beth had last seen her.

Beth hurriedly caught up with her and decided not to listen to her chatter. She needed these last few moments to concentrate on her own thoughts as she braced herself to see Joss again. As she followed the housekeeper's short little footsteps, she decided she was going to make it very plain how angry she was that he had gone back on his word. Yet she also hoped that while she made her case for River Valley, he would not be disappointed in seeing her again – if he even thought of her at all.

Joss took his place at the head of the table and looked about him. Seated around a long mahogany table were ten of the finest businessmen in Cornwall. Joss had handpicked each one before approaching them with this new venture. Each one had made a success of a failing business or started from nothing. Each one had passion and motivation, qualities that he had himself and that he also admired in others. This meeting was a culmination of months of planning and it was a good opportunity to introduce his brother-in-law to them.

'Gentlemen,' he began. The conversation about him hushed as they all turned their heads to acknowledge the speaker. 'We are here today as we all have one thing in common: a desire to diversify and take advantage of the revolution in maritime trade. My brother-in-law, Mr William Fitzpatrick, has spent his entire career on the sea working for the package ships and more recently he has been a captain of a trade ship. There is very little he does not know about maritime trade and his expertise and advice will be invaluable to us landlocked gentlemen.'

There was a ripple of laughter through the room. There was not a seafaring man amongst them but they had money and understood business. It would be good to have someone who understood the sea as part of their team.

'I can confirm that your investments are enough to buy our first ship. After long discussions with William we have identified several routes for trade.' Joss unrolled a map in the centre of the table. 'Gold has been discovered in California and Victoria and people from all over the world are moving there to make their fortune. We can take advantage of this. We are aware that mines in Cornwall are finding it increasingly hard to carry on. Highly skilled Cornish miners are much in demand and they are emigrating in large numbers overseas. Whilst we do not want to lose our men, emigrating to find work will mean they will be in a position to send money home to their families and help the economy of Cornwall. Canada is an alternative route. We can use the port of Padstow, and the trade route to Quebec, returning two months later with North American timber.'

A murmur went about the room as the information sunk in, but Joss had not finished yet.

'In the meantime …' Joss pointed to Egypt. '… a sea-level waterway is being constructed. It will take many years to build, but when the Suez Canal is finished it will open up trade links from Europe to Asia without having to navigate around Africa. We, gentlemen, are in the midst of a maritime revolution, and my brother-in-law can navigate us through the choppy waters to success. This is a pivotal moment, and what happens now will mark the course of our future—'

The door burst open and in marched Beth.

In shock, Beth stared at the sea of male faces looking at her. She had expected only two men, not as many as this. To make matters worse, they remembered their manners and all stood in unison at her entrance. They waited silently, looking at her expectantly, and she froze. At the far end of the table stood Joss, a frown upon his face, his expression unreadable. What should she do now? What did an illegitimate miner's granddaughter do to fool these men into thinking she had a right to be here? She felt like a schoolmistress standing in front of her pupils. Without thinking further, she took her inspiration from one, namely a Miss Prigg, who had been the headmistress of her own school. The words she uttered next would forever bring a blush to her cheeks when she remembered them. She flapped her hands slowly to indicate they could return to their seats.

'Good morning, everyone. You may sit.'

To her surprise, everyone obeyed. Everyone, that is, except Joss, who slowly straightened to brace himself. Beth had no option but to state her objection to the destruction of River Valley. Her opinion was valid and they must be made aware of it; her conscience encouraged her.

She cleared her throat. 'Gentlemen, I beg you not to go ahead with your plans. You must not destroy River Valley. Its destruction will rob future generations of its beauty.' Her audience remained silent so she continued. 'There are plants and fauna that rarely flourish in other areas. It is a haven for many species of butterflies and the clean fresh air provides the ideal place for rare lichen to grow ... or at least that is what my grandfather once told me. The valley provides an anchor, a place where the people who live locally can escape from the hardships of their daily lives.'

She looked at the blank faces staring back at her. Her speech was having little effect. In fact, they looked a bit bewildered.

'The valley is steeped in myth and legends and their tales have been passed on from generation to generation. Of course, there is the wishing tree, where ribbons representing the wishes of local folk blow in the wind. You cannot destroy the wishing tree.'

She was beginning to doubt the validity of her argument, an argument that sounded as if it was based on fairy tales and nothing that would impress these men. 'You cannot kill the wishing tree ...' she added lamely. 'I have wishes on it.' Heat rose up inside her and reddened her cheeks. She sounded like a child, a pathetic, whining child, rather than someone with a cause. She saw a slight curve at the corner of Joss's lips.

'Ma'am,' said the gentleman closest to her, 'I think you are misinformed. We know nothing of this valley you speak of. Our meeting is about shipping.'

Beth's eyes met Joss's, but it was only for the briefest time. Before he could speak she was out of the door and briskly walking down the hall – cursing in her frustration. She had made a fool of herself in front of gentry as she tried to enter their world. It was the thing she had feared most, and she had achieved it within three minutes of entering Joss's home.

Beth walked hurriedly along the corridor looking for the way out. Hearing footsteps behind her, she quickened her step, but whoever was following had broken into a run. She was about to turn around to see if it was Joss, when a steel-like grip caught the flesh of her upper arm and pinched it painfully before propelling her forward. In surprise she looked up to see Edward Nankervis looking angrily down at her.

'What do you think you are playing at? This is the second time you have come in here making demands. How dare you.'

Beth tried to pull her arm away, but his grip on her remained firm.

'You are a troublemaker. You are never to set foot in here again.'

Moments before Beth had been fleeing the building, but Nankervis's rough treatment brought the stubbornness out in her. She resisted again, digging in her heels to stop the momentum.

'Leave me alone. I will leave at my own pace. I will not be thrown out as if I am rubbish!'

Edward quickly masked his surprise at her retort with an angry frown. 'You have caused Joss nothing but trouble,' he said through gritted teeth. 'Refusing to leave his property, flirting with him to only turn around and throw his proposal back in his face. He is happy now. How dare you return and stir up trouble again.'

He grabbed her arm and marched her to the door. Beth tried to resist, but realised there was little she could do against his strength. She saw a vase of flowers on the side table ahead.

'It was not my intention to stir up trouble.'

'I heard you lecturing him and his business partners on what they must do or not do with the valley. Your interference is incomprehensible.'

As Edward manhandled her through the hall, everything became clear to Beth. 'It was never about the valley, not really. It was just an excuse to see him again.'

'He doesn't want to see you again. Leave him in peace. He is doing well without you. He does not need you.'

'Let me go. At least let me have the dignity to walk out alone.'

'Out!' shouted Edward.

Beth had had enough. No one had the right to treat her like this. As Edward renewed his forceful ejection of her she made up her mind what to do. Reaching for the vase full of water, Beth Jago fought back.

'Well, she was very passionate,' said one of the men at the table. Joss only heard his voice and he had no idea who had spoken. He was in shock and still unsure what had just happened. Had he really seen Beth come into the room and lecture a roomful of men about the benefits of a valley? Had she instructed them all to sit down? She had left so quickly it was as if she had disappeared in a puff of smoke, leaving him wondering whether she had really existed at all. He had not laid eyes on her since seeing her in the street at Killygrew, when he had hidden in the shadows like a coward. It was reassuring that someone else had also seen her in the room, and that he was not going insane.

'Do you know that woman?' asked William.

Joss nodded slowly, as he broke into a smile. 'Gentlemen, that was Miss Elizabeth Jago. If you will excuse me for a moment, I will leave you to continue the discussions about the various trade routes to adopt with my brother-in-law, who is well placed to head the meeting.'

William stood to take his place. 'Ahhh, so that is Miss Jago.' He smiled at Joss. 'Good luck, Joss.'

'Thank you. I think I may need it.'

With long, measured strides Joss passed the seated gentlemen and went out of the door that Beth had only moments ago fled through.

He heard Edward in the distance and quickly followed the sound of his voice, but it was not until he reached the main hall that he found Beth.

Beth stood proudly in the hall, holding an empty vase in her hands. She was too busy berating Edward to notice Joss's approach.

'How dare you treat me so badly? You are no better than me and I will not put up with it!'

Shoulders hunched, Edward stood in a puddle of water. His clothes were drenched and he was plucking flowers from his shoulders and hair. Beth placed the vase back on the table.

Joss looked at the scattered flowers at Edward's feet. 'What has happened?'

'She tipped a vase of water over me,' said Edward as he looked down at his wet clothes.

'Why?'

Beth looked at him as if it should be obvious. 'Because I didn't have a pan to hit him with,' she replied. Holding her head high, she turned, walked out of the door and did not look back.

Edward brushed off the last flower from his left shoulder. 'Well, that has got rid of her.'

'I don't want to get rid of her,' said Joss.

Edward looked up. 'What do you mean? She has caused you nothing but trouble and worry.'

Joss watched Beth walking down the stone steps and could not help but admire her composure after the humiliation earlier. She was heading for the river, and would not be able to go further. He would give her a moment to gather her thoughts. This time he would not rush in.

'I *want* to worry about her,' he replied. He turned to look at Edward. 'I know you mean well by telling her to leave, but I do not need you to protect me from her. I love her and I am glad she has plucked up the courage to come here ... even if it was for the wrong reason. I wish she were as passionate about me as she is about the damn valley.'

'I thought she was a nuisance to you.'

'She is not. There is no need for you to protect me, Edward. Stop feeling obliged to me for something I did years ago. Something that any other man would have done too.'

'Most men did not save my life. You did.'

'And your loyal friendship has repaid me a thousand times. Time moves on, we must move on.'

For a moment there was silence.

Edward raked a hand through his wet hair. 'She used the valley as an excuse to see you again.'

Joss raised an eyebrow, unsure whether to believe him.

'It is true, she said it herself. Go after her, Joss, before she wreaks further havoc. If you love her, I will not interfere. I am sure Miss Jago and I will become friends in the future ... even if we have got off to a shaky start.'

Joss shook his hand. 'I have no doubt that when you get to know her, you will like her. Now go and change into some dry clothing. You look like you have had an argument with a flowerpot.'

Beth's courage finally left her and was replaced by mortification. She had interrupted Joss's important meeting. If that had not been bad enough, she had also assaulted his closest friend. Joss would be relieved he was not engaged to her now. She left the main gravel drive, preferring to follow a footpath amongst the trees of the landscaped garden and hide from anyone's view. She began to remove the pins from her hair. With each lock of hair that fell, she felt as if she was shedding her foolish thoughts that she would ever be accepted in his society. And that realisation hurt, as she knew that her visit had just been an excuse to see Joss again and present herself as worthy of his station. She had ruined her chances before even starting.

The path took her towards the sound of a waterfall. It spilled into a river and she quickly realised that it was probably a diverted tributary from a natural river further away. Strangely, it appeared familiar, although she had never been in the area before. It reminded her of St Piran's Fall, and she found it oddly comforting to find herself surrounded by the noise of water tumbling into a slow moving, peaceful river. Just like the waterfall below Kynance Cottage, there was a recess and a path made of rock behind the wall of water as it fell from above. Hearing movement behind her, she quickly hid behind its white curtain as it glinted in the sunshine.

Beth held her breath as she saw the silhouette of a man emerge from the path in the woods. He came to a standstill, his feet planted firmly and square with his shoulders, just like a soldier. She knew it was Joss before he spoke.

'Don't hide from me, Beth. I know you are there.'

Although his familiar voice was calm and clear, she could not make out his mood. Beth remained silent, unsure what to reply.

'Perhaps I should call you Morzelah,' he added.

This time she heard a hint of amusement in his words and she let out the breath she had been holding.

'Years ago, when I returned from the war, I tried to recreate St Piran's Fall, and would come here to be alone. I think it may have saved my life in a strange sort of way.'

'Just like the river saved the life of the man Morzelah fell in love with,' said Beth, from behind the waterfall. The fact that Joss had come after her, and there was no trace of anger in his voice, gave her courage to face him. She emerged from behind the curtain of water and into the sunshine. 'And it is why she blessed the water. Only he left her and she suffered from a broken heart.'

'I will not leave you. I have never left you, even when you have driven me away.'

'We have not seen each other for almost a year. If your sister had not told me that you have plans for the valley, I would not be here today. I thought you had gone back on your word.'

'You have met one of my sisters?'

'I have met Karenza. I made a dress for her.'

Beth had used her Christian name with ease and Joss had noticed, but he would not be diverted.

'I do have plans, but I think you will approve. I have not gone back on my word.' Joss took a step nearer, and as she didn't move away, he took another and another until he was so near he could reach out and touch her. 'I waited for you to come to me, but you didn't. I had to wait until you were ready, but the more I waited the further you seemed to be from me. The less you needed me.'

'Becoming independent does not mean I would need you less.'

'Edward thinks it was not only about the valley.'

'Your friend is right.'

Encouraged, Joss took Beth in his arms. She laid her head in the nook of his neck and savoured the safety and strength his warm arms provided. He stroked her hair, now beaded with water droplets formed from the waterfall's mist. 'Being with you makes my heart happy, Beth. Morzelah went to her lover's spirit and brought him back to life. Have you come to do the same for me?'

Beth groaned in despair. 'I have made a fool of myself in front of your friends. Karenza said you were meeting her husband, not a room full of men.'

'Do not blame Karenza. She did not know that I was heading such a large meeting. She would not intentionally set you up to be humiliated. She does not listen to details regarding business; she is more interested in the affairs of the heart.' Joss eased a strand of her hair away from her face. 'They are men of business, who have worked their way up from humble beginnings. They appreciate motivation, passion and determination and they saw those qualities in your impassioned plea.'

Beth winced. 'I spoke of butterflies and rare lichen. They must think me mad.'

'You spoke of preserving a beautiful place for future generations.'

'I spoke of wishing trees and ribbons—'

'Which are extremely important,' Joss said quietly into her hair. She was aware he was trying not to laugh, but it did not make her angry. Instead she too found herself smiling. 'Besides,' he added, 'I don't want the tree to be destroyed either. I tied a ribbon to it and have no desire to lose my wish.'

Beth moved in his arms and looked up at him. 'Don't tell me your wish, it may not come true.' Before he answered, she felt his lips on hers. Gently insistent, his kiss caused her to melt inwardly and block out the world. She followed his lead and felt almost bereft when it came to an end.

His voice was as gentle and as sincere as his kiss. 'I don't need to tell you what it was,' he said as he stroked a stray strand of hair from her face. 'You already know.' He placed a kiss on her forehead. 'Will you marry me, Beth?'

'Yes. I have always wanted to marry you, Joss. I just didn't have the courage or belief I could accept until now.'

'What has changed? Me?'

Beth smiled. 'No. I have changed. Although I have come from humble beginnings, it does not mean I should let my start in life hold me back. I want to spend the rest of my life by your side and if you do not mind where I have come from, why should I?'

'It does not matter where we come from, Beth. What matters is where we are going and I know it will be a far better place if we go together, than if we go alone.'

Chapter Twenty-Three

Beth slid her arm through Joss's. After eleven months of marriage it felt natural to do so, and his gentle squeeze as he laid his hand upon hers told her she was right to feel this way.

'How many are there?' she asked quietly. The monument, made from solid, Cornish granite, towered above her and displayed the names of the young soldiers who had died. Behind each name was a man and a grieving family; behind each rank, no matter how junior, was a hero.

'Seven hundred and six,' replied Joss thoughtfully. 'Forever remembered, and their names now standing guard and facing out to sea.' He had chosen the site well for his final act of respect to his fallen comrades. The war memorial stood on the site where Kynance Cottage had once stood, surrounded by the beauty of the valley itself, its banks and cliffs protecting it like giant arms welcoming them home.

'How many people do you expect will come to see the unveiling?' she asked him, her voice threatening to break with emotion. She found reading the names almost painful. Although they were strangers to her, each one sounded familiar, each one felt closer to her than a man passing in the street.

'I don't know. I have sent out flyers and written an article for the news-sheet, but we will have to see. People are busy and the war ended seven years ago.'

'Karenza wanted to be here,' Beth said. 'But she is near her time and William insisted they remain at home. He is worried her age will make the birth a difficult one.'

'I would be upset with William if he had not insisted. Karenza is a law unto herself, and only William can control her.'

Beth smiled. 'I'm glad she is, or she may never have visited me at Harper's.'

In the distance they heard the breaking of twigs and rustle of fallen leaves. Someone was running down the track that led from the road. Edward came into view, his hair flopping across his forehead and a little out of breath.

'Beth! Joss!' he called excitably. 'They are coming! They have read about the monument and they are coming to pay their respects.'

She felt Joss's arm relax; until that moment he had been unsure if anyone cared enough to come. 'How many? A hundred?' he asked hopefully.

Edward shook his head, too excited to talk. Instead, he grabbed Beth and swung her around in his boyish joy. Finally he turned to Joss.

'They are coming in droves, Joss, on every road and across the fields from nearly all directions.' He laughed. 'Perhaps even west, but I have not looked for their boats. There are hundreds, my friend, and they are coming here.'

Beth saw a muscle work in Joss's jaw as he fought to control his emotions. Together, they faced the sea so they could look at the clifftop on either side of the valley. Still not sure if Edward was exaggerating as he was prone to do, they watched in silence for their arrival. After some moments, movement stirred the skyline. Gradually, people emerged, spilled over the top and followed one another down the winding, narrow paths that scarred the banks of the valley. They were varied in ages, gender and class and arrived on foot or by horse. Some led their children by the hand, others carried them in their arms. Eventually they paused, found a place to sit and waited. Despite the large number, no one spoke. Soon the valley, which formed a natural amphitheatre, was full of people and they were all waiting for Joss to speak.

Beth squeezed Joss's arm. 'It's time.' She was about to move away, when Joss stopped her.

He smiled. 'You're my wife, Beth. Stay. I want you by my side.'

Beth returned to him. 'There is no other place I want to be,' she replied.

Joss looked at the expectant faces in the quiet crowd. He remained silent, savouring the moment. Finally he began to speak. Beth's heart swelled with love for him, as she listened to his explanation as to why he had chosen to build a memorial to those who had died in a war on foreign land. The crowd listened in silence as his words carried on the breeze to reach even those who sat farthest away. Joss spoke from the heart as he told them that it did not matter how these men had died, whether by bayonet, bullet or from the epidemics of disease and starvation. These men had risked their lives to fight a war and had therefore died as soldiers.

'They left as sons, they fought as soldiers, they died as heroes,' said Joss. 'They are our history makers, and although the passing of time fades our memory of them, like footprints in the sand, this monument will bear witness that they marched to war, sacrificed their lives in the name of our country and that we will be forever in their debt.'

Joss paused. The valley remained silent as even the youngest child was listening to his words. He was telling them a story and it was as engrossing as any their parents had told them.

'There will be other wars,' Joss continued in a steady voice. 'Our history is littered with them. But unless we remember the past, we will not learn for the future. I hope we are up to the task.' Joss took Beth's hand. 'This monument bears witness to The History Makers of the 46th Regiment of the Foot. It is just one of many regiments, but it represents all those who died in the Crimean War. Seven hundred and six men are named here. They come from all ranks, and no matter how they died, they died as soldiers fighting on behalf of our country. In the darkest of times, these ordinary men did something extraordinary, and they must never be forgotten.'

The silence remained. Not a word, not a cough came from the crowd. Edward came to stand next to Joss as if to provide his support. Beth's mouth went dry with concern at the lack of their response.

'I can hear rain,' said Edward. 'Yes, heavy rain in the distance. The crowd will be running for cover.'

Joss searched for the black clouds in the sky but could see none. The rain seemed to be coming closer. The sound of heavy raindrops relentlessly hitting a tin roof – only there was no roof – there were no raindrops.

'Joss. Edward. It is not rain you can hear.' Beth touched her husband's arm. 'Look in the distance. See what they are doing? They are showing their thanks in the only way they know how. They are applauding.' The men followed her gaze. A wave of standing ovation came towards them from each side of the valley. They were waves of gratitude, of respect and of remembrance. As the applause came nearer, so did the volume increase. The noise was so loud and intense that when it finally reached and surrounded the former soldiers, it stunned them both and rendered them speechless.

Eventually the crowd dispersed, making it possible for Beth to slip away and make her way down to the river's edge. In the distance she could hear Edward and Joss talking, and she smiled to herself. To her surprise, she found herself liking Edward more and more each day. He was fun, excitable and unpredictable, yet a loyal friend to her husband. Joss had once said she and Edward had many similar qualities and now she could see what he meant. He behaved like a younger brother to Joss, and over the past few months he had slipped into that role with her, too.

Beth sat herself down on a rock and placed the flowers she had been carrying by her side. This was her moment to remember those she had lost. She had never had the time to grieve fully. Circumstances had taken over, and her feelings and emotions for her loss had become frozen. Now was her moment to do so. She picked up two flowers and addressed the river.

'Martha once said to me that if something is on my mind and troubling me, I should let the river take it away. In my life I have lost four people who were very dear to me. I did not have a chance to tell them how much they meant to me when they were alive. I did not have the chance to say my goodbyes. So I am here to send them a message.' Beth looked at the two flowers she was holding.

'A message for my mother, Anne Jago. Although my memories of you are marred by the workhouse, you always managed to retain your grace and elegance. It is these qualities that I remember about you the most.' Beth dropped the flowers into the water. 'Your loyalty, faithfulness and devotion to me are represented by these violets. You kept me with you when many would have given their child away and returned home.'

Beth watched the violets become entangled before they started their journey out to sea. Smiling, she watched them until she could see them no more. She sighed and picked up the next flower.

'Martha, you were my inspiration.' Her voice broke slightly as her emotions grew. She quickly kissed the flower and threw it in. 'Lavender for love, loyalty and devotion. To many you were a tough-talking fisherwoman. To me you were the most courageous and devoted woman I have ever had the privilege to know. Your devotion to Tom, the loyalty and love you showed him against the prejudice from others, will never be forgotten. I understand why you did what you did. It was to protect your child ...' Beth placed her hand on her own stomach. '... and I have come to understand that more and more with each week that passes.'

Beth blinked away the tears that were now threatening her vision. With renewed vigour she held her next flower up high to salute her grandfather in heaven.

'Honeysuckle, to represent our bond of love.' Beth lowered it and turned it in her hands as she remembered the times she had tested his patience. She could not help but break into a smile until her memories turned again to the last time she saw him. A little frown pinched her brows. 'As you lay dying,' she said quietly, 'you told me I had nothing to fear about my future. Did you have faith in Joss that he would take care of me upon your death? Or did you mistakenly think you owned Kynance Cottage and it would pass to me? I wish you had told me about Joss, Grandfather. You had already lost your daughter to a wealthy man, perhaps you were afraid that you might lose me to Joss too soon.' She threw the honeysuckle into the river and watched it float away. 'I will never know the truth of it, but I want you to know that I am no longer fearful for my future. I have a loving husband, a beautiful home and by winter your great grandchild will be born. I wanted to share my secret with you first.'

Beth gathered the remaining flowers that were left and eased herself into a standing position. For some reason, she felt that this last message required her to stand, yet she did not really understand why.

'Tom Kitto,' she said in a gentle voice. 'I bear you no ill will. I know that you found the world more confusing and frightening than any person found you to be. I know that you were not a bad person and that you didn't mean any harm.' Beth dropped a flower into the water. 'Chrysanthemum, to represent your cheerfulness. Your smile would light up a room and would bring joy to your mother's heart. Basil, to represent my good wishes to you. I never meant to hurt you, Tom. When I could not return your affections I withdrew, and that confused you more. I am sorry you were hurt.' Beth threw another flower into the water. 'Aloe to represent healing and protection as I hope that wherever your spirit is now, you are free from the limitations you had when you were here on Earth.'

Beth watched as the flowers gathered speed and were taken out to sea. She was glad she had said her goodbyes. She felt at peace now, the same peace that Joss had found since starting The Red Feathers' Fund. She heard him calling her name.

Turning, she saw Joss looking down at her from the earthy ledge above.

'Are you ready to go home, Mrs Roscarrock?' he asked, reaching out for her hand.

Beth placed her hand in his. 'Almost.'

Joss noticed the last remaining flower in her hand and raised an eyebrow as he pulled her towards him. 'What have you been doing?'

'I have been using flowers to send messages to the people I have loved and lost.'

'As you did when you threw them over Edward's head?' he teased.

Beth laughed. 'With a little more subtlety than that, I hope. Shall we visit the wishing tree before we leave?'

'Would you like to?'

'Very much.'

Joss took her hand and together they followed the trail of the river, before climbing the narrow track upwards. They arrived at the glade carpeted with sweet smelling lichen and moss. The sea pink thrift was just coming into bloom and the butterflies had yet to gather. They would come, as they had always done, and Beth made Joss promise to return later in the year to see them. They continued on. The track, although narrow and threaded with roots, was firm beneath their feet. Finally they arrived at the ancient tree, twisted, but still standing strong against the Atlantic breeze. Their ribbons were still there, side by side and twisted together as they curled and fluttered in the breeze. They were a little more faded and frayed at the ends, but they were secure, strong and defiant in the wind.

Beth withdrew a white ribbon from her pocket and tied it to the branch.

'Are you making a wish?' asked Joss from behind her.

'Of course.' Beth stepped back to watch it lift and wane in the breeze beside the others.

'Why did you choose a white ribbon?'

Beth lifted the remaining flower in her hand. 'Because Orange Blossom is white.' She placed the flower in his buttonhole and patted it into place. 'Orange Blossom represents fertility.'

Joss searched her face. 'You wished for a child?'

'No. I am with child.'

Joss took her in his arms. 'I love you. My life felt empty for many years. I believed I had no purpose, no reason to be still here when my friends had died. Having you in my life has filled that emptiness and I was prepared to live my life as a contented man for the rest of my days. But having a child, our child, gives a purpose to my life in a way that is hard to explain.'

Beth lifted her gaze to his and touched his cheek. 'There is no need to explain, Joss, for I feel it too.' She kissed his lips. 'I love you.'

He touched his forehead with hers and smiled. 'And now that we have said our goodbyes and made a wish for the future are you happy to leave River Valley?'

'It will always remain special to me, but a home is where you are loved. It is not a place or a building. It is the warmth that is wrapped around you when you feel safe and content.' Beth stepped from his embrace and took his hand. 'Take me home, Joss. Take *us* home ... so we can start our future together.'

Together, side by side, they made their way along the track leading out of the valley. They passed the site where the cottage once was and where the war memorial now proudly stood facing out to sea. They did not notice threads of spider silk forming on the granite block or the Cornish breeze turning on a penny to tear it free, as their thoughts were of their future together and their unborn child. The breeze lifted the gossamer higher, swirling the fragile web before it carried it down the valley and out to the Atlantic Ocean. Fragile as any memory, it followed the flowers out to sea, never to be seen again.

Author's Note

In English, the current prevalent spelling for the port in the Crimean peninsula is Sevastopol. The spelling Sebastopol was formerly used. The clasp representing the siege on the British Crimean Campaign Medal uses the spelling Sebastapol, therefore this spelling is used within the novel to reflect the period in which it is set.

The Legacy of the Crimean War

Prior to, and during the Crimean War, the British Army was led by gentlemen, as it was considered that they had a stake in the nation and would make better leaders. Generally commissions and promotions were bought rather than based on merit or experience. They were expensive, which therefore deterred all but the wealthy. Officers with experience and the skills to lead were often overlooked in favour of gentlemen with the means to pay.

As a direct result of the disastrous decisions that were made by the leaders, the Crimean War was the most mismanaged campaign in British history. Following the war, new reforms were carried out and administration was radically reorganised. The system for appointing, training and promoting officers in the British Army would never be the same again. For the first time it would be based on merit and not personal influence or wealth.

Over 20,000 British soldiers died in the war, and more than 16,000 of those deaths were from disease. The Crimean War was the first war to be covered by reporters. News of the errors made, the death and destruction endured by all and the bravery and courage of ordinary soldiers were reported home for the first time. Prior to the war only senior officers were awarded a medal for military prowess. As a direct result of the Crimean War, and the reporting of the bravery of the ordinary soldier, a new medal was commissioned that would be awarded to any rank who had shown valour in the presence of the enemy. The Victoria Cross remains Britain's highest military award for gallantry and it was once believed that they were cast from the metal taken from Russian cannons that were captured at the siege of Sebastopol.

The 46th Regiment of Foot

Created in 1741, the 46th Regiment of Foot fought in the Crimean War between 1854–1856.

In 1881 the regiment merged with the 32nd Cornwall Light Infantry Regiment of Foot to form the Duke of Cornwall's Light Infantry (D.C.L.I). At the end of the 19th century, and during the 20th, their soldiers marched to war again, fighting in the Second Boer War (1899–1902), WW1 (1914–1918) and WW2 (1939–1945). Several further mergers occurred in later years. Its lineage and history continues today in The Rifles.

Thank You

Thank you for reading *The Daughter of River Valley*. I hope you enjoyed Beth and Joss's story, as they learn to trust one another, fall in love and gradually realise that their past does not define who they are today and their future together.

River Valley is a fictitious location; however it was inspired by Rocky Valley, near Tintagel in Cornwall. Although I have used my artistic licence and renamed and changed many things about the valley, including its location, Rocky Valley is still a very special place and well worth a visit. Strangely, when I visit the valley that inspired my novel, I feel as if it is really Beth's former home and can imagine her falling in love with her unwanted guest, hidden from the world by the rocky banks.

However, now Beth and Joss's story is published it is no longer confined in the fictitious valley. Today it is out in the big wide world and hopefully it will remain there and be shared with others for many years to come. Positive feedback and word of mouth recommendations will help determine its success or failure and ultimately its longevity. With this in mind, if you enjoyed *The Daughter of River Valley*, I would be so grateful if you could take a moment to write a review on the retail site where you bought it. A review can be as short as one sentence or longer if you are so inclined. Your opinion and recommendations really do matter.

Thank you again for taking the time to read the third novel in the Cornish Tales series. I do hope you enjoyed the story, because I enjoyed writing it for you and I truly believe that Beth and Joss enjoyed having your company too.

Love

Victoria Cornwall

P.S. In *The Daughter of River Valley*, Beth confides in Joss that her Aunt Amy was unable to have children and had adopted a young runaway boy, who caused them "no end of trouble". The troubled boy grew into a man and you can read his story in *The Captain's Daughter*.

About the Author

Victoria Cornwall grew up on a dairy farm in Cornwall. She can trace her Cornish roots as far back as the 18th century and it is this background and heritage which is the inspiration for her Cornish based novels.

Victoria is married and has two grown up children. She likes to read and write historical fiction with a strong background story, but at its heart is the unmistakable emotion, even pain, of loving someone.

Following a fulfilling twenty-five-year career as a nurse, a change in profession finally allowed her the time to write. She is a member of the Romantic Novelists' Association.

For more information on Victoria:
https://twitter.com/VickieCornwall
www.facebook.com/victoria.cornwall.75
www.victoriacornwall.com

More Choc Lit

From Victoria Cornwall

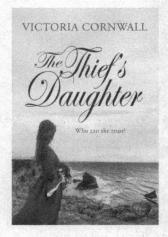

The Thief's Daughter

Hide from the thief-taker, for if he finds you, he will take you away ...

Eighteenth-century Cornwall is crippled by debt and poverty, while the gibbet casts a shadow of fear over the land. Yet, when night falls, free traders swarm onto the beaches and smuggling prospers.

Terrified by a thief-taker's warning as a child, Jenna has resolved to be good. When her brother, Silas, asks for her help to pay his creditors, Jenna feels unable to refuse and finds herself entering the dangerous world of the smuggling trade.

Jack Penhale hunts down the smuggling gangs in revenge for his father's death. Drawn to Jenna at a hiring fayre, they discover their lives are entangled. But as Jenna struggles to decide where her allegiances lie, the worlds of justice and crime collide, leading to danger and heartache for all concerned ...

Available in paperback from all good bookshops and online stores. Also available as an eBook on all platforms and in audio. Visit www.choc-lit.com for details.

The Captain's Daughter

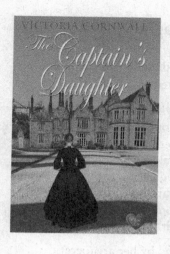

Sometimes you need to discover your own strength in order to survive …

After a family tragedy, Janey Carhart was forced from her comfortable life as a captain's daughter into domestic service. Determined to make something of herself, Janey eventually finds work as a lady's maid at the imposing Bosvenna Manor on the edge of Bodmin Moor, but is soon caught between the two worlds of upstairs and downstairs, and accepted by neither, as she cares for her mistress.

Desperately lonely, Janey catches the attention of two men – James Brockenshaw and Daniel Kellow. James is heir to the Bosvenna estate, a man whose eloquent letters to his mother warm Janey's heart. Daniel Kellow is a neighbouring farmer with a dark past and a brooding nature, yet with a magnetism that disturbs Janey. Two men. Who should she choose? Or will fate decide?

VICTORIA CORNWALL

Daughter of the House

The daughter of the house is often overlooked …

Evelyn Pendragon is spirited but lonely, and largely ignored by her parents whose attentions are taken up with her brother, Nicholas: the expected heir to the family's Cornish estate and the one who will carry on the Pendragon name.

Stifled by her aristocratic existence, Evelyn finds companionship in an unlikely place when she befriends Drake Vennor, an apprentice gardener on the estate.

But when Evelyn's life is thrown into turmoil by a tragedy, she realises just how much she has come to rely on Drake. Will family expectations and the burden of the Pendragon name mean she must turn her back on him when she needs him the most?

Available as an eBook on all platforms and in audio. Visit www.choc-lit.com for details.

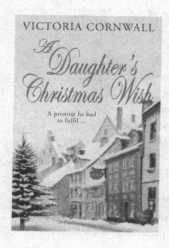

A Daughter's Christmas Wish

A Cornish Christmas wish sent across the ocean …

Christmas, Cornwall 1919.

A promise to a fellow soldier leads Nicholas to Cornwall for Christmas, and to the teashop managed by Rose, the youngest daughter of a family whose festive spirit has been blighted by their wartime experiences. But as Nicholas strives to give Rose the best Christmas she could wish for, he begins to question whether his efforts are to honour his friend, or whether there is another reason …

Available as an eBook on all platforms and in audio. Visit www.choc-lit.com for details.

Introducing Choc Lit

We're an independent publisher creating
a delicious selection of fiction.
Where heroes are like chocolate – irresistible!
Quality stories with a romance at the heart.

See our selection here:
www.choc-lit.com

We'd love to hear how you enjoyed *The Daughter of River Valley*. Please visit **www.choc-lit.com** and give your feedback or leave a review where you purchased this novel.

Choc Lit novels are selected by genuine readers like yourself. We only publish stories our Tasting Panel want to see in print. Our reviews and awards speak for themselves.

Could you be a Star Selector and join our Tasting Panel?
Would you like to play a role in choosing which novels we decide to publish? Do you enjoy reading women's fiction? Then you could be perfect for our Tasting Panel.

Visit here for more details…
www.choc-lit.com/join-the-choc-lit-tasting-panel

Keep in touch:
Sign up for our monthly newsletter Spread for all the latest news and offers: www.spread.choc-lit.com. Follow us on Twitter: @ChocLituk and Facebook: Choc Lit.

Where heroes are like chocolate – irresistible!